MONSTERS

a love story

MONSTERS

a love story

LIZ KAY

G. P. PUTNAM'S SONS
NEW YORK

PUTNAM

G. P. PUTNAM'S SONS
Publishers Since 1838
An imprint of Penguin Random House LLC
375 Hudson Street
New York, New York 10014

ISBN 978-1-10198-247-1

Printed in the United States of America
1   3   5   7   9   10   8   6   4   2

Book design by Gretchen Achilles

For Ken and Anne

MONSTERS

a love story

NOVEMBER

THE PHONE RINGS. The landline. I hate the landline. In the weeks after Michael died, it was constantly ringing—the sympathetic neighbors, the PTA moms, everyone wanting to know how I was doing. *You don't need to know how I'm doing,* I'd think. Michael died eight months ago, so it doesn't ring that much anymore. I guess I'm still not doing well.

"Stacey," the voice sings into the machine, "pick up your goddamn phone . . ." It's my sister, Jenny.

"Hang on," I say as I pick up. I hold the phone away from my mouth and call down into the basement. "Time to brush teeth, boys. Get ready for bed."

"You guys want to come here on Friday? We can stream a movie, make milkshakes?"

We've spent almost every weekend at her house. The boys are probably expecting it, but I'm starting to feel trapped. Michael was so big on routine, and now I feel like I've fallen into another one. Sometimes I just want to wing it. I don't know how to tell her that.

"I don't know," I say. "We should let you guys get back to your own lives. I mean, we'll be fine."

"No, we love having you!"

I know she means it. She was born to mother—her own kids, me, the boys. This past year, she's been amazing, and I know in some ways she loves it. Being so necessary.

I wander back into the living room and sit down in front of my laptop. I got it out earlier to look at job postings, but with my background—an advanced degree, two published books of poetry, and no real work experience—it's discouraging how little I'm qualified for. I could be a barista maybe.

Jenny keeps talking, but I'm not really listening. I'm checking my Facebook, my e-mail. I have a separate account that comes in from my author's website, but I haven't been paying attention to it. I haven't been writing anyway, and besides, it rarely has anything in it. But today, there's something there. The subject line reads, *Interested in your book,* so I open it. The note is short.

"Listen to this," I say, interrupting my sister, and I read her the e-mail. *Dear Ms. Lane, I just had the pleasure of reading your novel-in-verse,* Monsters in the Afterlife. *I'm wondering if you have an agent who represents you. I'd be interested in discussing the film rights.*

"Seriously? That's so cool! Who's it from?"

"Alan something-or-other. Probably some nobody," I say, but I'm already plugging the name into Google. "Is this the same guy? Holy shit." The list of credits is long. Really long, and I recognize a lot of it. "Oh my god. What do I say? I don't have an agent."

"Then answer, 'Thank you, that sounds amazing, but no, I don't have an agent because there's no money in poetry.'"

It's true. My first book, *The Seduction of Eve,* came out with a tiny press, but the reviews were good and it sold close to six hundred copies, which for poetry is really not bad at all. It wasn't a novel-in-verse like *Monsters*, but it was thematic, and each section opened and closed with poems titled "The Seduction" that retold this one moment, but the perspectives, the voices, kept changing. Some of them were really beautiful, like love poems, but in others the language turned dangerous, dark. The day the box came with the first copies of the book, I just sat on the floor and read it cover to cover, like it was something new, like it wasn't even mine.

"Wow," Michael had said when he'd come home. "Congratulations." And he picked up a copy and flipped through it, not to read it, just to see if it was real.

"One more chapter?" Stevie begs.

I look at the clock. It's late, past their bedtime by ten minutes, but I say yes anyway. I like reading to them. I feel like I can fall into the book, and then I'm giving them what they want, but I don't have to think. I don't have to find my own words. When the story's over, I kiss Stevie first, leaning into the bottom bunk to tuck him in. "Give me a squeeze," I say, and he does, his little arms tight around my neck. "Who's my favorite monkey?" I say, and he squeaks, "Me!"

I step on the rail and pull myself up to kiss Ben. I smooth his Hulk blanket across him, ruffle his hair. "Thanks for being my kid," I whisper, and he smiles. "Thanks for being my mom." We do this every night. Every touch, every word the same. I love the ritual of it, the few minutes when I feel like I'm my best self. I feel like I'm getting it right. I flip off the lights and stand in the hallway outside their door, leaning against the wall, listening to them talk. Some part of me is always expecting to overhear something painful or profound, to hear them talk about Michael or me. Most nights, they don't. Tonight Stevie is talking about Spider-Man, imagining new powers he thinks would be better, what if he could fly, what if he could be invisible too?

"Invisible all the time?" Ben asks. "Or just when he wants to be?"

I walk down the hall to my bedroom, and Bear pads along behind me. He curls up on the big fleece mat in the corner of the room. It's funny to think he's as settled as ever. It's the boys and I who are floundering. Just in different ways. They want nothing more to change, and I want everything to.

Last week while the boys were at school, I packed up all of Michael's things. It seemed pointless to keep hanging on to it all, the T-shirts, the electric razor. I went to a grief session once, in the very beginning, but one of the other women was talking about how she couldn't wash her husband's clothes, how she held on to the smell of him. Some days, she said, she spent hours on the floor of their closet, trying to breathe him in, and I thought, *I shouldn't be here, this isn't for me.*

I packed one box for each boy using old pictures. *Here is the tie your father wore for your christening. Here is a T-shirt he was wearing one day at the park. In the photo, he's pushing you on the swing. Here is a wallet, a watch.* I didn't know what to do with his wedding ring, so I just put it in a velvet jewelry box with mine.

The upshot is that now I have all this empty space to fill. I tried spreading my clothes between both dressers, but I couldn't find the right balance. Everything feels disordered. I can never find what I want.

I walk down to the kitchen and pour myself a glass of wine. At first I'd felt weird about drinking alone, but I have a rule about stopping at one glass, so I think it's okay. I do use my biggest glasses and I pour them pretty full, but I always stop after one.

Michael and I met in Boston, in graduate school. He was studying actuary science. I was studying poetry. He had a job lined up months before graduation, and when he proposed, he said, *Marry me, Stacey. God knows you can't afford not to.* Then he laughed. We both did. We were really young then, and happy.

We moved to Omaha right out of grad school, the year we got married. It's where Michael grew up—flyover, landlocked, just about as far as you can get from either coast, which is where I'd always lived—Boston, and before that San Francisco. First one coast and then the other, and now I'm right in the center. I don't feel very centered. I used to. I don't anymore.

I take the wine out to the living room and sit on the couch. My laptop is still sitting open, but the screen's black, timed out. *You realize your book could end up a movie?* Jenny had said before we hung up. *I wonder what they'll pay you.* In my best year, just last year, I made three thousand dollars. *Look at you,* Michael said. I think he thought it was cute.

He did risk calculation for an asset-management firm. *It's not really risk if you understand math,* he used to say, but I don't understand math, not even a little, so he told me not to even look at the numbers when we bought our first house. It was this sweet little bungalow in Midtown with wood accents and dormers. Michael didn't love it, but he liked the commute, and he liked that I liked the built-in bookshelves next to the fireplace.

"It's close to the university," he said. "Maybe you could teach."

"I don't think we can afford this," I said, running my hand along the dark wood of the shelves. "Maybe we should rent."

"Maybe you should trust me," he said.

There were not any jobs at the university. There never are, but for a while I did part-time development for an arts nonprofit. I wrote some grants and sat in on a few board meetings, but it didn't pay much and I wasn't very good at it. When Ben was born, Michael said I should just stay home.

I'd walk Ben in the stroller for blocks and blocks through Happy Hollow and Dundee with all the big brick Tudors and overgrown lawns and one-way streets. We'd stop at this cute little corner market and I'd buy Ben grapes most afternoons. Plums when he got a little older. Some nights we'd walk down to this offbeat vegetarian place, though Michael liked to tease me that if I was going to be a Nebraskan, I was going to have to learn to eat steak. I wasn't sure, really, how I felt about Nebraska, but I loved Midtown.

"We need a bigger house," I told Michael after Stevie was born, and what I meant was a big brick Tudor with ivy. But all he saw were the detached garages and the radiators and the retrofit piping for central air-conditioning.

So he bought this house, or rather it just *fell into his lap*, a corporate relocation deal that he couldn't pass up on.

"I don't want to live out west," I said.

"It's closer to my parents."

"I hate your parents." But he convinced me.

So we moved west. All the way west, past the cornfields at Boys Town, away from the narrow streets to the part of town that's all pedestrian malls and golf courses. We have a three-car garage and a lawn service. We have a monitored security system and a stacked slate fountain by the front walk. We don't have any ivy.

Not that any of that matters now. Michael set everything up years ago, *so you won't have to make any decisions,* he'd said. And there had been all these papers for me to sign. I just remember him saying, *Life insurance . . . trust account . . . annuity.*

I know I should be grateful. It's probably for the best. I'm not all that good at decisions, and a job is a long shot. Still, it would be nice to have some direction.

According to the boys, Jenny's husband makes the world's greatest milkshakes. I wouldn't know. I've never tried one, though he's made them a million times. Todd is this big, burly guy who can't go five minutes without offering you a snack or a beer, the ex–football player type you see a lot of in Nebraska, though he is not Nebraskan. Jenny and I have known him since we were kids. They moved here *so our kids could be cousins like the kind we never had,* Jenny said. But I think Todd fell in love with the lawns mostly. We didn't have lawns this big in San Francisco. The kids are close though. Jenny has three, two girls around the same ages as my boys, and then her littlest, a boy still in preschool.

Jenny jostles the pot on her stove, waiting for the popcorn to pop. Todd's in the great room, fixing the surround sound.

"No, the other remote," I hear Todd say for the third time.

Jenny wrinkles her nose. I turn away from her, move to look out the window. It's late enough that the sky is a heavy gray.

"So speaking of movies, this thing with your book sounds insane. I mean good insane. But, you know, crazy."

Behind me the kernels start to pop, dinging loudly against the metal of the pan. There's the sound of the heavy pot dragging across the grate of the stove as she shakes it and shakes it, then the rustle of her pouring the finished popcorn into a bowl. The bowl is the color of butter and it reads *Popcorn* in big white letters. I have a matching bowl, but I don't ever use it.

"Can you imagine what Michael would say? I mean, he would be like, 'This is insane.'"

"Wow. It's like you're channeling him." I lean closer to the window, peering out. "I think we're in for more snow."

"You know, refusing to talk about him is never going to make this any easier," she says.

"Well, with you around, how will we ever find out?" I turn around and she's scowling, one hand on her hip. "I'm kidding," I say, but she doesn't soften at all. "You're right," I say. "He'd be thrilled."

I'm making dinner late again because I haven't been paying attention to the clock. Stevie had finally asked for a snack and I said, *You've already had one,* and he said, *Yeah, but I'm hungry again,* and when I looked up it was already seven o'clock. Lately, I've been doing this a lot. I cradle the phone against my ear while I heat tomato soup. Ben doesn't really like it, but Stevie does, and it's the fastest thing I can do. It's almost their bedtime.

"I don't really understand all of this, Mom," I say. "They're buying a six-month option, whatever that means, but they're sending me a check for fifteen grand and flying me out to work on the script." I don't really need the money, but I like the thought of making it. And more important, they're flying me somewhere. More important, I get to leave.

"Jenny says this producer seems like a big deal," she says. "Maybe you'll get into screenwriting and move out to L.A. and we'll actually see you once in a while."

"You're seeing us for Christmas. We'll be there in a month."

"You know what I mean. I don't know why you don't just move home."

"To San Francisco?" I laugh. "Sure. The boys would love it. If we sell the house we could swing an efficiency apartment over someone's garage."

"That's a little hyperbolic, Stacey." She's using her best professor voice.

"Anyway, Jenny would kill me if we left." They moved out here three years ago when Todd got a job with the railroad. The hours are long, but the benefits are amazing, and the cost of living's so low, Jenny's able to mostly stay home. She used to teach French full-time. Now she gives private lessons.

"I'm just saying this could open some new doors."

"I wouldn't get carried away," I say. "From what I understand, these options almost never pan out. Honestly, Jenny shouldn't have even told you yet."

DECEMBER

THERE ARE FOUR SEPARATE FLIGHTS to get to the island, first to Denver, then to Newark overnight. We land in Turks and Caicos early evening, but then there's still a little island-hopper flight. The plane is tiny, with just a handful of people on it. The whole time we're in the air, I sit with my legs crossed, my right foot hooked around the back of my left calf. It makes me feel smaller, more steady. I balance my book on my knee and flip slowly through it. I've been away from this book so long I don't know if I can slip back into its voice, and that's what they're asking me to do. *We love it as a skeleton,* he'd said, *but of course we need some of the scenes you left out. The things you implied, well, now we need you to write them.* They're bringing in a screenwriter too.

The landing is less than pleasant. The plane tips heavily to one side, and I throw my hand out to brace myself. "Fuck!" I look around to see if anyone else looks nervous, but no one seems to have noticed me or the plane's sketchy maneuvering. Just then the wheels hit and the seat I'm clutching shudders hard and begins to vibrate as the plane struggles to slow itself. I close my eyes and clench every muscle until the shaking stops. When it finally does, I pull out my phone and switch it off airplane mode. I text Jenny, *Landed. How are boys?* and then slip it back into my pocket.

On the tarmac, there's a man waiting for me with my name on a sign. He takes my bag, and then we're in this Mercedes, and we're driving through hills and past beaches, and we finally pull up to this huge gate. He types in the code, and the gates open, and we drive up to this massive stucco house with a Spanish roof. The double front doors are wooden and open, and when we walk in, the whole place is full of light. The back of the house is all glass, doors and windows, and they're all open to this enormous terrace overlooking the ocean. It reminds me of a hotel Michael and I stayed at in Kauai. *I love it here,* I said the first night. I wanted to stay out late and drink too much and walk barefoot in the sand and kiss in the moonlight. Michael was tired though. *I'm still on Central time,* he said.

"You must be Stacey." The voice comes from the left, and I turn to see a man walking toward me, hand extended. He looks about fifty. His head is shaved and the top is pink from the sun. He's got a full, round face, thin lips. His graying eyebrows are obscured by the black frames of his glasses. His hand, when he grabs mine, is soft and firm.

"I'm Alan. Welcome. Welcome," he says. "Can I get you a drink?" He turns to the driver behind me and says, "Put those bags in her room." He looks back at me. "Ready to get started?"

"Sure," I say. "Yeah." I'm not ready at all. I need to catch my breath, to look around.

"I'm just kidding. We'll let you settle in first. We'll start tomorrow. Joe got here this morning. He's the screenwriter. Great guy. I've worked with him a ton. He's got a working draft. Just a sketch really.

Needs a lot of work." I realize he's leading me slowly into the room as he talks. "So you want that drink?"

I shake my head. "No, thanks. I'm good."

"And you call yourself a writer?" He pours himself a smallish splash of something—bourbon, maybe—and puts the bottle back. He pats the bar. "Tommy's got a hell of a bar here, so help yourself. This is his house, by the way, but you probably knew that. He gets in tomorrow."

I have no idea who Tommy is, so I just nod.

I wake up to the sound of the ocean. I barely slept all night. I just lay there staring at the ceiling, the walls, but then sometime around five, I closed my eyes. Now it's light out, and I'm not sure where I am for a second.

My hair is curling from the humidity, but it doesn't look bad. It's always curly, though not quite this full. I pull my fingers through, half untangling it, half checking for grays. I don't feel like I'm old enough, but stress can do that. I found one last week, a little wisp of silver against the brown.

I pull on a clingy white tank and a pair of shorts. They're looser than they were last year, kind of hanging off my hips. I don't mind this part at all. Grief is terrible, but it looks amazing on me. If Michael were here, he'd grab my ass and try to pull me back into bed. He's not here though, and I need coffee. It must be nine o'clock, but no one seems to be up. I know there's staff here. Someone unpacked my bags and cleaned up from dinner last night, but now there's no one around. There's a cappuccino machine that I don't know how to work, but I find a regular coffeemaker too. I brew a full pot and take a mug out to the terrace.

I sit cross-legged on a sofa holding the coffee in my lap, and I close my eyes. I'd forgotten how good the sun can feel. I think, *This is what happy feels like,* and I think about how people say you should just let the good feelings wash over you. But then I think, *No,* and I open my eyes. The coffee tastes kind of stale and bitter, and I wonder why this Tommy doesn't keep better coffee in his house when he has such an amazingly stocked bar.

I hear footsteps behind me.

"Well, don't you look gorgeous, all sun-kissed and fresh?" When I turn to look, it's someone new. He's young, maybe late twenties, skinny, his short black hair swept to one side. He holds his hand out. "I'm Daniel. Tommy's assistant. I do everything. Well not *everything* . . . ooh, coffee." He grabs my mug and takes a sip. "Jesus, who stocked this?" He looks around like there should be someone there to answer him. "I'll get you something else, honey. Don't drink that shit." He sits down in the chair across from me and leans forward, resting his elbows on his knees. "So you're Stacey?"

"I'm Stacey, yeah." I smile.

"Tommy's in the shower. He's a mess as usual. I got him on the plane at four, and other than crashing out on the flight, he hasn't had much sleep." He makes an exaggerated face. "Models. At the hotel last night. It was not a good scene." He shakes his head. "I was like, 'You know we have an early flight,' and he was all, 'Shut the fuck up,' and I was like, 'Whatever, as long as you sign my paychecks.'" He sighs. "Actually, I sign my own paychecks, so it's a good thing I'm honest. I mean, I should give myself a bonus anytime I have to drag his ass out of some strange bed that smells like morning-after pussy."

I laugh, but it's more fucked-up than funny. Daniel raises his eyes above my head. "Well, there you are, sunshine."

The voice behind me is a low grumble. "Fuck off." He moves around the couch and drops next to me, bumping my leg. He's wearing jeans, a gray T-shirt, damp at the collar from his hair, which is dark, very dark, almost black, and it's combed back from his face, which I can't really see because his hands are at his temples like he's trying to hold his head together. Then he drops his left hand to my knee in this apologetic pat, and *Jesus Christ*, I can't even think, but it's fucking Tommy DeMarco. "Sorry," he mumbles without looking at me. He looks like shit. I mean, gorgeous, of course, but like hell.

Daniel leans across and hands him my mug. "Have some coffee."

Tommy stares at it. "It's cold."

"Just drink it." Daniel digs through a bag next to him and pulls out a prescription bottle. He shakes a pill into his palm and hands it to Tommy. He looks at me. "Vitamins."

Tommy takes it and swallows half the coffee. "This is terrible."

"Your life? Yeah, it's a mess. Just drink the coffee. I'll get you an espresso in a minute, but only 'cause I'm making one for her." Daniel nods in my direction as he walks away.

With that, Tommy looks up at me, and he smiles this amazing little smile, and suddenly, he doesn't look like some hungover piece of trash. He looks like a movie star. I mean, he is a movie star, but right now he looks like something out of a movie, and he winks and says, "I don't travel so well." I laugh, and he holds his hand out and takes mine. "Tommy. And you're Stacey." He's still holding my hand, not so much shaking it as just holding it, and I really, really hope I'm not blushing.

"I loved your book, by the way. Obviously, or we wouldn't be here. But really, it's beautiful. Awful, but beautiful. And it really challenges the whole idea of what monstrous is. What makes a monster? And who or what is responsible? Or are we all? It's just great. I loved it."

"Wow." I hate it when I don't know what to say. I mean, I'm a writer. I should be good with words, and instead I'm like, *Wow.* "I'm flattered. I didn't realize many people had bothered to read it, much less get that much out of it, so that's really generous of you."

"Oh, a lot more people will read it now. Once the publicity machine starts rolling for the movie, people will get interested in the book. Your sales should pick up quite a bit."

Daniel reappears with the espressos and sets one down in front of me. "Here you go, sweetie." He looks at Tommy. "And you, fucking degenerate."

"I should fire you. I swear to god, man." He takes a sip of the espresso. "That is good though. Really good." He closes his eyes, leans his head back, and rubs his jaw. "It's bright out. You have my glasses?" Daniel pulls a leather case out of his bag and hands the dark glasses to Tommy, who puts them on over his closed eyes. "Jesus, I could die. Do we have anything to eat?" He gives my leg the little apology pat again. "Sorry. I'm not usually this bad."

Daniel's already on his way to the kitchen, but he calls back over his shoulder, "It's true. He's usually worse."

The script is much, much worse than not very good. We're sitting on the terrace, and I'm thumbing through the hard copy in my lap. I'm the only one still reading, though I'm not reading so much as stalling. I'm not sure where to start. "I think one problem is that you've sort of taken the poems and turned them into dialogue. I mean, you've plucked out all the good lines and given them to different characters."

Joe nods. "Obviously, we'll have to add to it." He looks older than me, which probably means we're the same age, mid-thirties. I'm always surprised by my own age. Sometimes I feel older, sometimes younger. I never feel right.

I glance at Tommy. He's stretched back on the couch next to me. He has his head tipped back, his glasses on. I mean, he could be asleep.

Alan is definitely not asleep. He's watching everyone. I'm not sure how this all works, if he works for Tommy, if Tommy works for him. I do know that I don't want to piss either of them off, but I don't want to let them break my book either.

"Right. But it's more than that. I mean, this basically reads like kind of a typical Frankenstein movie," I say, holding up the script.

"Your book is Frankenstein," Joe says. "Kinky Frankenstein with this Frederick psycho building himself a girl."

Tommy makes this grunting laugh. I guess he is awake.

"Okay, but this isn't based on the movies. This is based on the book, the whole nature-of-man discussion?"

Joe looks at me blankly.

I feel myself slowing down, pausing between words, waiting for some recognition to show on his face. "So, where Frankenstein's creature has a fully human soul in a physically corrupted form, my monster has a beautiful exterior, but she's evil."

"I thought the monster was always bad?" Joe looks at Alan and shrugs.

"The creature only turns when Frankenstein rejects him. But that book is about the corrupting influence of religion. Mine is about gender ideals and sexual power dynamics."

"Great"—Joe smiles a deliberately strained smile—"a feminist manifesto. That'll make a great flick."

17

———————

"How'd you get your book in their hands?" Joe asks as everyone's heading in for lunch.

Alan's already at the bar. He catches my eye and raises a bottle in my direction with a questioning shrug. It's barely even one. I shake my head.

"I have no idea, really. I just got an e-mail one day."

"You're kidding me." Joe says this like he might be kind of pissed.

"No. Why?"

"You just 'got an e-mail'?" He shakes his head. "You are one lucky bitch."

Tommy opens three bottles of wine over dinner, but I don't think he finishes more than a glass. Alan has quite a bit. Maybe more. And Joe, Joe has a lot. He seems to be holding on to some anger from the day. Tommy and Alan spent the afternoon holed up somewhere, talking about I don't know what, which was not so good because Joe and I need a translator. The only language he seems fluent in is asshole, and in the past few hours, we've gotten nowhere but pissed off.

"Well," Joe says, pushing his plate back and refilling his wine yet again, "I think we're fucked. Or you are, anyway." He waves his glass toward Alan and Tommy. "It's not my money on the line."

Alan leans forward and tries to do this calming motion with his hand, but it hardly seems to work. "Whoa, let's not get carried away. It's a rocky start is all."

Joe looks at me and shakes his head. "She doesn't get it. Controlling bitch if you ask me." He sort of sneers drunkenly. "How do you even keep a husband anyway? Seriously, how does he even put up with you?" Because, of course, it's right there, at the back of the book, my whole life boiled down to a paragraph. It reads, *Omaha . . . husband . . . two sons,* and I don't even know how to start correcting him. I don't even know which parts are still true.

Tommy laughs. "Joe, you're a handful, man." He stands up from the table. "Brandy?" He points to Joe, then Alan, then me.

"Please, yes, I'd love some." I get up and follow him to the bar.

Tommy lines up four snifters and pours two fingers in each.

"Let's talk outside." He hands me a glass and gestures toward the terrace. He points me to the couch and then sits across from me. "Don't worry about Joe," he says. "He's an asshole and a drunk, but he's really, really good. No one would put up with him if he wasn't. I think he hasn't quite figured out your vision yet, but he'll get there. We'll make him get there. Promise." He rests his hand on my knee and smiles. I think it's supposed to be a reassuring gesture, but I just feel hyperaware of his fingers and maybe a little flushed, which is ridiculous because I'm not the sort of woman who gets flushed. "Just don't let him push you around."

"Do I look pushed around?" *God, I hope not.* I take a sip of the brandy and try really hard not to look rattled. Or look at his hand, which is still just resting there on my leg.

Tommy laughs and leans back in his chair, taking his hand with him. "I don't know, honestly. You're hard to read."

In the morning, I walk out to the kitchen and find a full pot of coffee and a tray of sliced fruit. I pop a piece of pineapple in my mouth and take a cup of coffee out to the terrace. Tommy is already there. He's sitting with his feet propped up on the table. My book is in his lap, and he's writing in the margins. I feel strange standing there, out of place.

He looks up. "Coffee's good today," he says. "Daniel took care of it. There should also be some breakfast in there if you're hungry."

"No," I say. "Just coffee's good."

"So I'm making notes. I think if we look at these poems in terms of scenes, and then work from there. Who else is present for this scene and what will those characters say and do? Your monster is so fleshed out, so real, the rest of them need to come to life, give her some balance."

"Right." I nod my head a little and stare at my coffee. The steam rises in a slow, looping swirl. "You know, I don't know if I can do this," I say finally.

"Sure you can."

I set the coffee on the table and sit on the couch, cross-legged, holding both feet next to my hips, my fingers tight around my ankles. I look out over the water to the point where it merges with the horizon. When I finally turn back, Tommy is looking at me. He must have shaved this morning. They like to picture him with stubble, maybe to scuff up the pretty. That's really the word for it. Aside from the hard line of his jaw, he has the face of a pretty girl—high cheekbones, wide green eyes. He lets the book fall closed in his lap. I just shake my head.

"I know that you can." He puts this emphasis on the word *know*. Like it makes a difference. Like a person can know anything. Like knowing helps.

"I don't have room in my head for the others. Hers is the only voice I hear."

"That's bullshit." He stands up and grabs his cup. "I need a refill. You?"

"No," I say. "Thanks."

He turns toward the house and then turns back. "I can hear them in there. Right in the book. There are snippets of them, moments. You just keep them on too tight a leash. You've got to let them loose. You've got to give in to the chaos."

I try to laugh. "I don't like chaos."

"No shit?" He steps closer and leans down until we're face-to-face. I feel myself shifting backwards, trying to make space. "Jesus. You are wound so tight you're gonna break something. But you are not"—he raises his hand to point in the direction of the book where it sits on the table—"you are not gonna break this." He stands up and walks into the kitchen, and I turn my head back out to face the ocean and close my eyes as tight as I can and hold my breath.

It's getting later, and the sky is slowly darkening. It doesn't gray like back in Nebraska, it just turns a deeper blue. It's been a long day, with not much progress to show for it. *See,* I thought about saying to Tommy at one point, *I can't do it.*

Alan and Joe took off half an hour ago, headed out for burgers.

"Thanks, no, I'm a vegetarian," I said when Alan asked, and Joe just looked relieved.

I snap my laptop closed and lean back into the couch.

Tommy comes out to the terrace with a bottle and two short glasses. "Scotch," he says, setting the bottle on the table. I wrinkle my nose, but he says, "You'll like it." He sits down on the couch next to me and pours a little in each glass, hands one to me. "To finding chaos."

I roll my eyes, but I take a sip. "Jesus. This tastes like lighter fluid."

He laughs. "That's a four-hundred-dollar bottle of scotch."

"It's awful."

"Keep drinking. It'll grow on you."

It does. By the time the sky's completely dark, I feel like I could melt right into the couch. Tommy's telling me a story about his favorite uncle. He's telling it like there's a lesson in it somewhere, but I'm having trouble concentrating.

"Where'd you grow up?" I ask.

"Texas. Didn't I say that?"

"Maybe." I shrug. "Did you like it?"

"No." He shakes his head and takes a sip of the scotch. "No one likes their childhood. At least, no one likes their childhood and then ends up here."

"Really?" I turn to face him, adjusting my body so I'm sitting sideways. "Why not?"

"Isn't that what drives us? Getting away?"

"Not me," I say. "I loved my childhood."

"Tell me about it," he says.

"It was great." I pull my right leg up and hug it into me, resting my chin on my knee. "My parents both taught at USF."

He makes a face because he's obviously never heard of it.

"University of San Francisco. I did my undergrad there. Free tuition." I shrug. "Anyway, we lived a few blocks away. We didn't really have a yard, so my dad would take us down to the campus on the weekends, and my sister and I would roller-skate. My dad would say, 'Sunny, don't dig up the grass with those skates.'"

"Your dad called you Sonny? Like Sonny and Cher?"

"Sunny, like sunshine."

"Right. Because of your sunny disposition," he says.

"My older sister was Boo. Pale. White-blond hair."

"Like a ghost?"

"Like Boo Radley," I say, and Tommy laughs.

I'm smiling now. Just smiling. Then Tommy smiles, and then he leans forward and kisses me. It's this soft, slow kiss, just his lips on my lips, and he's got one finger under my chin tugging me closer and then his hands are on either side of my jaw, and he's pulling me toward him. I scoot my left leg across his lap, and then I'm kneeling over him, and his head's tipped all the way back. I've got his bottom lip in my teeth. He runs his hands up under my shirt and along my back all the way to my neck, and he presses his fingers into my hair and pulls his mouth away from mine, brushing his lips against my chin, and it feels like an electric shock, and I suck in my breath and scramble backwards as fast as I can and walk in the house.

In the kitchen, I brace my hands on the counter, but I can't keep myself up. I drop down into a squat, curling over my knees, my arms up over my hair. "Oh god. Oh my god. Fuck."

I can hear his footsteps coming closer. "Look, I get it," he says. "Some girls are married, and some girls are fucking married. Whatever. Let's not make a scene."

I'm rocking from my heels to my toes. I'm trying to breathe.

"Jesus. You're a disaster. You need to get your shit straight."

I'm fine. I'm fine. I'm fine. I'm fine. I stand up in one fluid motion and push my hair out of my face. "I'm fine," I say.

"You call this fine?" He's got a glass of scotch in his hand, and he's pointing it at me. "What the fuck is wrong with you?"

I take a really slow breath. I can do this. I can handle it. I'm fine. I press my lips together. It might look like I'm smiling. I try looking him in the eye. "My husband is dead."

"What?" He shakes his head like I've said something impossible. It's not impossible.

"My husband." I say it slower this time. "He's dead."

"Like . . . recently?"

I nod. I think I look like I'm smiling again. I might be trying to smile. "Mm-hmm."

"Oh Jesus, honey, I'm sorry." His jaw relaxes, and he takes two steps toward me and pulls me into him. He's cradling my head in the crook of his elbow, holding the glass of scotch next to my ear, and he's making this rocking motion like he's shushing a baby. He brushes my hair back off of my face with his other hand.

Tommy sits me down in the living room and goes out to retrieve the scotch. "We're gonna need more of this," he says, handing me my glass. He sits on the floor in front of me, one leg stretched out. He leans back into the couch and closes his eyes. "All right, let's hear it."

"There's nothing to hear," I say. "He just died." I take a drink of the scotch. I'm not so much sipping it anymore as sucking it in. "In March. He was in a car accident. Dead on the scene. Thank god. I mean, that it was fast. Not that it happened, just that it wasn't some lingering thing. You know?"

"How long were you married?"

"Ten years."

"And your kids?"

"They're six and nine."

He reaches one arm back over his head and squeezes my knee.

Then I'm crying, and I haven't cried in months. I cried a lot in the beginning, but it made the boys so sad, and now I don't cry anymore, and I'm telling him this too, like he'll believe me when I tell him I'm not crying, even though I'm sobbing and my hands are covered in snot. Through it all, he just sits there, shaking his head occasionally and pouring me more scotch.

I remember waking in Michael's room in his apartment in Boston, watching him dress. He was still so young then, his face like a baby's, but he had the body of a man. He stood at the dresser, buttoning his shirt, buckling his belt, fastening his watch around his wrist, and I thought, *This is how a man moves in the world, how he fills the space around him.*

I hadn't intended to go home with him. I'd just been tagging along with a friend. She wanted to go home with him, and he was really more her type. Clean-cut, businessy, athletic. We left the bar in a group. I hadn't been angling to be the one riding back to their place on his lap. I was just the last one in the car, and it was a small car, and then he patted his legs. I was wearing this short skirt, so when he draped his arm around me, his hand was resting on my bare thigh. My flight home for the summer was three days away, so it wasn't like we were starting anything. It was just for fun, just a fling.

I didn't plan to think about him through the summer, but I did. I thought about his hands. He had these big, strong hands and this sweet boyish face. He looked like a Boy Scout. He looked like the kind of guy you'd want with you if you were lost in the woods, worried about bears. I remember feeling lost that summer, and very much alone. Jenny had moved in with Todd by then, and my parents spent most of it traveling.

I had an assistantship, so I was teaching that fall when I got back to Boston. The second week of class, I walked out of the building, and there he was, sitting on the wall by the front steps.

"I would have found you sooner if you'd told me your last name," he said.

"Would you?" I said.

He jumped off the wall, and I walked toward him, and I dropped my bag at his feet.

"You know my friend tried to set me up with this girl, and I said, 'I'm seeing someone. Or I will be once I find her again.'"

I probably would have married him right then. Michael always made me feel found.

I feel like someone is hammering nails into my temple. I turn my head to get away from it, and it feels like my skull is cracking open. I have to stay still. Everything is broken. Everything hurts.

"Hey." There's a voice in my ear, and someone is touching my head. "You've got to get up now. You're gonna have to move."

Hurts, I try to say, but it doesn't come out.

"Jesus, Tommy. What did you do to her? Just get out of my way," I hear another voice say. "Sweetie? It's Daniel. I'm gonna help you, okay?"

I try to nod.

"Here's the thing, honey. You've been poisoned."

"She's not poisoned," Tommy says.

I just whimper. I have been poisoned. I think I might die.

"I'm gonna need you to drink something for me. Can you do that?"

"Uh-uh." I can't open my mouth at all. I think if I do, all my organs will come rushing out.

"We've got to sit her up," Tommy says. He pushes past Daniel and slides onto the couch next to me. "Help me pull her up."

"No, no, no, no, no," I mumble as they pull me into a sitting position.

None of my muscles seem to be working, so they just prop me against Tommy, and he grabs me by the chin. "Open your eyes. You have to open your eyes."

I do, but it hurts. It hurts so much. Daniel is smiling at me though, and he looks happy to see me. "Yay! Baby's awake!" He claps. "Okay. Now I want you to drink this." He hands the mug to Tommy. It's clear I'm not holding anything. "You just take a sip."

I shake my head. "I'll throw up," I say.

"Just try." Tommy holds the mug to my lips. I try to swallow. I do swallow. But then he tips the mug into my mouth again and it's too much. My stomach seizes, and I feel everything start to come back out. I slap my hands over my mouth, but it just runs through my fingers, down my shirt, all over Tommy. And then I start to cry. Again.

"Jesus Christ. Ah, god, get some towels," Tommy says. I wish I were dead.

"Oh, honey." Daniel pats me on the arm. "It's okay, sweetie. Girls throw up in his lap all the time. You'll feel better now."

"Fucking towels, man!"

Daniel runs down the hall, and Tommy pats me halfheartedly on the back. "Don't worry about it," he says, but it doesn't sound very sincere. When Daniel comes back, he has these fluffy white bath sheets. They look expensive, but he just wipes my face and hands, mops up what he can. Tommy dabs at himself with another towel and stands up. "Get her showered off and put her in the sauna. She needs to sweat some of this shit out." He walks off down the hall, still wiping at his hands with the ruined towel.

Daniel gets me back to my room and turns the shower on, and I stand under the water for I don't even know how long. I can't lift my arms to wash my hair or anything. I just stand there, hoping I'll come out clean.

When I finally come out, I find a robe hanging by the door and pull it on.

"You decent?" Daniel calls through the crack in the door, but he doesn't really wait for me to answer. "Brush your teeth, sweetie." He fusses over me like a mother, finding my toothpaste, combing my hair. "All right, let's get you out to the pool house. Sweat lodge time."

It's early. The sky is a dusty blue and the sun's just barely over the horizon. In the pool house, the sauna is on but empty. Daniel plants me on the bench and promises he'll be right back. I let my head fall back against the wall and close my eyes, waiting.

I hear the door open, but I don't bother moving.

"How're you doing?" It's Tommy's voice this time. I wish he weren't here. I don't want to look at him. I don't want him to look at me. I keep my eyes closed and just shake my head, and I feel him sit on the bench next to me.

"You'll live," he says, sighing. I finally lift my head and turn to look at him. He's bent over, resting his weight on his knees. He's just got a towel on, fresh from the shower. His hair is wet, falling forward around his face. He glances up at me. He looks tired. He looks wrung-out. "Sometimes I have bad ideas." He shrugs.

Just then, Daniel comes back with two mugs in his hands. "Coffee."

"I don't want coffee," I say.

"You want this coffee," he says. "This is prescription strength." He hands me a mug and passes one to Tommy.

"I'll check on you in twenty," Daniel says. He reaches across and pats me on the knee. "You're gonna be fine. But drink that. All of it." He ducks out and closes the door.

It's sweet as hell. Full of sugar. I don't really do sugar. "I don't really do sugar," I say, half to Tommy, half to the mug.

"You couldn't drink it without the sugar. It's so full of Oxy, it would taste like shit."

"It's full of what?"

"OxyContin. He crushes the pills and stirs them in. Works faster that way."

"Seriously?"

"Just drink it."

I do. It helps. But the less I hurt, the worse I feel. "I'm so sorry about all of this."

"You're fine." He rests his hand on the back of my neck, gives it a quick squeeze. "I'm the one who fed you all that scotch. I knew where we'd end up."

"You must think I'm such an asshole."

He laughs. "Yesterday, I thought you were an asshole. Today, I like you. Today, you're just as fucked-up as the rest of us."

I turn my head to look at him. He's folded over again, resting his elbows on his knees, holding his coffee in both hands. He has a tattoo on his right shoulder, and this close I can see how some of the edges are blurring, like it wasn't outlined very well.

"You didn't like me yesterday?"

"No." He shakes his head. "But I like you now."

By the time Daniel retrieves me from the sauna, the headache has subsided into a dull but persistent throbbing. "How are we doing?" he says.

"Mortified."

"No reason for that. Usually, he gets them naked at night, and they spend the next day crying. This is much classier. You're raising the bar."

"Stop it," I say.

"Seriously, honey, Tommy told me about your husband. You needed a little meltdown. You earned it." He kisses me on the cheek. "I'm going to take you back to your room, and we're going to get you dressed, and I have some drops for your eyes, and by the time we come back out, you'll look totally human, totally beautiful."

I do not feel totally beautiful by the time I come back out for break-fast, but I do feel like I can stand up at least. From the hall, I can see that Alan and Joe are already at the table, and when I see them, I start to panic.

"Jesus." I turn to Daniel. "Do they know?"

Daniel follows my gaze to where they're sitting and shakes his head. "First of all, there's nothing to know. You had a few drinks and cried about your very legitimate grief. So what? And second"—he leans in like he's telling a secret—"those two were so shitfaced last night, they wouldn't have noticed if the two of you had been fucking on the coffee table."

I let out the breath I've been holding, and for a second I rest my head on his shoulder. He smells clean, like soap and shampoo. He smells like someone who has his shit together.

When I reach the table and sit down, the two of them don't even look up. Alan is holding a cup of coffee up to his mouth but not drink-ing it, and Joe's eyes are closed. Daniel sets a plate in front of me—fried potatoes, eggs, a piece of toast. Daniel points at the fork and says, "Eat." He brings me a new cup of coffee. This time it's black and sugarless. By the time I've eaten half the toast, Tommy walks in.

"Good morning," he says loudly, and everyone sort of grumbles in return. "Sorry to make you all get up so early. Especially you two." He waves his hand at Alan and Joe. "You guys look like you had a lot of fun last night." Alan kind of half smiles and nods in agreement. "Either way, we have a lot of work today. Alan has some potential investors coming in tomorrow. They're gonna want to see some pages."

By noon we have exactly two of those pages, and Tommy says there's no way we can break for lunch. He has Daniel arrange for the house-keeper to put out a tray of food on a side table.

"Grab something," he says to all of us, "and then it's back to work."

I don't feel like eating, and he obviously doesn't either, but Alan and Joe have finally recovered enough to be hungry, and they converge on the table like vultures. Tommy's been standing most of the morning, moving from me to Joe, looking over our shoulders, pointing at our screens, shaking his head. Now he sits down next to me. "How's your head?" he asks.

I shrug. "Better. You?"

"I've had better days," he says, "but I've had worse too."

"I'm really so sorry," I say.

He makes a dismissive face. "Forget about it. It's nothing."

"It's humiliating."

"What is?" He narrows his eyes like he's concentrating. "Oh, right." He reaches over and raises a strand of my hair like he's inspecting it. "Did you get all of that shit out of your hair?"

I slap his hand away. "Fuck you. God."

"Hey, you're the one who wants to wallow in it. We can wallow. I'm all over the wallowing."

"You are a dick," I say, but I do laugh.

"I'm a goddamn saint. I totally took care of you. I didn't even have sex with you when you were passed out."

"Wow," I say. "Thank you for not being a sexual predator."

"What?" He looks at me like I've lost my mind. "Have you not seen me? I mean, c'mon. Consent is implied."

"Seriously?" I say. "Do you come by asshole naturally, or do you have to work at it?"

"I don't really have to work for much of anything, honey." And I know he's just teasing, but the expression on his face, his eyebrow slightly raised, his tongue just at the corner of his lips, this expression is totally filthy. I think I might blush.

"I must have forgotten," I say. "You're like the sexiest man alive, right?"

He presses his lips together and holds up three fingers. "Technically, no. Not this year. This year I'm number three."

"Hard to believe," I say, shaking my head. *Hard to believe.*

Joe looks right at Tommy. "I think we need to go back to the name thing. I don't care what little miss poet says, the main character in a movie needs a name. How 'bout Matilda?"

Tommy sighs and rubs at his brow.

"She can't have a name," I say. "She's representative of all women."

"This isn't some art film. We want this shit to sell, right?" Joe looks at Tommy. "Or you just doing this for fun?"

I take a deep breath, pinch my lips with my teeth. "Okay, but you know what? The creature didn't have a name in *Frankenstein* either."

"Yeah," he says, his voice a little louder, "and that's why everyone thinks the monster's named Frankenstein because people need a fucking name."

"No, it's because they're illiterate." I toss my pen on the table. It clicks against my glass, and Joe looks pointedly at it and then raises his eyebrows.

"Enough," Tommy says. He raises his left hand, his palm pressed flat in Joe's direction. "We've wasted enough time on this. Don't bring it up again."

Joe throws his hands up. "I don't even know why I'm here. Bitch is always right, huh? What, did she blow you or something?"

I open my mouth, but Tommy sits up straight and puts his hand on my arm.

"You got a problem, Joe?" he says. "You feel like you need some more attention?" He's raising his voice. "You want to fucking blow me? Or you want to do your goddamn job?"

By the end of the day, my back is in knots. Daniel slipped me something he said was ibuprofen over dinner, but I'm pretty sure it was something much stronger. Still, it's like the stress of holding up my head is just too much. I roll my shoulders, twist my neck.

"Hurts, doesn't it?" Tommy says.

We're inside, and I'm sitting cross-legged on the couch. It's raining, but it's still hot, and the back door is open. We're watching the water spill across the terrace in warm waves, listening to it drum.

Tommy says it won't last long. He walks to the window and leans against the wall, looking out.

I lift my hair up off my neck and massage it, try to force out the tension. Alan and Joe are at the bar fixing tomato juice and beer. "You want one?" Alan yells, but I just wince, and Tommy shakes his head.

"I am not a believer in that hair-of-the-dog shit," Tommy says, but he's not talking loud enough for them to hear. He walks back and sits on the arm of the couch, resting his feet on the seat beside me. "You gotta walk through the pain sometime, and you may as well do it now, or when you wake up, it'll just be sitting there waiting for you."

I wonder if this is supposed to be some kind of pep talk. "Is that like a metaphor for grief?"

He looks confused for a minute and then laughs. "No. I was mostly talking about alcohol poisoning, but it was pretty profound, wasn't it?"

"Not really," I say.

The investors show up on Saturday in time for lunch, and the table looks amazing. In the center is a platter of smoked salmon, a basket of bread, a huge glass bowl of mixed green salad. The bowl alone is ridiculous. It's blown glass, a pale, pale blue. It looks like it's made of ice. In anyone else's house, this would be a display piece, and to Tommy it's just a salad bowl. I bet he wouldn't care if it broke. He's pouring wine for one of the investors, a woman. I think her name is Marie. She's pushed her glass toward him, and he has his hand on hers, touching it for longer than he needs to. She looks close to fifty, but beautiful, patrician. Her hair is a dark brown, and she wears it swept back from her brow, a little silvering at the temple. It doesn't look natural, or really it looks too natural, like a young actress aged for a role. Her face isn't unlined exactly, but she certainly doesn't have wrinkles, just softening around her features, a little crinkling around her eyes, a little accentuation around her smile. Whoever does her face must be worth a fortune.

The other investor's her partner, at least that's what I think. No one's bothered to explain anything to me. He's much younger, maybe just thirty.

From across the table I watch Marie work Tommy, or maybe he's working her. It's hard to tell. He's leaning in, focusing. Whatever he's saying is only meant for her. She clearly loves it. She's laughing, but just gently, for effect, and she rests her hand on his arm, and when she pulls away, she does it slowly so that her fingers trail the length of it, and I think, *Jesus Christ.* But then I think, *Whatever, it's not like I care.*

I pick at the salad, choose wine over bread. It's a very dry white. Not much sugar, which is good. Around me, the conversation is picking up, turning to business.

"Who are you thinking for the lead?" the partner asks. I still haven't caught his name.

"Sarah," Alan says. "Sarah Nixon."

I look up because I know who this is. She'd be perfect. Tommy catches my eye and raises an eyebrow. I know he's asking if I approve, and I nod and look at him like, *Jesus, of course,* and he must get that because he kind of laughs. This is the first time Marie looks at me. She smiles like she hates me already. *Good.*

She turns to Tommy. "And, of course, you'll be in it."

He nods. "Frederick."

I make a scoffing noise. "Are you serious?" He can't be serious. I shake my head.

Marie says, "Well, obviously you'll have to do *a* role."

"I'll do that role," Tommy says.

"Absolutely not." There's no way he can do Frederick. It's insane.

"Are you saying I can't play it?" He smiles, but it's the kind of smile you'd give a child, the kind of smile that says, *Isn't she cute? Isn't she cute with the talking?*

"I'm saying you shouldn't." I take another sip. This wine is good. I feel like I should have more. "Frederick," I say slowly, "is basically a pedophile."

Marie sits back in her chair. Just the word has made her uncomfortable.

The partner speaks up now. He says, "I didn't realize this movie was about child rape . . ."

"It's not," Tommy says, in a tone that very clearly states that the partner has not been invited to speak. He doesn't bother to look in his direction. He's still looking at me, and he doesn't seem to think that I'm cute anymore. "Don't do that. Don't dumb down the book to win an argument."

"I'm just pointing out that you"—I wave my hand at Tommy—"are not what people want to imagine in that role. They want to see you looking handsome, maybe a little dangerous, but not so much with the raping of little girls, you know?"

"You know," Tommy says slowly, "that's why it should be me. Because we don't believe in attractive rapists, do we? If he's attractive, how can it be rape? If he's so attractive, why can't he just find a living girl? I mean, the trope for a character like Frederick is that he's driven to it. He's the poor, rejected bastard who can't get laid. But that's not the story we're playing with here. It isn't about sex. It's about control." He holds my gaze for a long moment.

I look at him. I look back at my wine. It's nearly empty, which is probably how I got into this mess. "I'm not saying you wouldn't be good for the role," I say finally. "I'm saying the role wouldn't be good for you." I shake my head again. "I think it's a mistake."

It's still early, even earlier back home, and I think I can catch the boys before they're off to sleep. "Are they still up?" I say when Jenny answers the phone.

"Yup," she says. "Just finished brushing their teeth."

It's only the second time I've talked to them since I've been away. Stevie is the first to get on the phone.

"I made my Christmas list," he says. "But Ben says Santa might not find us at Noni's."

"I already told Santa where we'll be. I sent him a letter last week." This will be our first Christmas away from Omaha, without Michael, and the boys have been worried about it.

I want our regular Christmas, Ben had said. As if anything's regular these days.

"I saw you guys built a snowman," I say.

Jenny had texted me a picture, though I couldn't really see their faces. It could have been anyone's kids all bundled up for the snow. I recognized the jackets, of course, the mittens, the hats. Stevie in the green coat. Ben in the blue.

When I wake, it's still dark. I don't know what time it is. But I know the boys are two thousand miles away, and Michael's even farther and the truth of that feels too huge. It feels like a rock on my chest. I need to move, to get out from under it. I slip out of bed and roll out my yoga mat to stretch. I think about going for a run or a swim. I'm afraid I'd get lost if I went out through the front gates, that I'd never get back in, but there's a treadmill out in the pool house by the sauna, and I think if I get on it and turn it as high as I can, I might feel better. I might be able to breathe.

When I make it to three miles, my lungs feel like they're working, like I'm filling up with air. Everything is arms and legs and air and space, and I fit inside it. I feel like it's closing around me like a neat little box, and I know where all the walls belong.

When Marie comes out for breakfast, she comes from the right. I don't know this house well, but I know the only room down that hall is Tommy's, and I think, *Fuck.* Whatever, it's none of my business. I really don't care. She'll be gone by this afternoon anyway.

Tommy is sitting at the head of the table reading a newspaper, and as she walks past him, Marie stretches her hand out, brushing his shoulders in this lingering gesture. He doesn't look up, but she doesn't seem to mind. The dress she's wearing is this soft linen shell, sleeveless, and it just floats over her body. I think she must live in a yoga studio. She sits down across from me and smiles.

"Good morning," she says brightly, and I think, *Yeah, I bet,* but I smile anyway.

"There's coffee," I say.

"Oh no." She shakes her head a little too emphatically. She looks around at Daniel. He's standing at the counter, checking something on his phone. "I'll have some green tea," she says, like he was just waiting to take her order. "Very hot."

This little muscle in Tommy's cheek tenses, but he doesn't say anything.

"Sure," Daniel says, "absolutely. Let me just get that for you." He sets his phone down and picks up a mug. He comes back in a few minutes and sets it in front of her. "Watch out. It's very hot." He catches my eye and raises one eyebrow behind her back.

"So, I understand you're from Nebraska," she says, putting a little emphasis on *bras*.

"My husband was."

"And you don't like it?" She takes a sip of her tea but startles. She seems to have burned herself.

"No, I like it," I say. "I'm just not from there."

"Hmm." She doesn't seem to care where I'm from now. She seems to have really been hoping it was Nebraska. "Well, maybe all this will be your ticket out."

"I'll keep my fingers crossed," I say.

The investors left hours ago, and no one else seems to be around. In the living room, there's a wall full of books, and I finger my way through the titles. I take one finally and curl onto the couch to read. I read and read and read. It's a beautiful book, the kind that makes me a little jealous. All the pieces are lining up, and I can see the ending coming, but it doesn't even matter. A book like this isn't about the plot.

"Hey," Tommy says, and I look up. I hadn't even heard him come in. "You like that?" he says, gesturing toward the book.

"I do," I say. "It's great."

He drops onto the opposite couch on his back, throwing his legs up over the arm of it. "Have you read any of his other work?"

"No." I shake my head.

"That one's the best, definitely. Probably the darkest too." He smiles. "Not dark like your book, but close."

"My book isn't dark. It's a constructed examination of gender and power."

He laughs. "You're so full of shit."

"What?"

"Your book is so raw. But then in person? Totally zipped up. I just expected you to be more . . ." He shakes his head. "I don't know. But that was like half a bottle of scotch to get you to open up."

"Go to hell," I say, and I stand up to go.

He holds one hand up defensively. "I'm not criticizing you. I mean, I see you're just holding shit together. I get it. I do. I'm just saying the result is"—he waves his hand in a circle like he's taking in all of me—"a little uptight."

I throw my hands up. "What do you want me to do with that?"

"I don't want you to do anything. I'm just telling you. Jesus. Don't get all worked up."

Half a decibel I raised my voice, and already I'm getting this. I smile, soften my tone. "So what you're saying is you want me to share my feelings more, except for those times when my feelings might make you in any way uncomfortable?"

He laughs. "That would be perfect. Can you do that?"

"Of course," I say. "How do you think I stayed married so long?"

"So he makes this monster, and she's beautiful, right?" Joe leans back, spreading his arms wide along the back of the loveseat in that sort of pose men use when they're trying to make themselves look bigger.

"Right." I nod.

"So why's he keep chopping her up? Replacing parts? I think that's why this scene isn't working. I don't see the motivation."

"He's not satisfied," I say. "Women are held to impossible standards, so even though the moment he finishes making her, he calls her his new Eve, his Aphrodite, he's also noticing all these things he wants to change about her."

"There's that," Tommy says, pressing one palm in my direction. "I mean, that's a very real theme, but in terms of plot, there's also the fact that when she opens her mouth, nothing good comes out. She's fucked-up on the inside, and Frederick still thinks he can fix that."

Joe leans forward onto his knees. "Trust me, I see the appeal of cutting out a woman's tongue. That's a good scene. I like that scene a lot."

Tommy laughs. "He doesn't want her quiet. He just wants to control what she says."

"Frederick is the inversion of Frankenstein," I say. "Frankenstein doesn't want the responsibility of being a god to the creature, but that's exactly what Frederick wants. He wants her to worship him, and she won't."

"Does he want her to worship him?" Tommy says. "Or does he want her to love him?"

"To Frederick?" I shrug. "Same thing."

Tommy shakes his head. "See, that's where we're getting stuck. You're so fixated on what he represents. There's no complexity to him. He wants worship. He wants sex." He kicks his feet up on the table, closes his eyes. "Let go of the symbolism for five seconds and let him be a person."

"I wouldn't mind a little worship," Joe says, half under his breath.

"Yeah, it's not as fun as you'd think," Tommy says.

———

I've promised to stay for ten days, but I think, if we can just get finished, I can leave, I can get out, and I mention this to Tommy after dinner. He's pouring me another glass of wine.

"You want to go home?" he asks.

"Feels like it's time."

"Miss your kids?" He hands me the glass and sets the bottle down on the terrace wall. We're both resting on the wall, looking out, though it's too dark to see much of anything. I'm listening to the waves.

I kind of laugh, but it's a sad laugh, and I shake my head. "I don't know what I feel. I do, but then I don't. It's hard to be around them these days."

"Yeah. I get that," he says. He has a daughter, a teenager, and I know this. Everyone knows. Her mother's an actress. Famous. More for having Tommy's daughter than anything she's done on her own. I feel strange knowing all of this already. "My daughter," he says. "I hate it when she's with her mother." He takes a drink. "But I also hate it when she comes to live with me."

"Why?"

"I don't know." He sighs. "When she's around, I feel like I'm on, like I'm playing a part." He's quiet for a long time. "My dad was pretty shitty," he says finally. "I don't want that for her, you know? So ever since she was a baby, I've been like, 'Here is a scene in which I play a good father.'" He shakes his head. "Doesn't come naturally, you know. It doesn't feel real."

I don't mean to say it, I really don't, but it comes out anyway. "That was me as a wife sometimes."

I can feel him watching me now. He puts his hand over mine, rubs his thumb lightly across the back of it, but he doesn't say anything, and I don't turn to look at him, and after a minute, he pulls his hand away. I think that's probably a good thing. I think it's probably for the best.

I get home late, just after ten, and Jenny is waiting, though the first one to greet me is Bear. He wants me to pet him hello, and so I do, scratching under his chin and behind his left ear.

Tomorrow's a school day, and the boys have been asleep for hours. I wanted them home though. I wanted to look in on them sleeping in their beds, so Jenny brought them here.

"Thank you," I say. "Thanks for taking them."

"You owe me," she says, but she doesn't mean it. She closes her book, sets it in her lap. "So tell me everything," she says.

"It was surreal," I say. Jenny's sipping tea and there's a kettle of hot water still on the stove. I pull a mug from the cabinet and drop a teabag into it. "I mean, Tommy DeMarco."

She already knows he was there. I told her over the phone. Still, she shakes her head like she doesn't believe me. "That is insane," she says. "It's like . . . it's like something out of a movie."

"Literally. He is literally something out of a movie."

"It's insane," she says again. "Is he as hot in person?"

"Oh god. Yeah. Definitely." I dunk the bag in and out of the water. I almost smile. *I kissed him,* I could say. I wonder what she would think about that.

"And you're actually available now." She stops. "I can't believe I just said that." She stands up and crosses the room and puts her arms around me. "Like it's a *good* thing you're . . . Like you would ever . . . God. I'm so sorry. I didn't mean it like that."

"It's fine," I say.

She steps back and nods toward my mug. "Switch to wine?" She walks to my wine rack and pulls out a bottle. "I'm so sorry," she says again.

"Just drop it, Jenny. It's nothing." Nothing worth talking about. I walk over to where she's set her book down. "What are you reading?"

"Don't be dismissive," she says. "It's for my book club."

"Ugh, your book club." I went with her once, and only half of them had even picked up the novel. Hers is more of a drinking club.

"Hey, I like it, and they're fun."

"You know you could skip the lame books and just drink here."

"I do drink here." She raises a glass and hands it to me. "I'm drinking here right now."

When she leaves, I rinse the glasses, set them beside the sink. I take a clean rag and wipe down the counters though no one's eaten here all week. But it's after midnight, and I'm not tired, and I'm not going to sleep. I cork the open bottle and set it back on the shelf, and then I send a text to Daniel. *Tell Tommy thanks for the hospitality, but now, by comparison, all my booze tastes like shit.*

A few days later, a case of wine is delivered, and with it, a very expensive scotch that's labeled *For emergencies only.* I don't plan to open it.

JANUARY

I PULL UP TO THE SCHOOL and park in one of the visitors' spots. Stevie's class is learning about poetry, and he volunteered me to his teacher. *My mommy can come,* I imagine him saying. *She writes books.* Of course, she e-mailed me, so here I am with these haiku handouts and armpits full of anxiety sweat. I'm glad the sweater I'm wearing is black.

Stevie's teacher is finishing up reading one of those giant flip books about Lewis and Clark. It must be part of their Nebraska history curriculum. I think about saying, *Can you tell the kids about their contributions to genocide?* but instead I just wait in the doorway.

"Now, kids, we have a very special visitor today." All the kids twist in their seats to look. "And I know you are all going to do your very best to use your ears and your eyes, but not your . . . ?"

"Mouths," all the kids say.

"That's right. Now maybe, Stevie, you could greet our guest and introduce her to the class?"

Stevie's still little enough to hug me in front of his friends. He takes my hand and pulls me to the front of the class. "This is my mom," he says.

"Mrs. . . . ?" says the teacher.

"Mrs. Lane," Stevie says. I smile at him, and he sits back down.

"Hi, guys," I say, and I wave my hand. "So, Stevie asked me if I would come and talk to you guys about poetry because that's what I do. Poetry is kind of my job." *Jesus Christ,* I think, *I sound like an asshole.* "I thought maybe we could start by talking about metaphors. Has your teacher told you what a metaphor is?"

It turns out that Bashō is not the biggest hit with first-graders, and their little confused faces make me even more anxious. I wish the teacher would just cut me off like I can tell she wants to, but she just lets me talk and talk, and then I get the kids to help me write a haiku on the board.

"Why don't we write a poem about one of the animals we've been studying?" the teacher says, and a boy in the back says, "Ooh, a bear, a bear."

"That's great," I say, and I write *bear* on the board. "Now, how do we want to describe it?"

The teacher says, "What are some good adjectives for a bear?" and then we end up with *furry,* which I don't think is a particularly interesting adjective, but what do I know?

"Okay," I say. "What's something surprising we could compare a furry bear to?"

"A garbage truck!" someone yells, and I'm like, *Nice,* but then the teacher says, "I didn't see a hand." She's a real stickler.

Stevie puts his hand up, and I think, *Yes,* because I'm doing this for him, or maybe I want him to do it for me. I don't know, but he says, "A monster," and I'm like, *Really?* I start to make a face at him like, *Maybe not,* but then the other kids all start saying, "Yeah," and the teacher is telling them all to settle back down, so I write *monster* on the board. Then the teacher hands out paper and they all copy down *Furry bear monster of the dark woods*, which is not exactly seventeen syllables or a very good metaphor. They're drawing giant brown bears and trees, and I'm just ready to get the hell out of here.

"Well, thank you so much for coming," the teacher says to me.

I slip around behind Stevie and hug him goodbye. His *furry* is missing an *r*, and his bear looks like a boulder with ears. "Bye, sweetie," I say. "Thanks for letting me come to your class." He nods, but then he kisses me on the cheek with his soft, tiny lips and I feel like I could cry. I don't though. I just stand back up and leave.

When I get in my car, I pull my phone out to turn the ringer back on. I have a text from Jenny and a voice message from Daniel. I hit *play*.

"Hey, it's Daniel. Call me as soon as you can."

He picks up on the first ring. "Hang on," he says. "Here's Tommy."

"Stacey, hey. How's it going?" He sounds nice. He sounds like we're friends.

"Good," I say, though I'm suddenly feeling anxious again. "What's up?"

"I need you to come out to L.A."

This is not what I was expecting, not that I knew what to expect, but if I had, it wouldn't have been this. "Okay. Why?"

"So I've got my friend Jason coming in to talk about directing. I think he'd be perfect, you know. I don't know if you know his work? Jason Collier." He pauses like I'm supposed to answer, and I don't say, *Are you kidding me?* I just say, "Yeah."

"Anyway, I think he's interested, but I want you to be here. I mean, Jason's a genius, but so much of this comes from you. I want to make sure we're shaping his vision, you know, that we get this right."

This is flattering, and it is January in Nebraska, and the thought of leaving sounds great. "Okay. When?"

"That's kind of the thing. Jason's coming over at eleven tomorrow, so we could have you on a plane at, hang on." He holds the phone away, and I hear him say, "Daniel, what time is that flight? Four o'clock," he says.

"Are you serious? That's not exactly time for me to figure out my kids." I lean my head back against the headrest, chew on my lip. "Let me call my sister. I'll see what I can do."

"Look, the minute Jason's on board, we get the green light on this. You've got to be here. You have to come out."

Out the window, the sky is a dull gray. It's been just warm enough that some of December's snow has melted. Beneath it all the grass is brown and dead. *Dormant* I guess is more accurate, but it just looks dead.

Daniel picks me up at the airport and takes me back to Tommy's. His house in L.A. is nothing like the house on Parrot Cay, but it's definitely as dramatic. The gates are tall and the whole place is hidden behind walls and shrubs, and when we pull past them, it's this modern beachy-looking spread. It looks expensive, of course, but inviting. Just inside the entrance there are these open, floating stairs to the right, and then this long wide hallway that leads straight back toward this tremendous fireplace, and halfway down, double doors that lead to a living room on the left.

Tommy is in the living room, and he throws his arms out and says, "Hey, you're here." He crosses the room and catches me in a hug.

"Hi," I say. "Good to see you."

"You look like you need a drink." He lets go of me and walks to the bar in the corner. "Red?" he says, holding up a bottle he's already opened. "Daniel? You staying to drink or you headed home?"

Daniel shakes his head. "I've seen this show before. And I'm guessing I'll need to be here early to feed you ibuprofen and make sure you're presentable."

"I'm presentable. I am always presentable." Tommy pours two glasses and steps out from behind the bar. He carries both glasses in his left hand, the bottle in his right. He holds the glasses out toward me, and I take one.

"Don't stay up too late. Don't open another bottle." Daniel points his finger at Tommy and then at me.

Tommy just smiles, and Daniel squeezes my arm and says good night.

I turn to move toward the couch, but Tommy says, "Come this way. I want to show you something," and he presses the hand with the wine bottle against my back and takes me through the doorway into the dining room. Beyond that is the kitchen and this enormous great room, which is where the fireplace is, and then there's this wide hallway. The first door opens into a study that is just lined with books. I mean, there are shelves all the way around it, and then there are stacks of books on almost every surface. There's this small loveseat at one end of the room and a desk at the other. Tommy sets the wine on the table in front of the loveseat and retrieves a laptop that's sitting open on the desk.

"Sit," he says. He sets the laptop on the table and sits next to me. His leg presses right up against my leg, but it doesn't seem to bother him. It is bothering me. I take a big sip of the wine, a really big sip. It might be more like a swig.

"Okay," he says, "so I have all of this shit on Frederick, and I want to see what you think."

There are pages and pages of notes, this whole backstory on the character that I obviously never wrote, and then there are just these random lines and quotes. I only recognize a few, but there's Eliot, Rilke, Nabokov obviously. As I'm reading through them, Tommy says, "I felt like I needed to get some male voices in my head, you know?" and I nod.

"Where did you get all of this?"

He sort of holds his hands out like, *Look around.* "Well, it's great," I say. "I mean, it all feels right."

He lets out this tremendous sigh like he's been holding his breath, and he puts his arm around my shoulders and leans his head against me. "Oh thank god. I was sure you were gonna fight me on this again."

"No. I mean, if this is how you see him, you see what I see."

"Okay," he says, and he leans forward, grabbing the laptop, balancing it on our knees. "So look at this."

He has all of these short video clips. Some are him, but mostly it's other people. He's been using them to figure out the walk, how he'll move his hands, how he should talk, and everything he shows me has some little shadow of Frederick, and he's trying to explain how he'll layer them together. He wants me to look at the screen, but I keep turning my head to watch him talk, and he has to keep pointing me back. He has a lot of this to show me, so we do go through the wine, and Tommy does open another bottle, but by then I don't even mind how close he's sitting or the way he keeps touching my hand when he makes a point.

When he finally closes the laptop, I pull my left leg up and hug it into me and then my right. I'm trying to unkink my hips.

"Fuck, no wonder you're so tense," he says, and I think, *What? Why? Is it obvious?* "You've been stuck on a plane all day, and now I've got you all cramped up in here." He rests his hand on my back and rubs his thumb along the edges of my spine right between my shoulder blades. Up one side, down the other. I try not to flinch.

"I should get some sleep," I say. "It's like three a.m. for me." I smile. "You're a terrible influence."

"I hear that a lot. Come on." He stands up and pulls me to my feet. "I've got a room for you upstairs."

When I wake up, there's a pale yellow light coming in through the window. The curtains are just these thin beige panels, and they don't keep anything out. I can see now that there's a shade behind them that I could have pulled down, but of course I hadn't noticed. It doesn't really matter. It's always hard for me to stay asleep.

In the shower, I let the hot water run through my hair for a long time, try to massage away the fog left by the wine.

I walk back into the bedroom and pull my clothes out of the bag. Packing for this was confusing. I mean, what do you wear to a business meeting that's in someone's house? And what if the person you're meeting is really powerful but they're more of an artist? I don't know. That's too many variables for me, so I brought these black pants with a wide leg, but they hang really low on my hip like they could be casual. The top is this sleeveless, mossy green knit, and it's got this nice flow to it and a low neck, which now that I have it on, shows kind of a lot of skin. I wish I'd brought a tank or something to put under it, but I didn't, so I'll just have to live with it.

———

Tommy is already in the kitchen when I get downstairs, and he looks fine, refreshed even. He's sitting at the counter reading a newspaper. I don't know how he can live like he does and still look like that. It took a lot of work to disguise the circles under my eyes.

"Morning, lazy. Thought you were gonna sleep all day."

"Please. It's not even nine. Coffee cups?"

He points to a cabinet, and I open it, take down a mug to fill. The coffee smells perfect, all earthy and rich. "Actually, I've been awake for hours." I lean back against the counter across from him. "I don't sleep all that well."

"Ever or just the last year?" He sets his newspaper down like he's giving me his full attention.

I shrug. "I guess it's probably gotten worse."

"Daniel can get you a prescription if you want to try some Xanax or something." He gives me this look like he's actually a little concerned. "That, or maybe you just need to get laid."

"Wow, you're like a doctor or something, aren't you?"

"You'd be surprised how much it helps."

"Well, you look like the picture of health in any case." I look back down at my coffee. I bring the mug up to my lips, but it's still too hot, so I just blow on it.

He picks his paper back up, refolds it to a different page. "Honestly, honey, with you looking like that, it would not be hard to arrange."

"Wow. Isn't that the highest compliment? 'I bet there's someone willing to fuck you.' You've made my day."

"Jason's going to love you, actually, which might work in our favor." He sort of gives me this nod like, *That would be great.* "I don't know if it'll really help your sleeping problem because he is married. Third wife though, so who knows?"

"You are such an asshole," I say, and I stand up and walk to the other side of the island, which is actually closer to where he is, but I can't figure out another direction to move.

"I'm kidding. Jesus. I forgot how uptight you are." He stands up and walks toward me with his arms kind of raised like he wants to give me a hug, and I take a step back.

"Oh, come on, Stacey. Lighten up. I'm just giving you shit." He reaches me and throws his arms around me and slides his head right down next to mine. "You really need to learn to relax. No wonder you can't sleep."

Tommy is leaning against the wall by the front window watching for Jason, who's about fifteen minutes late.

"Lunch is ready to go whenever you want it," Daniel says to Tommy.

"Perfect," Tommy says. "Sounds great." It actually sounds like Tommy's not paying much attention.

"Also, I was checking your calendar, and it looks like you have a reservation tonight. Dinner plans. What do you want to do about that?"

Tommy knocks his head back against the wall. "Shit. I forgot. You're gonna have to call Hannah. Tell her not tonight. Maybe some night next week."

"Great," Daniel says, and he makes a face at me. "That's gonna be a fun call." He rolls his eyes.

I laugh. "Are you really so important you can't break your own dates? That's kind of shitty."

Daniel nods. "Isn't it? He doesn't like to 'make his own arrangements,'" he says, making these dramatic air quotes.

"Daniel knows my schedule better than I do. I don't need to talk to her, and she doesn't need my number."

"Wow. You really are a dick."

Daniel nods. "This is what I'm trying to tell you. He is un-fucking-believable."

"Okay, hold on, it's not that I don't want her to be able to reach me, but I don't need my number getting out. If she wants to talk to me, she can just call Daniel."

"And I can tell her he's 'not really available right now,'" Daniel says, punctuating with his fingers again.

"Exactly," Tommy says.

It's horrible, but I laugh. "God, you're an asshole."

He shrugs. "But I sleep like a baby."

"No. I bet you do because in my experience babies sleep like assholes who interrupt everyone with their random, selfish demands for more tit."

Daniel laughs, and Tommy just smiles. "That was pretty good, Stace. I'm gonna let that one slide." He turns to Daniel. "Keep the reservation. I'll take Stacey."

"I don't want to go to dinner with you."

"Shut up. It's a nice place," he says. "You'll like it." He looks out the window again. "Jason's here."

Jason is awfully cute but a little short. I know he's in his mid-forties, but he could pass for my age easily. He has this curly brown hair and a sweet baby face and this one great dimple on just the left side. When he shakes my hand, he smiles really wide, and it makes me smile too.

"So you are Stacey," he says, leaning his arm against the bar. Tommy is fixing us something to drink. "I have to admit, I didn't know what to expect." He makes an apologetic face. "Your book is a little scary, you know." He laughs.

He doesn't seem to think I'm scary though. His eyes keep dropping to my chest, but I pretend I don't notice. I don't actually mind.

"Jason, I know you're having scotch. Stacey?"

"No. No scotch. Maybe vodka."

"Tommy tells me you live in Omaha," Jason says. "You don't strike me as all that Nebraskan."

I put my hand up to take the drink that Tommy holds out, but I keep my eyes on Jason. "Really? You can't picture me out with the tractors and cows?" I raise my eyebrow.

"Not really." He laughs. "Should we have a seat?"

He motions to the couch. He sits on one end, and I sit on the other, but I turn sideways, sit on my hip, so my knees are pointing toward him. I lean my arm against the back of the couch. I take a drink. The vodka is nice and cold. The vodka is great.

"So tell me about yourself," Jason says.

I smile. "There's not much to tell."

He reaches over, picks a copy of my book up off the table. "So where did all this come from?"

I laugh. "I have no idea. I couldn't tell you how it all works." I pull my bottom lip in with my teeth, but not in a nervous way. I'm doing this on purpose. Jason smiles.

Tommy crosses the room and sits in the chair across from us. He

LIZ KAY

leans forward, rests his elbows on his knees, and looks at Jason. "So, what are your thoughts?"

"Well"—he turns to Tommy—"I've read the script, and I like it. I do. I think it has potential."

"But?"

Jason tosses his hands up. "I don't know. There's some fucked-up shit in this thing, no offense." He reaches across the couch like he means to pat my hand, but there's a lot of space between us. He doesn't even come close.

"I think," I say, "you're focusing on the wrong things."

Jason looks back at me. I swirl the vodka in my glass, watch the ice spin and settle.

"The story isn't about the things that happen. It's about the people they happen to. All of this violence that sort of builds up around them, that isn't the story, Jason." When I say his name, I look back at him. I look him in the eye. "It's just the lens through which we discover these characters, who they are, what makes them, what tears them down."

Jason takes a breath, he raises his eyebrows, he looks at my breasts. I lean and stretch my arm to set my glass on the table, and when I sit up, I may shift my shoulders back a bit.

"Okay, keep talking," Jason says, and I do. I talk about the characters and the book and the script. I talk about Tommy, how much I trust him with this, how much I'm willing to trust Jason because Tommy says I should. Tommy is watching me too, but I only look at Jason. Jason I can handle. Jason I've got.

By the time Jason leaves, he and Tommy have a handshake deal that they've sealed with yet another round of drinks. In the foyer, Jason kisses my cheek a little sloppily, and his hand slides a bit lower on my back than his third wife would probably like.

When Tommy closes the door behind Jason, he leans his head against it for a moment, lets his hand rest on the door frame. "Oh shit," he whispers. "We've got him. We've fucking got him." He turns around, and he's smiling. Not just a smile really, more like a grin. "And you." He walks toward me, grabs me by the shoulders. "Jesus, who are you? Why have I never met this Stacey before? I have to hang out with boring, uptight, pissed-off-all-the-time Stacey, and he gets fun, sexy Stacey. That's kind of bullshit."

"Fuck you," I say, shoving him backwards and turning toward the living room.

"See? There's my girl. There's the Stacey I know."

I drop down on the couch, lay my head back, close my eyes, but I feel him sit in the spot where Jason had been. I hear his feet thunk onto the table.

"You look beat. Go lay down," he says, and he sets his hand on my leg, so he must be sitting closer than I'd thought. "We've got hours before dinner. Go get some sleep."

When I open my eyes, the light from the window has faded. It's seven forty-five, and we're supposed to be leaving at eight. I didn't bother to set an alarm because I can never sleep. Except today, which is brilliant.

I'd at least had the good sense to take my clothes off and lay them over a chair in the corner so they wouldn't get wrinkled. I slip them back on, walk into the bathroom to touch up my eyes, my lips, pull my fingers through my hair. I shake it out and let it fall around my shoulders. *This is not about Tommy,* I think because of course it isn't. I just like to make a good impression.

Tommy must have spent the rest of the afternoon not drinking because he drives, which is not what I expected. There is something about sitting in the passenger seat of a man's car that feels a little exhilarating, a little dangerous, and because the man who's driving is Tommy, I try to look out the window a lot.

"You really were great today," he says. He pulls to a stop at a light and reaches over, grabs my hand. "And what you said about trusting me with this meant a lot." He tugs on my hand like he wants me to look at him. "I promise I'm not going to fuck it up."

They seat us at a table near the back, and as we walk through, there are lots of people not looking at us, conspicuously so. There's a lot of quickly lowered eyes, deliberate not-staring. I feel a little dizzy, like I might trip.

It's a circular booth, and while Tommy sits at an angle from me, he's close enough that our knees are almost touching. There's a bottle of wine open to breathe on the table. I'm guessing Daniel called earlier to set it up.

Tommy must come here a lot because the waiter is totally relaxed with him, and Tommy orders for both of us without even looking at the menu. When the waiter steps away, I take a sip of my wine, look around. The place is packed, and I can tell by the way people are sitting, holding themselves so carefully, barely turning their heads, that everyone has noticed Tommy. On the far side of the room, one couple is openly gaping, which is unsettling, but at least it's honest.

"How did you even get started in all of this?" I say.

Tommy looks at me over his glass. When he sets it down he says, "You mean like all of it, all of it? I don't know. I just caught a break."

"No, I mean, what made you want to try?"

"Oh," he says, and he takes another drink. He looks like he's deciding whether to answer me. "I guess I was running away."

I keep my eyes on him like I'm waiting for the rest.

"Really?" he says, and he kind of laughs. "All right. Fine. I had a fucked-up family. My dad was mean and drunk and usually broke. I never did very well in school, and frankly, I didn't have any other options, so it was either this or who knows." He holds my gaze for a minute. "So anyway, I got out here, and I looked like me, which didn't hurt," but he says this in a tone like he's deliberately being an ass. "And you know, I'd been playing roles my whole life, trying to dodge all the shit. I guess it all just clicked."

"Huh," I say. "Interesting." I hold my glass on the table, twist the stem through my fingers.

"You sound like a shrink."

"No, it is," I say. "It's interesting. And you know, that's kind of what I do, think about what shapes us, where we end up. It's kind of my thing." I smile.

"Maybe your next book should be about me."

"Mmm. I don't know. I don't really write smut."

"Right." He laughs. "But think of all the research opportunities."

"Oh my god, yes. So many opportunities." I nod. "Like syphilis."

"Ha!" He shakes his head. "People don't get syphilis anymore."

"No," I say. "I'm pretty sure they do."

———————

When we get back to the house, Tommy opens a bottle of red wine and pours us each a glass.

"I don't know," I say. "It's late. I have to fly tomorrow."

"Who cares? It's not like you're gonna sleep."

He leans against the bar, holds the glass out to me and waits. And of course, I take it. It's like I have no self-restraint. I take a taste, but then I set the glass on the bar. I wrap my left hand around my right arm and try to stretch out my shoulder, roll it around in the socket.

"All tense again?" he says.

"I'm always tense," I say, and I frown at him. "I'm uptight. Remember?"

He steps toward me and puts his hands on my shoulders, rubs his thumbs along my neck. He works his fingers along my collarbone, up the top of my spine. He's standing close enough that his breath rustles my hair. He holds my neck in his palms and tips my head upward with his thumbs, catches my mouth with his lips.

"I think you should go to bed with me," he says, his lips still against mine.

Actually, this sounds like a terrible idea, but again I have no self-restraint, so I say, "Okay," and he laughs. He says, "Wow, Stace, you're really blowing me away with the enthusiasm."

"Never mind, then." I brace my fingers against his stomach and start to pull away, but he catches the back of my head, winds his arm around my waist, tightens his grip. "Honey, I'm just teasing you," he says. He slides his hand up under my shirt, traces the edge of my rib cage with his fingers, and he coaxes my mouth open with his teeth. And then he pulls away and grabs my hand. "You want to bring your wine?" he says.

"Not really," I say, and he says, "Good."

He pulls me through the house to the master, which is in the back, past the study, and there are even more of his stacks of books, and there's one book lying open on the middle of the bed, and it's mine. It's not *Monsters* though. It's my first book, and I don't even know what to think of that, but Tommy just moves it off to the side table and sits down on the bed. He pulls me to stand in front of him, and he catches my legs between his knees, works his hands under my shirt, and rubs his palms along my waist. He slides his hands up, lifting my shirt over my arms, dropping it on the floor behind me, slips his fingers under the straps of my bra, rubs his knuckles along them. He presses his mouth into the space between my breasts, moves slowly up my neck and to my mouth, pulling me down onto him. I move my knees up onto the bed on either side of him, and he grabs me tight around the waist, holding me up. "You doing okay?" he says into the side of my neck, and I nod. He lifts me by the hips, rolls me over onto my back, grabs his shirt by the collar and tugs it off. He leans into me, pressing his skin against my skin, and I let my head fall back, let him bury his face in my neck. His fingers are working at the waistline of my pants, which are loose enough not to unfasten. When he pulls hard enough, they just slip off. And he kisses me again, catches my knee with his hand and lets his fingers trail all the way along my thigh, and when he slides his finger inside me, I catch his lip with my teeth. "Oh, baby," he says, "you don't feel uptight anymore."

The morning that Michael died, when I came down the stairs, he was in the dining room, sitting with his laptop. He had his planner out, working already, and it wasn't even seven o'clock. I hadn't bothered to get dressed yet, but it was one of those mornings when my hair looked all slept in and sexy, and Michael was wearing this dark striped button-up that I liked.

"You look kinda hot this morning," I said, and he said, "You too."

"You're not even looking."

"I don't have to. You always look hot." His right hand was still on the trackpad. I could hear it clicking. His eyes were on the screen.

I walked around him, straddled his lap from the left, stretched my arms over his shoulders, kissed his jaw.

"Babe, come on," he said, and he put his hands on my shoulders, pushed me over far enough that he could see around me. "I'm leaving in five minutes. Save it for later."

"Maybe you should go in late," I said, and I leaned in again, this time kissing his lips.

"Why are you always like this when I'm busy?" he said, and he put his hands on my hips, nudging me to get up.

I narrowed my eyes at him, pushed my lips out into a pout. "I hate you," I said, and then he did kiss me, but only lightly, not with any interest, and he said, "I know."

When I wake, it's dark out, and Tommy is still curled around me, his hand tucked between my thighs, but I slip out without waking him. In the upstairs shower, I lean my face against the cool tile and let the hot water run on my neck. I stay like that for a long time, and I keep my eyes closed tight, but I don't cry.

It's close to eight when I hear Tommy's bare feet scuffing on the tile floor behind me.

I say, "Morning," but I don't turn around.

He walks around the island and goes straight for the coffee. He's just wearing these low jeans, no shirt. "You didn't sleep any better?" he asks, turning to face me.

I smile, but I shake my head. "Not really."

"I gotta tell you, that's a little insulting." He frowns. "You could at least fake it."

"Maybe I did."

"Good one," he says. He takes a sip of his coffee. "Flight's at noon? Before you go, I want you to read through a new draft of the script. Joe sent it yesterday while you were sleeping." He pulls a banana off a bunch sitting in a bowl on the counter and snaps the peel. "Banana?"

"No," I say. "When you say 'new draft' . . ."

He takes a bite of the banana, shifts it to his cheek, and talks around it. "You'll just have to look at it." He walks around the island and across the room, toward the study. When he comes back, he drops a stack of pages in front of me. "Start on page eighty-seven." And then he stands there next to me, leaning against the counter, half naked. *Christ.* "Sure you don't want some of my banana?" He smiles.

"No. I really don't. Thank you."

"Come on, just a little bit." He pulls a piece off and holds it up to my mouth. "Just the tip."

"You are a pervert," I say, pushing his hand away.

"Come on. One bite."

"Then will you go away so I can read this?"

"Absolutely."

I open my mouth, and he holds the piece of banana up, and I take it with my teeth.

"Jesus, Stacey, not the teeth. It's very tender."

"Oh my god. You are like a twelve-year-old. Go away."

I hear the front door open and close, Daniel's feet in the hallway. He walks into the kitchen, and he takes one look at us, Tommy leaning on the counter, his foot on the rung of my stool, both of us eating the same banana, and he says, "Jesus Christ. Tell me you're not that stupid."

"You're fired," Tommy says, and he takes another bite.

Daniel walks around to the coffeemaker and pours himself a cup. He adds sugar, walks to the fridge, pulls out the milk, stirs.

"Stacey," he says finally with a kind of sigh as he turns to face me, "I'm not gonna lie. I'm disappointed."

"I know," I say, frowning at him. "I'm kind of disappointed in myself."

"Oh, fuck you both." Tommy stands up and walks back around the island, throws the banana peel in the trash, and picks his coffee back up.

Daniel shrugs, shakes his head at me with this sad frown. "I'll be in the study if you need anything, sweetie." He walks around the island and rubs my arm. "Like some penicillin," he says, and I laugh.

"Just read the script," Tommy says.

I pick it up, flip the pages across my thumb, looking for eighty-seven. "I feel like you're very demanding, Tommy."

"Yeah? I feel like I'm very fucking generous."

"I feel like your 'generous' is mostly about being demanding." Then I look up. "What am I looking at?"

"Dialogue sounds off." He's right, most of the script is really lyrical, and in this scene, a lot of the rhythms are stilted, flat. "You should take that with you." He nods at it. "Read the whole thing. I think it's good, but read it. See what you think." He crosses the kitchen, leans over, resting his elbows on the island. He's directly across from me, but it's a big slab of granite. We're still a few feet apart. "Can you fix it?" he says.

"On paper? I can fix almost anything."

It's already dinnertime when I pull up to Jenny's house to get the boys. She's made whole-wheat spaghetti with fresh mozzarella, and the kids are crowded around her kitchen table, sucking the noodles up through their puckered lips.

"Look, Mom," Stevie says. The skin around his lips has an orangeish tint.

"Nice job," I say, kissing him on the head.

"I know you haven't eaten yet," Jenny says, putting a plate at the breakfast bar.

"No, I'm starved," I say. "It looks awesome."

"So, how did it go?"

"Great." I twirl a few noodles onto my fork. "Fantastic. We got the director Tommy wanted, so it all worked out. And I have a new draft of the script to look at, make a few tweaks." I take a bite.

"And then you spent the rest of the day just hanging out with Tommy DeMarco," she says. "Remember that time we went to see *Destructions* and Michael was like, 'That guy seems like a real . . .'" She glances at the kids and makes a face. "You know."

Michael hated that movie. He hated all of Tommy's movies.

"I remember," I say.

"So what's he really like?"

"Nice." I wave my fork like, *Nothing to tell.* "Tommy's always really nice, and his house is gorgeous. Really modern, airy, lots of glass. Beautiful place." I take the last bite of pasta and stand up. "We should really get going though. It's a school night," I say.

Ben has a birthday party to go to. It's a bowling-alley thing. When the invitation came, Stevie cried and said, *I never get invited to anything,* and I promised we could go and play in another lane. We end up at the far side of the room, far enough from the party that I can see Ben but not hear him. Stevie wants an orange ball, but all the balls that are light enough for him to manage are pink.

"It's okay, Mom," he says. "I know it's not your fault."

They've got these automated rails that go up for all of Stevie's turns and retract for mine, so the end result is that all of my balls go straight in the gutter, and Stevie always manages to at least hit something.

"It's just a game, right?" Stevie says.

It is loud as hell, and there are at least three parties. One of them is in the lane next to us, and the boys look about six. The kids that don't seem scared to be here are chasing one another in circles around the tables. One table is piled with gift bags and packages with ribbon. The table for Ben's group looks very much the same, so I feel a little bad about his yellow envelope with a generic robot birthday greeting and twenty-dollar gift card.

"Mommy, watch this," Stevie says. He uses both hands to roll the ball from between his legs, and it bounces from the right rail to the left to the right to the left. It knocks down four pins, and Stevie says, "Yes!"

"Good job, baby," I say.

One of the dads from the party next to us wanders within talking distance. "Some Friday night, huh?" He's wearing a red golf shirt, tucked in, and it's pulling a little at the beginnings of a beer belly. He smiles. "Greg," he says, holding out his hand.

"Stacey." I stretch my hand out, palm down, and let him squeeze it.

"This pro bowler over here your boy?" he says, nodding at Stevie.

"Yeah," I say. "He is." I point toward the party across the room. "And I have another one over there."

"Oh yeah?" he says. "Mine's with this group. Pretty loud, aren't they?" He's wearing a ring, a gold watch. His hair is thinning at the top.

"Is yours the birthday kid?"

"No. His mom just makes me stay. She's a little, you know, nervous."

"Oh," I say, and I smile. It's a really good smile. I don't know why— probably because my night's just so dull. "Moms can be so annoying."

Stevie tugs on my arm. "Your turn."

I brush my hand against Greg's forearm. "I better go throw another gutter ball."

I don't look back, but I'm sure he watches. I only look at Stevie, who yells, "Mom, you got one!" and throws his arms around my waist. "Good job, Mommy," he says.

I almost wander back to Greg, but I feel my phone buzzing in my pocket. There's no name, but the area code looks familiar. I pick up and say, "Hello?"

"Hey, it's Tommy."

I feel a little sorry for Greg, who seems to be hanging around on the edge of the party, waiting to see if I come back.

"I hope you don't have more work for me," I say.

"Why? You don't like getting paid?"

"Not when all this extra shit is lumped into a flat rate."

"It's a hell of a flat rate, honey. Daniel just mailed your check today." Two hundred thousand dollars. It's a nice number. It's not exactly going to change my life, but it's a nice number. And it means that the movie's officially a go. I watch Stevie roll his ball, and when he turns around I give him a thumbs-up. *Great job!* I mouth.

"Where are you? It's loud."

"I'm bowling with my kid. Hang on." I lean down to Stevie. I pull the phone away from my mouth. "I have to take this call, honey. Can you do my turn?" He gives me a high five and grabs a ball to roll. Of course the bumpers are down for my turn, so he's not going to hit a single pin. "All right, what do you want?"

"Wow. Good to talk to you too."

"Come on. What is it?"

"Nothing, Jesus," he says. "I read your changes. Thanks for doing that."

"Yeah, of course. You know I really will work on it anytime. I'm just, you know, giving you shit." I scuff my toe along the floor. "Hey, is this your number you're calling on?"

"Yeah, why?"

"I don't know, Tommy. Do you think I should have it? I mean, what if I try to call you when you'd rather be 'not really available'?" I try to make Daniel's air quotes with my voice.

"Very funny. You're hilarious," he says. "I'll be available."

Poor Greg is standing at an angle like he's not really facing my way, but he's not really into the party either. He turns far enough to make eye contact. He makes a little half-smile, and I smile back.

"I'm not actually going to call," I say.

"Wow." He laughs. "Who's the asshole now?"

"I know. I'm sorry. I know that's kind of your thing. I don't really mean to step on your toes." Stevie gets a spare with the rather significant help of the bumpers. "I should go. He's going to start pouting if I don't take my next turn."

"Yeah, you have fun with the bowling. That sounds really fucking exciting." But then he says, "Hey, Stace, thanks again."

"Anytime," I say, and then I hit *end*.

Stevie's standing at the return, waving his hands over the little vent. "I can get your ball for you," he says when he sees I'm off the phone.

"I would love that, buddy. That would be great."

Stevie and I finish our games way before the party ends, and I know he's going to be jealous about the cake, so I buy him an ice cream, and we sit in the dining area. There's a bar, and I think about ordering a vodka, but I feel like it would be weird.

"You're not having ice cream?" Stevie says.

"I don't really like ice cream."

It's soft serve, a twist, and he's holding the cone in his hand, licking it on just one side so that it's dripping on the other. He's got streaks of chocolate and vanilla on his knuckles.

"You can have a lick," he says, holding it toward me.

"That's okay, baby. It's for you."

"Do you think Ben's having ice cream too, or just cake?"

"Probably just cake," I say.

"I like ice cream better than cake," he says, "but I like pie the best."

"Like your dad," I say, but then I think, *Shit, why did I say that?*

Stevie doesn't look sad though, just interested. "What was his favorite pie?"

"Coconut cream," I say.

"Me too," Stevie says, though I don't think he's ever had it. "We're the same."

Some days the boys walk to Jenny's after school, and I meet them there. We let the kids play for a little bit while Jenny and I have coffee. She has this very formal front parlor, and there's something nice about sitting on her little Victorian loveseat, drinking coffee out of our grandmother's china.

Jenny is in the kitchen pouring the coffee when my phone rings. It's sitting out on the coffee table, and I see the screen light up just as it starts buzzing. It's my editor, who honestly never calls. I haven't talked to her in forever. Even with the movie, it's been strictly through e-mail. They don't technically have anything to do with it because they don't own any of those rights, but obviously I've kept them in the loop. She's said sales have already been picking up.

"Hi, Erin," I say. "How are you?"

"Oh, Stacey, good, great. I'm so glad I caught you."

"Sure. What's up?"

Jenny walks in with our coffees on this little tray with a plate full of butter cookies. Neither of us is going to eat them. We'll just leave them for the kids. She gives me a look like, *Who's that?* and I shake my head.

"Well, we've got an opportunity we want to talk to you about," Erin says. "The L.A. book festival is in April, and you know the panel proposals all had to be in months ago, but I was talking to the festival director about how their registration has been really down this year, and how they really need some kind of buzz."

"Yeah?" I already don't like where this is going.

"And anyway, we got to talking about you and your movie project, and well, we'd really like you to fly out for it. People are always interested in hearing about screenwriting. Especially in L.A. Everyone wants to get into the movies." She's talking fast. She always does when she's trying to convince me of something. "So you could talk about the project and how it all went and maybe someone from the movie would be willing to join you? That would really be something."

"You mean like Tommy DeMarco?"

Jenny makes another face at me like, *What the hell is going on?*

"Well, that would be fantastic, but we'd honestly be thrilled to have anyone who could speak to, you know, their end of things."

"Look, I don't know, Erin. You know how much I hate these things, and asking for this favor, this all puts me in a strange spot."

"I know. I know. But you have to think about how much the book deserves this attention. It's a fantastic book. We all really went out on a limb for it. That's how much we believed in it, and sometimes you have to go out on a limb for it too."

I close my eyes. "Look, I'll ask," I say finally. "E-mail me all the dates and specifics."

I hear this little intake of breath on the other end. "I'm sending you everything now. Call me the minute you know. And Stacey? I really appreciate this."

I end the call, and Jenny says, "What was that about?"

"It's just this book festival thing, and they want me to go and ask Tommy, and I just . . ." I shake my head. "The whole thing is not what I want to do."

I'm feeling a little sick. I don't want to call Tommy, but I also don't want to put it off. The longer I wait, the more I'll have to think about it, so I thumb over and scroll through my contacts. He's texted me a few times, but we haven't talked in over a week, not since the bowling alley.

"Are you calling him now?" Jenny says, and I nod. "You have his phone number?"

"Yeah," I say, tapping it and holding the phone up to my ear. He picks up on the third ring.

"Hey," he says. "You know, I'm not really available right now."

"Oh, sure, no. That's fine, I'll just send you an e-mail." I close my eyes really tightly, press my thumb and forefinger to the bridge of my nose.

"I'm just fucking with you, honey," he says. "I thought you weren't gonna call."

I make this exasperated sigh. "God, you're an asshole."

Jenny makes a little *oh* sound and holds her hand up over her mouth.

"You keep saying that," he says.

"You keep acting like one."

He laughs. "I know. So what's up?"

"Look, my editor just called about doing this thing for the L.A. book festival, talking about the book and making it into a movie. Anyway, it's in April, and I don't know what your schedule is like, but, I don't know, I just thought I'd see if you want to do it with me." I think I'm talking fast too. I might sound like an idiot.

"Yeah, totally. I'm in."

"Well, let me send you the date and see if it works for you."

"No, I'm in. I'll just rearrange shit if I have to. Send it over to Daniel, and we'll get it set."

"Seriously?" I look at Jenny like, *He said yes!* and she claps silently.

"Yeah. I'm happy to."

"My editor is going to be thrilled. You're the best."

"That's what I keep trying to tell you, Stacey, but you don't fucking listen."

"I'm totally listening now. You're fantastic. You're amazing. I could absolutely kiss you." I kind of wish I hadn't said the last part, but he just laughs and says, "Of course you could."

I take this deep breath and let it out slowly. "I'd better call my editor back, but seriously, thank you."

When I hang up, Jenny gives me these wide eyes and says, "How close are you two?"

"Tommy?" I try really hard to look confused. "I mean, we're friends. It's not like we talk all the time or anything, but you know, I guess we're friends." I lean forward and take my coffee from the tray, hold the saucer in my left hand, take a sip. "What?"

"You sounded a little flirty," she says.

"Oh god, yeah, of course. I mean, Tommy's super flirtatious. He's kind of a bully with it actually. It's just, whatever, it's like how he is."

"You sound like you like him," she says.

"Oh, come on, Jenny, who wouldn't? I mean, he's gorgeous and smart and funny and mostly very nice, but he's also just a tremendous asshole to women and his life is ridiculous. I mean, yes, of course I like him, but it's not like it's real." I take another sip of the coffee. I like the way the cup and saucer keep both my hands busy. "I'd better call my editor."

FEBRUARY

"I DON'T WANT the kind with stickers. I want the kind with candy," Stevie says.

"Honey, everyone's going to be giving out tons of candy. Maybe we should do something different. How about pencils?" I say. I hold up a box of Valentines. They come with silver pencils with blue and pink hearts.

"Those look girly," Stevie says.

The shelves on either side of the aisle are a mess. There are plenty of Valentines left, but lots of the boxes are in the wrong place. There's a bag of candy hearts on the floor. I watch a woman in the aisle with us nudge it out of the way with her foot, and I'm like, *Seriously?*

"They have blue ones too," I say, and I hold the box close to him so he can see through the little plastic window. "Half of them are pink, and half of them are blue." Ben's favorite color for a long time was purple. Then he graduated from preschool into kindergarten, and he didn't want to carry his purple umbrella anymore. For a while he said it was his *secret favorite color*, but by the time he got to first grade, it was through.

"Hearts are girly," Ben says.

Stevie walks to the end of the aisle and comes back with a box in his hands. "I want these," he says.

"Sweetie, it's just so much sugar . . ."

"No one even likes pencils," Stevie says, and he starts to cry. "You just want everyone to hate me."

"Baby," I say, and I squat down, rub his arm. I know I'm supposed to say no here, and there was a time I was pretty proud of never being manipulated by tears, but since Michael died, it's hard to say which ones are genuine.

The boys dump the boxes of cards out on the dining room table. It usually has some sort of school crap strewn across it. We never eat there anymore. I print out their class lists and dig through my desk for a couple of sharp pencils.

"I can't give this one to anybody," Ben says. "It says, 'I'm sweet on you.'"

"I'll take that one," Stevie says. "I don't care if it's mushy. Nobody cares in my grade."

"They do in mine," Ben says.

"So give all the mushy ones to your brother, and Stevie, you give the not-mushy ones to Ben."

"Is 'Sweet Stuff' mushy?" Stevie says.

"I don't know," Ben says. He looks at me.

"It's just objectifying," I say.

"What does 'objectifying' mean?" Stevie says.

"Nothing, never mind, I was just making a joke." They're all mushy. And stupid, and when has "Be Mine" or "Sweet Stuff" ever worked on anyone? *Would you please just put the names on the candy and let's get this done with?*

"But what does it mean?" he says again.

I hear my phone ring inside my purse in the kitchen, and I say, "Hang on, baby. I'd better get that." It's Daniel.

"Hey, what's up?"

"We've got a problem. It's the script. Jason and Joe. I don't know. You have to come out."

"What are you talking about? What happened?"

"I don't know. Tommy just wants me to set up a day to get all four of you together."

"Seriously? I thought the script was done."

Daniel laughs. "Oh, sweetie, you're cute. They'll be changing shit every other minute. Okay, so, get your calendar out. Jason and Joe can do the thirteenth or the seventeenth."

"This Friday the thirteenth? Jesus, Daniel, you guys never give me any notice."

"I know. I know. So which one?"

"My kids are having their Valentine's parties on the thirteenth, so not that day." I'm one of the party moms.

"Seventeenth it is. Meeting'll be early, so I'll book you a ticket for the sixteenth."

"Are you kidding me?" I slam the script down on the table. We're in Tommy's study. He's standing in the center of the room, watching me, his arms crossed in front of him, one hand on his mouth.

"I knew you wouldn't like it."

"This goes way beyond not liking it, Tommy." I prop my feet on the edge of the table, but then I drop them back down to the floor, lean my elbows onto my knees. "Goddamn it."

"Let me get you a drink," Tommy says.

"I don't want a drink."

"Well, I want a drink if I have to listen to you." He walks out of the room.

By the time he comes back, I'm pacing. He's got two small glasses of vodka in his hands, the bottle tucked under his arm.

"Drink this," he says, handing me one.

"I don't want it." I set the glass on the table next to the script. I think about dumping the vodka out onto it.

"All right, let me explain Jason's position." Tommy straddles the arm of the loveseat, balances his glass in front of him. "He's not asking to give her a happy ending. I mean, it's not like he's looking to tie things up, but the original ending is so fucking desolate . . ." and I glare at him, so he holds his hand out and adds, "which I love. But Jason wants a more open ending, not happy exactly, but with the possibility—and I'm quoting him here—of redemption. He thinks it would be easier on the audience. Better for the bottom line."

"I don't care about making things easier on the audience." I cover my face with my hands and talk through them.

"And better for the bottom line."

"That's your problem."

"Yeah, Stacey, it is. That's why we have to have this conversation."

"Great." I cross my arms, look at the floor. It's covered with this expensive Persian rug, all shades of beiges and browns and deep maroons.

"Look. It's not just my money, or I'd say fuck it, let's see what happens." I can hear the ice tumbling in his glass as he takes a drink. "A lot of people have money in this. People I don't want to screw."

"You promised you wouldn't fuck this up, and now you're going to." I shake my head.

"Slow the fuck down, Stacey. If I wanted to fuck it up, you wouldn't even be here. We'd have just done whatever we wanted, and you would have had to live with it. Let's remember that you don't have any actual rights here, so maybe you should be nice to me for keeping you involved."

"So you're what, asking for my approval?" I may sound a little bitter, a little snide.

"I'm asking you to make your fucking case." He takes another swig of his drink, and then his voice softens. "Look, you know I'm on your side, but I can't just lay down the law here, or Jason could walk. Nobody wants that."

I don't say anything. I lift my arm up, slide my fingers deep in my hair, make a knot of it in my fist.

"Tell me why it's better your way. Convince me, convince Jason, convince Joe. Well, fuck Joe. I don't care about Joe."

I laugh a little, more to release the tension than anything. I drop to my knees, sit cross-legged on the floor in front of the table, pick up the vodka, but I don't drink it. I just hold the glass in my hand, rub my thumb through the condensation on the side.

"This isn't a Disney story. I mean, we're exploring this whole system of privilege and oppression and then you want to turn this into 'Oh, she's a plucky heroine, so she's fine, she saves herself in the end.' That's not real, that's not true." I turn the glass in my hand again. The ice is melting. I finally take a sip. "We have to take the reader, the audience, whatever, all the way. We have to make them feel complicit."

Tommy sits for a minute. Maybe he's waiting to see if I say more. Maybe he's just thinking. "Okay," he says. "But you'd better sound a hell of a lot more eloquent tomorrow. And with Jason, you know, it wouldn't hurt if you wore something a little more revealing."

"If you think it'll help," I say. "But you're with me on this?"

He nods, sets his glass on the table. "I always was." He reaches his hand out, pulls me to my feet. "You want me to take you to dinner?"

I hate being in public with Tommy. I hate feeling watched. "I don't know. I've been traveling all day. Can't we just stay here?"

"We can do anything you want, baby." When he says this, he gives my hand a little tug and raises his eyebrows. "Or did you want to wait till later?"

"Jesus, you are obnoxious." I try to say this like it isn't a relief to have the question answered.

"You didn't think I was gonna have a room made up for you, 'cause I most certainly did not."

"Wow," I say, pulling my hand out of his. "That's a hell of an assumption to make."

He moves toward the door. "The word 'assumption' implies the possibility that I could be wrong, and you know, you'd think as a poet you'd be more mindful of your vocabulary."

"You'd think as a human being you'd be more mindful of being a dick."

"You'd think, yeah"—he turns back toward me and nods—"but you'd be wrong."

I wake up around five, which is seven o'clock back home. It's practically sleeping in. Tommy's arm is under my head, sort of on my hair. It's hard to get free without waking him, but I do. It's so early no one will be here, so I don't really bother getting dressed. I just pull on my T-shirt and slip out to the kitchen, make coffee, take a mug of it into the study, and sit with the script. I read the whole thing. I start on page one, and I read and read and read. Sometime around seven, I hear Tommy in the kitchen, and when I look up, he's leaning against the door frame.

"What the hell is wrong with you?" he says.

"Can't sleep." I lean forward for my coffee, but when I pick up the cup, it's almost empty.

He walks behind the couch, massages my neck, works his fingers up into my hair. "You should try staying in bed."

"It just makes me feel anxious."

"Then you should try going back to bed." He leans down, kissing the curve between my shoulder and neck. He works one hand through the neckline of my T-shirt, rubs his thumb across my breast.

I say, "I'm trying to work here."

"Yeah, me too."

He takes the script out of my lap and tosses it on the table in front of us, and the pen I had tucked in the middle of it falls to the floor. He reaches both hands around me, his fingers massaging the insides of my thighs.

"Jesus, Tommy."

"You can keep fighting me," he says, his mouth against my ear. "I mean that's a lot of fun too, but they're coming at eight-thirty, so if you want time to shower, you're gonna have to give in soon."

When I come out, Daniel is bustling around the kitchen, setting everything up. He fills a carafe with coffee, sets it on a tray with cups and spoons, a little pitcher of milk, and a sugar bowl, and when he turns around, the tray in his hands, he sees me and smiles. He sets the tray back down and circles the island toward me.

"So good to see you," he says, kissing me on the cheek. "There's toast, yogurt, fruit. What can I get you?"

"I'm good," I say, and he frowns at me. "I'll grab something in a little bit."

He picks the tray back up and carries it across the room. "Meeting's in here," he says. "Tommy says it's more intimate, it'll bring down their defenses."

And it is. If the living room is clean and spare and modern, the overstuffed leather couches by the fireplace are absolutely cozy, positioned closer together than they'd need to be in a room this size, the heavy wooden coffee table weathered-looking, the sort of table where you feel comfortable putting your feet. The fireplace is oversized and old-fashioned and wood-burning, and there's a small fire crackling away. It's not like it's cold here, not compared to Nebraska, but it's all for show. The ceilings in this room are high enough that the extra heat shouldn't matter.

Jason and Joe walk in together. I've already folded myself into the closest corner of one couch. They'll have to walk past me to sit down. Tommy greets them both in the kitchen, but I don't stand up. I just glance over and wave. As Jason approaches, I hold my arm up toward him, and he leans over the back of the couch to kiss me on the cheek. I know he looks straight down my shirt, but it's okay. I'm kind of inviting it.

"I hear you want to fuck up my book," I say just as his lips touch my cheek. I feel him startle against me, but he laughs, pats my shoulder.

Joe does not kiss me on the cheek. He sits down heavily on the couch across from me and says, "Hey. Good to see you." He says it like he absolutely does not mean it.

Jason looks like he's moving toward the opposite couch, but Tommy circles the long way around and steals the spot, so Jason has to sit beside me, close to the fire.

Joe has already poured himself a cup of coffee, selected a Danish. He looks thoroughly uninvested. Jason looks a little uncomfortable. Maybe the fire's too hot, but Tommy's sitting right next to the fire too, and he seems completely relaxed. He has one foot resting on the opposite knee, and the script open in his lap. He's flipping through the pages near the end of it.

"So," Jason says finally, looking from me to Tommy and back again, "if I understand correctly why we're here today, it's that Stacey isn't happy with the changes to the script."

"Can't say I'm totally sold either, brother," Tommy says, but the expression on Jason's face makes him hold his hand up and add, "No, no. I haven't made my mind up. I'm here to be convinced." He looks totally sincere about it, but he'd better be acting.

"Goddamn it," Jason says, and he looks at me. "You know it's not that big of a change. It's one scene."

"Jason"—I keep my voice soft, but I hold his gaze with mine—"you say that like that scene isn't important, and if it wasn't import-ant, you wouldn't be trying to change it."

"Look, I'm not saying your way wasn't right for the book. It was great. It was artsy. It was perfect. But we're trying to sell a movie here. We can't push the envelope as far." He looks back at Tommy. "I mean, I think we're already pushing it, but you know, people go to poetry to expand their minds and shit. They go to movies to be entertained."

Tommy nods, and if he was close enough, I'd kick him for it.

"I think you know," Jason goes on, still talking to Tommy, "I'm willing to go to some pretty dark places, but the ending to this thing isn't even dark, it's fucking bleak. It makes me want to blow my brains out, you know."

"Gee, thanks," I say.

He turns back to me. "Look, it's different on the page. You have some distance, some space to digest it. In the theater, across this giant screen, with the music and the lighting and the whole experience of it, I just don't think we have to go as far." He sighs.

Joe cuts in. "Seriously, we're just looking to cut the one scene. One scene, Stacey. One fucking scene."

"I can actually read and count, Joe, but thanks for clarifying."

"Stace," Tommy says, and he gives me this look like, *Be cool.* "Come on, we're all on the same team here." Which is bullshit, we absolutely are not, but he had damn well better be on mine.

We go back and forth half the morning. I can tell Jason is wearing down, but Joe keeps digging his heels in. Such an ass. He's got no dog in this fight. Just before lunch, Tommy and Jason have a call, so they duck into the study and leave me alone with Joe.

They've barely closed the door when Joe says, "Seems you had plenty of time to work Tommy over before we even got here. Didn't you get in last night?"

"What's that supposed to mean?"

"Nothing at all, Stacey. Nothing at all. Although if I could go to a meeting with my tits hanging out, I probably wouldn't have to work so hard either."

84

"Are you that scared of me, Joe? Is the possibility that maybe I could be right so terrifying that you have to turn this all into some sexist bullshit?"

"You trying to tell me that you're not willing to fuck whoever you need to to get your way? 'Cause we can all see the type of woman you are."

"The type of woman I am, Joe, is not stupid enough to think that Tommy DeMarco gets laid so infrequently that a blow job or a nice pair of tits is going to change his position on a multimillion-dollar decision. If you think that's why Tommy listens to me, you're high or delusional."

It's true. I don't think that's why Tommy listens to me, but I feel like we're dancing way too close to something, so I just throw my hands up and say, "I can't be in a room with you. Misogynistic piece of shit."

I stand up and walk straight down the hallway to the front door and out into the sunlight. It's chilly, but not like Nebraska. I won't need a jacket. There's a stacked stone wall that flanks the sidewalk leading down to the driveway. I sit on it, lean my elbows on my knees, drop my head into my hands. I feel sick. My stomach is in knots from all the stress and the coffee. I probably should have eaten something. I should have had some fruit. I hear the door creak open, but I don't look up.

"You okay?" It's Daniel.

I raise my head and smile at him. "I just hate Joe. I'm okay though."

He sits down next to me, pats my hand. "And how are you handling this shit with Tommy?"

"Is this in your job description? Girls crying on your shoulder?"

"Usually, yeah."

I lean my head against him and he wraps his arm around my shoulders. He feels warm and the shirt he's wearing is soft. I don't know why this makes me feel like maybe I am going to cry.

"I would quit that job," I say.

Daniel laughs. "No. Tommy's pretty great to me. I don't get a lot of time off, but you should see my paychecks. He's just . . . I don't know. He's a very popular guy, but he's pretty isolated. And the thing is, honey, he's used to it, and he's gotten to like it that way." He squeezes my arm. "I just don't want to see you get hurt."

"I am so far past hurt these days. I am just so far past it."

He sighs, leans his head against mine. "Well, if you're looking for a distraction, Tommy is pretty distracting. Just don't let him get you all spun out. He can come off all romantic lead, but, you know, he doesn't usually mean it." He squeezes his fingers into my shoulder again, and again I feel like I could cry. "Did you get anything to eat?"

"No," I say, "and I'm starving." This is not a lie. I feel a little woozy.

Daniel loops his arm through mine and pulls me to my feet. "Come on. Lunch is ready as soon as they're off that call, but I can grab you something."

There's a basket of rolls out on the counter, and Daniel pulls one out. "Whole-grain?" he says, and I say, "Lovely."

I tear a piece off and put it in my mouth, chew it slowly. I lean back against the counter and look out across the room. Joe is still at the couch, but he has his laptop out now, and he doesn't look up. I glare at him anyway.

"I've got to go take care of a few things," Daniel says. "You good?"

"Perfect," I say. I pinch another bite of bread between my fingers and twist it free, roll it across my tongue. The door to the study opens, and Tommy walks out. Jason follows behind him and walks straight to the couch, but Tommy comes toward me.

"Hey," he says, walking around the island to where I am. "You look pissed."

"Joe's a dick." It's a big room, but I say it quietly, almost under my breath.

"I knew that," he says. "Why now?"

"He thinks I'm sleeping with you to get my way with the script."

"You told him you're sleeping with me?" He seems a little annoyed. It makes sense. I'm sure a lot of girls brag about it, which is ridiculous because as far as I can tell, it's pretty easily accomplished just by proximity.

I tear off another piece of the roll, pop it in my mouth. "You really think I'd want anyone to know?"

He scowls like I've offended him, but underneath it he looks relieved.

"He just thinks that as a woman, the only thing of value I can contribute is a vagina."

"Well, that's obvious, isn't it?" He opens the cabinet to the right of me and takes down a glass. "You want water?" he says. I nod, and he takes down another. "So what did you say?"

"I told him that I think you probably get laid often enough that you wouldn't be easily swayed by a blow job."

It's good that he hasn't taken a drink of the water yet, because he nearly spits. "Fuck, Stacey." He's still laughing as he fills both glasses and hands me one. "Maybe we should back up though. Just how good is this blow job?"

"Shut up."

He lowers his voice a little. "You know none of that has any bearing on how I see your work or what I think is right for the movie, right?"

"It doesn't matter. The minute someone like Joe finds out, all the work I've put into this gets dismissed."

"Joe is not on my list of confidants, so I don't think you need to worry about him finding out, and shit, even if he did, you're brilliant, Stacey, you're super fucking talented. You're not that easy to dismiss."

I don't answer him. Tommy leans against the counter, looks back over his shoulder toward the two of them sitting at the fireplace.

"You might still have to sleep with Jason though," he says, turning back to me.

"Fuck you. Christ, you're as bad as Joe."

"Nah," he says, shaking his head, "I'm nothing like Joe. Joe is an asshole. Me? I give you everything you want."

I do actually get everything I want—from Jason too. He promises to rework the ending to stay more "true to the original vision."

When he says this, I look at Tommy. "I'll drink to that," I say.

"Hell yeah," he says, standing up from the couch. "What's every-body having?"

Joe looks at his watch. "I've got to head out. Ex is dropping the kids off tonight." He stands up too. "I'll catch you guys later. Stacey, always a pleasure."

"Isn't it though?" I say, but I don't even try to make my expression friendly. I'm fooling no one.

Tommy follows Joe out toward the front door, and Jason turns to me. "Shall we head to the bar?"

"I'd love to." I hold my hand out and let him help me up.

"You know, Stacey, for someone with no actual leverage, you're a pretty tough negotiator."

I just laugh, rest my hand on his arm. "You want to hire me?"

"Maybe for my next divorce settlement," he says.

"You have one in the works?"

"Nah." He waves one hand dismissively. "We're very happy, but you know, all good things . . ."

"I love the optimism."

We reach the bar before Tommy does, and Jason walks behind it to help himself. "What are you having, Stacey?"

"What are you pouring?"

"Scotch," he says, and I say, "Not that."

"Stacey's a vodka girl," Tommy says, walking in behind us, "but I'll take a scotch."

Jason pours the two scotches and my chilled vodka on ice and lines the glasses up on the bar.

"You have to cut me off after this one," he says to Tommy. "I'm supposed to go to my daughter's soccer game." He pulls his phone out of his pocket. "See, Trina's already texting me now. I told her this morning that I'd meet them there." He starts typing with his thumbs. "That should buy me all of five minutes." He sets the phone down and picks the scotch back up. "Fucking marriage, right?"

Tommy laughs. "Why you keep roping yourself into it then?"

Jason shrugs. "I'm just a romantic, I guess." He tosses back the rest of his drink. His phone buzzes again, and he picks it up to check. "She wants to know who you're bringing tomorrow. She's making place cards," he says to Tommy, and then he turns to me. "My wife's gotten into this whole formal dinner party thing. Boring as death." He points at Tommy. "But you're coming and you won't tell her I said that. Who's your date?"

The vodka is cold in my hands, but right now, it burns going down.

"Hmm? Uh, Kim," Tommy says, sliding his glass back and forth across the slick surface of the bar. "Kim Revell."

Jason whistles. "Nice. *I* or *y*?"

"How would I know?" He takes another drink of the scotch. "Trina can Google it."

Jason laughs and sets his glass down, shoves his phone in his pocket. "See you tomorrow night, then. And Stacey, I'm looking forward to the next time." I smile. "No, no," he says to Tommy, "I can let myself out."

When the door closes, Tommy looks at me and furrows his eyebrows apologetically. "Sorry about that."

I look back at my glass, which is emptier than I'd like. "Come on," I say, and I try to make my voice sound like, *It's nothing.* I think I'm doing pretty well. "I assumed you'd be fucking some actress tomorrow night." I turn to smile at him like, *See, I don't care.*

Tommy smiles back. "She's not an actress," he says, shaking his head. He finishes the scotch in his glass. "She's a lingerie model."

"Oh," I say, and I feel my smile slip. There's nothing I can do about it. "Well, that does suck, then."

He laughs, and reaches across the bar for the bottle of vodka to refill my glass. "She's not very smart though, so really, you're much hotter."

"Mmm, that's great," I say, but I can't seem to get my lips to unpinch themselves.

"How much of this do you want?" Tommy says, starting to pour the vodka.

A lot, I think. *I want so much.* But of course I don't say that, I say, "Just a touch."

MARCH

I WAKE UP and look at my phone. Today is one year. Michael has been dead a whole year, and it feels like the longest time. It feels like forever. I walk downstairs, and Bear meets me at the bottom. I scratch his head while I turn off the alarm. When I put him outside, I lean my head against the glass of the back door. It's still winter, and cold. The last week has been nothing but wind. The other night, Stevie showed up in my bed. He said, *It sounds like the house is breaking.* And I said, *No, baby, it isn't.*

When Bear comes back, I let him inside. I start my coffee and cut an apple into very thin slices to have for breakfast. I hear the boys upstairs talking, making their morning noises, and I think, *We'll be okay. We've made it this far.*

APRIL

MICHAEL'S MOM WANTS US to come for her Easter luncheon, which is a nightmare. I've never liked the woman, but since Michael died, she's been this weepy, pathetic mess. She makes the boys uncomfortable. *It's really important to us to spend time with our grandchildren, especially now that we've lost our boy.* She actually breaks down on the phone. I'd like to say, *For Christ's sake, I am not your family.* Jenny, of course, says that I have to go.

I take a big pasta primavera salad for me and a bottle of cheap white wine for her. She's not a very classy lady. I'm trying to play to her tastes.

I make the boys wear nice collared shirts and slacks, and when Carol opens the door, she doesn't let us in so much as she pushes her way out and throws her arms around them. "You look exactly like your dad when he was little," she says, and Ben stiffens.

"Can we go in?" I say. "My hands are pretty full."

She moves out of the way and holds the door open. I walk in and head for the kitchen. The whole place smells like ham.

"I made your favorite—twice-baked potatoes," she says, rubbing Ben on the head.

"That's not my favorite," he says, and I give him a look. I may not like her, but he doesn't have permission to be an asshole.

"You liked them last year," she says.

"Is Lisa coming?" I like Michael's sister, but of course Carol says, "No."

"But Josh is," she says, opening the oven and letting out this tremendous wave of sugar and pig.

Great. Josh is an asshole. Josh I hate. When Michael and I were still dating, Josh got drunk at a family Christmas and put both hands on my ass as I was coming back from the bathroom. He'd cornered me in the back hallway. "I will tell your brother," I said, and he backed away. So, yeah, I'm thrilled about seeing him.

"You look so handsome, you two," Carol says to the boys, and she sniffles again. "Are you just coming from Mass?" They look at each other. They look at me.

"We don't go to Mass, Carol."

"What?" She's holding this giant meat fork, and she turns and sticks it in the ham.

"Boys, go say hi to your grandfather," I say, and they trudge off toward the living room, where they're bound to find him in front of the TV.

"I'm not Catholic," I say, and she says, "Well, Michael was."

She stands back up, closes the oven. She's holding the fork in her hand, staring at me. I can see little droplets of fat on its prongs—*juice*, she would probably call it.

"Don't you think it's disrespectful not to raise the boys the way he would have wanted?"

"He wouldn't have expected me to take the boys to church."

"Well, I bet he would have liked it," she says, her lips pressed together in a thin mean line. She slams the oven open and pulls out the potatoes. They're loaded with bacon. She just loves me. She always has.

The only dish on the table that doesn't have meat is my pasta salad. She doesn't even have the decency to put out some plain rolls. I know she does this on purpose, but as she brings out the last two trays she says, "Oh gosh, Stacey, I guess you can't have this either. I don't know what I was thinking."

I do, but I just smile. "It's okay, Carol, I've always hated your cooking," and then I make a face like, *I'm just kidding.*

"We brought a Jell-O salad?" Josh's wife, Lee, says.

"Mmm, gelatin. No thanks. That's made from animals."

"It is?" she says.

Josh says, "It's like hooves and bones or something, right?"

"Not exactly," I say, but close enough.

"Are the kids eating in the kitchen? I'll just make them some plates." I give them mostly pasta salad, small pieces of ham, some of those bacon-covered potatoes, a little Jell-O. I hope they haven't heard the bit about hooves. Once they're settled, I spoon some of the pasta onto my plate and sit in my usual spot. That's the thing about Carol's, we all know our place.

"So Mom tells me you've got some movie deal going?" Josh says.

"I do, yeah. One of my books." I spear a noodle and a strip of carrot with my fork.

"Making a lot of money off that?"

It's not any of their business, really. "Is it polite to talk about money at the dinner table?"

"Come on, we're family," he says.

I give him a look that very clearly says, *No, we're not,* but then I say, "I'm making enough."

"Enough that you don't have to work?" he says, holding this slab of ham up to his face.

"Michael left Stacey enough that she doesn't have to work," Carol says.

Which is true, but I say, "This is work, Josh. That's why they're paying me." I turn to Carol. "Did you open that wine?"

"Not yet. I have an open box of blush in the fridge. You want a glass?"

Of course, boxed rosé. That sounds delicious, but I say, "Thanks, Carol, that would be great."

"Anyone else?" she says.

"I'll take a glass," Lee says. "Let me help you."

"No, no. You just relax," Carol says, waving her off. She's always loved Lee. Lee is totally her favorite.

"I'll have another beer," says Stan, Michael's dad. These are the first words I've heard from him all day. There's a good chance they'll also be the last.

"Me too," Josh calls after her.

"So tell us about this whole movie thing," Lee says. "It sounds exciting. Have you met any famous people?"

"I have," I say. "The director is pretty famous, and the actor producing it too."

"Who is it?" she says, her eyes big.

There is really no way to prepare them for the name-dropping that's coming. Normally, I feel uncomfortable about it, but I hate these people. Well, I don't really hate Lee, but she's married to Josh, so I probably should. "Jason Collier. Tommy DeMarco."

"Holy shit," Josh says. "No wonder you don't have to work."

"Josh," Carol says sharply, coming back in the room with two beers and a glass of wine for Lee. "I don't like that language in my house."

"Sorry, Mom. Thanks," he says, grabbing the beer and taking a swig.

"What's he like?" Lee says.

I know who she's asking about, but I say, "Jason? Sweet. He's lovely. I like him a lot." I take another bite of my pasta, wonder how long I'm going to have to wait for my wine.

"No, Tommy DeMarco." She says his name in the tone that all women seem to use when they talk about him. "I mean, you've *met him* met him?"

I think, *Yeah, I've definitely met him,* but I say, "Sure, I just talked to him yesterday."

"He calls you?"

"Sometimes." I nod. "Yesterday, I called him." I had a good reason, a legitimate question, but then we just stayed on the phone for a long time. I smile. "You want to call him? I'm sure he's around." I wouldn't do this if I thought she'd take me up on it. She just giggles.

Carol finally brings my glass of shitty wine, but she doesn't hand it to me. "You know," she says, and I can tell she's about to pull some crying shit. "When my son died, I did not expect to see you, sitting at my table barely a year later, giggling about some other man."

Clearly, I am not the one giggling, not that that matters to her. When Michael died, I thought I could be done with these people, but here I am. Right now, I'm so pissed at Michael. When he was alive, he handled Carol for me.

"Carol, these are people I work with. I was talking to Tommy about a book panel we have to do at the end of the month. But, you know, the fact is, he's famous, and I'm sure that's all a little exciting when you first hear about it. For me, this is just a job."

"You're going out of town?" Finally she hands me my wine.

"Yeah, just overnight hopefully. Why?"

Carol looks at Stan and then back to me. "Well, we could keep the boys while you're gone."

I nearly choke on my wine. "That's nice of you, Carol, but they can stay with my sister."

"You never let the boys stay here," she says. "Don't you trust us?"

No. Fuck no. Michael didn't either. She wants me to respect his wishes? Well, on this, I am. "Of course I trust you. You're their grandmother. But it'll be a school day, and Jenny's kids go to the same school. It just makes things easy. You know?" I smile really sweetly.

"What about some other time? What if we took them for a weekend?"

I look at Stan. He doesn't say anything. You can barely tell he's listening.

"Sure," I say. "We could do that." I hope she can't tell I'm lying. "I'm sure the boys would think that was fun." Actually, I don't even know what they'd do here. They don't even keep any toys in the house. What kind of grandparents don't have toys?

On the way home, Stevie says, "I don't like ham. It's too wet."

I wonder if Carol even cooked it all the way. Leave it to Carol to poison my kids with parasitic meat. And she wants them for the weekend.

"Don't be rude," Ben says.

"I'm not rude. You're rude. You're the rude, stupid one."

My head hurts. Maybe it's the wine. I only drank a glass of it, but it tasted stale. Or maybe it just tasted like wine from a box. Either way, it was crap.

"Gramma Carol says she's going to take us to the zoo," Stevie says.

"Really?" I say. I don't bother saying that she's not, that I won't allow it, that I wouldn't let her take them in a car for anything.

"We'll take you down and leave you with the alligators," Ben says, and Stevie starts to cry. The alligator exhibit is really scary. Even I won't go in it.

"Ben," I say, "don't start with him. Can't you two be nice?"

Usually they are. Usually they're the sweetest boys, but lately Ben's been agitated and Stevie's an easy target. Ben can't seem to help himself.

I get into LAX about ten a.m. and go straight to the festival. We don't have to actually do the panel until mid-afternoon, but I have nowhere else to be, and I know if I wander the book fair I'll see people I know. I've been to this thing before, and as busy as it is, the poetry world is pretty small. An hour into the thing I realize that, as usual, I didn't wear the right shoes. I always think I'll feel more steady if I look a certain way, like people will think I know what I'm saying if I wear black jeans and a tailored jacket. Of course it's too hot, and I have to take the jacket off and stash it in my bag, so now I'm just wearing this sleeveless violet shell, which I'm hoping is dark enough to hide whatever anxiety sweat I'll be dealing with all day. But the shoes are a problem. I mean, they didn't seem too high at home, but Michael would have talked me out of them for sure. *You'll call me crying about your feet by noon,* he would have said, and he would have been right. The balls of my feet feel bruised.

When I reach the room for the panel, there's no way I can get in. I get there fifteen minutes early and already the place is packed. I say, "I'm supposed to be on this. Do you think I can get through?" to the people jammed in the doorway, but there's nowhere for them to move. I feel a little panicked. I step back into the hallway, moving away from the crowd, looking for someone official-looking, someone to help me.

"There you are," a man says behind me.

I can't remember his name, but we've met. By *met* I mean he came by my publisher's table this morning and stayed for a long time, and at one point, he made a comment about my shoes. "That's some sexy footwear," he'd said, which was creepy both for the word *footwear* and for the fact that he is super unattractive. But he is on the festival board, so I smile like I really need him, and I say, "I can't get in."

"Let me take you through the service hall," he says, and he takes me through a door marked STAFF ONLY and down a hallway with none of the polish of the rest of the place. He's trying to talk to me the whole way, and I laugh politely a couple of times, but I'm not really listening now. I'm just responding to his tone of voice.

I don't know the moderator. She's a short, heavy, gray-haired woman in this awful beige dress. "I'm Sandra," she says, shaking my hand. Her palm feels doughy, maybe a little wet. "So we'll go ahead and get you settled."

They've brought in a portable stage and skirted it in maroon fabric. She points me to the rickety stairs in the back. The table is long and similarly skirted to hide its folding metal legs, a white cloth stretched across the top. I try to keep my focus here, on the stage. Beyond it are too many people, too many bodies pressed into the chairs and standing along the walls, but the ceiling is high, and when I look straight out, keeping my eyes over their heads, I can tell myself the room is filled with air.

"So you'll sit here," Sandra says, pointing me to a black folding chair at one end of the table.

There is a second chair beside it and a tabletop lectern at the opposite end of the table—mic'ed, of course—and there's another mic between the chairs, its cord running dangerously close to the pitcher of water they've set out. I pour myself a glass, take a sip.

"So I'll introduce you and then I thought you could read a bit from the book, maybe ten minutes?"

"Sure," I say. I can read. I can read all day. It's the answering I'm not looking forward to. I'm better with a script.

"And Mr. DeMarco is still . . ." She must be getting nervous. We've only got a few minutes left, and people bailing on panels and readings is pretty common. Sometimes it's last-minute travel problems, but often they're just assholes. Writers don't get invited to much, so when they do, they tend to overschedule.

"I'm sure he'll be here," I say. I slip my phone out of my pocket, slide it to unlock to see if I have any messages.

Sandra says, "Oh," next to me in this sort of surprised tone, and I look up and there's Tommy. He's in the doorway, shaking a woman's hand, talking, nodding. He leans in close like he's trying to hear her. She can't seem to stop talking. And then he nods toward the stage, stepping backwards, holding her hand a moment longer, letting it go. He turns toward me, and when he sees me he smiles. There are four steps. He takes them two at a time, and as he rises onto the stage, there's a hum of voices across the room. I feel conspicuously frozen, but Tommy moves as naturally as ever, catches me in a hug, kisses my cheek. He leans back, still holding me by the waist.

"Good to see you." He presses his thumbs against my stomach and lets his eyes roll over me. "You look great."

"This is Sandra," I say, turning toward her and away from his hands. "She's the moderator."

"Oh, yes, so. Wow. It's so nice to meet you." *Poor flustered Sandra.*

Tommy must feel sorry for her too because he takes her hand in both of his. "Walk me through the plan," he says because he seems to understand that she needs some direction, someone in charge of telling her what to do.

"Yes," she says. "So, you'll sit here, and I'll introduce both of you, not that you really need an introduction." She laughs a little stupidly. "And then Stacey will read for a few minutes, and then I have a few prepared questions, and then we'll open it up to the audience." She rounds her eyes like she's asking a question. "Sound good?"

"Sounds great." Tommy smiles again and lets go of her hand and turns back to me. "I've never heard you read," he says as we sit down.

"Mmm," I say. "I'm pretty amazing." I'm just excited to be sitting, and for the fact that I can kick my shoes off under the table without anyone seeing.

Now that everyone is looking at Tommy, I feel like I can look out into the audience. Whatever the fire code is, we've broken it by a lot. Some of the girls are grinning, giggling, holding their hands over their mouths, bouncing in their seats, and Tommy doesn't look away. He waves to them like to someone he recognizes, mouths, *Hi, Hey,* over and over, the occasional *Thank you.* He holds his hand over his heart. It's ridiculous actually, but even I would probably fall for it. He is really, really good.

———

The girl at the microphone is adorable and very young. She's got one of the festival bags slung over her shoulder, and I can see from here that it's heavy. She must have picked up a ton of books.

"Hi," she says. "I just want to say how much I loved your book. I read it in my first grad seminar, and it just totally changed my life as a writer."

"Gosh, that's . . . Wow, thank you." I hate this. I feel awkward. I know most of the people in this room are here because of Tommy, but it is a book festival after all, so most of the questions have been for me. I spread my fingers across the white tablecloth and touch the edge of the water ring seeping out around my glass.

"I'm really looking forward to seeing how this works as a film," the girl says.

"Me too," I say, and everyone sort of chuckles politely.

"So what I'm wondering is how you handle the vulnerability that comes with allowing all these other people, these other influences, into your work?"

Tommy's been sitting back in his chair, his arms folded across his chest, relaxed, just listening. Now he leans forward, up to the table mic positioned between us, and he says, "Well, she didn't fucking handle it well." Everyone laughs.

"I don't know if it's so much about vulnerability," I say, giving him a sideways glance, "and actually, I'm going to argue with you on that word." I smile. "I've spent a lot of time thinking about the interplay of vulnerability and power." It's true. This is basically what my first book is about. "And we tend to think of vulnerability as weakness, or a willing weakness maybe, but it's an illusion, isn't it? I mean, the more power you have, the more vulnerable you can allow yourself to be, but you're never really giving up that power, are you?" I shake my head. I think I'm getting off track. "And in this scenario, I definitely didn't have any power. I don't know if you know this, but poets don't generally have agents, so when they were drawing up the contract, I didn't really have anyone negotiating this for me, and the end result was that I found myself in a position where Tommy was saying, 'You're lucky I'm so cool with you, because I own this shit now,' so, yeah, I really don't think 'vulnerable' is the word."

Tommy laughs. Loudly. And he leans forward and says, "I definitely never said that."

"Maybe not word for word."

The next girl, they're mostly girls, wants to know what Tommy saw in the book. "Do you read a lot of poetry?" she says. "And what made you fall in love with this book?"

"I don't. I don't read a lot of poetry necessarily. Well, I guess sometimes I do. I read a lot. I read whatever people give me." He pauses. "And why this book? I mean, it's beautiful, isn't it?" He says it like he assumes everyone in the room has read it. I'm betting it's more like three. "I mean, it's full of rage and grief and loss and all of the mess and ugliness of human experience, but it's beautiful too, you know, and there's that conflict, that tension, and I just saw a lot of power in it. It just seemed true."

His hair has fallen forward into his eyes, and he lifts his hand to push it back. He looks serious and a little tired. Then he notices me looking, and he pulls his mouth into a smile, and he's just delicious Tommy again. He could be on a fucking poster.

———————

"You were fantastic," Tommy says. "That reading was gorgeous. We could just film that."

We push through the doors into the service hall, and while it's not totally empty, compared to the room we're coming from, we're practically alone.

"Sure, yeah, you'd make a ton of money on that."

"I don't know, Stace, I think people would pay to watch you." And he raises his eyebrows, changes the tone of his voice. "I mean, I would."

I just roll my eyes.

"What now?" he says. "You have to stay? You want to get a drink?"

"I do want to get a drink. I want that very much." I slow down, look around, trying to get my bearings. "You know, I left my bag at my publisher's booth in the book fair. I can just run back. You want to meet me at the car?"

He shrugs. "I'll just come with you."

"Are you kidding me? It's already a madhouse in there, and then to throw you into it? Jesus. That's like my worst nightmare." I can already feel my jaw tensing up.

"Aw, honey, stop with the sweet talk already. You're gonna make me blush." His mouth curls up on one side. "I mean, it's nice to hear how much you enjoy spending time with me."

"It's not you. It's just, you know, all of this and them, and, just, all of it." I shake my head, press my fingers to my temples.

"You know what?" He takes my hand and starts pulling me toward the door that leads out into the main hallway. "It's like that therapy where they make you hang out in a room with spiders or whatever shit you're afraid of. It'll be good for you."

"No, come on. I really don't want to."

"We'll probably see friends of yours, and you can introduce me." His hand is on the door now. He's starting to push it open. "We can make out a little. People will take pictures."

"Seriously, Tommy." I try not to step forward, but he tightens his grip.

"Seriously? You're gonna want to stay very close. Don't look up. Don't make eye contact. Keep talking."

Then we're through the door and into a crowd of people. So far, no one seems to have noticed, but it's only been maybe two seconds, and now a woman ten feet away does a double take. *Great.*

The booth is being staffed only by interns, and they are absolutely losing their shit over Tommy, but I introduce them, and he's super gracious and friendly. He looks through the books, asks them which are their favorites, and he buys a few. My bag is tucked in the corner under one of the side tables next to some boxes. I throw it over my shoulder, but when I step out of the booth and we start moving away, Tommy pulls the strap off my arm and takes it from me.

"Thanks," I say.

He smiles. "I'm just trying to get you into bed."

"You're really sweeping me off my feet."

"I think we both know it's easy to get you into bed. It's just hard to get you to stay."

We're talking quietly, but there are people everywhere, and of course everyone's paying attention to Tommy. "Would you shut up? Jesus, people can hear you."

He laughs and pulls my arm under his again. "No one can hear me." He holds up the books he bought. "These any good?"

I've only read one of them, and it was pretty dull. I guess it was well done, but it's just these long contemplative essays on place. I shrug. "I've read that one. It's eco-lit, which I think is pretty boring. I mean, the language is nice, but I don't know, maybe you'll like it. It wasn't really my thing."

"Really?" He looks disappointed. "Find me a book I'll want to read."

"I have no idea what you like to read," I say, but I think I know exactly the book. I spent almost an hour talking with the author this morning. "Fine. We need to go this way."

The crowds are getting thicker, which is good on the one hand because only the people right around us can see Tommy, but bad because it's hard to make our way through. I pull my arm from Tommy so I can walk ahead of him, weave my way in and out and around. The table I'm looking for is just a few rows away.

"Oh my god!" I hear a voice behind me squeal. "Oh my god!"

Sure enough, when I turn around, this woman is on him. Her fingers are curled around his biceps, which honestly is just insane, like she has some innate right to touch him. He's being cool about it, of course. I hear him say, "Oh yeah? That's so sweet. Really, so kind of you," but he keeps glancing in my direction. Then more people start milling closer to him, and some guy says, "Hey, Tommy, loved you in *Destructions*, man," and Tommy nods and waves. When he looks back at me, I give him this look like, *I knew it,* but still he can't seem to pull himself away.

"Excuse me, sorry." I push my way through and grab his wrist. "I'm so sorry," I say to the people around him. "We're on a schedule."

Tommy makes an apologetic face. "Handlers," he says, so they're all annoyed with me, but at least they let us through.

"I told you to stay close," he says. "That was not my fault."

I still have my fingers around his wrist, and I might be digging them in a little. He pulls away, takes my hand in both of his, and pats it in this patronizing way. "Have we talked about the possibility of getting you on some Xanax?"

By now we're at the row with the table I'm looking for, but I can't remember exactly where it is. I'm scanning the banners in the front. I know it's on the left side. "There," I say, and I point.

"Hey," I say to the guy working the table. He's too busy checking me out to notice Tommy, who's sort of half turned away anyway. "I'm looking for Ben Merriman's new collection of essays. Tell me you haven't sold out."

"We have." He gives me a little frown. "I know he's around here though with more copies. If you can find him."

"Uh, yeah, I'm on my way out. Shit." I turn to Tommy. He's on his phone, looking busy. "They don't have it."

The guy at the table looks up and says, "Oh shit. Are you . . . ?"

"Yeah," I say to him, but I think I roll my eyes. "Look," I say to Tommy, "I'll order a copy for you later."

"You know, I actually have a copy myself," the guy says. "I mean, I could sell you that one, and I'll just grab another from Ben."

I don't know why he didn't offer this when he thought it was for me. It's kind of insulting.

"That would be awesome, man. I really appreciate it," Tommy says.

"Don't enable him. He can wait," I say, but the guy's already digging it out of his bag.

"I mean, it's signed to me, but, if you don't mind . . ."

"Jesus, don't give him your signed copy."

"No, it's cool. I mean, I know Ben, so he'll sign another one. It's fine."

Tommy's got the book in his hands now, and he flips it open to the inscription, which is actually really personal and lovely, and I look at the guy like, *You can't give him this,* but Tommy just laughs. He says, "This is awesome, man. I love it."

"This is bullshit." I hand the guy a twenty. "No, it's cool, keep the change. I love your press."

"Did you just buy this for me?" Tommy says, and he looks at the guy. "See, she really does like me."

Getting to the car is like the biggest relief of my life. Tommy drops my bag in the backseat, and I slide into the front and hold my palms up over my eyes.

"That wasn't even that bad," Tommy says.

"I don't like crowds."

He laughs. "Where to? You hungry?" He backs out of the parking spot, pulls toward the front of the garage.

"It's barely four o'clock."

"Yeah, but you're on a different time zone, so . . ."

I shake my head. "I'm fine. Let's just get a drink."

"See, you're like the woman of my dreams."

"Mmm. Right. Actually, can we swing by the Sheraton? I still have to check in."

"What?" He turns to look at me. He's sitting in the exit lane waiting to turn into traffic. It's clear, but he doesn't pull out. "What the hell are you talking about, 'check in'?"

"It's a hotel," I say. "People sleep there."

"That's stupid, Stacey. You're staying with me."

"It's fine. This isn't for the movie, you know. This is all, like, through my publisher."

"Honey, I don't care why you're here. When you're here, you stay with me." He smiles, then turns his head to the left and pulls out of the garage. "Forward your reservation to Daniel. He'll take care of it."

"You know, you're sweet, but really, I've missed the cancellation—"

Tommy cuts me off. "Forward the fucking information," he says. "How many times do I have to say it?"

I press my lips together and pull my phone out to scroll through my e-mail for the confirmation. I'm not exactly sure what to say, so I say, "Thanks."

He reaches over and squeezes my leg. "You want to stop for a drink or drink at my house?"

"Your house, definitely. I've had enough of people today."

I slip my shoes off, curl my feet up beside me on the couch, and rub the ball of one foot and then the other with my thumb. Tommy is at the bar, opening a bottle of wine. He brings the open bottle and two glasses to the table and sets them down.

"That needs to breathe. You want a vodka while we wait?"

"God, yes." I smile. "Sometimes you're just the best."

When he comes back, he sets my vodka on the table and sits next to me, picks up the book of essays from the table.

"I can't believe you let that guy give you that," I say, rubbing my feet again.

"People like giving me things. I just let them. It's mutually beneficial." He flips the book open to the first page, then glances toward me. "Feet hurt?"

"Like hell. I want to soak them in a tub full of vodka."

"Shoes were pretty hot though. They might be the kind you should only wear to bed." He holds the book in his right hand, his thumb holding it open, and while he's reading, he reaches with his other hand and pulls my left foot into his lap, presses the tips of his fingers in circles across the bottom. "Have you read this whole book?"

"Uh-uh. I've read a few of the essays in magazines, but I just picked up a copy this morning. That first one, the title essay, is gorgeous."

"Yeah? Even the opening line is sharp." He keeps reading, flips the page with his thumb, keeps rubbing my foot. "You ever write essays?"

"No. Never. I don't write anything but poetry."

"Why not?"

"I don't know. I just don't have it in me. Maybe I can't sustain anything past twenty lines. Maybe I'm lazy."

He laughs. "You don't strike me as lazy, honey. Maybe you're just too intense."

"Is that the same as uptight?"

"It's very fucking similar, yes." He nods. "So what are you working on these days? What's the next book?"

I hate this question. I really do. "I'm working on nothing, Tommy. There may not be a next book."

"Don't be stupid. Of course there'll be a next book."

"No, I'm serious. I haven't been able to write." I take a sip of the vodka, but right now, it's not really helping.

"What do you mean you can't write? You write for us all the time." He looks at me like I'm crazy.

"That's just tweaking, revising, playing with words and shit. This is different. I can't draft anything new. I can't get started."

"Since your husband?" he says, and I just say, "Yeah."

"Interesting. I'd always assumed he was the one cutting your tongue out, but maybe you're doing it to yourself."

"The book's not about me."

He laughs. "Right. You've said that before, but you're clearly full of shit."

"She's a constructed identity based on contemporary gender ideals."

"And those ideals don't affect you at all. That's why you go to a poetry reading in fuck-me shoes." He runs one fingernail along the arch of my foot as he says this. I pull my leg back, but he grabs my ankle and laughs. "I'm just giving you shit, Stace. I like the shoes."

"Gee thanks, Tommy, because I'm really desperate for male approval."

"I know. It shows." He closes the book and holds it up. "Thank you for this. I like it. I'm putting it on the top of my stack."

Sometimes the way he can shift so quickly into what looks like sincerity is a little dizzying. Or maybe it's just him that's dizzying. That's a distinct possibility.

"You're welcome," I say.

He sets the book down and takes my foot in both hands. He presses his thumb into the arch of my foot, trails the fingers of his other hand around my ankle, slides his hand up under the leg of my jeans.

"Are you trying to seduce me?" I say, and he shakes his head.

"I wouldn't have to work this hard. I'm just trying to show you how much I like you."

"I don't like you at all."

"You're a terrible liar. You would never make it in this town."

"You're a terrific liar. You're like the best."

"Shut up and finish your vodka," he says. "I'm ready to pour this wine."

When I wake in the morning, Tommy's hand is splayed across my stomach. I try to slip out from under it, but he slides his hand around my waist, pulls me back against him. "Uh-uh. Stay. Go back to sleep." He presses his lips against my shoulder. I can't sleep obviously, so I just lie there, breathing, thinking. Michael has been dead for thirteen months, long enough that I feel like maybe it's okay for me to be naked in a bed with someone, but not long enough for it to be Tommy. It would take years for that. It might take a whole lifetime. I think, *If Michael were here now,* but he isn't. He obviously isn't, so I tuck myself farther into Tommy's arms, and I close my eyes, and eventually I fall back asleep.

When the plane coasts to a stop in Omaha and I turn my phone back on, it buzzes and buzzes with notifications. There are two texts from Tommy, one that says, *Feeling well rested?* and another that reads, *God, this book is phenomenal. How do you know this guy?* There's one from my editor that they sold out of my book, and they're upping the size of the next print run. Jenny says Stevie has lost a tooth, and she follows it up with a picture of him grinning around a bleeding hole in his gums. I don't reply to any of them. I just grab my bag from under the seat in front of me and scope out the people around me. I wonder if I'll be able to slip off the plane quickly. I'm so tired of traveling, of being up in the air.

JULY

IN THE AFTERNOON, I take the boys to the cemetery. It's Michael's birthday. We didn't last year. It was too new, but we came once in the fall when the plaque was done. It was easier because Jenny and Todd came too.

I like an old-fashioned cemetery with big gravestones, but this is just flat stones with bronze plaques listing names and dates. *Easy for mowing,* Michael had said. His grandparents are buried here too. I intend to be cremated, but Michael left specific instructions, so it's a double plot with a shared stone, and my name is on a little plaque next to his. It's a strange feeling, looking at your own grave. Not that I'm going to be buried here, or anywhere, so it doesn't count.

"I made him a card," Stevie says, pulling it out from where he's hidden it under his shirt like it's a surprise.

"That's not fair!" Ben yells. "I didn't . . . no one told me." He crouches on the grave, scrunches his hands into fists, and holds them against his eyes.

"It doesn't matter," I say. I squat next to him, my hand on his back. "You can make him a card tonight."

"It's not the same," Ben says.

Stevie lays his card in the grass. It says *Daddy* in big red and blue letters. The last time Stevie made him a card, I had to write the letters for him. He traced them with marker, but you could still see the black line of my pen underneath spelling out *Happy Birthday Daddy.* Then he'd covered it with hearts.

"Benny," I say.

"Don't call me that," he growls.

"Okay," I say, and I nod.

I rub my thumb across his shoulder blade, but he shrugs my hand off. Sweat pools behind my knees and the dry grass bites at my ankles.

"How long are we staying?" Stevie says. He's swinging his arms, wiggling his hips. "Can we look for Gran and Pops' grave too?" He's never going to remember Michael. Not really.

I have an hour while the boys are at swim lessons, so I figure I'll stop at the store. As usual, I've forgotten my list, but I know I need spinach. I'm making quinoa, and I run through the recipe in my head. I pick up onion, garlic, shallots. I hold a tomato up to my nose. It doesn't smell like anything. It doesn't smell real.

In the checkout, I see Tommy on the cover of a gossip magazine, not the lead story, but in one of the little bubbles with the heading *New Romance?* In the photo, he looks like Tommy, but also not. He looks more like a character from one of his movies. He has his arm wrapped around the very small waist of a blonde that I think I've probably seen before. She's beautiful, like a porcelain doll, and very,

very young. I think I was probably in high school by the time she was born. He has his head turned toward her, almost in her hair, like they caught him turning to whisper something in her ear.

I think about calling him, just to see what he's doing, but I think that would be weird, so I just text him the title of a book I keep hearing about. *Have you read this? Should I?* I type, and I know he'll call me by the end of the day. He usually does. I doubt he ever calls the porcelain doll. Not that it matters. None of this matters. Because the reality of my life is organic juice boxes and baby-carrot snack packs. It's just weird seeing these stories, though I see them a lot.

Besides, next month, I'm going out to see him, or not to see him, exactly. I'm just going out.

"There's a ton of shit going on, final casting, set design, storyboard should be done. I want to get your take," he'd said when he called.

"I don't know," I said. "It's hard to get away. How long are you talking about?"

AUGUST

THE BOYS ARE COMING WITH ME just till Tuesday. Tommy says they'll be fine hanging out with Daniel for a few days, but I don't know how I'll handle having them there. I don't like to feel divided. They'll fly with me and spend a few days at Tommy's, and then my parents will drive down from San Francisco. It's a day's drive, but they can take them to Disneyland and then I'll meet them all back at my parents'. They've been bugging me to bring the boys out anyway.

The boys are totally excited because they know Tommy has a pool, and this is the single greatest thing they can imagine. He's not home when we pull up, but Daniel is, and he stands in the front doorway with his arms crossed while I'm still trying to get the boys out of the car. They've brought backpacks, and the backpacks could not go in the trunk, and now Stevie's gotten his caught on the seat belt.

I turn toward Daniel, hold my arms out for a hug. He looks me over a little too closely. "You look thinner."

I don't say thank you. I know he doesn't mean it as a compliment. "I've just been busy."

"And this must be Ben." He holds his hand out, and Ben shakes it.

Stevie finally tugs his backpack loose and trudges out to stand next to his brother. I can tell he's nervous because he's trying to hold Ben's hand. It's an old habit, and Ben's old enough now not to like it, but he still puts up with it.

"Stevie?" Daniel asks, and Stevie nods. Neither one of them has said a word yet, and I wonder how long it's going to take. "Your mom says you guys like swimming." They both nod. "You want to see the pool?" Stevie looks at Ben, and Ben looks at me.

"Go ahead," I say.

Daniel puts his hand on Stevie's back and nudges him toward the house. "Now, don't go jumping in with your clothes on," he says. "But I bet after lunch you can get changed and go in. By the end of the day, you'll look like a couple of prunes."

They do get changed after lunch, and I go out to the pool deck to sit and watch them. They don't swim so much as jump in, flail their way to the side, and do it again. But they're happy. They're squealing and dripping all over the tiles. I like watching them. The sun is out, but it's not too hot, and I think I could just sit here all day. I dangle my legs in the water and lean back on my elbows, letting the sun slowly warm my neck and chest.

"Hey," Tommy calls from behind me, and I tip my head backwards to smile at him.

He kicks his shoes off and sits next to me. "They look like they're having fun."

"They are," I say. "They're loud though." Today, though, the loud doesn't bother me. Somehow, out here with all the sun and air, the loud feels fine.

He watches them for a minute and then calls out, "Hey, you Stacey's boys?"

They stop and look at him, and Stevie says, "Yeah."

"I'm Tommy," he says. "Nice to meet you."

They're standing at the edge of the pool, just dripping. They don't really look at him or me. They don't seem to know what to do. They're sort of jockeying to see who can stand behind whom.

"I'll give five bucks to whoever makes the biggest splash," Tommy says.

Stevie sort of hops. Five dollars is a big deal to him.

"It's got to be a really big splash though. It's got to come all the way over here. You're gonna have to get your mom wet."

I kind of groan, but the boys throw themselves into it, wearing themselves out, and by the end of it Tommy and I are drenched, and I haven't yelled at them, and the boys think Tommy is the coolest guy they've ever met. They're talking to him now, telling him all sorts of stories and things that they think are jokes but that aren't really funny. It's the kind of talk that I tend to zone out, so they have to repeat it a few times, ask, *Mommy, did you hear me?* He can tell when they want him to laugh, and so he does, and as they're drying off, he gives them each five dollars, and they totally love him.

For dinner, the boys are eating sandwiches with the crusts cut off, which I would normally never allow. Stevie had said, "Do we have to eat the crusts?" which he always asks, even though I always say, "Yes," and I did say, "Yes," but then Tommy took their plates and cut their crusts off and gave me this look that said, *Stop being such an asshole.*

"My dad taught us how to swim," Stevie volunteers after a while, which isn't even true. He made them take lessons.

"Yeah?" Tommy says. "Well, you guys are great at it."

Stevie looks at his sandwich for a minute. I can tell he's working up to it, but I don't know how to stop him. "Did you know my dad's dead?" he says finally.

"Shut up, Stevie," Ben says. "You'll make Mom sad."

Tommy gives me a look like, *Jesus*, and I'm sure he's thinking that I've broken my kids.

"Your mom's pretty tough," he says to Ben. "But I bet it makes you sad."

Ben doesn't say anything.

"You know, I did know about your dad," Tommy starts again, this time talking to Stevie. "I'm really sorry."

"It's okay," Stevie says. I don't think he really has anything to add. I think he'd just wanted to say it. It's like he needs to, every so often. Sometimes I hear him talking to his friends at school, *Can you come play on Friday? Did you know my dad is dead?*

Once the boys are in bed, I head back downstairs. Tommy is in the great room on one of the overstuffed leather couches with a bottle of wine, and I drop down next to him, prop my feet on the edge of the table. He hands me a glass of wine and doesn't say anything. He's just sitting there, his legs loosely crossed, his foot on his knee, watching me, and it feels like he's waiting for something.

"You think I'm a bad mom," I say finally.

"No." He shakes his head. "I think you're a great mom. I think you have great kids."

I try again. "You think I'm smothering their grief."

He takes a drink, stalling probably. "I think"—he turns to look at me—"I think the three of you are not the best at grief."

"I know." I set my wineglass down, bury my face in my hands.

"How long has it been?"

"Almost a year and a half."

"And you think, if you just gut it out, at some point things will get better?"

This is exactly what I think, but I shake my head. But then I say, "Maybe. I don't know."

"It might work like that for you, Stace, but it's not going to work like that for them." He reaches across the couch and grabs my hand. Already I feel like there's too much in my head, like how am I supposed to think about Michael and the boys and all of this grief when Tommy's sitting here looking at me? How am I supposed to remember to breathe? He tugs on my hand. "C'mere."

I tilt my head. I frown. "I can't sleep with you with the boys in the house."

"Honey, you can't sleep without me."

"What if they go looking for me upstairs and they can't find me?"

"It wouldn't matter if they could. You're a mess, Stacey. You're no good to anybody." He moves closer, slides his fingers deep into my hair, pulls my mouth against his. "Let me help you. Let me fix you up."

My hair is still wet from the shower. I have my clothes draped across the bed, but I don't know what to put on. We're going to the production office today, and thinking about it makes me feel anxious. I pick a pair of gray jeans. They're skintight, any tighter they'd bruise my hips, but I feel held together. I feel defined. I pull on a tailored navy cotton tee. It looks simple, but it cost a fortune. It's cut a little lower than I remember, and while it's not see-through, it hints that maybe it could be. I squirt a bit of mousse into my palm, finger it through my hair, and I pull out my makeup bag, smooth a little lotion over my face. It's true that I don't look as tired. This morning it was nearly light out when I woke up. Sleeping with Tommy doesn't help in the long run though. It just makes me even more restless when I get back home.

When I get downstairs, there are dirty cereal bowls on the counter, and Tommy and Daniel are both in the kitchen. Tommy's reading the paper. Daniel's on the phone. He must be on hold because he just twists it away from his mouth. "Morning," he says. "There's coffee. Boys have already eaten. They're in the media room, watching cartoons. You want some breakfast? I bought you plain yogurt."

I lean behind him, kiss him on the cheek. "You are my favorite person ever."

"Excuse me?" Tommy says, tossing his paper on the counter. "I think I do some shit for you that's way better than picking up yogurt. I mean, we could talk about some of the shit I do for you."

"Oh god, please don't," Daniel says. "I can't hear this kind of talk about Stacey."

"Yeah, you know, I feel like no one needs to hear this kind of talk about Stacey," I say. "Maybe what you could do for me is have a little discretion."

Tommy laughs. "Why? You embarrassed?"

"I'm not embarrassed," I say. "It's more like I'm deeply, deeply ashamed."

Daniel nods. "You should be, honey."

"Oh, shut the fuck up, both of you," Tommy says. Then he smiles, but his mouth seems stretched a little tight. "For you, Stacey, I have been nothing but discreet."

He stands up and walks behind me toward the door, but then he stops, takes hold of my hips. He pulls me back against him and leans down, says in my ear, "But as long as you're dressed like that, people are still going to think you're a slut."

"Go to hell," I say.

"I feel like I'm there already," he says, but he pats me on the ass as he moves away. "We're leaving in thirty."

"Don't take this the wrong way," Daniel says when Tommy's gone, "but you being here all week makes me sick to my stomach."

"Is there a right way to take that?" I say, pulling the yogurt out of the fridge.

"Never mind," he says. "It's none of my business anyway."

"Jason," I say when we walk in, and he jumps up from the desk. "The script is amazing. I love it."

Jason is not a groper, exactly, but he doesn't keep his hands still when he hugs me. Over his shoulder, Tommy raises his eyebrows and kind of laughs. Quietly though. He's not the type to call Jason out on it. I put my hands on Jason's waist and gently push him back.

"Pull up a chair." He waves toward the desk. "I was just looking at casting tapes. I'm down to the last few decisions, but I'll show you the people we've already locked in."

"Contracts signed on all of them?" Tommy says. He's already moving a chair for me.

"Yeah." Jason nods. "Sarah's in, obviously. And we've got Allen for the neighbor." He looks at me. "You know Allen Hayes?"

I know he means do I know of him, but I don't, so I shake my head.

"He's good. Not much of a résumé yet, but good." He goes on listing names I don't know, but Tommy seems happy with them. "So we're down to the last few key roles and the extras, of course, but I don't really dip my hands in that."

"He just fires the ones that don't work out," Tommy says.

"Yeah," Jason says. "I do do that." He motions toward the chair. "So sit down, I want to show you our cast."

He sits down too, and he starts pulling up all these clips on the screen in front of us. Tommy stands behind us. I can feel his hand on the back of my chair. We watch a lot of these, and honestly, I don't know what I'm looking at, so I just say a lot of *yeah*s, and *sure*s, and *seems greats*. Tommy seems super invested though. He keeps leaning forward to point at the screen, and every time he does, he brushes against me. If I was trying to pay attention, it would be very distracting.

"Who's this?" he says at one point.

Jason flips through a stack of paper on the desk for a second, but he gives up quickly. "Can't remember her name. She's no one yet, but we've got her down for the neighbor's wife."

"Yeah," Tommy says. "She looks good." And she does, she looks great, and maybe all of nineteen. "I like her for this role," he says.

Tommy's daughter gets in from her mother's before we make it back to the house. She's apparently been holed up in her room all day, and when Tommy insists she come down for dinner, she holds her phone in front of her plate and spends the entire time texting. She barely eats. I count, and she takes a total of five bites. Three of the spinach salad. Two of the potatoes. I can tell she's counting too. Her plate looks untouched even after the boys have been excused.

"Why don't you put the phone down?" Tommy says in this soft, understanding tone.

She acts like she doesn't hear him.

"Honey?" he tries again. "Sadie, honey?"

"What?" she snaps. "Jesus, Dad, can you give me like a minute's peace?"

He pauses, takes a breath. "Have you noticed that we have company? Maybe you could say hello."

She sighs and sets her phone down loudly. She looks at me and says, "Hi, I'm Sadie, and you must be fucking my dad." She picks her phone back up and turns to Tommy. "Can I go?"

Tommy drops his head forward, folds his hands at the back of his neck. "Fine."

She walks out, and I put my hand on his arm. "Well, she's got a lot of spunk," I say, in my best *Let's look on the bright side* tone.

"Yeah." He nods. "I knew you'd like her." He rubs his face with one hand, but then he pulls on this relaxed smile. "Hey, buddy, what's up?"

I turn, and Stevie's standing in the kitchen doorway.

"Ben pushed all these buttons and now the movie won't play."

"I didn't!" Ben says from where he's hiding around the corner. I can hear in his voice that he's trying not to cry.

"Not a problem, man. I can fix it." Tommy pushes his chair back and stands up, walks into the kitchen. He rubs his hand through Stevie's hair as he walks past him. "You guys want some popcorn?"

"They just had dinner. They don't need any popcorn."

"Go tell your mom we're gonna make popcorn," Tommy says, and I hear Ben giggle.

Stevie looks at me, his eyes wide, and I shrug like I'm giving up.

"She says okay!" he yells, and runs after Tommy.

I take my glass of wine and walk into the living room.

"My dad really likes little kids." I hadn't seen Sadie, but there she is, sitting in the corner, curled up on this upholstered linen chair. It looks like the kind of spot a little girl would curl up in to read. I bet she's been hiding there for years. She makes a face. "I mean, not like that. Not creepy. But he likes them." She looks down at her phone but doesn't pick it up. "Probably because they believe all his bullshit."

The rest of the room is arranged facing away from the chair she's in, so I just lean against the back of the couch. "I'm not sleeping with your dad," I say, but Tommy's right, I am a terrible liar. I'm sure she doesn't believe me.

"Whatever," she says. She doesn't look up at me. She's staring at her fingers. She's found a loose thread at the edge of the chair, and she's trying to tug it free. "I guess you're a little old for him anyway. Most of my dad's girlfriends are like barely older than me."

It's like she wants me to hate her. "You want to tell me why you're so mad at him?"

She shrugs. She's such a pretty girl. Sharp angular bones, thin skin. She looks like she's made of glass. She shifts her feet, and I see these thin white scars around her ankles. They look old, but I wonder if Tommy knows. If I had to guess, I'd say no.

I wait, but she doesn't say anything. "If it makes you feel any better, I think he's an asshole too."

She smiles, but she's trying not to.

"Let me know if you change your mind," I say. I stand up and move back toward the dining room.

"Hey," she says as I reach the door.

"Yeah?" I turn back to look at her.

She's standing now and starting to move out of the room. "I'm sorry about dinner."

"It's okay," I say. "I know."

We carry a bottle of wine out to the pool deck and lie on the lounge chairs. "To kids." Tommy raises his glass in a toast.

"At least mine will be leaving tomorrow." My parents will get in town late afternoon, and they're taking the boys straight to Anaheim. They have a reservation at the Disneyland Hotel.

"Maybe Sadie could go with them," he says.

"Sure." I nod. "My parents would take her. But it might cost you."

"Name your price," he says.

We just sit for a while, quietly. It's cooling off, and there's a breeze. I tuck my feet under me to keep off the chill.

"So did you always want kids?" I say finally.

"No," Tommy says. "I didn't want them at all." He pours another half-glass and holds the bottle out to me, but I shake my head. "Sadie's mom really hounded me on it. She really, really wanted a baby." He sighs. "And then we split up before Sadie turned two." He raises his glass. "So great fucking plan, huh?"

"I've heard worse. You weren't married, were you?"

"Uh-uh. Thank god." He shakes his head, smiles a little, but it's a tired smile. "She's cost me a small fortune in child support. I can't even imagine what a divorce settlement would have looked like."

"That's very calculating of you."

"Not calculating," he says, "realistic." Then he laughs. "That's not why I didn't marry her though. It just adds to my relief."

"Huh," I say. I finish the wine in my glass, hold it out for him to fill.

"She was just very, I don't know, motivated," he says as he leans back, setting the bottle on the ground next to him.

I raise an eyebrow. "Motivated is bad?"

"No. I mean, she was very serious about making the most of every opportunity for publicity, whatever." He shrugs. "If I told her ahead of time where we were going for dinner, she'd tip off a photographer."

"Seriously?"

"That's not even"—he waves one hand—"most of the women I've been out with would . . . or do. It just gets old."

"You poor thing," I say. I shake my head, push my lip into a pout. "All those gorgeous young women taking advantage of you."

"You're hilarious." He drains his glass, picks the bottle back up, and then he turns toward me, sitting sideways on the lounge chair. "This was different though. We were living together. We had a kid. And then when we split up, she was like . . ." He shakes his head. "She was doing all these interviews about 'life after Tommy' and making sure there were all these shots of her on vacation with Sadie. We had to get lawyers involved. She was selling pictures of my kid."

"She wasn't."

"Oh yeah." He nods. "She's a great mom."

He's leaning forward, resting his arms on his knees, holding the bottle of wine and his empty glass between us. I reach over, rest one hand on his arm.

"Sorry," I say.

"I'm used to it." He tips the last of the bottle into his glass, and I pull my hand away. "Honestly, the fact that you're just back in Nebraska doing your own shit, that's one of the things I like best about you."

"Are you sure you're not a poet? Because that's like the start of a sonnet—'The thing I like about you is that you're so far away.'" I lean back into the chair and pull my knees into my chest. "Please, keep going."

He laughs. "You know what I mean. Just that you're not caught up in this whole . . ." He waves his hand in a sweeping circle like he doesn't know the word for it. "I like that you don't want anything from me."

"That's not entirely true." I gesture toward the empty bottle with my glass.

"Okay, then I like that you're only using me for my wine cellar," he says, standing up and walking toward the house.

"It's a good wine cellar," I say. I close my eyes and listen to the door open and close behind me, and I think, *Fuck. I shouldn't even be here.*

We drink a lot of wine, and by the end of it, I'm feeling sleepy. My eyes keep fluttering closed.

"C'mon," Tommy says, standing up. "We have to get you inside before the kids find us passed out here in the morning." He offers his hand and pulls me up, and when I'm on my feet, we're standing close, inches apart, and then Tommy's mouth is on mine. I think how Tommy is like a planet, a center of gravity, throwing everything off-balance. I pull back, and there's just a whisper of air between us. Nose to nose. It's as far as I manage to go.

"Sadie would kill me," I say.

"You're probably right," he says. "But she sleeps late. I think we'll be good."

"No," I say. "I feel weird about this."

I step backwards, pull my hand out of his, but he grabs my wrist and draws me back. Kisses the skin along my jaw.

"I'm serious, Tommy."

"So am I, Stacey. Don't piss me off." He kisses me again, and when he does, he holds my lip between his teeth. He doesn't really bite me though, and even if he did, I wouldn't mind it. I kind of like things a little rough.

We spend most of the day at the production office with Jason, but my parents are supposed to be on their way for the kids. I keep checking my phone and texting them. I don't know if they're running late or if they just aren't looking at their phones.

"We should go," I say to Tommy finally. "I don't even know when they'll be here. If they show up to get the boys and I'm not there, my dad'll flip."

Jason looks up from his computer. Tommy's been sitting next to him, and they've been super intense about whatever it is they're looking at. I'm relieved that Tommy stands up to leave as soon as I ask.

"You still scared of your dad, Stacey?" Jason says, smiling. "Seem a little old for that."

"Watch it," I say. "I don't seem old for anything."

"Right. Right," Jason says. "I misspoke."

"My dad just gets worked up pretty easily. I don't like to upset him." But then I smile. "My dad's adorable. My dad's pretty great."

"No wonder you're not into Tommy," Jason says, and Tommy turns to give him this *What the fuck?* look. "Tommy only appeals to girls who hate their dads."

"Who says Stacey's not into me?"

"Stacey's too good for you," Jason says, and he gives me this smile like he hopes I'm not too good for him. His third wife must be on the downhill slide.

I laugh and shake my head. "Let's just go." I wave to Jason as we're walking out.

Tommy opens the car door for me, and as I slide in, he says, "You seem pretty into me."

"Not really," I say. "I'm just bored."

Tommy gets in and starts the car.

"You know, maybe you should just drop me off." I wave my hand back and forth between us. "I mean, if they thought anything . . ."

He turns to look at me. "You're serious?"

"They're my parents."

"And they're a little conservative?"

"Hardly." I turn to look out the window. "My parents are like, I don't know, intellectual hippies. My dad's an ethnologist. He studies cultural variations on kinship structures. Actually, he co-teaches a lot with the Women's Studies faculty. Not that it's called that anymore. It's Gender and Identity or Gender and Sexuality? I can't remember."

"So that's where your work comes from?"

"Probably, yeah." I nod. "A lot of it anyway."

"And your mom?"

"Art history. Mostly folk art."

"So dinner at your house was like a fucking college course every night."

"Definitely not." I laugh. "They were both working a lot. It was mostly me and Jenny."

"I thought you had this great childhood?"

"I did. My parents just weren't home for a lot of it."

"Sounds idyllic."

"Jesus, Tommy, they just . . . They were very progressive. They were encouraging. They gave me a great education. So we didn't do a lot of family dinners. So what?"

He lifts one hand from the steering wheel in a quick wave. "Don't get defensive. It's just finally making sense. I mean, it's always seemed kind of weird that your work is all 'Fuck the patriarchy!' but then you're like this suburban housewife."

"See? They're gonna love you. Please, call me that in front of my parents so they can lecture you on the denigration of traditionally female spheres. While you're at it, maybe you could say something about not doing chick flicks since you want your work to be taken seriously."

Tommy laughs and pulls left onto the street that leads to his house. "I make a lot of money doing chick flicks." He hits a button on the opener clipped to his visor and the gate to the drive swings open.

"No car yet," he says as he pulls in and parks in front of the house. He shuts the engine off and turns toward me. "All right, so here's the plan for your very progressive parents."

"You're leaving?"

"No, that would be rude." He sets one hand on my knee and slides his thumb along my thigh. "I'm just going to act like I'm not fucking you, and you're going to act like you're not damaged by it."

"Fuck you." I reach for the door handle, pop it open.

"Oh, come on, Stace," he calls after me. "That was a good one."

The boys come flying down the stairs and launch themselves at my parents almost the minute they're through the door. Everything's running behind schedule, but still the boys haven't packed up the last of their things. I send them back upstairs, and Sadie offers to help them. Today, she's being super sweet. She seems to have fallen in love with Stevie, and it's mutual. He's holding her hand.

"Can I get anyone a drink?" Tommy says.

"Please," I say, nodding, but he just stands there waiting, his hands in his pockets.

"What can I get you?" he says finally.

"Mom, you want some wine?" I say, setting my hand on her arm.

"No," she says. "Do you have any scotch?"

"Definitely." He walks behind the bar and pours a scotch, hands it to my mother. "Stacey, red or white?"

"Red," I say. "Dad?"

He shakes his head. "I've gotta drive your kids to the land of bull-shit and cultural stereotypes."

"I think it's supposed to be magic and fairy tales, Dad."

"A good fairy tale has a purpose. A message. It's not afraid to get bloody. It's not just some trip through la-la land."

"You're a good grandfather," I say, patting his arm.

Tommy sets a wineglass on the bar. "So I've got a bottle of Cab and a Syrah right here, but if you'd rather check the cellar . . ."

"Either of those is fine." I shake my head.

"Which one?" he says.

"Whichever. So, Dad . . ."

"Let me show you the labels," Tommy says, holding one bottle across the bar to me.

"Syrah," I say. "I'll take the Syrah."

"Good choice," he says. He pours the wine, then sets the glass at the edge of the bar. He leans forward onto his elbows, facing my mother. "So, Stacey tells me you're an art historian."

"Mm-hmm." She nods, the glass of scotch still at her lips. "I study mostly folk art, but you have some beautiful contemporary pieces. You're a collector?"

"Hardly." He shrugs. "I know a lot of artists, and I'm in the position to buy things."

"A patron," she says. She smiles a little, but I know she means this dismissively. I take the wine from the bar and sip it. It has a bitter, almost smoky finish that I don't particularly like. I set the glass back down.

"I wouldn't say patron." Tommy shakes his head. "I just get paid too much for ridiculous reasons, so when I see something I like, they know they can gouge me."

"Because you simply must have it," she says, her smile much more genuine now. My dad likes altruism, but my mother has an artist's heart. She's interested in passion.

"I'm entirely selfish," Tommy says.

"We had heard that," my dad says with a sort of quiet laugh.

Tommy nods, letting his shoulders slouch just a little. "Right," he says. "I'm sure you have."

"Not from Stacey," my dad says quickly.

"Stacey says you're very smart," my mother says. "Surprisingly well read."

"Surprisingly?" Tommy laughs, but it's not a normal laugh for him. He smiles at me with just a quick shrug of the lips, disturbingly platonic.

"Very gifted too," she says, and my dad nods.

"I'm flattered," Tommy says. He looks right at me. "That's really nice to hear. Thank you."

I'm going to have to get drunk, I think, but just then Ben appears in the doorway, and Sadie's behind him, holding Stevie on her hip like he's a baby. She doesn't look big enough to carry him, but he's a tiny slip of a kid.

"Well, I guess we're on our way." My mom finishes the scotch and sets the empty glass on the bar. "It was nice to meet you," she says.

"Nice to meet you too." He's still leaning forward on his elbows, and he doesn't move to take her hand.

"Come give me hugs," I say to the boys. Sadie lets Stevie down and he dashes to me. Ben sort of shuffles behind him. I hug both of them, brush my thumbs across their cheeks. I say, "I know you're going to be good."

"Come on, come on," my dad says. "We need to hit the road." He kisses me on the cheek. "Kids'll be fine."

I follow them out to the front and watch them drive off. I blow kisses and wave. Through the windows, they all look happy, even Ben.

When the gates close behind them, I hug my arms around myself and walk back in the house. Tommy's drinking my wine, and he's opened the other bottle and poured me a glass.

"I knew you wouldn't like the Syrah," he says, holding the new glass out to me.

I don't take it. He stares at me for a minute and then he shrugs, sets it down. He leans against the bar across from me. "I don't act with you if that's what you're wondering."

"Everyone's acting," I say. "You're just better at it than the rest of us."

Tommy wants me to read this novel that he swears I'm going to love. We're on the couches in the great room, but we're sitting opposite each other, our feet propped up on the table. Sadie keeps ducking in and out of the room. She clearly wants attention.

"What are you up to, honey?" Tommy looks up from his book, turns his head back to look at her.

"Nothing," she says. She wanders over like she's not sure where she's headed and leans her elbows onto the couch behind him. "I'm bored."

"Read a book," Tommy says. "Read one of Stacey's books."

"No," I say. "Don't do that."

Sadie makes a face at me. "I've already read them," she says.

I raise an eyebrow at Tommy. "Boundaries?" I say.

"What? She's a smart kid."

"Yeah," she says. "I am." She comes around the couch and sits next to Tommy. He holds his arm up and she slips under it, leaning against him. "What are you reading?" she says, after a minute.

Tommy turns the cover toward her.

"Is it good?"

"That's why I'm reading it," he says.

She sighs a little dramatically, but then she's quiet for a minute. She pulls one foot up and picks at the flaking polish on her toes. "What was your husband like?" she says, without looking up.

"What?" I say.

Tommy sort of grimaces an apology and looks back at his book.

"Was he a writer too?"

"No," I say. "He wasn't."

"I kind of pictured you with an artist, in like a loft apartment or something."

"Michael was in finance. We live on a golf course."

"That's so weird," she says. "How'd you meet him?"

"Grad school," I say. She's leaning forward now, a little expectantly, like I must have a great story to tell, something dramatic or romantic. Everything feels dramatic and romantic when you've just turned fifteen. "We met in grad school. And then we got married. And we had a couple of kids."

She smiles a little sadly. "Do you think you'll get married again?"

"I hadn't really thought about it," I say.

"I'm never getting married," she says, in the tone of a little girl who can't wait to get married. She looks at Tommy like she's daring him to challenge her, like she wants him to say, *Someday you'll find the right person . . .*

"Good call," he says.

I try to finish the book over coffee in the morning while Daniel sits on the stool next to me, sorting through a stack of mail.

"Look at this," Daniel says, holding up this envelope covered in lipstick. "Disgusting."

I just smile and turn back to the book. "He has very passionate fans."

"Yeah. But I'm the one who has to open this shit. I swear someday I'm going to catch something."

His phone rings, and he sort of jumps to pick it up. "This is Daniel," he says, hopping down off the chair and walking toward the doorway. I can tell he's trying to lower his voice, but as he steps through to the dining room, I hear him say, "You know, I don't know if he's really available right now," but I can't hear what he says after that.

I close my eyes for just a second, and I take a deep breath. Daniel's probably gone five minutes, and when he does come back, I'm still on the same page. I keep running my eyes over the words, but I can't hold on to them long enough to figure out what they mean.

"That was Tommy's agent," Daniel says, sitting back down.

"I'm not stupid," I say, though I am. I obviously am. *I don't act with you,* he said, and it feels like I believed him.

Daniel sets the phone on the counter. He clicks the screen on and then off, on and then off. "No. You're not stupid," he says.

I'm drinking coffee by the fireplace when Tommy comes out of the study. He slams the door behind him.

"Not a good fucking start to the day," he says. He walks fast, his feet heavy on the tile, toward the kitchen.

"What?" I'm sitting cross-legged on the couch, but the tone of his voice makes me want to fold my knees up, hide behind them.

He tries to pour a cup of coffee, but he tips the pot too fast, and the coffee splashes over onto his hand. "Fuck!" he yells, and he turns and throws his mug against the wall. The coffee leaves a trail of drips toward the counter, the pieces of shattered mug. I do rearrange my legs now, hug my knees into me. I don't ask again. I just wait. He grabs a towel and wipes his hand. He holds it up to his mouth like he's blowing on it. "Fuck," he says again, but quietly. He takes down another mug, pours the coffee slowly this time, and walks over to sit on the opposite couch.

"There's just a lot going wrong today. It's all money and contracts and insurance and shit." He sets his coffee down, rubs his face with his hands. "None of it's anything you need to worry about. I'll take care of it, but you should probably just stay here. Maybe Sadie can keep you company," he says, and he gives me a look like, *Sorry.*

"I'm sure we'll be fine." I put my feet down on the floor and lean forward to pick up my coffee.

"I better go," he says, and he stands up and starts to walk out, but before he reaches the door he turns back. "If you want to go anywhere, keys are in the closet next to the garage. Sadie knows where they are. Take anything you want."

Sadie thinks we should totally go somewhere. She's sitting at the counter, eating the one slice of dry toast that apparently makes up her breakfast.

"Let's go to the beach," she says, and I say, "There's a pool."

"We could go shopping."

"Or, and I think you'll like this, Sadie, we could stay here and play chess."

She rolls her eyes at me. "Come on, my dad has like the coolest fucking cars."

"Sadie, do you have to talk like that?"

"Sorry, I didn't mean to swear. I just keep forgetting because you're so cool." She gives me the most manipulative smile. "Like cool enough to go somewhere fun."

"I am not driving your dad's car."

"You have to. He never lets anyone drive his cars, so, I mean, if you get the chance, you can't not take it."

"Of all your arguments, this is the least likely to work." I shake my head. "Do you know how much anxiety that would give me? I would absolutely, and I mean absolutely, get in an accident."

"So? He's insured."

"Sadie. No. I don't know why we're still discussing this."

She sighs heavily and stands up. She hasn't even finished her toast. "Jeez, Stacey. I thought you were fun."

"I am so fun," I say, "and I'm totally going to kick your ass at chess."

"You suck," she says. "You're lamer than my dad."

"I told you to take a car." Tommy pulls a sparkling water out of the fridge, twists the cap off, and takes a drink.

"I am not going to drive one of your cars. Christ. They're worth more than my kids." I set the book I'm reading on the counter in front of me. If it were mine, I'd set it down open to save my place, but it's Tommy's. I don't want to crack the spine, so I close it, hope I remember.

"They're just cars, honey. They're insured."

"It doesn't matter." I shake my head. "I don't know my way around here anyway."

"You don't have navigation on your phone? You have like a flip phone or some shit?" He's grinning at me. He seems to like it when I get flustered. Apparently, it's hilarious. "I just don't know why you'd want to be stuck in the house with a stir-crazy fifteen-year-old all day." He takes another swig of the water. "She says you made her play chess."

"I did. She's not bad." I suck in my lower lip and chew on it because she's much better than not bad.

"She says she kicked your ass."

I shrug. "I'm not a mathematical thinker."

"Is there math in chess?"

"I don't know. There must be. It's the only thing I'm not really good at." I look down at the book, run my fingers across the letters in the title. "How did things go for you today?"

He grimaces. "Expensive. Probably would've helped if you'd crashed one of my cars. I could use the insurance payout."

"That bad?"

"Nah, it's fine." He drains what's left in the bottle. "It'll all work out. It's nothing you need to worry about."

Sadie is spending the night at a friend's house because she *just can't be in this house every minute*, and when she'd said this, she'd glared at me. She doesn't mean it though. She likes me. I've even let her borrow a shirt.

"That's a little sheer on her, don't you think?" Tommy says after she leaves. He sits across from me in the living room.

"It's fine. She looks sweet."

"She probably won't be back by the time you leave tomorrow."

"So she can keep it."

He's tapping his heel up and down, jiggling his knee.

"What's with the anxiety, Tommy? You look like me."

"I know. It's gross, isn't it?" He stands up abruptly and walks to the bar. "It's Sadie. You know. She's a mess. It's not like I don't see it. I mean, I see it. I just don't know what I'm supposed to do about it." He pours himself a bourbon, a vodka for me. "Should I just bring both these bottles over?" he asks, but he doesn't bother waiting for me to answer. He just tucks them under his arm.

"So what the hell do I do?" he says, sitting back down next to me.

"Maybe you should ask someone who's good with their kids." I take a sip of the vodka. "You want to call my sister?"

"Kind of." He laughs. "I kind of do. Maybe we could work out a trade, you know. I'll keep your boys, and you take Sadie."

I nod. "That could work, but you'd have to run it by her mom."

He laughs, shakes his head. "She doesn't take my calls."

"How do you coparent and not speak?"

"It's not really a collaboration," he says. "There are a lot of lawyers. A lot of legal fees. It's, uh, it's not really good for us to talk."

"Because of the publicity stuff?"

"Nah. She's just unreasonable." He shrugs.

"Wow. What the hell did you do to her?" I cross my legs and lean back into the corner of the couch because this seems like it'll be a good story.

He smiles. I can tell he's stalling. "I don't think it was that bad."

"Mm-hmm, go on."

"Fuck, Stace." His glass isn't empty yet, but he refills it anyway. "So, I was on location for a long time, like six months, and this shoot was hellish. I couldn't really get away. I made it home like three times for less than twenty-four hours, and every time I did, I just spent every minute with Sadie. Every time I came home, she was this totally new kid. It was awful. It was miserable, lonely."

"And you fucked around on her?" I say, but it's not really a question.

Tommy takes a sip of the bourbon, and then he shakes his head. "She fucked around on me."

"Really?" I say, because this *is* a good story. I like stories with surprising twists.

"I came home, and she just broke down. She gave me this whole weepy confession, and she was like, 'I'm so, so sorry.'" He pauses, takes another sip of the bourbon. "And this is how much of an asshole I am, because after all of that, I said, and I'm quoting, 'It's okay. I get it.'"

"Seriously?"

"Yeah, she flipped. She was so pissed. She went completely crazy, like she tore up the house, and I just scooped up Sadie and went to a hotel, and she hasn't said a civil word to me since."

"Because you forgave her?"

"Because I wasn't mad in the first place."

I hold my hand up and twist my fingers around my lips. "Yeah," I say after a few seconds, "when you put it like that, it's a little shitty."

"It's not that shitty."

"Oh, it's pretty shitty," I say, and I lean forward and pour more vodka over the ice that's left in my glass.

"Whatever. I'm sorry I'm so fucking understanding." He tosses back the last of his bourbon. "I'm hungry. Let's go to dinner."

OCTOBER

Now that he's ten, Ben's old enough for pee-wee football, which in Omaha is a really big deal. The parents on this league are insane. Like they tailgate. Who tailgates at pee-wee football? Anyway, there are only a few weeks left, and I must be feeling generous because I invited Michael's parents to come to this week's game. Stan's not a problem, but Carol keeps talking to me. If anything, you'd think she'd help keep Stevie busy, but she doesn't. She keeps telling him to sit still, which is ridiculous. He's seven. "Why don't you look for roly-polies?" I say, and this keeps him occupied for at least the first half of the game. When my phone rings, I'm so relieved to have the excuse to step away.

"I have to take this," I say to Carol, and into my phone, I say, "Hey."

"Who is that?" Carol says because she's always so nosy.

"It's Jenny," I say, and on the other end of the line, Tommy says, "This is getting insulting. I mean, discretion is a nice change, but you're going a little overboard with the secrecy."

"That's just Carol," I say, "Michael's mom." The fact that Carol doesn't call me on this proves how dumb she is. I mean, if it was Jenny, she'd know who Carol is. "She came out to watch Ben's game."

"Oh. Yeah, no, I'll give you a pass on that one. That one makes sense."

"Thanks," I say. "That's very generous of you." The kids are heading back out to the field, but I don't see Ben with them. The coach tries to send him out as little as possible. "What are you calling for anyway?"

"I don't know," he says. "I'm just bored. I'm guessing you're not really up for phone sex with your mother-in-law right there?"

"Jesus, you're fucking horrible," I say, but I laugh. It's totally funny. Carol turns to look at me though, and she doesn't look happy.

"Careful, honey. You talk to Jenny that way?"

"Sometimes," I say, but it's actually pretty rare.

"And here I thought I was special."

"Not really." When I look up, I see the number 27 on the back of one of the kids on the line. I am ninety percent sure this is Ben. "I gotta go," I say. "Ben's playing now. I'll call you later."

I've volunteered to help with Ben's class's Halloween party, but only because they don't have enough parents. The spots filled up just fine in Stevie's class, because they're littler and still cute, and half the moms haven't gone back to work yet. I said this to Tommy, and I must have sounded kind of dismissive because he laughed and said, *You don't exactly have a job either.*

Anyway, the lead mom is super into it, and she has this plan where the kids will have to race to pull all of the gummy worms out from a scoop of chocolate pudding, but they'll have to do it with their hands tied behind their backs. It just sounds like a mess to me and probably to the teacher too, because she asks us to bring plastic tablecloths to spread on the floor. The kids love it though. They march in their little costume parade around the school, and when they come back into the room, we've got all the bowls of pudding ready. They have to race in waves because there isn't that much room on the plastic sheet. By now most of the kids have their costumes half on and half off, and I keep worrying someone's going to rip something or leave their mask behind. They still need it all for tonight.

"Well, I think this is a success," lead mom says to me, and I nod.

"Seems like they're having fun."

"I just love Halloween," she says. "I wish I could still pretend to be a princess once a year."

I say, "Yeah. I kind of hate pretend." She sort of frowns at me though, so I force a laugh.

"Where did your son get that mask?" she says, gesturing to the one in my hand. "It's awesome."

"This?" I say, holding it up. "It's a prop. I have a friend in the movies. He sent a bunch of stuff like this to the kids." It's not from our movie, just an assortment of crap he had lying around. The boys were making me crazy not deciding on their costumes this year, and Tommy said, *I'll send them some ideas.* "They never used it, but I think this was supposed to be in some alien movie? I don't really know."

"Wow, that's a cool friend to have," she says.

"Yeah," I say. "He's the best."

I haven't seen him since the summer of course, but we talk a lot, almost every day. *I miss you,* he's started to say, but I have no idea when I'll even see him again, so he clearly doesn't miss me enough.

NOVEMBER

SATURDAY NIGHT THERE'S A THING, and I have to get a sitter. She's a new girl, and I make her a list of phone numbers to keep on the fridge. I let her make the boys dinner, which Michael never would have allowed. She's sixteen. She knows how to cook a frozen pizza. She's not going to burn down the house, but I can still hear Michael arguing in my head, *What if she leaves the oven on? What if they choke?*

It's a fundraiser at a gallery downtown, the kind of place I almost never go, but they're raising money for a new arts program in the schools. I'm supposed to give a reading. They promised it could be quick.

There's a cash bar, and I really need a drink, so I order a glass of white. It feels a little safer, more responsible.

"Stacey?" I turn at the sound of my name. It's Craig. He's a friend, I guess. A poet. We've done workshops together, and the guy is always around. He runs this little poetry mag that he keeps asking me to send to, but of course I don't because who wants to publish in some shitty little magazine out of Omaha? He moves to kiss me on the cheek, and I feel like I have to tilt my head down a little for him to reach it. "Hello, hello! Looking beautiful as ever. Radiant!"

I smile.

"And you'll be reading?" he says. "Which is fantastic. Something from *The New Yorker*, maybe?" I've never been published in *The New Yorker*, and I know Craig knows that. He also hates to hear me read. He's probably pissed that he wasn't asked. He's a little competitive, kind of a Napoleon complex. "You know Phillip?" He turns to the man next to him, who stretches out his hand. "Or shall I say Dr. Phil?" Craig laughs.

Phillip smiles and takes my hand. "Just Phillip," he says. He has a very nice smile, bright eyes, a strong jaw, blond hair cut short and clean. I catch myself looking for a ring.

"Do you already have a drink?" he asks.

"I was just getting one."

He signals to the bartender. "I'll get hers," he says, "and I'll take a Jack and Coke." He turns to Craig. "You?"

"On the good doctor? Your finest cognac, sir!" he says to the bartender, who stands there looking bored. "Ha! Just a joke, man! Jack and Coke sounds great."

Phillip pays for the drinks and drops a couple dollars in the tip jar. "Have you two walked through the silent auction?" he asks.

"I've put some bids in," Craig says. "And now I think I will circulate, if you don't mind." He makes what I'm assuming is an ironic bow and backs away.

"How about you?" Phillip asks. "You up for a spin through the tables?"

"I'd love to," I say.

There's a painting of the Old Market area, an antique ring, a weekend at a B&B. I feel like I should bid on something, but there's nothing

I want. Phillip must feel the same because he leans over and says, "Tell you the truth, I'd rather just write them a check."

I laugh. "How about the wine?" I say, pointing to a pair of bottles, one white, one red. The current bid is ninety.

"Maybe I could talk you into drinking them with me?" Phillip says, picking up the pen.

"I can usually be talked into drinking."

Phillip writes *$150* on the next line, and I think, *Not bad.*

"So you're a Ph.D. or an M.D.?"

"M.D. I'm an allergist."

"Nice. Probably not a lot of middle-of-the-night emergencies."

"Yeah, that's what pushed me over from ob-gyn. Well, that and the likelihood that I wouldn't be able to get a date."

We keep moving through the tables, and Phillip says, "So what do you do, Stacey?"

"I'm a writer," I say. "A poet."

"Right, I know that," he says, "because you're reading tonight," and I make a face like, *Right, of course.* "But aside from that. Do you teach?"

"No, I don't." I shake my head. "I'm just a writer." I'm sure he's wondering how I can afford to eat, but I just let it drop. "So are you from Omaha?" I ask.

"No, but I've lived here forever, almost ten years."

"Oh, me too," I say.

I feel my phone buzz in my pocket. "I'm so sorry," I say, pulling it out. "I have to check this text. I wouldn't normally. I just . . . I have a new sitter."

"Oh, sure. Yeah," he says.

But it's not the sitter. It's Tommy. I should have known. There's a whole chain of messages under his number because we text a lot and

I never delete them, though I probably should. This time it says, *Read the hairless cunt poem. That'll go over well in Omaha.*

"Kids okay?" Phillip asks.

I look up. "Oh, yeah. It was"—and I don't know what to say—"work." I shrug.

We've reached the end of the tables, and I'm out of wine. "Can I return the favor? Buy you a drink?" I say, gesturing toward his glass.

I read a few pieces from *Monsters* because god knows I don't have anything new. I keep it short, maybe fifteen minutes, and when I walk away from the microphone, Phillip stands up from his chair in the front row and brings me my wine. I'd asked him to hold it. Seemed like a good move.

"That was terrific," Phillip says. "Really great." I can tell by his tone that he didn't understand a word of it. It's probably better that way.

Craig comes up to me from behind, touches my shoulder. "First rate," he says. "Love that second piece. It's one of my faves."

I know this is a dig. *Why don't you have any new shit?* is what he means. It's true, this book is three years old. Phillip doesn't care though. He thinks I'm great, and when I decide it's time to leave, he walks me to my car. He holds the driver's door open for me and asks for my phone number, and when I give it to him, he writes it down with a pen. It's really cute.

It takes Phillip almost a week to call me. It's Wednesday, mid-morning, which is weird. I wonder if he's calling me from his office and what his office looks like. I wonder if he's wearing a white coat.

"Stacey? It's Phillip. From the fundraiser." He sounds nervous. Out of practice.

"Oh, hi," I say, trying to sound surprised.

"I won the wine," he says, "that I bid on. I think I promised you a drink."

It's a cute touch. I like it. I think he's doing pretty well. "You did," I say. "You absolutely did."

"I don't know what your weekend looks like?"

It looks shitty. Ben's got a friend sleeping over on Friday, and Saturday I have my sister's kids.

"This weekend's pretty lousy," I say. "But I'm free the next?"

He groans. "I'm in Philadelphia for a conference. Let me grab my calendar. The nineteenth? No, wait, I'm out of town for the holidays. First week in December?"

"I'm in L.A. Work."

"Seriously?" He laughs. "I think this used to be easier."

"I know, right? Maybe we could just say coffee? Next week?"

"How about Tuesday morning? Around ten? My office is just off Pacific. I could meet you at Countryside."

"Perfect, yeah. I'll be there," I say.

I have a date, I think when I hang up. I'm going on a date. And I guess I don't have any reason not to.

Phillip is already waiting when I get there. He must have come early because I'm not even running late. He stands up to greet me, and sort of air-kisses me on the cheek. He motions for me to sit down and says, "I'll grab you a drink. What'll you have?"

I say, "Vodka?" but he doesn't seem to get it, so I say, "I'm kidding. Coffee, black, would be great."

I look around and realize this is a shitty place for a date. In the corner is a business meeting, probably sales. Some guy's blustering, and the rest of them are nodding along. The table across from us is a mommy with her kid. She's probably just looking to get out of the house, read a paper, have an excuse to comb her hair. I get it. The little girl looks about two, and she's fully into her muffin, picking out the chocolate chips. Phillip returns with the coffee, and I smile a thank-you. He looks nice, a little straitlaced but nice, and definitely cute. He looks like a very nice, cute allergy doctor. I wonder if my sister's ever taken her kids to him.

"So what's taking you to L.A.?" he asks as he sits down.

I blow into my coffee but don't take a sip. "Film adaptation."

"A movie?" he says.

I nod. "One of my books. I've been working on the script." I blow across my coffee again and watch the steam swirl off. "They want me to come out for the start of filming, but I won't stay long."

"Wow, that's incredible." He looks genuinely impressed. "Is it like a big-budget thing?"

"I have no idea, really. They don't tell me the budget." I laugh.

He makes a little *Of course* shrug. "So is there anyone I would know in it?"

I don't say Tommy. I say, "Sarah Nixon is the lead."

"No kidding?" He shakes his head, smiles. "Wow, that's really cool."

I just shrug. "So tell me again what brought you to Omaha?"

"I did my residency here." He sits up a little straighter, looks a little more serious. "And then my wife, my ex-wife, her family is here, so we stayed."

"Mmm." I take a sip of my coffee finally. "How long have you been divorced?" I don't know if this is a safe date question or not.

"Almost two years. You?"

I shake my head. "My husband passed away."

"Oh, jeez, I'm sorry. Craig said you were single. I just assumed . . ."

"No, you're fine." I feel like this would be easier if we were drinking. "Do you have kids?"

"No. No kids." He looks down at his coffee, and for a second I'm afraid he's going to tell me some awful story about how they tried, but he doesn't, and I'm totally relieved.

"And you're off to Philadelphia, is it? For this conference? If it's anything like a writer's conference, you'll be hungover for a month." I laugh, but really I'm thinking, *Jesus, how hard do I have to work?* But this one takes, and he laughs, and he tells me a few stories about drunk doctors and guys who get busted for fucking around on their wives, though he doesn't use the word *fucking*. Whatever, it's working, and I think, *We could do this. I could see him again.*

DECEMBER

DANIEL RUNS UP just as I'm pulling my bag from the carousel. He grabs me by the shoulders and presses his cheek against mine. "I just texted the driver. He'll swing through." He steps back. "Tommy wants me to take you straight to the set. You okay with that?" he says as I'm popping the handle on my roller bag. "I can stall if you need to rest. It might be kind of a long day."

"I'm fine," I say.

By the time we walk outside, the driver's pulling around. Daniel opens the back door and nudges me in, sliding in behind me. "I brought you a protein bar," he says, digging into his bag. "I know you haven't eaten yet, and the shit on set is not going to work for you."

"Peanut butter? I love it. I wish you lived with me."

"I know," he says, patting my hand. "I better text Tommy we're on our way."

I tear open the wrapper and take a small bite, folding the paper back over the end of it. I shake my head. "I already sent him a text when I landed."

Daniel raises one eyebrow. "You two still text a lot?"

"Daniel, please don't start."

"You're right," he says. "Never mind." He pinches his lips together, folds his arms, but after a minute, he pulls his phone out and says, "You know, I'm just gonna text him anyway."

We ride for a long time with our arms crossed, looking out separate windows. The sky is so hazy, so beige. Not like Nebraska, where everything's so blue and wide and clear.

"I mean, you do get that he doesn't do relationships, right?"

"Daniel." I close my eyes, press my tongue against my lips because of course I get that. "I have a dead husband and two sad little kids. I've got more relationships than I can handle, so the fact that Tommy's not particularly invested really works out pretty well."

"Jesus, Stacey, you know that isn't how I meant it. Don't make him sound like that."

"I wish you'd make your mind up, Daniel."

"Yeah? I wish lots of people would." He sighs heavily, shakes his head. "I'm not saying he doesn't give a shit. I'm just saying he's not really equipped for this."

"There's no 'this,' Daniel. It's just . . . it's easy."

"Really?" he says. "You just keep telling yourself that. And then when this shit blows up, don't come crying to me." He shifts his whole body toward the window, and I do the same.

"Take her things back to the house," Daniel tells the driver as we step out. "I'll text Tommy that we're here," but he doesn't actually need to.

I hear Tommy's voice behind me calling, "Stacey," and by the time I turn around, he's in front of me, and he wraps me in this tremendous, tight hug. "Jesus, how come you haven't been out to L.A. in forever?"

"I don't know," I say. "You haven't given me an excuse."

The first person I see when we walk in is Sarah. Well, she's not the first person I see, but the first person I can't stop looking at. She's in costume, and it's like she stepped right out of my head. When she turns toward us, she smiles at Tommy, but then she looks back at me for a second. "Oh my god," she says, "is this Stacey? Oh my god!" and she comes rushing over and swoops me into a hug. "Tommy's told me so much about you," she says. Her head is by my ear, and I look over her shoulder at him like, *You didn't,* because someone like Sarah thinking of me as just another girl that Tommy fucks is really more than I can stand. But he just barely shakes his head.

"So I want Jason to rethink the blocking on this scene. Who's going to talk to him?" I don't know if she's talking to me or Tommy now, and I don't know if she does either. She loops her arms through ours and starts leading us toward the set.

They're still filming at six o'clock. They do, I don't know, a million takes of this one microscopic scene, and when Jason turns and catches my eye, he gives me a thumbs-up, and I smile, but really I'm like, *I think I'm in hell.* Tommy must be able to tell. Between takes he whispers, "You want to go?"

"Don't you have to be here?"

"Nah, this is Jason's baby now. I'm just an actor, and they're not shooting any of my scenes this week." He nods toward the door. "Let's get out of here."

Tommy's parked right out front, so we're in the car and off the lot in just a few minutes.

"So what do you think?" he says finally.

"I think your job is exhausting," I say. "You should try my job. I can do it in bed."

He laughs. "No. How do you think it looks?"

"Sarah looks amazing, like I dreamed her."

"Yeah. I thought of her the first time I read your book. She's perfect for the part." He pulls up a hill, and I think it looks familiar. I think we're almost there. "And she loves it. She's really excited about it."

But we're not almost there. I'm just imagining landmarks. He's just pulled through some side street, and now we're back on a main road, deep in traffic, stopping at a red light. "Speaking of excited," he says, and he reaches across with his left arm and grabs my head, pulls me toward him, and leans in to kiss me. "I've wanted to do that all day." But then traffic starts to move again, and he lets go and kicks the car back into first.

The door's barely closed when Tommy wraps his arm around my waist from behind and pulls me back against him. He twists me to face him and buries his hands in my hair, and he pulls me up against his mouth.

"There's no one here," he says, and he doesn't move his mouth away from mine, but he walks me backwards, presses me up against the wall, and he starts unbuttoning my shirt.

"Jesus, Tommy."

"I can't help it, baby. You've been gone too long. You can't stay away from me like that." He pins my right hand to the wall just above my head and leans into me, pushing his knee between mine. He holds my earlobe between his teeth and the feel of his breath against my neck makes me laugh.

"Slow down," I say. "Let me get in the house at least."

"Uh-uh." He grabs me hard around the waist, lifts me off the floor, and I wrap my legs around his hips. "I'm tired of waiting," he says.

Tommy brings dinner and a bottle of wine to bed. Dinner being a box of crackers and some insanely strong blue cheese. I don't like it at all, and he says, "You have an undeveloped palate."

He keeps slipping me little bites of it between kisses, and when I say, "I seriously hate this cheese, Tommy," he says, "You'll get used to it."

"You say that about a lot of shit," I say, and he laughs and says, "I'm right."

The wine I do like, and I keep letting him refill my glass.

"I hope I have another bottle," he says.

"You have another bottle of something," I say, and he says, "Yeah, that's true."

He rolls to his back, pulling me on top of him, and I lean down to catch his mouth with mine when there's a knock at the door, and this little voice calls, "Dad?"

Tommy pushes me off him and jumps out of bed, pulling on his jeans and wrestling his way into his shirt. "She won't just come in here," he whispers, but I slide as far down under the sheets as I can. Then I remember that half of my clothes are out in the hallway. At least they're by the garage. I'm guessing she came in the front entrance. Still.

"Tommy," I whisper, "my clothes are out there."

He closes his eyes like he's trying to wish this fact away. He holds one finger up for me to wait, and he opens the door. He doesn't walk out though. He just stands there, totally relaxed, holding the door open, like it would be fine for her to come in. At least the door is between us, blocking her view of the room.

"Hey, I thought you were at your mom's tonight."

"I just came to see Stacey. Isn't she here yet?"

"Yeah, you know, Daniel had to bring her back this afternoon. She had a migraine. I think she's still sleeping."

"She okay?" She sounds worried.

"I don't know, hon. Hopefully it's just from traveling. I guess we'll find out in the morning. You staying the night?"

"Yeah, Mom's driver just dropped me off."

"You want some dinner? Want me to take you out?" I can't believe he says this. This would take them right past my discarded clothes, but he must know she'll turn him down.

"I ate already. I think I'll just go up to bed."

"Try to be quiet. I don't want you bothering Stacey."

"I'm not going to bother her, Dad, god."

"I'll see you in the morning, honey." Now he does duck behind the door to hug her.

When he closes the door, I sit up in bed and drop my head into my hands. Tommy throws himself onto the bed next to me.

"I feel like such an asshole," I whisper.

He pulls my hands away from my face. "We're not doing anything wrong." Then he sort of twists his mouth and says, "I mean, aside from the lying."

I smile, and he smiles, and we both start to laugh, and then we're laughing really hard, and he pulls me down against him and covers my mouth with his hand. "Jesus. Shut up. She's going to hear you."

I feel like an asshole again in the morning when Sadie comes down for breakfast all dressed and ready for school.

"Stacey," she says, and she throws her arms around me. "Dad said you had a migraine. Are you feeling okay?"

"You're sweet, honey. I'm fine." Having never experienced a migraine, I don't even know how to play this off, and over her shoulder, Daniel is scowling at me. Of course Tommy had to fill him in. How else could he cover for us? *Disgusting,* he mouths.

When she lets go of me, I say, "Daniel stocked us up on yogurt. You want some?"

"Like flavored?" she says, and by this I know she means *sugared,* because that's how I mean it too.

"Plain. It's Greek. Lots of protein. I'll get you some."

I start to stand up, but Daniel says, "No, let me. You should take it easy today."

"Yeah," Sadie says. "You don't need another migraine."

"Okay. Then can someone refill my coffee?"

"Oh, I don't know." Daniel turns back from the fridge with the tub of yogurt in his hand. He reaches into a cabinet for a bowl. "You should probably go light on the caffeine today." He makes a face.

I know the only way I'll get a headache is if I don't get enough caffeine. "Daniel," I say.

"Caffeine can be a trigger," he says. I don't even know if this is true, and I'm sure Sadie doesn't either.

"You know what? I'll just get myself a refill."

Sadie puts her hand on my arm and says, "Really, I don't think you should." She looks so sincere, so absolutely worried, I just say, "Okay, I'll skip it, but if I fall asleep at lunchtime, it's on you," and she smiles. She absolutely beams at me, and she eats her yogurt, almost half a cup, and I even talk her into adding a third of a banana.

"Go get your stuff together, sweetie. You don't want to be late," Daniel says as she finishes the last bite.

She leaves, and Daniel leans across the counter, sighs heavily.

"I know you don't want to hear this, but it's not fair for you to show up for a week and play house or whatever this thing is that you and Tommy do. I don't care how secretive you think you are, this affects more than just you."

"Daniel," I say quietly. "I think you're reading too much into things. I think . . ."

"Would you stop lying?" he says. "At least to me."

"That," I say to Tommy as we're getting into the car, "was the longest day."

He laughs. "It's barely after five. That's not even close to a long day."

"Yeah, but I'm a poet. I work like forty minutes a week. I have a very short attention span."

Tommy turns to look at me. He hasn't started the car yet. "You're writing again?" He sounds happy about it, so I feel like I'm letting him down.

"No," I say, "I'm not." I turn away from him, look out the window. "I guess I work zero minutes a week."

"Have you tried?"

"It doesn't work like that." I shake my head. "It's like a radio station, and I just . . . I can't tune it in. It's nothing but static."

"I knew you heard voices," he says, and I know he's just teasing me, but right now, I'm not in the mood. I haven't been in a good mood all day. I've been thinking too much.

"It's not funny," I say. I cross my arms in front of me.

"Stacey, come on, honey, don't be like this. It'll come."

He takes my hand and kisses it, which I know is supposed to be sweet, but we're sitting right here in the middle of the parking lot. I mean, anyone could see.

"Can we just go?" I say, pulling my hand away, and I can hear the tone in my voice. I don't mean it, really, but it is kind of sharp.

"Hey," he says. He grabs my hand again, but this time he's got me by the wrist. "I don't know what your problem is, but you have been acting like a fucking bitch all day."

"Tommy," I say, and I try to pull away, but he's not letting go.

"No," he says. "I have been nothing but good to you, Stacey. I don't need this shit."

He does let go now, starts the car, turns in his seat to look out the rearview window as he backs out. He pulls forward to the edge of the lot, and stops, waiting to pull out.

"You hungry?" he says. His voice is softer now, and he sets one hand on my thigh.

I still don't want to talk to him. I have nothing to say. But there's no point in fighting. There's no point starting an argument with him, so I say, "I don't know. Are you?"

I fix my hair, touch up my makeup in the room upstairs. Sarah's coming for drinks after dinner, and she's bringing her husband, who is apparently really powerful but all behind the scenes. I think he might be a studio exec or maybe he just finances shit. I don't know. I can't follow half of what Tommy tells me, but from what he says, they're loaded, crazy rich, and they live way out of town, in Colorado or something on some kind of ranch, and they don't have any kids.

I sit on the bed I don't sleep in and call the boys to say good night. Their bedtime is minutes away. I'd almost forgotten the time difference and missed them entirely.

"Thanks for being my kid," I say to Ben, and he says, "Yeah."

When I hang up, I catch up on a few other messages and e-mails and a voicemail that turns out to be from Phillip. He says, "I know you're in California, but I wanted to say I hope we have a chance to have coffee again soon. Or dinner. Maybe we could have dinner when you get back." I think, *Maybe.* I do like him, and the voicemail is sweet.

When I come down, they're already in the living room. I can hear Sarah laughing. She sounds like a bell. I walk in, and she throws her arms up, walks toward me. "Stacey!" she says, and she hugs me. "Come meet John."

John does not look the least bit imposing, and he's not exactly handsome, just regular, nice. He's sitting on the couch, and he doesn't stand up to greet me, he just lifts one hand in a sort of wave. It doesn't feel rude though. It feels better, normal, like none of us have to be on our best behavior.

Tommy's opening another bottle of wine, which is good because my glass is almost empty. All day, my nerves have felt like cut glass under my skin, but now everything is softening again.

"So we're on location, we're . . . was it in France?" Sarah looks at Tommy.

"Honey, I don't even know what story you're telling." He pulls the cork out and holds the bottle up to me, raising his eyebrows. I nod.

"Anyway, we're on location, and we're staying in this little local inn," she starts again.

Tommy groans. "Sarah, come on, not this one." He covers his face with his hand, shakes his head.

She waves him off and leans toward me like I should be on the edge of my seat. "And we get back from dinner one night, and the crew is all packing up, but it's like, we're not done, we have a week left of shooting, and we're all like, 'What the hell is going on here?'"

"Sarah, Jesus, can we not?" Tommy says as he fills her glass. He glances up at me with this look that says, *Sorry*.

"And the owner comes out, and he's screaming at us in French, which I of course don't speak, so I'm still totally confused, but I think, like, someone hasn't paid him or we've broken some family heirloom." She pauses, she purses her lips for effect. They form a little pink bow. "But it turns out, our friend Tommy here has been fucking his little girl."

"Okay." Tommy holds his hand up. "You say 'little girl,' but clearly she was an adult. I think she was actually older than me." He looks at me and sort of smiles apologetically. "And this was, what, twenty years ago?"

Sarah makes this face like, *Don't look at me*. She says, "I'm just filling in your backstory. I'm revealing your motivations."

"Motivations," he scoffs. "We were in the middle of nowhere. I was just looking for a way to pass the time."

"Tommy"—John cuts in, and we all look at him because he hasn't said much all night—"is probably the loneliest man I know." He gives Tommy this knowing nod. "But he gets laid an awful lot, so that's something."

Tommy laughs this short, single-noted laugh. "You guys are killing me." He holds the bottle up, refills John's glass. "I think we need a statute of limitations on Sarah's mouth."

John kisses me on the cheek, his hand on my elbow. "It was nice meeting you, Stacey."

Over his shoulder, I can see Tommy and Sarah making their goodbyes, which seem ridiculously overdrawn for people who are going to see each other tomorrow. Sarah's clearly drunk. She has Tommy's face in her hands, and they're talking very close.

"Those two," John says, turning to stand next to me so we're facing the same way, "they've known each other since they were basically kids. It used to make me crazy, but they're like brother and sister."

"Hmm," I say, smiling at him with my best *Why are you telling me this?* face. I cross my arms in front of me, look at the floor.

Tommy glances up then and sees John waiting. He takes Sarah by the shoulder, starts moving her toward us, and when she's close enough, John takes her arm and Tommy lets go. She's like a baton in a relay, and once John has her, he keeps her moving. Tommy closes the door behind them and when he turns around, he throws his hands up like, *Fuck, whatever.*

"Wow," I say. "That was very entertaining."

"Not my fault," he says. "You know you wouldn't have to listen to all that shit if you weren't so secretive. If she had any clue there was anything going on between us, she'd have the decency not to tell those stories."

"If she had any clue, I'd be one of those stories, Tommy."

"No, you wouldn't." He laughs. "Sarah likes you. I mean, she'd tell people, yeah, but I'd be one of the stories she tells about you. That's very different."

"Yeah, that's a lot better," I say. "Besides, you know I don't care." I uncross my arms, dig my thumbs into my pockets.

"Really?" He crosses the foyer, reaches through my arms to grab me by the ass and pull me against him.

"It's not like I'm learning anything new. You are a dirty, filthy whore, but whatever, I'm used to it. I don't give a fuck what you do."

Maybe I've had too much wine though. Maybe I don't quite pull it off because Tommy just sort of looks at me for a minute, and so I smile, and I shrug, and I say, "What?"

I sit down at the edge of the bed, finger through the screens on my phone to set the alarm for six. Sadie has school in the morning. If I'd taken five minutes longer this morning, she would have caught me coming out of Tommy's room. I don't want to cut it that close again.

"Isn't it a little late to be calling the boys?" He crawls into the bed behind me, wraps one arm around my waist.

"I'm setting an alarm for the morning."

"You are not." He laughs. "I can't believe it."

I set the phone down on the bedside table. "I have to be up before Sadie." I know the point he's trying to make, but I'm pretending I don't.

He pulls me back onto the bed and crawls over me, pins my wrists with his forearms, wraps his hands around my throat, and he pushes my chin upward with his thumbs. He kisses my neck. "I'm so good for you," he says. "I'm like anxiety medication. You need me like a fucking drug."

"Jesus, Tommy, you're ridiculous." But I don't bother trying to push him off. I couldn't if I wanted to, and I don't actually want to anyway.

"How are you gonna go back to Omaha? How are you ever gonna sleep?"

"I'll find someone else," I say, and Tommy laughs. He says, "No, you won't. Not like me."

Tommy has a call after dinner, and Sadie and I crash out in the living room reading. Well, I'm reading. She's perched in her chair with her phone and a book that she's barely looking at. I sit sideways, look over the back of the couch at her. "What are you reading?" I say.

"*Ariel*," she says, and I think, *Shit, Plath?* but of course. It makes sense.

I raise an eyebrow. "Right. 'The boot in the face,'" but she doesn't seem to get the reference, and I think, *Really, with all your issues, you're sitting there with a poem in your lap called "Daddy," and that's not the one you're reading?*

"I like 'Morning Song,'" she says.

"About the baby? That's a beautiful poem."

"Yeah," she says in this kind of sigh, and something about it makes my stomach clench, and I just think, *No. Oh god. No.*

"I was so crazy when the boys were babies." I really emphasize *so*, and I shake my head. "All those hormones, they really mess with your head. They make you do stupid things." I try to make my voice really soft, really safe. Then she starts to cry, and she's telling me everything, and by then I'm sitting on the floor in front of her, holding her hands, and she says, "Please don't tell my dad," but of course both of us know I don't have a choice.

I stash Sadie in her room, literally tuck her into bed, and I have her put a movie on her laptop and put her earbuds in. I'm not exactly sure how Tommy's going to take this, but I know there will be yelling. Before I leave, I push her hair back from her face and kiss her forehead. "You're gonna be fine, honey," I say, and she smiles, but it's a sad, weepy smile. I might be lying.

When I walk downstairs, Tommy is in the living room on the couch, reading. He has a glass of bourbon in front of him on the table. I can't decide if I should wait for him to finish it, or if that would be worse. I sit down on the couch, facing him, crossing my feet up into my lap, and I hold my ankles with my hands.

"Tommy," I say, "we need to talk."

"Jesus, you look serious. Should I get the scotch?" He tries to laugh, but I put my hand on his arm and say, "Stop."

"Goddamn it, Stacey." He sighs, looks at the ceiling, rubs one hand across his jaw. When he turns to look at me he looks disappointed, almost angry. He looks exactly how I'd expect him to look if I were to sit him down and say, *This is what I want, Tommy. This is what I need from you.*

"We need to talk about Sadie," I say, my tone a little colder than it should be.

"What?" he says.

"It's about Sadie," I say, a little softer because it is about Sadie and it's going to get bad.

His jaw tightens, and he sits up straighter. "She's not cutting again?"

When he says this, he reaches across to grab my arm, and I shake my head. I look down at my hands and try to catch my breath.

"Jesus Christ, Stacey. Just tell me."

I look up, and I give him this look like, *God, I'm so sorry.*

He closes his eyes. "Is she pregnant?"

"She was," I say, and I look down again. Right now, I would rather be literally anywhere else. "I don't think she's doing okay."

"A fucking abortion?" It comes out in a whisper. I nod, or at least I think I do. My neck feels stiff. Tommy just stares at me. "Are you telling me my daughter had an abortion?"

He drops his head in his hands. He's sort of rocking forward and back. I set one hand on his shoulder, and he leans toward me like he's going to lay his head in my lap, but then he doesn't. He sits straight up.

"She's fifteen, Stacey!" he yells, like this will change anything. "She's fucking fifteen!" He braces his foot on the edge of the coffee table and kicks it over. His glass hits the floor and shatters. There are shards of it everywhere. I don't have any shoes on. It's going to be hard to get out. Tommy stands up, kicking the table again.

I try to fold myself smaller. I try to tuck myself away.

"Fuck!" He holds his head in his hands, stalks back and forth across the room. "Fuck, fuck, fuck." On the last *fuck* he throws his fist into the wall, and I'm pretty sure it comes out bleeding.

I sit on the couch, my arms wrapped tightly around my chest, and listen to him leave. I don't know how long I wait. A long time. I hope I wait long enough. The floor behind the couch looks safer. I swing my leg over the back of it, walk in a wide circle, and manage to avoid all the glass. I walk to the bar and pull the vodka from the small freezer beside the wine fridge, and I pour myself a lot of it. I swallow it fast. I'm afraid of stalling, of losing my nerve. I set the empty glass on the bar and walk out through the kitchen to the glass door at the back of the house. I'd heard it open and close when Tommy walked out. The stone tiles are cold against my feet, but I walk out anyway. Tommy's sitting at the edge of the pool, his head in his hands, and I sit down next to him.

It takes a minute to get my voice to work. "I got pregnant," I say, "the night I met Michael."

"Ben," he says like it's not a question, and I say, "No." I turn my head to look at the water. "Not Ben."

"I didn't even know him," I say finally. "And then I was pregnant. I had this whole plan for my life." I take a deep breath. "It's funny because Michael was such a problem solver. Whatever went wrong, ever, he was just like, 'This is how we'll fix it.' And then I had this huge fucking problem before he was around to help me deal with it." I look over at Tommy, and I see that he's looking at me, and I try to smile. I pull my knees up, rest my head on them. "It's just not easy, you know. Right decision or wrong, it's not fucking easy. And she's just a baby, Tommy. She's just a little kid."

He rubs his face with his hands. The knuckles of his right hand are ripped open, bleeding.

"Let me get something for your hand." I stand up and walk into the kitchen and grab a towel from beside the sink, and I bring it back out. When I sit down, I take Tommy's hand in my lap. His skin is ragged, painful. "She thinks she's in love."

He pulls his hand away, digs his fingers into his hair. "I'll kill that piece of shit."

"Tommy, they're just kids. They're just stupid, stupid kids. You've gotta cut them some slack."

He just sits there for a long time. I wrap my arms around my knees and wait.

"What did he say when you told him?"

"What do you mean?" I'm not stupid. I know what he means.

"Michael. What did he say when he found out?"

I press my teeth together hard, wrap my fingers around and under my feet. "I never told him." I don't actually know if Tommy can hear me, but he must, because he says, "You never told him?" He turns to look at me, and he sounds almost angry. He makes this derisive sound. "You are a fucking piece of work."

"When was I going to tell him? When we were dating? When he proposed? When we brought Ben home from the hospital, or Stevie? 'Hey, I know this'll be really hard for you, and you'll never really look at me the same, but I just thought you should know . . .'" I turn my head, look out toward the water. I pay attention to how it seems to swallow the lights from the house, how it holds them under. "It wouldn't have been okay, Tommy. It just . . . it wouldn't have been." I pull my legs in tighter, rest my head on my knees.

I love you, Michael would say sometimes, and I'd think, *Maybe, but how could we know?*

"I'm gonna have to call her mother," Tommy says finally.

"She already knows." I suck my lips in, hold them with my teeth.

He turns his face up toward the sky and every muscle along his jaw and down his neck is tight. I count the seconds in each of his breaths. I say, "She did the right thing. She had to take her."

"She should have told me." His fists are still clenched. "You can't keep a secret like this."

I say, "I know," but I don't really mean it.

Neither of us talks for a while. It's cold, but it's still a beautiful night, and in the quiet, I can hear the water slowly lapping at the walls of the pool. I put my hand on his arm finally. "I'm tired," I say. "I'll sleep upstairs, give you some space."

He doesn't look at me, but he says, "No," and shakes his head. "I'll be in in a minute."

Tommy wakes me up crawling in beside me, and I roll toward him and then his hands are on my face, and he presses his mouth into me, hard, all lips and tongue and teeth. He pushes me onto my back and lifts himself over me. And he leans past me, to the nightstand for a condom, and tears it open. I reach down to pull off his jeans, but he wrenches my hand out of the way, pins it to the bed. He pushes himself inside me, his mouth by my ear, the button of his jeans pressing hard into my thigh. I say, "Tommy, wait," but he puts his hand over my mouth and turns my head to the side, leaning his arm hard against my neck.

After, Tommy spoons himself against me, presses his lips over and over into my hair, and I let him.

Next week is my anniversary. The second since the last. Michael had taken me to dinner. The usual place. I'd had three glasses of wine and when I'd ordered the third, he'd raised his eyebrow, said, "Really?" but that was it. Back home, as I was getting undressed, he'd come up behind me, wrapped his arms around my waist, brushed his lips across my shoulders.

"Sometimes," he'd whispered, "I think you don't really love me. I think you just love how much I love you."

And I said, "Of course I love you."

———

Sadie comes down as usual in the morning, but her eyes are red and swollen. Tommy's already been up talking to her. He went up the stairs at six o'clock, almost the minute that my alarm went off. I don't know if he woke her or just sat by her bed waiting. He'd looked pretty wrecked when he came back down, but he just poured himself some coffee, sat down at the counter with his paper. I felt like it was best to stay out of his way, but Sadie is different. She's just a little girl.

"Oh, honey," I say, wrapping my arms around her. "You know what? I don't think you should go to school today."

"What?" Tommy says behind me. I hear him set down his paper.

"Look at her. Her eyes are practically swollen shut. What are people going to say?" I turn around to face him, but I keep one arm around Sadie.

"You worry too much about what people say." He turns back to his paper.

"Maybe you don't worry enough."

"She's not your kid, and she's not missing school."

He says this so cold and low it makes my breath catch in my throat. I think about backing down, but then I feel Sadie's shoulders spasm inside my arm as she starts to cry.

"She can," I say. "She can miss one day. She can lie on the couch with a mask on her eyes for one day."

He looks up at me, his eyes narrow, and I think, *You owe me, you owe me, you fucking owe me,* and I let it show in my face.

It takes longer than I expected.

"Fine," he says. He stands up and walks to her, pulls her out of my arm and into his, and he rests his chin on her head. "Your mom home today?" he asks, and she nods. "I'm sending you back there. I don't want you staying here alone all day."

"I don't appreciate the interference," he says after about five minutes of brutally cold silence punctuated only by aggressive shifting. He's going to break something the way he keeps slamming the car into gear.

"Sorry," I say. I'm not though, I'm not sorry at all, and I think it's ridiculous that I'm the one apologizing.

"That's it?" he says. "That's all you've got to say?"

"What do you want me to say? She's having a hard time. I think you need to be a little gentler with her."

He grunts. "Well, I guess you're the expert on abortion, aren't you?"

I don't even answer him. I just lean my head against the window. I should have expected this. I should never have told him.

"I guess I should ask, have you had an abortion lately?"

I turn to look at him, and then I just turn back, study the houses we're driving past. He slows down and pulls the car over to the side of the road.

"Would you?" he says. "Would you just take care of it and not even tell me?"

"Probably," I say.

He grabs my arm and jerks me away from the door. "Are you fucking serious?"

"Fuck, I don't know!" I pull away from him and rub my arm, though it doesn't hurt as much as I'm letting on. "You know this isn't fucking about me, Tommy."

He takes my face in both hands and pulls me toward him. He

doesn't kiss me. He just leans his head against mine. "I think I'm losing my shit," he says, and I say, "I know."

I spend as much of the day as I can reading on the couch in Sarah's trailer because Tommy's realization that he's falling apart has done nothing to soften his mood. Even Jason seems a little afraid of him.

"Jesus, what is Tommy's problem?" Sarah says as she comes in between takes.

I know enough about Sarah not to tell her, so I just make my eyes really big and say, "I know, right? Fucking temper."

"Is something up with the movie?"

"I don't know. I don't think he had any calls this morning, but I wasn't really paying attention." I shrug and look back at my book.

"You're not much of a spy, are you?" Sarah says. "Jesus, it's so damn hot in here." She fans herself.

It is hot, but I have this thin sweater on, and I can't take it off because, thanks to Tommy, I woke up with this purple bruise on the inside of my arm. It doesn't matter. I bruise pretty easily, but it is hot. "I don't know," I say. "I'm kind of cold. Maybe it's just you."

Tommy comes in around two, and when he walks in he says, "Hey."

I'm lying on the couch with my knees up, the book propped against them. "Hi," I say, and I close the book but hold my place with my thumb.

"Sarah?" he says.

"Not here. You looking for her?"

"No," he says. "I'm looking for you." He sits down on the couch next to me, wraps one arm around my legs and rests his chin on my knee. "Stace," he says.

I reach up, touch my fingers to his arm. "It's fine," I say, and I smile. "I'm used to you being an asshole." Of course this is different, but it's so much easier to pretend that it's not.

"Let me take you to dinner tonight." He takes my hand, rubs his thumb across my palm. This is in no way the sort of apology that I'm interested in, and my reluctance must show on my face because he says, "Come on, I'll buy you the most expensive fucking wine." He starts to hold my hand up to his lips, but then we hear feet on the steps of the trailer, and he lets go and stands up, moves the two steps across the room.

The door opens, and Sarah walks in. "Ugh," she says, "so many takes," and then she sees Tommy and says, "Oh, it's you." She crosses her arms across her chest. "You come here to yell at people? Because you can get the fuck out."

"I'm begging forgiveness," he says, and he holds his arms out to her.

Sarah is easy because her posture softens immediately, and she steps right into him. "What's the matter, honey?" she says. "Is it the budget again? If you need more money, I'll call John."

"No, no," he says, and he kisses her on the forehead. "It's home. Sadie. Custody shit." Which is brilliant really. Close enough to the truth that she won't ask for more.

"Poor baby," she says, and she pats him on the arm as she pulls away.

Tommy manages to drag me out of the trailer for the next hour, but then he gets a call, and I duck away. It's tedious really. I mean, the first take is cool, but then it's over, and over, and over, and Jason's giving people notes, and then let's do it again. It's just like this year's music program at school. Stevie's and Ben's grades were back-to-back, and it was the same damn songs, the same stupid routines. But those were only half an hour, so this is so much worse.

I'm afraid it's Tommy when the door opens, but it's not, it's Sarah. I think, *Good, I get to stay here,* but she says, "Jason's looking for you," and I groan.

"Kinda handsy?" she says, and she wrinkles her nose. "I think he's got a thing for you."

I laugh. "No. Jason's fine. He's a sweetheart. He's married anyway."

"In this town, that almost never matters."

"I just don't feel like going out there." I shrug. "But I guess I will."

When I turn the corner, there's Tommy. He's got his back to me, leaning against the wall, talking very close with some young girl. Not an actress though. She's got a headset hanging around her neck, so she must be on the crew. As she's talking, very excitedly of course, this strand of hair falls over her eye, and Tommy reaches his hand up, tucks it behind her ear, and his fingers kind of linger against her cheek, and I just think, *Jesus fucking Christ.* I should have known. Things have been too intense, so it shouldn't be a surprise that he'd handle it like this. I almost turn around. I'm about to leave, but then there's Jason from the opposite direction, yelling, "Stacey, I've been looking everywhere," and I have to start walking toward him. Tommy doesn't move away from the girl. He's not one to overreact, but he does turn his head toward me, and he looks, I don't know, *caught.* I'm not sure how to act natural.

It seems stupid to smile, so as I pass him, I hold my arm up, point to my wrist like I'm wearing a watch, and I just say, "What time are we planning on leaving today?" It takes him a second, but he says, "Up to you." He's quiet though. I almost don't hear him.

At least the place Tommy takes me for dinner is so expensive that everyone here is rich enough to not be easily blown away. He's not even the only celebrity here, but he is Tommy, so he's obviously at the top of the list. The downside is that there are photographers absolutely parked out front, which is obnoxious, and super disturbing, but once we're inside, it's fine. The wine he orders is insane. It's very close to the number they quoted us when Michael wanted to send Ben to private school. Clearly, this is an apology wine.

"Shoot is going well," he says. "I know you think it's tedious, but everything's on schedule." He runs his thumb along the rim of his glass. "Jason's a perfectionist, you know, so we've got extra time built in. I was talking with Amanda about it." And he raises his eyes to mine to say that I know exactly who he's talking about. "She works with the script supervisor, you know."

"Mmm," I say. "She's adorable."

"Isn't she though?" And he smiles. "Very sweet too. Friendly." He says *friendly* with a lot of emphasis, and I'm thinking, *You fucking dick,* but I say, "Yeah? Just what you like."

"I do like friendly," he says, and he takes a drink of his wine. "That doesn't bother you, does it?"

I laugh, and it's the kind of laugh I make when I actually want to stand up and leave.

"Because you know, Stace, if it bothered you . . ."

He reaches across the table and trails his fingers around my wrist. I feel my shoulders tense, and I pull my arm away. I think, *Don't you dare. Not today. Not like this.* Because he doesn't mean it. I know he doesn't mean it. It's just more apology, more smoothing things over, more *Sorry I've been such a dick.*

"You know, Tommy, the last thing I want to be right now is the subject of a 'Tommy DeMarco seen with unknown woman' story."

It looked very intimate, an eyewitness will say. The last thing I want to be right now is one more in a string of those stories.

He frowns. "Stace, look. I know you're mad . . ." He stretches his arm farther, and I put my hands in my lap.

"Why would I be?" I smile as nicely as I can. "I'm leaving tomorrow, so I get that you have to start making plans for next week."

"Look at you, honey," he says, sitting up straight and reaching for his glass. "You're so understanding."

FEBRUARY

ALMOST THE MINUTE I got home, I was packing the boys up to spend Christmas at my parents'. It was already hard enough driving home at night to the only house on the block with no lights up. And then it was January, the longest, coldest month of the year, and Phillip called me a couple of times, and we went for coffee twice, and lunch, but it's all the way into February before we can find a date that works for dinner. Maybe I was stalling.

I drop the boys at my sister's for the night and head back home to get ready, try on everything in my closet, and finally settle on black jeans, a silk turquoise tank, and a fitted jacket. I have a pair of black stilettos in the back of my closet that I haven't worn in years, but I'm worried they're too much for a guy like Phillip. I can't remember how tall he is. I mean, I remember him as tall, but I also remember him as standing beside Craig, so I can't be sure. Lately, I don't feel sure of anything. The phone rings while I'm doing my eyes. No photo, just the little green robot and the number buzzing in. Tommy. We still talk all the time. I thumb it to answer and hit the speaker key.

"Sadie wants me to meet this kid," he says.

I'm pulling my eyelid, trying to make a straight line. "No way. Bad idea."

"Yeah, well, she's bringing him over. She's on her way."

"Tommy, you can't."

"What do you want me to do, call her? Tell her not to come?"

I look at the clock. Phillip will be here any minute. I don't have time for this shit.

"I don't know, Tommy. I think you're screwed." I've moved on to lipstick, but I think it's too red. I don't know. I don't know how to do any of this. "She won't believe you if you act like you like him, but you can't act like a dick either." I hear him grunt, and I say, "I'm serious, if you come down on this kid, Sadie's going to want him even more. She'll be like, 'My dad's such an asshole. He doesn't know what love is. Blah, blah, blah.' You're gonna have to play this really cool, really straight."

"Yeah, that'll be easy."

"You're the actor. She wants to see what'll happen when she puts you two together, and you've got to give her nothing. You've got to be dull as shit."

He laughs. "I don't really do dull."

"Yeah well, tonight you do." I slip the shoes back on and look in the mirror. My hair is too big, and I think I have too much eye shadow on, and I just feel too old for this. "Look, I've got to go," I say. "I have a date."

"A what?"

"A date."

"Like a date date?" He sounds incredulous. Like he's made any effort to see me in the past eight weeks. I wonder how long he expected me to wait.

"Jesus. Yes. A date."

He's quiet for a second. "I don't know how I feel about that."

Exactly, I think. *That's the whole fucking problem, isn't it?* Though I obviously can't say that.

"You don't get to feel anything about it, Tommy. It has nothing to do with you."

Then the doorbell rings, and the dog is barking, and my hair really is too big, and I say, "I've got to go." I hit *end call,* and I rush down the stairs to the front door and shove Bear out of the way with my knee. When I open the door, there's Phillip, and he has a bottle of wine from the auction, and when he steps in the house, he is tall enough and he looks totally, totally sweet.

He takes me for sushi, which is perfect. I have a seaweed salad, this vegetarian roll with sweet potato and olive oil, not exactly authentic, but whatever, and besides I think the whole chopsticks thing is sexy. And there's sake, lots of it, and it's totally warming me up. Halfway through, I slip the jacket off and swing it over the back of my chair, and when I turn back around, Phillip's eyes are all over me, and I think, *Oh, I've got this,* and from then on I feel absolutely fine.

I wait until dinner's over to check my phone. I've been really good, completely attentive, totally there, but the text from Tommy just reads, *Fucking nightmare,* and I feel like I want to call him right away.

"We could walk up the street, grab another drink?" Phillip suggests as we stand up. He holds my jacket and slips it up over my arms.

"Yeah, yes, I would love to," I say, but I hold my phone up apologetically. "I just have to make a quick call about this. Kids." I didn't technically say my kids, so I feel good about not lying.

"Sure. Of course. I'll just wait." He indicates the doorway like he's going to stand out in the entryway, and I say, "Great, I'll just be a minute," and walk back to the hallway by the bathrooms.

"What happened?" I say when Tommy picks up. He sounds a little drunk.

"This kid is an asshole, a total piece of shit."

"Tommy, what did you do? Jesus, you didn't hit him?"

"I didn't hit him." He sighs. "I threw him out of the house."

"Goddamn it." I lean against the wall, push the toe of my shoe against the baseboard, try to focus on that and not the sound of Tommy's voice.

"He's eighteen, Stacey. He's way older than she is. I mean, this is statutory rape, isn't it? I should press charges."

"Tommy, come on, you can't press charges. This is her boyfriend. She'll hate you."

"She hates me already to do this shit to me." He pauses. I can hear him drinking. Even over the phone he sounds sloppy. "Fucking punk-ass piece of shit. You should have seen it. He's got his hands on her the whole time, and not like he's being sweet with her. It's like he owns her. In my goddamn house." He's starting to yell, and I have to hold the phone away from my ear. "This little piece of shit comes in my house and puts his fucking hands on my daughter."

I let the side of my head rest for a second against the wall, but then I remember where I am, and it just seems kind of disgusting.

"So I told him to get out."

"What did Sadie do?"

"She was crying, and he said, 'Sadie, we're going,' and I said, 'Fuck you, she's not going anywhere, and if you talk to my daughter that way again, if you come in my house and talk to her like that, if you fucking touch her, I'll cut off your dick.'"

"Jesus, Tommy."

"And then I threw him out."

And here I am standing in a restroom hallway with the light above me flickering, and my feet hurt, and Phillip is out front waiting for me, and I don't know how to end the call. I don't know how to let go, so I just say, "God, Tommy, I don't know what to say, but I know it's not good."

"Everything okay?" Phillip asks as we walk out to the sidewalk.

"Yeah, just, you know." I shrug.

He smiles. "Well, should we go?" He nods in the direction of the bar up the street. He doesn't take my arm, but he walks next to me, and with the heels we're almost shoulder to shoulder. With the heels, I wish he would offer his arm like Michael used to. Michael always paid attention to my shoes.

When Phillip drops me home, I ask him in for a drink. He says, "I've probably had too much already." I think, *Jesus, are you that out of practice?* but I just say, "Coffee, then?" And he says, "Yeah, coffee would be great."

I start the pot and then turn around to face him, lean my hands back against the counter. The granite feels cold beneath my palms.

He smiles. He says, "You look really beautiful."

I think, *Finally,* and I say "Yeah?" I raise my chin a little. I kind of chew on my bottom lip, but he just stands there, all the way across the room, waiting. I hold his eyes for a long time and still nothing. I mean, there's only so much I'm going to do. The coffeemaker beeps, and I pour him a cup. "Cream? Sugar?" I say.

"Both."

And then he stands there and drinks the fucking coffee, like just drinks it, and I think if I had known that was what he wanted, I would not have invited him in.

When I walk him to the door, he hugs me, wrapping his arms around me in this awkward, safe mid-arm range. We're elbow to elbow. And then he kisses me good night in this really chaste, dry-lipped way, and he says, "I don't want to go too fast for you."

I'm thinking, *Really? This is fast?* so I lean my weight into him, pushing him back against the door, and I pull his lips open with mine. I flick his tongue with my tongue.

I lean back onto my heels and wipe my lipstick off his lips, and I say, "I think I'm fine. Really. I think I'm pretty good."

The boys are watching cartoons when I show up to get them in the morning. Stevie's lying on his stomach, propped up on his elbows. "Hi, Mom," he calls. He always notices when I come in.

"Morning, babies," I say. I squat down and they give me distracted hugs. They're both looking over my shoulder at the TV.

I walk into the kitchen, and Jenny pours me a cup of coffee. "I'm making pancakes," she says. "With chocolate chips. You want one?"

"I've already eaten." I lean against the counter to watch her.

"Bullshit."

"No, I have. I ate a cup of yogurt." Or half a cup. Whatever, it's not like I measured.

She turns around and ladles scoops of batter onto her griddle.

It's blackened, well-seasoned. She uses it a lot. "How was your date?" she asks.

I shrug. "Eh. He's a little slow."

She turns to look at me. "Like in the head?"

"Jenny, he's a doctor. He's not slow in the head. He's just a little, you know, not aggressive."

"Oh," she says, drawing it out like she's made a discovery, "like slow in bed?"

"Who knows? Maybe he's really quick in bed." I take a sip of the coffee. "But definitely slow to get there."

"Ugh." She makes a face. "I hate that." She turns back to flip the pancakes. They are perfect, golden, except where the chocolate's melted out. They smell like burnt cocoa.

"Anyway, he's nice," I say.

She waves me off. "Who cares about nice? Nice is overrated."

"No, nice is underrated. Hence Tommy, international sex god."

"Tommy?" she says. She sounds surprised. "You're not thinking about sleeping with him?"

"No! It's just, you know, the whole sexiest-man-alive thing. People seem to like that type."

"I always assume that type doesn't try very hard. Like you should just be so grateful . . ."

I laugh into my coffee. "Oh my god, Jenny, can we not? I mean, gross."

"Gross?" She leans back against the counter, folds her arms, the spatula still in one hand. "You brought it up. And I've seen you flirting and texting, so don't try to feed me this 'gross' line. It would be a stupid thing to follow through on, but you don't think he's gross."

"No, I mean, yeah, he's not . . ." I shake my head. "I meant 'Gross, we're friends.' Jesus, Jenny." I set my mug down. "And anyway, I thought we were going to talk about my date."

"You said you didn't like him. Too slow."

"I like him very much. That's why I was disappointed by the slowness."

She points behind me. "Hand me those plates."

She has a stack of little colored plates, so they know whose is whose by favorite color. She knows my kids' favorite everything. She's like Mary Poppins.

"Did he kiss you good night?"

"Yeah." I shrug. "I mean, it took a while, but he finally did."

"Was it weird?" she says.

And I realize that if we don't count Tommy, and of course we aren't, Michael was the last person I kissed.

"Yes," I say. "It was weird."

I get a text from Sadie in the afternoon. It says, *My dad is an asshole. I don't know what to do.* I think about calling her, but I'm in the middle of filling out papers for the boys' school. We've switched doctors and now no one can find their vaccination schedule. I've been getting calls from the school nurse.

I text back, *I agree. He is an asshole, but he really loves you. Cut him some slack.*

I think she must be waiting by the phone because she replies immediately. I imagine her sitting in her reading chair, twisting the loose threads in her fingers, hiding her eyes with her hair. *He says I'm grounded, and my mom's in Europe and I have to live with him for the whole month and if he won't let me see Matt I'm going to scream. I'm going to kill myself.* I don't take this threat seriously. She's not the type to do anything quick. She'll sit and starve herself, but she's not going to pull a razor across her wrists. Well maybe, but not deep enough to matter.

Still, I reply, *Don't say that. Why doesn't he like Matt?* and then I text Tommy, *Sadie is freaking out. Why is she grounded?*

The replies come in so quickly it takes me a minute to tell what's from whom. Tommy says, *Because she thinks she's in love with this piece of shit,* and Sadie says, *Because he's an asshole (Dad, not Matt) and I hate him.*

I call Tommy. "You've got to let the piece of shit see her," I say when he answers.

"No way." I can almost see him shaking his head.

"I'm serious. As long as you're the dragon at the door, she's in a fairy tale, and Matt's her goddamn prince." I shuffle my papers around, try to copy the primary-care number from my insurance card. "You have to change the narrative. You have to make it boring."

"Right." Tommy laughs, but it's not a happy sound. "How am I supposed to do that?"

"You know, give them a bunch of rules. He can come over, but only when you're home, and they have to stay in the living room."

"No," he says. "I don't want this kid in my house."

"And then sit there and talk to him. Ask him where he's going to college, what he likes to do, just whatever. He will get tired of her if it means sitting in a room with you. You know he will."

"How is this your business anyway? Don't you have a date or something to get ready for?"

I hate his tone, but it's easier to deal with over the phone. "I don't know, Tommy. It seems like you want to talk to me about everything right up to the minute I disagree with you. You want to break them up? You want to keep her safe? Act like a father and not some possessive piece of shit. Jesus, Tommy, it's not about you. This kid didn't happen to you. He happened to her, so stop being such a narcissist. It's not your pride on the line. It's her fucking life."

I hang up and press my hand over my mouth, pinching my nose closed with my fingers. It's like I can feel him yelling even with the phone sitting off on the table in front of me. After a minute, I text Sadie, *Your dad is an asshole.* But then I add, *I'll do what I can,* which is nothing, frankly, but at least Sadie doesn't know that.

Mornings are so loud, and then the boys are off to school and it's quiet again. Then much too quiet. I used to write in these quiet stretches. Now I have nothing to do. I sort of stand in the living room with my coffee, and then I think about dusting. I'm studying a shelf when the phone rings.

"Sarah," I say. I haven't talked to her in probably two weeks.

"Jason made us come in at three this morning." She yawns audibly. "I'm so exhausted. And now he doesn't need me for the next hour."

"Take a nap."

"I've had too much coffee," she says. "I'm like bone tired, but when I tried to lie down, I felt like my heart was going to beat right out of my chest."

"So you're calling me 'cause you're bored?" I laugh.

"And my heart might explode," she says. "How's Nebraska? Distract me from my impending death."

"Nebraska's amazing. It's like forty degrees outside, and later I might go to the store."

"Frigid," she says, and I say, "No, forty is warm."

She laughs. "Oh, hang on. It's Tommy." Her voice gets quieter like she's moved the phone from her mouth. "I'm talking to Stacey, love. You want to say hello?"

And in the background, I hear him say, "No."

Phillip asks me out the following Thursday. It's a doctors' thing, some dinner, and he needs a date. "Absolutely," I say when he calls. "I'd love to."

He picks me up around five. I've toned the hair down. I've got less shadow on my eyes. I'm wearing a sleeveless sheath that it's still way too cold for, but my arms look really good, and my legs are already bare, so what the hell. I've got a warm coat.

"You look beautiful," he says as I slide into the car.

I smile, and he backs out of the driveway. It's a nice car, very doctorly, very sturdy. Four doors, leather interior, heated seats. I sit on my left hip so my knees are pointing toward him, close enough to touch, but it's not a stick shift, and he keeps his hands on the wheel.

"So where are we headed?" I ask, and of course it's a steakhouse, but it doesn't really matter as long as they're serving wine.

We walk in, and to start there's a mixer, and I'm there with all these midwestern doctors' wives and I think, *Not a fit, this is not a fucking fit.* But whatever, I've lived here a long time. I know how to blend in. Phillip orders a scotch and soda, and I say, "I'll have a vodka on ice," and I feel like, once I drink it, things will be better.

Phillip has a little stubble coming in, a little five-o'clock shadow, and I like the way it looks on him. I decide I like the way he looks in general. I shift my body so our arms are just barely touching.

He says, "I should introduce you to a few people." This time he does rest his hand on the small of my back as he leads me through the room. He's getting better.

I can't keep all their names straight, but Janet is the one with the beige Coach purse, and she's married to the guy with the red tie. Alex is an internist, and his wife is pregnant and therefore not drinking. I feel sorry for her. Then there's the couple who are both doctors, and I didn't catch either of their names, but she's an OB, and he's an infectious-disease guy. Cara is a cardiologist, and her husband is named Mark. I don't know what he does, but he is also not a doctor, and he seems a little embarrassed about it.

"And what do you do, Stacey?" asks Alex's pregnant wife.

"I'm a poet," I say, draining the last of my vodka. I jiggle the glass like the ice might be hiding more.

"You don't say?" says red-tie guy. And then he laughs and says, "You must get good alimony then."

I think about saying, *Actually, I don't get any alimony because my husband fucking died,* just to be an asshole, but Phillip says, "She does a little screenwriting too. She has a movie coming out. When is it, Stacey?" and I just sort of shrug.

"They're still filming," I say, and I jiggle my glass again and wonder if he's going to notice.

"Yeah, she was just in L.A. a few weeks ago on set," and he says *on set* like he's making air quotes, but he doesn't actually. He keeps his hands down, and his left hand is still on my back, which right now is the only thing that's going right.

"Really," says Cara. "That sounds exciting," but she says it like it absolutely does not.

Phillip notices my glass and says, "Can I get you another?" and I flash him my very best smile. I say, "Please."

"So what's the movie called?" Mark asks.

"I don't know," I say. "There's been some argument about the title"—there's been some *Joe is a pain in my ass* about the title—"but the book was called *Monsters in the Afterlife.*"

Suddenly Janet is interested. She says, "Hey, I think I've heard of that! With Tommy DeMarco?"

"And Sarah Nixon," I say.

"Holy crap, that's a big deal," she says.

I just shake my head. "You know, they had to pay me, so that part of it was pretty nice."

Phillip returns with my drink and presses it into my hands. He rests his own hand back on the small of my back, and I think, *Good boy,* and I turn and smile at him.

"Thank you," I say, and I take a sip of my drink. I lean toward his ear. "I was really glad when you called."

But then Janet asks, "So have you met Tommy DeMarco?"

"We've been in some meetings," I say. I don't add how he doesn't appear to be speaking to me since I called him a narcissist. I know he's taken my advice though, because I've heard from Sadie, and Matt's already been over for dinner.

Phillip says, "I didn't realize he was involved."

"Mmm," I say, and I nod. "And Jason Collier."

"Wow, you really undersold this," he says. He turns toward the rest of them. "She just said, 'Oh, I'm working on this little movie thing, I guess.'" He shakes his head. "Jason Collier."

Mark says, "Collier is a great director, but I've never thought much of DeMarco. He does some weird stuff. Didn't he do that movie where he's a drug addict who thinks he's killed his girlfriend but then it turns out that really he didn't?"

I say, "Yeah, that's Tommy," and then that seems too familiar, so I add, "DeMarco," but it feels like I did it too late.

"He seems like a real playboy," red-tie guy says, and I laugh because who says that, and then I say, "That's putting it nicely," and Janet says, "Really?" in this really engaged tone, and everyone is looking at me a little more intently, and I feel like I've just turned into a walking tabloid.

"I mean, he has a pretty bad reputation," I say, and then I shut my mouth and focus on the vodka.

Phillip pulls into my driveway and stops the car.

"If the kids weren't home, I'd ask you in."

"That's okay," he says. He turns in his seat to face me. "Can I kiss you good night?"

"I'd be mad if you didn't."

He leans toward me, holds my neck with his left hand, and he parts his lips this time. I am marginally impressed. I put my hand on the top of his thigh and press my thumb across it, and I feel him shift in his seat. His mouth moves with a little more assurance, a little more need. I twist my chin to the left to free up my lips, and I trace the stubble along his jaw with the tips of my fingers. "I like this on you," I say, "a little rough against my chin."

He says, "I like you," and he turns his mouth to find mine again, and this time he uses his tongue to tease open my lips. I think, *Of course you do.* I think, *Who wouldn't?*

MARCH

"CRUNCHY OR CREAMY?" I say, holding the pantry door open.

"Creamy," Stevie says.

Ben's having scrambled eggs for breakfast, but Stevie wants peanut-butter toast. I set the jar on the counter in front of him and walk back to the stove.

"Do you have a boyfriend now?" Stevie says.

I turn to look at him, but he's focused on spreading the peanut butter. "You mean because I went to dinner last night?"

"And two other times too."

"You're right, we did go two other times. So I guess I have a friend I sometimes go to dinner with."

"Is that why you're not talking to Tommy anymore?"

I turn back to the stove. Ben's eggs look a little dry. I slide them onto a plate. I'm so stupid. Of course they would have noticed. We talk all the time, and sometimes my hands will be full, and my phone will start ringing, and one of them will pick it up for me. Stevie always hands it right over, but Ben will talk for a minute or two.

"I'm not not talking to Tommy," I say. "He's just been really busy with the movie. It doesn't have anything to do with me having dinner." I set the plate of eggs in Ben's place. "Can you go tell your brother his breakfast is ready?"

"Okay," he says, and he hops off the stool and heads down the hallway.

I turn toward the sink, run cold water into the pan.

"Mom," Stevie says, so I know he's back. "I really like Tommy."

I shut the water off, but I don't turn around. I say, "I know, baby. I really like him too."

I don't hear from Tommy for three weeks, and when I do, I wake up to see a text from him that reads, *I forgive you.* I pick up the phone and type, *Go fuck yourself,* and then hit *send.* I'm in line at the post office when he calls. I'm shipping a box of books. I see his number come up, and I hit *answer* and hold the phone to my ear.

He must realize I've picked up because after a second he says, "Stacey?"

I scuff my foot along the floor. I shift the box of books onto my hip.

"Okay," he says, "you were right."

"How's Sadie?" I say, but I make sure my tone stays pouty. I don't want him to think that I'm not still pissed.

"Better, maybe. I don't know." He sighs. "You were right. I'm a terrible father."

"I didn't say you were a terrible father. I said you were a narcissist."

"Same thing."

I'm almost to the front of the line. I say, "I should go. It's not a good time."

"C'mon, Stacey, what are you doing?" he says.

"I'm mailing a package," I say, and I shift its weight to keep from dropping it.

"You know," he says, "sometimes people argue and then if they aren't complete assholes, they figure out a way to patch shit up. So, you know, stop being a complete asshole."

I set my package on the counter and try to smile at the woman behind it. I'm trying not to let anything slip. I shift the phone a little away from my mouth and say, "I need to send this to Minneapolis. Media rate."

On the other end of the line, Tommy says, "Oh, fuck you," and hangs up.

When I walk out to the car, I don't get in. I lean against the trunk and let the sun warm my face. We're having one of those early springs when it's already warming up in March. I have always loved spring in Nebraska. When Michael wanted to talk me into moving here, he brought me out in the spring, and the whole city was so green, and the trees were budding, and Michael and I were starting a new life, and I said, *Yes, let's do it here,* and so we did. And even here, in the post office parking lot, it feels like the air is filled with possibility. It feels like the very beginning.

I take my phone out, and I call Tommy, and when he answers, I say, "I'm lousy at apologies," and he says, "You suck at forgiveness too."

"I know," I say, "but you're good at it, right?"

"I am," he says. "I'm like fucking magnanimous."

APRIL

PHILLIP IS TAKING ME to dinner for the fourth time on Friday, and once again, Jenny's offered to take the kids. He seems more relaxed this time. He's actually wearing jeans, and he wants to hit this Mexican place in the Old Market. He tries to order me a margarita, but I say, "I like my tequila straight." He gives me a look, but the thought of all that sugar makes me feel nauseated. I sip my tequila and rub my leg against his.

When he hands the check to the server, I lean close to his ear. I let my breast press against his arm, and I'm sure he notices. I whisper, "When are you going to show me your place?"

He lives in a condo in an old converted warehouse. It's small but very, very nice. Hardwood floors, high ceilings, top-of-the-line everything. It looks like it came furnished because I can't imagine him picking out any of this. It's lots of glass and chrome and leather. We stand in the kitchen, and he pours me a glass of wine. I remember the two tequilas at the restaurant and promise myself that this will be my only glass. I don't want to regret it in the morning.

He says, "We can go up to the roof deck?"

I say, "I like it here," and I set my wine on the counter behind him and turn toward him, and tip my head up and kiss him on the chin. He puts his arms around me. It's more hug than passionate embrace. He keeps his hands very still. "Are you going to give me a tour?" I whisper into his neck, and he says, "Yes, oh, yeah, sure."

He takes my left hand, and I grab the wine with my right because I feel like I'm going to need it. I feel like this is going to be a long night. And of course, he shows me the whole goddamn place, a little balcony, and off the hallway there's a bathroom with a very expensive sink. I say, "Is this a one-bed, or two?"

And he says, because I'm realizing he's really an idiot, "It's a two-bedroom. There's a small guest room down this hall."

"Where's your bedroom?" I say, and I use my huskiest voice, which frankly, I don't do very well or often, but I'm running out of ideas.

"Just up these stairs."

I realize he looks a little nervous. And I know this isn't the first time since his divorce. I know he dated a woman for almost six months last year. It must be me. It must be the widow thing. I walk in front of him and take his hand and pull it close behind me, and when we reach the top, it's an open loft with a double bed and beyond it a wall of windows with an amazing view of the city. I walk over to look, and when I turn around he's next to me. I take his hand and place it on my waist. He kisses me again, and I unbutton the top button of his shirt and then the next, kissing the skin underneath. I drop his shirt on the floor.

He says, "Are you sure about this?" but I don't answer. I reach for his belt and unfasten it, unbutton his jeans. I let my fingers slip inside, trace the line of his pelvis. I push him backwards toward the bed, and when he reaches it, he sits down. I lift my shirt up over my arms and move his hands to the zipper of my jeans, let him strip them off. I push him flat on his back and lean over him and kiss him, and my hair completely covers his face. He pushes it out of the way. He says, "God, Stacey, you're beautiful," but I put my hand over his mouth. I make him kiss my fingers. He tries to roll me onto my back, but I push him down and climb on top of him. I think, *It's better this way.* I know exactly what I'm doing.

When I wake in the morning, Michael has been dead for two years, and there's a man twelve feet below me in the kitchen of this expensive loft downtown, and I can hear him making me coffee. I pull the top sheet off the bed, and I wrap it around me and walk downstairs in my bare feet. Phillip is in the kitchen in just his boxers, and when I see him, I don't regret a thing. He smiles and pours me coffee. I let him make me a slice of toast.

I sit on the couch and curl my legs underneath me, tucking them under the sheet.

"Do you mind if I grab a shower before I take you home?" he asks, and I shake my head, bite into the corner of the toast. "I'll be quick," he says, and he kisses me on the cheek.

My phone rings while he's in the shower, and my breath catches in my throat when I see that it's Tommy. It's early here, and barely five o'clock his time. "What's wrong?" I say when I pick up. "Is it Sadie?"

"Nothing. No. We just wrapped. We just shot the last scene." He sounds tired and excited. "We're packing up. We're going home."

"God." I let out the breath I've been holding. "You scared me."

"No, no. Everything's good. We're a week ahead of schedule. We cranked this shit out." I hear him take a deep breath. "And it's good, Stace. It's so good. I can't wait for you to see it."

I hear the water turn off upstairs. "Look, can I call you later?"

"Why? What are you doing? I know you weren't sleeping."

I twist the sheet through my fingers, think hard about what to say next. "I'm not actually at home," I say, and I bite my lip.

"What are you doing out this early?" He stops. "Oh fuck. Jesus, Stacey, I don't want to know this shit." He makes this disgusted shivery groan like he's just gotten a chill down his spine. "I can't believe you answered the phone. You are such an asshole."

"Jesus, Tommy, I thought it was about Sadie," I whisper.

"Still, Christ. You have no fucking tact." He's yelling now, and I think, *Really? Try reading about it in the checkout line.*

It does almost make me smile though, and I have to concentrate so that it doesn't show in my voice. "Just call me when you wake up," I say, and I hang up.

I hear Phillip's feet on the stairs and look up. He looks good coming out of the shower. His hair's wet. He's pulling a T-shirt on. "Who was that?" he asks.

"They wrapped the movie," I say. "Just now." I stand up and walk around the couch. I meet him at the bottom of the stairs. I run my fingers through his hair and say, "I'd better get dressed."

On the drive back to my house, Phillip tries for small talk, but it's awkward, so he settles for holding my hand. He seems distracted, and he nearly misses the expressway. It's light out, but cloudy and gray, and it's hot already.

"Tornado weather," Phillip says, pointing to the clouds stirring in the west, but he's wrong. The real storms come on clear days. The real storms come when the air is very, very still.

"Everything okay?" Phillip asks.

"Everything's great," I say, and I pull my hand away from his, run my fingers through the hair at the back of his neck, but I'm getting tired. I didn't sleep well. I cross my legs, fold my hands around my knee, and turn to look out the window. There's not much traffic. This shouldn't take long.

I grab a quick shower before picking up the boys. Bear lies on the floor watching me, looking pouty. He's feeling neglected. Like it's not enough that I pay the neighbor kid to let him out. Jenny lives close, less than a mile, and I don't believe it's actually going to rain just yet. I decide we can walk. When he hears the jangle of the metal collar he perks up. I can see that he wants to flip out, spin in circles, but he's way too big for that. We had to train him to stay steady, to rein it in. He sits, but he sort of shivers in place with all that energy. It's hard to fasten the clip without pinching one of us.

When Jenny opens the door, she says, "Well?" and I shrug. I say, "Hey."

I don't want to spend the day on this. I just want to get the boys and make it home before it rains. There's a reason I brought Bear. Now I can't come inside. Jenny just opens the screen door and steps out to sit on the stoop. She says, "Uh-uh, this is how you pay me for taking the kids." Bear sticks his giant nose in her face, and she scratches him for a minute before she pushes him away.

I know she wants to know everything. She wants to know about feelings and heartache and love. She's a romantic, but more important, she's a family girl. She wants me to get married so we can go back to the Sunday dinners and shared vacations. She and Michael were like a matched set. *Let's rent a cabin. Let's take the kids on a cruise.* Sometimes I think she misses him more than I do.

"So do you like him?" she says, and she rests her head in her hands. She looks at me expectantly. Her eyes are big.

"I do," I say. "I think he's really sweet." I feel like I need to give her something, so I say, "And he made me breakfast."

She makes this giddy cooing sound and smiles behind her hands. She bounces her knees.

"Oh, I'm so happy," she says, and she reaches out to squeeze my hand. "I don't want you to be lonely."

I want to say, *I'm not lonely,* but I'm not good at lying. I'm better at just not telling the truth, so I say, "I should really get them home." I look at the sky like, *Any minute now. Any minute these clouds could break.*

Tommy calls late, so late I've already finished my glass of wine and poured another. I'm making an exception. I take my time answering so he won't think I've been pacing the house with my phone in my hands, which of course I have been. Though when Phillip called three hours ago, I didn't answer.

"So," he says, "you're officially fucking around on me."

I smile, sink into the couch, because the tone in his voice makes me feel like I can finally relax.

"I don't think there's anything official going on here. And you're working on the assumption that I intend to keep sleeping with you, which I don't."

"You can intend or not intend whatever you want, honey. We'll see how you manage to follow through."

"Because you're so irresistible?"

"I think I've demonstrated some talents that you would miss. I mean, it's like if you need some work done on your house and you've had this really talented carpenter, not just any carpenter, like an artisan, and you're gonna go from that to just some handyman in the phone book?"

"So you're like a master craftsman now?"

"I know my way around some trim work, yeah."

I laugh. "You know, I don't even know what that's a euphemism for, but it sounds filthy."

"I know, right? See, even over the phone, baby, I can get you like halfway there."

"Fuck off," I say, but I say it softly. I say it like everything's fine.

"Seriously, who is this guy?"

I shake my head, like he can see me. "Just someone I met at a fundraiser. Divorced. A doctor."

"Oh, a doctor." Tommy's brilliant, but I don't think he even has a GED. Not that he needs one, but sometimes he's a little sensitive. "Like some cocky surgeon type?"

I laugh. "No," I say. "He's an allergist."

"A what?" he says, and I don't like his tone.

"An allergist," I say again, but slowly.

"Are you kidding me? Like he spends his day writing prescriptions for Zyrtec and shit?"

"I don't know how he spends his day, Tommy." But I can see where he's going with this.

"Wow, Stace, that's exciting. That is some exciting shit."

"Okay, you know what, fuck you. He makes a good living at it anyway," and then I immediately regret it because Tommy really laughs now, and he says, "That's fantastic, because I have this beach house I've been trying to unload."

"Jesus, would you stop being such an asshole?"

"I can't help it, baby. You're making me crazy with this. You're driving me out of my fucking mind."

Then do something about it, I think, but I don't say that. I say, "I'm sure you can find something to distract you."

MAY

TOMMY PICKS ME UP at the airport. They've got a rough cut, and he wants me to see it. That's the excuse anyway. I walk out past the security gates and I think, *Shit, why didn't you send Daniel?* He's just leaning against the wall, waiting, and there are all these photographers snapping pictures. *Tommy, can you give us a smile? Tommy, are you coming or going?* He's just ignoring them like they're not even there. He keeps looking down at his phone. I don't even want to go over, but he spots me immediately. He says, "Hey!" and he stands up straight and walks toward me, and the photographers just sort of move enough to let him pass, stepping backwards, keeping him in focus. He hugs me, kisses me on the cheek. "How was your flight?"

"Um, okay." I'm having a hard time tuning all of this out. I can't seem to block out the flashes and clicks.

He rolls his eyes. "Don't let them freak you out." He grabs my bag and throws it over his shoulder and takes my arm. "So how are the boys?" he says as he starts walking toward the doors, and he talks really quietly, really close. I don't know if it's to keep people from overhearing or just to force me to pay attention.

"Good," I say. "They're with Jenny for the weekend. They're going to eat popcorn and pancakes and fucking sundaes."

"I feel like I need to meet this Jenny. Think she'd make me pancakes?"

"I think a lot of people would make you pancakes."

Then one guy comes in really close. I feel like he's going to walk right into me, and I take a step backwards and trip. If Tommy wasn't holding on to me, I'd fall over. I think maybe I wore the wrong shoes. The whole time, the guy just keeps snapping pictures, and he says, *Who's your friend, Tommy?* Tommy puts his hand up and shoves him hard in the chest. "Fucking space, man!" he yells. "Fuck! I am always cool with you guys, but give me my goddamn space!" And the tone of his voice makes the muscles at the back of my neck tighten. The tone of his voice makes me want to curl up in a ball.

My phone rings just as I'm getting in the car, and the photo that comes up is the same as Phillip's profile from his clinic's staff page. Tommy leans over to look. "Is this the guy?"

I wave him off and pick up, and he mumbles, "Jesus, you're answering it?"

I just roll my eyes and say, "Hi!"

"Land safely?" Phillip says. Like he doesn't already know this. Like I didn't text him when I saw Tommy outside the security area, *Just grabbing my bags. Call me in 20?*

"I did," I say. "I just got in." I use my brightest voice, and Tommy wrinkles his brow like, *Who are you?* He pulls out into the line of cars leaving the airport.

"That was fast," Phillip says. "You must not have had a layover."

"No," I say. "They flew me direct. They're really very good to me." I smile at Tommy when I say this, and he mouths, *Fuck you.*

"Are you staying downtown? I know a few great spots you might like."

"No, um, I'm staying, uh, with one of the producers, actually."

Tommy throws his hands up and mutters something under his breath. I make a face at him and mouth, *Shut up.*

"Oh, okay." Phillip seems to be searching for something to say. "Well, have a great time, and call me if you have a few minutes free."

"I will, yeah." And I reach across and slap Tommy on the arm because now he's mimicking me.

"I'll be thinking about you," Phillip says, and I say, "Yeah, me too," and then we're both kind of quiet, and it feels really weird and not at all worth it, so I make a quick excuse and hang up the phone.

Tommy pulls out of the airport and into traffic. He just shakes his head, cocks his chin forward. His jaw looks tight. "That," he says, "was ridiculous."

"Whatever." I turn my head away from him and look out the window.

"I can't believe you took his call. You know I don't take calls in front of you."

"Because Daniel doesn't put them through. You can hardly take credit for that." I turn back to face him, smile. "And you know I always take your calls too."

He glances at me, then back at the road. "I think it's in your best interest not to remind me of that little incident." From the expression on his face, I feel like this is probably true.

I wave my hand like, *I get it.* "Let's just drop it."

He does at first. He doesn't say anything for a while, but once something's under his skin, he can't let it go. At least when he brings it back up, he sounds fine. He sounds like he's just teasing. "What's with this 'Oh, I'm staying with one of the producers'?" he says in this falsetto voice. "You can't be like, 'I'm crashing with my friend Tommy'?"

"Um, no." I shake my head. "I think that would make him uncomfortable."

He glances to the right before switching lanes. He seems to be driving a little fast. "You know, I think it's great that you're so invested in protecting his feelings. Have you considered the possibility of sometimes lying to me?"

"I don't have to lie to you. You don't have any feelings. Besides, I'm in a relationship now, so this shit between us is off the table."

"Oh, so this is a 'relationship'?" He does use air quotes, but I ignore him. "And this"—he tucks his hand between my legs, gives my thigh a little squeeze—"baby, this is never off the table." And he gives me this really ridiculous impish smile, and he winks at me, and I think, *Goddamn it, Tommy, what the hell are we doing?*

Tommy says the rough cut is fantastic, but I think it looks awful. I think it's a goddamn terrifying mess. We walk out of his screening room, and I say, "I need a drink."

"You just don't know what you're looking at," he says, and I know he's trying to sound reassuring. "There's still a lot of editing left."

"Great." I raise one eyebrow. "I'm glad you showed it to me then."

For a second, I think he's going to say something shitty, but then he puts his arms around me and laughs. "God, what am I going to do with you?" He sort of shakes me around. "I'm trying to keep you in the loop here. I'm trying to show you some fucking respect."

I just sigh and let my head fall against his chest. "I know," I say.

Then I notice the feel of him against me and how he smells, and I think I need to back away, but he's still got a hold on me, and his mouth is by my ear, and when he sighs, I can feel his breath.

He says, "You just don't trust me," and I nod because I really don't. How could I?

Matt is coming for dinner, and Sadie swears I'm going to love him. She's dressed in jeans and this pale yellow top. She looks pretty, but I can tell she's not wearing a bra.

"Honey," I say, waving my hand across my chest, "maybe let's not give it all away, huh?"

She shrugs her arms across her chest and says, "Stacey, oh my god!"

"You want your dad to see that?"

"See what?" Tommy says, walking into the room. He's got an open bottle of wine, and as he passes the bar, he picks up two glasses, hangs them off the fingers of his right hand.

"Nothing, jeez," Sadie grumbles, but she crosses her arms tighter and storms off toward her room.

Tommy looks at me, but I just shake my head. I don't want to embarrass her more than I need to. I just want her to put on a damn bra. Tommy steps into the hallway to look after her, and when he's sure she's gone he turns back and says, "Wait till you see this kid." He sets the glasses on the table and pours them half full. I love how he always starts the evening like a moderate.

"I can't wait."

"You won't believe me though." He smiles. "I'm like a changed man. I really apologized for flying off the handle, said that I knew I wasn't being fair to him. I lied my ass off." He raises his glass in a toast to me. "Sadie probably thinks I'm saving up for their wedding."

"Good." I sit back on the couch with my glass. "You should make him think that too. Nothing kills a young boy's libido like thinking about a wedding."

He laughs. "Don't I know it."

The doorbell rings, and I can hear Sadie skipping down the stairs. She's so light I'm surprised she makes any noise at all. I hear the front door open, and she says, "Hi," in this really pathetic and lilting tone, and I look at Tommy like, *That's disgusting,* and he mouths, *I know.* And then they're standing in the doorway, and Sadie's holding his right arm with both hands, tucking herself behind his shoulder, hovering nervously on her toes. She says, "Stacey, I want you to meet my boyfriend, Matt," and she says under her breath to Matt, "Stacey's like my dad's really good friend."

I want to kill the kid immediately, and now I can't blame Tommy for ever trying, but Tommy steps toward him and claps him on the shoulder and says, "How's it going, man?" and I honestly don't know how he does it. The kid is tall and pretty lanky, and he gives Tommy this cocky *Hey, man* nod, and I suck on my lip to keep from saying, *Jesus, who do you think you are?* Even the way he moves makes me angry, the way he positions himself so that the arm Sadie's hanging on to keeps her a half-step behind him, away from Tommy and me.

He looks at me and says, "Hey, nice to meet you. Sadie says you've been real good to her." I can tell he's trying to make his voice deeper.

It takes me a second, but I channel my very best midwestern, and I stand up and walk across the room to pull his arm away from Sadie.

"I've been waiting all day to meet you, come have a seat." I nudge him into the corner of the couch, so there's no room left for Sadie on his other side. I glance back at Tommy, and he looks like he wants to take me to bed right then. He looks as grateful as I've ever seen a man.

"So tell me how you met," I say, and Matt says, "School."

"I know that," I say, and I laugh, "but I want to hear the story." I know he doesn't have a story. Sadie's probably memorized every minute that's passed between them, and I doubt he remembers more than five. Depends how many times they've managed to have sex. I pick up my wine and take a drink. I'd like to swallow the whole thing, but I don't. I hold my glass in front of me and look at him like I'm waiting to hear what he has to say.

"Um, I think we met at a pep rally," he says, and when I look at Sadie I know he's gotten it wrong.

"English class," she says, "first semester." Of course. They probably read *Romeo & Juliet*. They shouldn't read that in high school. That play really fucks up little girls. And what the hell were they doing in the same English class? Is he stupid? Is he taking remedial shit?

"That's so romantic," I say, nudging him with the back of my hand. "And you saw her sitting there, with her cute little nose in a book, and you were like 'That's the girl for me,' right?"

He just kind of shrugs and says, "I guess."

———————

After dinner, Tommy lets them have the living room to themselves, but he makes it clear we're going to be just outside the door. "So no getting carried away," he says to Matt, and he winks at him. He should get an Oscar.

I sort of lean against the dining table and look through the door at them. They're sitting on the couch, and Sadie's trying to kind of cuddle up to him, but he's having none of it. I feel terrible for her, but also glad. Tommy's standing with his back to them, so they can't see his face. He looks at me, and he lets the whole act drop, and his eyes just fill up with loathing and his jaw looks tight. He whispers, "I could kill him. I could seriously cut his body up into little pieces and bury him in the yard."

I say, "You're doing amazing. You're doing great." I reach out to squeeze his arm, and when I do, he grabs my hand. He twists his fingers tightly through mine. It doesn't feel like affection. It just feels like he needs something to grab on to.

When he lets go, he sighs. "I hope he leaves soon. I plan on getting drunk."

We do. We get very drunk. By the end of the night, we've got four open bottles, and I'm starting to worry about the morning. Tommy's lying back on the arm of the couch, and he's got his legs stretched out toward me, and he's swirling the wine in his glass. Not like a connoisseur, exactly. More like a drunk. He looks at me, and he says, "We need to get some food in you, or you're not gonna make it."

I shake my head. "I'll be fine."

He gets up and walks off toward the kitchen, and when he comes back, he's got a bag of tortilla chips.

"I don't eat that kind of crap," I say.

As he's pushing past me to sit back down, he says, "Stacey, you don't eat." Which is bullshit, and not something that people are supposed to say anyway. I must look pissed because he pats me on the leg and says, "It's cool, honey, I'm used to it." He shrugs. "I mean, it's fucking L.A."

I just glare at him, but he opens the bag and tips it toward me. He's sitting next to me. His leg's pressed right up against my leg. "No, thank you," I say.

He laughs and bites into a chip. He holds another one up to my mouth, uses the corner of it to poke at my lip. "Come on," he coaxes. "They're delicious."

I brush his hand away. "I don't want a chip, Tommy."

"I don't really care what you want. You're gonna eat it because I don't feel like cleaning you up in the morning. I have been there, and done that, and it is no goddamn fun." He waves another chip in front of my mouth. "C'mon, baby, open up. Do it for me."

I try to sink farther into the corner of the couch, but he just leans closer, his whole body pressed against me now, his hand braced against my thigh. "We can do this the hard way if you want to, honey. It's a whole lot easier if you just say yes."

He makes me eat eleven chips, which is ridiculous, and then he tosses the bag on the table. He reaches across me and grabs my thigh, pulling it toward him over his lap so I'm straddling him, and his chin is between my breasts. He tugs the neck of my shirt down with his teeth.

"I'm not going to bed with you," I say.

He holds my hips in his hands, presses me down against him. "I think it's so cute when you talk that way."

"I'm serious, Tommy. I'm seeing someone."

"It's cool, baby. I'm seeing lots of people, but I save all my best shit for you." He grabs the skin of my neck with his teeth, and I let my head fall back. I don't have a lot of resolve left, and he's already pulling off my shirt.

"Tommy, I mean it," I say, and he pulls my mouth against his and pushes his tongue between my teeth and, of course, I kiss him back because I always do, because I can't seem to help myself, and when he pulls away he says, "I think I'll decide what you don't mean and what you do."

I wake to Tommy's lips on my cheek. "You look like shit, Stace."

This is appropriate since it's exactly how I feel. I just groan, hold my hands over my eyes.

"How long till my flight?"

"Three hours. Here, sit up. I brought you coffee."

I do sit up, but maybe too fast. My head is pounding already, and the motion sends a jolt through the top of my skull. I might sway a little, or maybe the room does, but Tommy wraps an arm around my shoulders, holds me up straight. "Easy, honey," he says, and then he holds his hand out. "Pills?"

I look at him like, *Christ,* but I take them. I say, "God, Tommy, what are you doing to me?"

He just laughs, takes a mug from the bedside table, puts it in my hands, and lies back on the bed next to me. He trails his fingers along my spine. "Sure you want to fly today? You know you can stay if you want to," he says, but I can't see his face. I can't tell what he means, if he just feels like he should offer.

I shake my head. I say, "I'd better get back."

Tommy moves behind me, wraps his arm around me, grabs hold of my breast. He presses his lips against my back, and for a second I think he must be trying to convince me, but he's not, because his mouth is still on my skin when he says, "Yeah, okay."

Phillip picks me up when I land in Omaha. The airport is tiny, and I'd told him to just pick me up at the curb. They won't let you wait, but he must have driven in circles until he spotted me, because when I walk out, it's like he's right there. He gets out of the car and takes my bag from me and puts it in the trunk. He opens the passenger door, and as I move to get in, he stops me and gives me a long kiss. I'm glad to see him. He makes me feel like I can catch my breath. I get in the car, and he closes the door behind me, and then he walks back around to the driver's side and climbs in. He puts the car in gear, but before he pulls out, he takes my left hand and kisses the back of it and holds it in his lap as he starts to drive.

"I'm happy you're home," he says, and I smile and say, "Me too."

Traveling from L.A. takes like all fucking day, and I'm still hungover, and I just want to get home, but when he says, "Can I take you to dinner?" I say, "Sure."

"So how was the movie," Jenny says, holding her mug out for me to fill.

"Pretty awful."

She frowns at me. "Really?"

I shrug. "I don't know. I'm sure they'll fix it."

"I can't wait to see it," she says, and she turns to look out the window at the kids. They're playing this game with Bear where they run screaming away from him, and he knows he's supposed to run them down hard, that that's what they want. He always slows down in the end though, veers to the side, lets them win.

"So is Tommy really dating that Vivian Kells?" Jenny says, turning back to me. I don't even have time to think. I'm too busy trying not to react. "She is so cool. I've loved her forever, ever since she was in that movie *Caroline*, remember? I loved that movie." She shakes her head. "Doesn't really seem like his type though. I mean, she's like forty, right?"

"I don't know," I say. "I think probably everyone is Tommy's type."

"He didn't talk about her?"

"Tommy doesn't really talk about that kind of stuff with me." I shrug.

"I thought you two talked about everything."

"Yeah, but not that." I take a sip of my coffee. "I'm not really interested in who he's dating."

"The kids say you talk to Tommy a lot," she says slowly. "Pretty much every day."

"I talk to you every day."

"What is that supposed to mean?"

"Just that, you know, there are lots of people I'm close to." I move to refill my cup. "I talk to Sarah a lot too."

"Okay," she says, and she sets down her mug. "I guess I'm wondering if maybe you have some feelings?"

"For Tommy?" I force a laugh.

"I'm just asking," she says.

"Okay." I take a deep breath. "I adore Tommy. I do. And he's been really good to me. But it would be stupid to have those kinds of feelings for someone like Tommy. Wouldn't it?" I want her to say no. I want her to feed me some bullshit line about how you have to follow your heart, or be true to yourself, but she doesn't say any of that.

She says, "Yeah, it would be really stupid." She holds out her cup for me to fill. "That's why I'm glad you have Phillip now."

I nod. I say, "Me too."

JULY

STEVIE'S BASEBALL TEAM is having an end-of-season potluck, and of course I'm going to take him. He's excited. He's wearing his team shirt. I can see him smiling in the rearview mirror. "Do you think I'll get a trophy?" he asks Ben.

"Everyone gets a trophy," Ben says, but he doesn't say this as a dismissal. He's being reassuring, and this is exactly how Stevie takes it. He wiggles in his seat.

I feel out of place even pulling up to the house. The boys climb out of the car, and I hand Ben a package of organic juice boxes. I made hummus, and I've sliced up carrots and bell peppers. I don't want the boys to just fill up on chips. Stevie races to the front door, but he doesn't ring the doorbell. That would be asking too much. He just hops up and down on the step.

It's a nice house, and the neighborhood is prime, but inside, it's a little out of date. There's a wallpaper border above the kitchen cabinets. There's an awful lot of oak.

"You can just set your food in the dining room, and if the boys are hungry they can go ahead and grab a plate," the hostess tells me.

There are a lot of moms and dads here, and while I've been running into them twice a week for the past two and a half months, I don't know any of their names. It's Stevie's first year, and none of these kids even go to the same school. I think we got put on the wrong team. Everyone else seems to know each other, and none of them have ever talked to me, and I think, *That's fine. I don't need friends who bring frosted sugar cookies and potato chips to a potluck. How about a salad? How about you don't try to give my kids diabetes?* But maybe I'm just defensive.

The boys are eyeing the table, and Ben says, "Mom?" I glance over it. The other kids are piling their plates with mostly chips, half barbecue, half plain.

"Ten chips, lots of veggies, and you can split a cookie," I say.

The woman across from me raises her eyebrows.

"I'm a vegetarian," I say, "kind of a health nut. I try to be pretty mindful about what they eat."

I think this may be why people like her don't like me. She's squirting a lake of ketchup onto her kid's plate. I think about saying, *You know that shit is mostly corn syrup,* but I don't. Instead I say, "Which boy is your son?"

"Gavin," she says, and nods at a redheaded kid.

The truth is I haven't actually been paying attention at most of the games. The thing about baseball is that you only really have to watch the few minutes your own kid is up to bat. I mean, sometimes I glance up when he's in the outfield just in case he's looking, so I can wave, but they put him way the hell out there. The kid can barely catch. In any case, I spend a lot of the games reading or texting, and maybe the other parents have noticed my lack of investment. This may be the other reason they don't like me.

"Did you have fun playing baseball, Gavin?" I say, even though I don't care. I'm just trying to fit in.

"Gavin loves it," his mom says, rubbing his head. She actually smiles at me, and I think, *Oh, look at that, I'm doing okay.* "His dad played baseball in college, so he got some extra coaching. Right, buddy?"

Gavin nods.

She just waits for a minute, and I know she's waiting for me to say something about Stevie's dad and whether he's really into sports, but most important whether he still lives with us. I know they all think I'm divorced, which in Omaha is not okay, at least not in this neighborhood. You can be divorced, but you have to live in Midtown, and your kids can't play in this league. I almost wish Stevie would make one of his announcements.

"I'm so sorry, I didn't catch your name," I say, and I hold my hand out.

"Lynn," she says, and she shakes my hand.

"I'm Stacey," I say, and she smiles.

"And these two are both yours?" she says, nodding toward the boys.

"They are. And you have Gavin? Is he your only?"

"Oh no," she laughs. "We have five."

I say, "Oh, you're Catholic," and then I think, *Shit, why did I say that?* I make a little face like, *I'm just kidding,* but I think it's too late. She kind of laughs, but it's the kind of laugh people use to tell you you're an asshole.

I say, "Well, I should probably fix a plate."

―――――――

I sort of position myself at the edge of a group of parents, and I turn my head so it looks like I'm really intently watching the kids. There must be three dozen of them in the backyard. They're swarming the wooden playset, falling in the grass.

The dads behind me are talking sports now, mostly about the Huskers, and I think, *I wish Michael were here. He would know how to do this.* Actually, I think Phillip would too. I can see where he would fit between these two guys in their golf shorts. I wouldn't let him wear golf shorts, but he could stand there. He could bridge the gap between us.

I walk out to get the boys, tell them it's time to go, and as I walk up behind Stevie and the boys around him, I hear them all talking. They want to have a pool party. They're asking a couple of the other moms.

"We'll see," one says, and then she turns to her friend. "Let's just get through this one first."

Stevie says, "My mom's boyfriend has a pool. He's a movie star. He lives in a mansion."

"Stevie!" I say, and I look at the other women. I kind of shake my head. I say, "I don't . . . he's just . . . ," and then I think, *Fuck it.* I say, "His dad died."

I drop to squat beside him, take his arms in my hands. I say, "Honey, Tommy is not my boyfriend. He's just a really good friend."

Stevie just says, "Oh," but he looks like I've just told him Disneyland burned down. Even to Stevie, Tommy's a big deal. I can feel these moms looking at me, and I think, *God, how can I deal with this here?* I pull Stevie into a hug, and I say, "Hey, it doesn't mean you can't still see him, right? Because he's one of my very best friends, and he would love for you to come stay with him and go swimming." I smile up at the other moms, but they're both making this sad, sorry face like they feel like they should bring me a casserole. It's Nebraska. It's the only thing they know to do.

When I tuck him into bed, I think about telling Stevie how proud Michael would be, but it feels like something I don't want to start. It feels like an intrusion, so I just say, "Who's my favorite bug?" and Stevie says, "Me."

In the kitchen, I throw out the leftover hummus, which is most of it, and wipe down the counters. There aren't really any crumbs, but Bear comes running anyway, snuffles along the floor. I lean forward over the island, let the edge of it press against my stomach, rest on my arms. The granite feels damp still and cool, but I don't really care. Everything else in the house feels too hot. I keep forgetting to turn on the fan. Across the room, Stevie's trophy sits on the mantel. He's already polished it twice, standing with it over the sink with an old washcloth.

Looking at it makes me feel raw, and I think how, in the opposite corner, on the shelf with painted wineglasses and crystal decanters that are really only filled with colored water, just for display, is Tommy's bottle of scotch that I never planned to open, but I think tonight might be a good night. It might be just what I need. I pour a little into a glass, not even two fingers, and I swirl it. I hold it up to my nose. I don't know if you're supposed to do this with scotch, and it smells terrible. I know it's going to taste bad too. It's like trying to swallow gasoline, but I do like the way it leaves my tongue feeling numb. I like how it feels against my teeth. I pour a little more in the glass, raise the level back up. I'm just topping it off, so I don't feel like I have to start counting. I feel like this just makes it one. With each sip, the fist knotted around my spine is loosening its grip. I set the glass in front of the bottle and snap a picture of it with my phone, and I label it *fucking godsend* and text it to Tommy.

When the phone rings, it's been twenty minutes and I'm staring at the trace in my glass, wishing it wasn't almost empty. It's too late now to call this topping it off. I'm curled in the chair by the fireplace, and my phone is across the room, back in the kitchen on the counter. When I walk, I don't feel wobbly, but my joints feel loose.

"I hope you're not alone," Tommy says when I answer. "You need a babysitter with that shit."

"I'm just having a little," I say, "just a little, little bit," but I do pour another small splash in the glass. I decide to call it one and a half.

It's loud wherever he is. I can tell he's not at home. "What's wrong?" he says.

"Nothing. You should go back to your party. I've just had a long day." The voices behind him get louder and some of them are calling his name. "Seriously, though, you should go. You can call me tomorrow." I don't actually mean this, and I'm afraid the scotch lets it show in my voice. This is what I don't love about the scotch. It's not that it makes me let my guard down. I'm still trying to hold it up, but with each sip it just eats a little more of it away.

"I hate most of these people anyway." The noise behind him fades a little like he's moving out of range.

"It was just this stupid baseball party for Stevie and all these parents and their mayonnaisey salads and their 'Why don't you have a husband?' looks. I just . . . I can't blend in."

"Why would you want to? They sound like assholes. Only assholes eat mayonnaise." I have actually seen Tommy eat mayonnaise, but him I forgive.

"I don't know, for the boys, I guess. Don't they need a regular mom who makes friends with all the other moms, who isn't like some kind of pariah?"

"Pariah?" Tommy says, and I think he laughs at me. "Come on, honey, the boys are fine."

"Yeah, they're totally fine. This is why Stevie announced to a whole group of them that 'my mommy's boyfriend is a movie star,'" and then I think, *Fucking scotch,* because I wasn't going to tell him that part.

"Me?" He laughs. "That's pretty cute."

"No, Tommy, it's sad. It's a sad little story made up by a little kid who doesn't have a dad, and that's what all these awful moms were thinking, and they're just standing there looking at me and wondering what the hell I'm doing that he's making up these crazy stories and how I must have a lot of men coming around anyway, or where else would he get the idea."

"Jesus, take a breath," he says. "He's not pulling this shit out of thin air, you know. So are you pissed off that he caught you or that his interpretation of reality doesn't line up with yours?"

"Reality? We don't have reality, Tommy. We have, I don't know, vacation sex."

"Wow." The laugh he makes now does not sound happy. "You just keep taking the asshole up a notch, don't you? You're the one who's always on vacation, honey. This is just my fucking life."

I should have stopped at the first glass. I maybe shouldn't have started. "I don't know," I say. "I don't even know what I'm saying right now."

He doesn't say anything, and I can hear the noise behind him picking up again. I'm sure there's some very pretty girl waiting for him in that crowd. There always is.

I try to take the boys to the pool a few times a week. We go in the late afternoon, so when we're getting there, it's the busiest time, but it thins out pretty quickly as everyone's heading home for dinner. I can usually find a shady spot to camp out. It was more fun when they were littler and needed me to stand at the bottom of the waterslide, needed me to catch them. Now they're such good swimmers. They jump and jump off the diving board. I watch for a while. Then I usually just sit and read. I'm right in the middle of a chapter when my phone rings, so I almost let it roll, but when I glance down, I see that it's Erin, my editor.

"I'm putting together all the book promo stuff to send to this conference in Chicago, and I need an updated bio. The one I have doesn't even mention the movie. They want it fast though, so I need it by tomorrow."

"What are you talking about?" I sit up and let the book fall closed in my lap.

"I thought you knew." She sounds nervous now, like she knows I might back out. "Okay, it's nothing crazy. It's just a weekend in Chicago."

"*What* is just a weekend in Chicago?"

"It's a publishing conference. More of a pitch event really, and the panel you're on is acquisitions, what makes a project stand out. It's with one of your movie producers, so I doubt you'll really have to say much. Very low-stress, but it's a good chance to move some books."

"Right. One of the producers," I say. "When's this supposed to be?"

"Late September."

The lifeguards blow their whistles for break, and I look up and see that Stevie still has his head underwater. I'm sure he'll be the last to come in.

"Look, Erin, I have to go. I'm at the pool with the boys."

"Don't blow this off, Stacey. And send me that bio," she says. "Today."

I tuck my book back in my bag so they don't drip on it, and pull out towels to wrap around them. It's a hot day, but I know they'll feel chilly in the shade.

The boys sit on the lounge chair next to mine. "Did you bring any snacks?" Stevie says.

"Apple slices," I say, and I dig them out of my bag.

"Did you see my flip?" Ben says.

"I did. You went really high." He landed on his back though. It looked like it stung. "Dry off a little. I want you to get more sun-screen on."

The break is ten minutes, and the whole time I'm watching the second hand tick on the giant clock that hangs over the door leading to the showers. I'm counting down to the whistle, to the boys run-ning back to the water, to calling Tommy.

When he answers, I say, "What the fuck did you do?"

"I'm not sure who you're talking about, baby, but whoever it is, she means nothing."

"Really, Tommy? That's hilarious. What is this Chicago shit?"

"Jesus, you're worked up about that? It's a weekend."

"You could have asked me first."

"I don't need to ask you, honey. You always make it work. And anyway, we're doing this for Daniel, so don't make a thing about it. He's already freaked out."

"Daniel?"

"Yeah. You don't think this little Chicago deal is really my league? He wants to start doing more, maybe finding his own projects. He needs to start meeting people, agents, making some contacts."

"Daniel's leaving you?"

"Leaving me." He laughs. "Whose money you think he's gonna spend? He's not leaving me, he just wants to change his job a little."

"Who's going to run your life?"

"Fuck if I know. Not me. I'm not really qualified."

AUGUST

MATT STOPS CALLING Sadie in early August, and Tommy says she's in a tailspin. He says she's lost ten pounds. I have had a few weepy texts from her, but of course she didn't mention the weight loss. She's stupid, but not completely.

"Jesus, from where?" I say.

"Exactly." He sounds like he's going to cry.

I'm in my kitchen, sorting the boys' back-to-school supplies. Two boxes of crayons in the yellow backpack, three packs of pencils in the blue.

"Tommy"—I take a deep breath—"how's she been dressing?"

"Trying to hide it. Wearing all this baggy shit, but it's not like it isn't obvious. I mean I can see it on her face."

"No." I can't remember which color of scissors belongs to whom. I think Stevie picked red. "I mean how much skin is she trying to cover. Is she wearing shorts ever? Long sleeves?"

He doesn't say anything for a minute. "How do you know about that?"

I say, "You told me," even though he didn't really need to. You'd have to be trying pretty hard not to see.

"I don't even remember that," he says.

"You wouldn't," I say, sliding a ruler into each bag. "It was a pretty bad night, Tommy."

"Yeah," he says, "it was." But he says it really quietly, like he doesn't want to think about it, and I can't blame him. I don't either.

"So?" I say. "It's summer, Tommy. What's she been wearing?"

And then he says, "Shit," but he says it in this voice that's kind of cracking. He says, "I don't know what to do."

"Have you thought about a treatment program?" I say. "Maybe something inpatient."

"I don't know, don't you think it would just make her mad?"

"Better mad than dead." Then I think I shouldn't have said that. "I'm sorry, I shouldn't have said it like that."

He sighs and says, "No, you're right, she's a mess. And her mom isn't helping. Her mom's like, 'Why doesn't that guy like you anymore? What did you do?'"

"You're kidding me."

"I don't know. She's in the middle of a divorce, and she's got all her own shit mixed up in this."

"Well, you're gonna have to find a place you can put Sadie," I say. "She needs full-time help. Like a nutritionist and a fleet of shrinks help." I open the package of glue sticks and separate them into two piles. "I'm sorry. I really am," I say. "I wish I could fix this for you."

Jenny wants to have a barbecue on Labor Day, and she wants me to bring Phillip. She says, "I'm cutting you off on babysitting until I meet this guy." We're standing in her kitchen, and the kids are all outside.

"I don't know. The kids haven't met him yet." I sit down at her table where I can still look out the windows. They're covered in these horizontal wooden blinds, and my view of the boys is sliced into layers. It's like looking at a grid. *Here is a section of leg. Here is an eye.*

She sits next to me. She has a wide elastic band twisted around her wrist, and she pulls it off, uses it to tie back her hair. She's older than me, just by a year, but her skin is so light and pretty. She doesn't show her age at all. Every time I look at her, it makes me feel tired.

"It's been almost six months," she says. "Don't you think it's time?"

"He doesn't have anything to do with them. I just . . ." I shake my head. "I don't see the point."

"You are an asshole, Stacey. A total asshole." She points her finger at me like she's being all emphatic. "This guy is serious about you. You encourage it, but then you turn around and keep him at arm's length." She shakes her head. "That's kind of shitty, Stacey."

"Oh, fuck you," I say, but I say it in a soft tone, not really like *Fuck you*, just like *You're wrong*.

"Seriously, Stacey." She gives me this really tough mom expression. "Bring him over and act like a decent person."

SEPTEMBER

I MAKE PHILLIP drive over separately, and we get there before him. He brings a six-pack of craft beer that Todd likes, and it's perfect because it's what I told him to do. I take him out to the backyard, and Todd is at the grill. It smells like smoke. It smells like burning meat.

"You must be Phillip," Todd says, shifting his tongs into his left hand and holding out his right, "and you brought beer? Nice! Welcome to the family." He winks at me. "I got a brat right here with your name on it, Stacey. You like 'em a little charred?" I just roll my eyes, but I love Todd.

The glass door slides open, and Jenny steps out. She'd gone downstairs to get a bottle of chilled white from the bar. "Hi!" she says brightly, and I can tell she's giving Phillip this whole body scan, but she's pretty subtle with it. Jenny's always been slick.

The kids are all up in the playhouse, and they won't come down until they run out of potato chips, so Jenny decides she can speak freely. "So you're the guy keeping my little sister so busy?"

I think Phillip almost blushes. He's still standing there, holding that stupid six-pack of beer. It's kind of awkward, really. If I were him, I'd want to leave.

"Here," I say, taking the beer from him. I pull one out and grab the opener that Todd keeps hanging from his grill. I pop the top off and hand the bottle to Phillip. "You're going to need this."

"Hot dogs!" Todd yells in the direction of the playhouse, and the kids all echo him in squeals.

Jenny's fixing their plates because of course she already knows who wants ketchup, who wants mustard, who wants the hot dog but doesn't want the bun.

"Wash your hands," I say when the boys are close enough, and Stevie holds his up like, *They're not even dirty.* They don't argue though, they just open the door and head in.

When they come back out, I hold my hand out toward Phillip and say, "And this is Dr. Keller."

He squats down in front of them. "You can call me Phillip," he says.

"Hi," Ben says. He takes his plate from Jenny and holds it in both hands. He looks up at me. "Can we eat in the playhouse?"

"No." I shake my head. "Crumbs and ants."

Ben rolls his eyes and heads for the picnic table.

"What kind of doctor are you?" Stevie says.

"Oh, uh, I help people with allergies."

Stevie frowns.

"He means hospital or school," I say. "Dr. Keller is a medical doctor, sweetie."

"But you can call me Phillip," he says again.

"Okay," Stevie says as Jenny hands him his plate.

Phillip stands back up. "I think that's one of the first things you asked me too."

"We need to know if you can perform CPR or you just really know your way around a library."

"And the library's more important," he says.

"Obviously."

Jenny gets her three settled at the table and comes back to stand by us. "So I have been bugging Stacey for the longest time about bringing you over," she says to Phillip.

"Great," he says. "No pressure then?"

"Actually, I have this rash," Todd says, turning half around. "Maybe you've got an ointment or something?"

"He's joking," I say.

Todd's trying, but he can't keep a straight face. "It's on my ass. You want to look at it?"

"Oh my god, you are such an embarrassment." Jenny smacks him on the arm.

Phillip laughs and takes a sip of his beer. "That's not really my specialty," he says. "But I'll get you a referral."

When we leave, Jenny hugs me, and she whispers in my ear. "I love him," she says. "He fits right in."

OCTOBER

I'M IN THE PICK-UP LINE in front of the boys' school when the phone rings.

"Come to New York with me next week," Sarah says. "John's busy, and I hate traveling alone." Some movie she shot last year is coming out, and she has to do the morning and late-night shows.

"I can't," I say. "I just got home. I had that conference in Chicago."

It was nothing, like a fifty-minute panel, and I barely even had to talk, but then Tommy wanted to take me to dinner and buy me drinks and kiss in the elevator, and after two nights of that, I felt completely unwound. Though it's not the nights, really, that get to me. It's the mornings, how the mornings drift into afternoons. *What's with you?* he said. *You're so fucking down.* And I shrugged and said, *I don't know. Maybe I'm feeling guilty?* But Tommy didn't really want to hear it. He laughed after a minute though, and he said, *You should, you know. I hope you feel like shit.*

Sarah sighs. "I love that you'll go places with Tommy, but not with me. Come on, Stacey. It's just for a few days."

"I would, really, but I've got parent-teacher conferences next week."

I have a feeling I'm going to be hearing a lot of *concerns*. Last week Ben's teacher e-mailed to ask if I'd gotten her notes about his missing assignments. I haven't seen any of these notes in his backpack, but Ben swears he didn't throw them away.

Sarah makes this annoyed groan. "Now I'm just going to feel stressed-out."

"Pack your Xanax," I say, and she says, "I was going to."

I hear the bell ring and turn to watch the kids filing out of the building. Stevie's classroom is toward the front of the school, so he's always in the first group. When he spots the car, he waves.

"Well, maybe I'll just stop on the way back to see you."

Sarah here? I think that could be a mess. But I say, "I would love it."

"And then I can meet this Phillip," she says. "We'll have dinner."

I think about Phillip in the room with Sarah's big mouth, and I say, "No fucking way."

The conferences are even worse than I expected. Stevie, it turns out, has drawn a family portrait that is mostly just him and Ben and Jenny. There's an arrow pointing to the house that reads, *Mommy*.

"When I asked him who was in the picture, he added that label. He said you were inside," his teacher says, and she gives me this concerned look. At least he didn't draw Michael floating over everyone in the sky.

Ben is not drawing pictures, but he is failing math. *Of course he is,* I want to say. I can barely count. How am I supposed to help with his homework?

When I get home, I call Tommy, and I say, "I think I broke my kids."

"This doesn't surprise me, honey. You are determined to break shit."

"I'm being serious," I say, and I tell him about the picture, the math.

"Who needs math?" Tommy says. "We'll hire someone to do his math. It's not like he wants to be an architect." He wants to be a football player, and Tommy knows this. Neither of us believes it will work out. The kid is as scared of the ball as he is of the other players, but he reads a lot of football books, and they seem to make him happy.

I sit on the edge of the couch, fold my body down against my knees. "And what about Stevie?" I say. "With the unavailable mother?"

"You're not unavailable. You're just trying to figure things out. But how lucky is he that he has Jenny? That's the thing about family, Stace. It means you don't have just one person to lean on. He's fine. I promise. Honestly, that picture says more about you."

"Great. That's just perfect."

"What? We already knew you were a mess. This sounds like good news."

I offer to pick Sarah up at the airport, but it's a charter flight, and she says it's just as easy for them to send a car. She'll meet me at the hotel, she says. She's only staying the night. I almost don't recognize her when I walk in. She's known for her long blond hair, but she's spun it up into this messy bun. And she's got glasses on. I don't think she needs them. She's wearing jeans and a loose beige sweater. She's still beautiful though. She has to work hard to dull it down.

She jumps up and runs over to hug me, and she says, "Stacey, hi!"

but she does not use her bell voice. She's almost doing an accent. I can't quite place it, but it's definitely not her.

"Jesus, do people ever recognize you?"

She shakes her head. "Only in L.A. No one would think to look for me here."

"How do you feel about sushi?" I say. "There's a place close by. We can walk."

She squints behind the glasses. "Fish in the middle of the country? Is that even safe?"

"How would I know?" I say. "I don't eat fish."

She laughs and says, "Let's do it."

We walk arm in arm to the restaurant. "I talked to Tommy this morning," she says. "He said to tell you hi."

"Oh?" I say. "How is he?"

She sighs. "I don't know. He seems particularly gloomy. I guess he tends to get like this when a project is winding down. I don't know that he has anything new lined up. John sent him the script for this action movie he's involved with, but Tommy turned it down."

"That was John's?" I say, and Sarah frowns.

"Tommy tell you about it?"

"He mentioned it, yeah. In Chicago."

I'm not going to say that I spent Saturday morning reading the script in Tommy's bed. *This isn't very good,* I said. He was just coming out of the shower, and he crawled in beside me, laid his head on my stomach, and said, *Yeah, I know.*

I call Jenny in the morning. "Why don't you guys come for dinner?"

She seems surprised.

"Are you inviting Phillip?" she says, and she's got that lilt in her voice.

"I don't think so," I say. "But I'll make something good. I'll make that Tuscan bean soup." It's cold. It's good soup weather, and I know it's one of Todd's favorites.

"Okay," she says, "yeah. I'll bring the wine." And I think, *Perfect,* because I've drunk all mine. I don't want to have to go to the store.

The kids run downstairs to the playroom. They've got a new video game, and they want to show it off. The soup is ready, but I've just stuck the whole pot in the oven to keep it warm. The kids need time to burn off some energy, and I need a glass of wine to settle my nerves.

"Open this?" I say to Todd, and I hand him the wine and nod toward the shelf where the corkscrew is.

"Sure," he says. "Shit, that's an expensive bottle of scotch."

"Help yourself," I say.

"No, I'd be afraid to. That's like liquid gold."

I grab the bottle and an orange-juice glass and pour a healthy ounce or two. "It's like drinking lighter fluid," I say. "Seriously, I don't want it."

"Really?" Todd says, and I can tell he really wants to try it, so I push it into his hand. "But first," I say, "open that wine."

We sit in the living room, and I try to look relaxed. I'm all twisted up though. My spine is in knots. I take a swig of the wine. I hope it helps.

"What's the matter?" Jenny says, and I just smile, shake my head. "I'm fine," I say.

"This scotch is really something."

I turn toward Todd. "I know, right? I don't really like the taste of it, but it packs a punch."

"Where'd you even find it?"

I shrug. "I don't know. Tommy sent it."

"Oh shit, this is a gift?" Todd looks back at the glass like it makes him uncomfortable.

"No, really, it's more like a joke." I wave my hand like, *It's nothing,* because to Tommy it really isn't. It's no big deal.

"That's a hell of a gag gift," Jenny says.

"More like a white elephant. I gave myself a pretty nasty scotch hangover. Tommy thinks he's hilarious."

Jenny frowns a little. I don't love her expression.

I take a deep breath because I'm trying to work up to something. "Stevie drew a picture of his family in school, and he forgot to put me in it."

"What?" she says, and she scoots forward a little on the couch.

"Yup," I say. "It's him and Ben, and you can tell it's Ben because he's holding a football, and you, and you're smiling, and then there's a house in the background, and I guess he forgot to draw me because he just drew an arrow and said, 'Mommy's inside.'"

Todd says, "Shit," and I just look at him like, *Yeah,* but Jenny scoots over to hug me.

"It's just 'cause they're spending so much time at our house. I bet it doesn't mean anything."

"I don't know," I say. Jenny looks like she feels a little guilty, so I hug her back, and I say, "I'm not mad or anything, I'm just worried."

"I think the boys are doing fine," Todd says. "I bet it's just all the traveling you do."

"Yeah, that's what Tommy said. Actually, he said, 'You're a disaster, Stace, but your kids seem fine.'"

"What does Phillip think?" Jenny asks.

"I don't really talk to Phillip about the boys." Jenny gets this look on her face like she just caught me in a lie or something, and I say, "I'm serious, Jen. I'm not ready for someone to get all involved with my kids."

"Okay. Okay," she says. She puts her hand up like she's actually going to be willing to drop it.

"I should probably call them up for dinner," I say. Tomorrow's a school day. They can't stay up all night.

NOVEMBER

OMAHA HAS this little film festival in November, and Tommy wants to come. The movie won't be released until December, but he says he'll bring a trailer, and we'll do some kind of Q&A.

"You don't want to come to Omaha," I'd said when he first brought it up. I mean, it's more of an arts town. It's nothing like L.A.

He didn't listen of course, and now I have an envelope in my hands with extra passes for Jenny and Todd, and I feel like this is a collision I can't let happen. I can already see everything spiraling out. *What about Phillip?* she'll say. *Why don't we bring Phillip?*

"I just got the schedule," I say when I call her, "for this festival thing. I don't think you want to come."

"What?"

"I'm going to have to be there for like ten hours and Tommy's actually got all these press calls scheduled that he'll be doing from the hotel room, so I'm just going to be hanging around waiting and then there's a short little Q&A and I don't know if we'll even have time for dinner or anything. I mean, you might get to meet Tommy, but probably not."

Bring your sister, he said. *I have a lot of questions.*

"I'm not coming for Tommy. I'm coming for you."

"Okay, but I won't even see you. I mean, I won't even know you're there."

"You sound like you don't want me there."

"No. That's not . . . I mean, I have the passes right here, and if you think it would be fun, then totally, you should go to the festival. I'm just saying, it doesn't really seem like something Todd would enjoy, but I'll give you the passes and if there's anything that sounds cool, you should go to it. You just probably won't get to see me much, so don't go as a favor to me. It's fine though. I can get a babysitter."

She sighs. "Don't get a sitter," she says. "They can spend the night at our house."

I walk into the hotel just after noon, and Daniel's waiting for me in the lobby. He's sitting on the couch, and he's got a pile of things stacked beside him. He jumps to his feet and hugs me, gripping my shoulders, pressing his cheek against my cheek. "Look what I have!" he says, pointing back. "Posters!"

He picks one up and unrolls it, turning it toward me. "This one is my favorite." It's Sarah, surrounded by shadows, and behind her is Tommy, but his eyes look cruel. "Someone from the festival is meeting me to get them. I should have sent them ahead, but the first batch were a mess. Fucking printers." He throws his hands up. "Anyway, I'll text Tommy. Tell him to meet us in the bar."

I glance over at the entrance, and it's not packed, but it's not exactly empty. I feel like it's a bad idea. I feel like Tommy appearing is going to cause a scene. But my nerves are on edge already and a drink sounds good.

Daniel seems to guess what I'm thinking. He pats my arm. "We can always leave. It's tonight you're gonna have to get ready for. Tonight's going to be a mob."

The trailer is spectacular. I haven't seen a clip since the rough cut, and this is completely new. It is not my book. It's something bigger, something more.

"How did you do that?" I whisper to Tommy, and he says, "Don't insult me. I promised you, didn't I?"

He's leaning close as he says this, his hand high on my back, tucked under my hair. I want to turn toward him, to ask, *Did you make that for me?* But then the lights come up, and I remember who I am and where we are. I remember everything.

I shift away. "I know people here," I say, under my breath.

It's late for dinner, but Tommy's hungry, and I haven't eaten all day. Daniel slips into a pub not far from the hotel and makes arrangements for a table in the back. It barely matters. Tommy is coming off six straight hours of adoration, and he can't seem to wipe it off. It's impossible not to look at him.

It's hard to order because the waitress is so busy fussing over Tommy. She's apparently seen everything he's ever done, even some seriously obscure shit, but we finally get our order in, and of course she comps it. I know Tommy's going to leave her some ridiculous tip.

I order a carrot dog, with no bun, and when she brings it, Daniel says, "Jesus, honey, what is that?" and Tommy wrinkles his nose.

"It's like a hot dog," I say. "They brine it." It comes with sauerkraut, which I like, and it goes well with vodka.

Tommy reaches across with his fork and takes a bite. He makes a face. He says, "That's not a hot dog."

I say, "Jesus, help yourself." And he says, "What? It's not like you were going to finish it."

And then we both look up because it's like we can feel someone walking toward us, and Tommy puts on his *I'd love to give you an autograph* face, but this time, it is not a pretty twenty-year-old girl. This time it's Phillip. Of course. He lives three blocks from here. It makes sense.

He says, "Stacey?" and I stand up and hug him. "Phillip," I say, and I try to sound happy. "Hi!"

Tommy says, "Oh shit, you're Phillip?" and he stands up and grabs him by the arm. "Hey, I've heard so much about you, man, good to meet you." He smiles a little wider than I'd like.

"And this is Daniel," I say, pointing to Daniel because I want him to not look at Tommy. Daniel waves. "And they are both in town for the film festival I was telling you about," I say, "which is totally exciting." I did tell him. I just neglected to mention Tommy.

Then our waitress comes back, and she's found someone to take a picture of her with Tommy, and Tommy says, "Of course," and steps away.

"I didn't realize you two were close," Phillip says kind of quietly.

I cross my arms over my chest. I say, "Tommy? Oh yeah, we're friends," and I give Phillip this really nice smile like, *Didn't I mention that?* But then Tommy comes back and as he walks behind me, he rests his hand on my back, and I can see that Phillip notices.

"Sorry," Tommy says. "It's like you really don't have any fucking celebrities around here."

"Just Buffett," I say, and Tommy laughs. He sits back down and says to Phillip, "Pull up a chair."

What do you think you're doing? I think, but I can't say anything. I can't even say it with my eyes. Phillip is watching me way too closely.

"I'm with people," Phillip says. "We were just leaving," and he leans over and kisses me on the cheek. "I'll call you later."

When he leaves, Tommy says, "Jesus, that poor bastard." He smiles though. He seems kind of happy about it.

Daniel shakes his head. "Fucking humiliating."

I take a big sip of my vodka, and I say, "What?"

"Stace, come on, what are you doing with this guy?"

"What? I like him."

"Uh-huh. You clearly like him a ton, honey," Daniel says. "We can tell 'cause you're like super genuine with him, totally at ease." He rolls his eyes.

"It was painful to watch," Tommy says. "I mean, I'm all for making friends, honey, but then have the decency to cut them loose."

"You're worse than Tommy," Daniel says.

"Yeah." Tommy nods. "You're worse than me." He reaches across to my plate again, takes a bite of the sauerkraut. "I can't believe I covered for you. I mean, it would have been a kindness to be like 'Hey, I'm Tommy. Totally fucking your girlfriend.'"

"Not today," I say, and Tommy just laughs.

"Look, I get that this guy is like a pet who comes when you call him and sits and stays and all of that, but that's not what you want, is it? That's not what you need."

"Fuck you," I say, and Tommy says, "You always do, baby. You always do."

"Jesus Christ," Daniel says. "Would you two stop? I don't know if you realize there's another actual person here, and he doesn't want to hear this shit."

I don't say anything more. I just look at Tommy and I think, *I hate you*. I know that he can see it, but he doesn't care.

When we get back to the hotel, I gesture toward the parking garage. "It's late," I say. "I'd better go."

Tommy laughs. He says, "You're not still pissed about dinner? Come on, I'll make it up to you. Let's get a drink."

"I've already had enough," I say.

"So you obviously can't drive," he says. He holds his hand out. "Come on. At least one."

The bar in the lobby is packed. I say, "I'm not going in there."

Tommy takes my arm like he's trying to steady me. I do feel like I'm losing my shit. He says, "It's fine, we'll have something sent up," and he steers me toward the elevator. People are watching, but he just positions himself a little in front of me, and I duck my head. Once the doors slide closed, I lean back and brace my hands on the rail. I feel like I can almost breathe. Tommy slides his arm around me. "Relax," he says. "You know I've got you." It really doesn't help.

When we get to Tommy's suite, Daniel picks up the phone and tells them to send up a bottle of vodka, well chilled. "I've got to head to bed," he says when he hangs up. "One of us"—he looks at Tommy—"never gets a day off." He crosses the room and kisses me on the forehead, and as he pulls back he gives me this worried frown. I smile back at him.

When the vodka comes, Tommy hands me a glass and sits in the chair across from me. He says, "I know you don't love this kind of shit, Stace, but you have to get used to it. It's going to get much bigger. Wait until you get to L.A."

I just sigh, put my hand over my face. "You don't need me for all of this, Tommy. Really. I don't need to come out."

"I want you there." He says it like it's final, like he gets the last say. "This is your baby. You need to see it through."

I don't answer, and I don't look at him either. Sometimes it's bad enough just knowing he's there.

"How's Sadie?" I say, because I'm interested, but also because I want to change the subject.

"Better. Her mom's got her in New York." He makes a dismissive face. "She's doing some off-off-Broadway thing, but I think the change is probably good for Sadie." He shrugs. "She's gained a little weight back anyway."

"Not that you would ever say that."

"No! Fuck no. I'm not an idiot." He laughs, but it's a sad laugh. "I don't say a goddamn word."

We don't stay up much later. He's got an early flight, and I feel completely frayed. I feel like I'm unraveling. I set our glasses on the bar in the corner, and as I walk back past the chair he's in, he stretches his arm out and catches me by the waist, pulling me onto his lap. He slips one hand up the back of my shirt, unhooking my bra, and I let him, but I say, "Tommy."

"I fly out early," he says, and he pulls my mouth against his. "I don't have time for all the sweet talk, but you know how I feel about you."

I laugh then, turn my head. "Do I?" I say. I drop one foot to the floor and lean my weight into it, standing up.

Tommy grabs my wrist. "Where you going?"

I just shake my head, and Tommy lets go. He drops his head back, stares at the ceiling. "Jesus, Stacey, what is it you want from me?"

"I don't want anything from you," I say, turning away. I reach back to refasten my bra. "Hasn't that always been the point?"

"What is that supposed to mean?"

I turn to face him, fold my arms across my chest. "What could I possibly want from you, Tommy? A reputation? Some confused shit I have to explain to my kids? I don't know." I wave my hand back and forth between us. "I mean, this is fun, but—"

"You leaving then?" he says abruptly, cutting me off.

I nod. I say, "Yes."

"Good," he says. "Great. That's just fucking great." He rubs one hand over his face. He shakes his head and stands up. "Call a cab." He pulls his phone from his pocket and throws it at me. I turn to dodge it, but it hits my arm.

I hold my hand over the spot and look him straight in the eye. "I'll just walk," I say slowly because Phillip lives close and Tommy knows that.

He moves toward me, his jaw hard, and I stumble backwards, hitting the wall. Tommy holds me there, one arm around my back, pressing my arms into the wall behind me. "Don't fuck with me," he says, and he leans into me a little harder, his elbow digging against my biceps. I feel my eyes starting to burn, and I close them fast. I say, "Tommy, you're hurting me."

"Not yet," he says, but he shifts his weight just enough that I can pull my arms free, and he leans down, kissing my neck. He catches at my skin with his teeth.

"Tommy," I say, my voice softening. I slide the fingers of one hand along the back of his neck, but then he bites me, hard, and I have to twist both hands through his hair to get him off.

"Jesus, Tommy, what the fuck?"

He takes two steps back and just stares at me for a minute, his mouth open, his tongue pressing into the corner of it. He raises his hand, pointing one finger toward me. "I don't know, honey. That's gonna leave a mark. I mean, I like the way it looks on you, but what's your boyfriend gonna say?"

"That you're a sick fucking bastard?"

"Nah," he says. "That's what he'll say about you."

"Fuck you," I say, pushing past him, but he grabs my wrist, dragging me toward him.

"Tommy, let go."

"What?" he says. "You don't like it?" And he doesn't relax his fingers. He pins my arm behind my back, pulling me close. He rubs his lips along my jaw.

I say, "Would you stop?" I twist my chin to push his mouth away, but he winds one hand into my hair, pulling my head back hard. I brace my free hand on his chest and push him. "That fucking hurts!"

"Does it?" he says, but he lets go. He takes a few steps back until he bumps into the arm of the couch. He sits against it, closes his eyes, rubs his fingers across his brow.

I press my lips together, try to catch my breath. I hold my palm against the dull ache in my neck, and I keep my eyes on Tommy.

When he looks up at me, he frowns, holds out one hand. "Stace."

"What the fuck was that?" I say, my voice barely more than a whisper.

"Baby, come on." He tilts his head, lifts both his arms to me. He looks as sincere as I've ever seen him, but he's a hell of an actor, really. "Don't try to put this on me. You have been throwing this guy in my face for months, and I think I've been very fucking cool about it. Haven't I?"

"I'm not throwing anything in your face. I'm trying to be in a relationship."

"No." He waves one hand back and forth between us. "This right here. This is the relationship you're in."

"This?" I laugh. "This isn't a relationship, Tommy."

He stands up and moves toward me, and I don't move away. I let him wrap his hands around my face, lean his head against mine.

"It's been almost two years. What the fuck do you think it is?"

I don't know. I don't know. I don't know.

I shake my head, rest my forehead against his chin.

"You can't see him anymore. This guy is out."

I laugh. I say, "That's rich, coming from you."

"Yeah, honey, but you don't care what I do." Tommy leans back far enough to look me in the eye. He pushes my hair back behind my ear, rests his hand on my cheek. "I care. Okay? I hate it."

I lean into him, tuck my nose against his neck, and for a few seconds, I just breathe and breathe and breathe. I press my lips to his skin.

"There she is," he says. "There's my girl."

He kisses me like he means it, working his fingers deep in my hair, and I almost say *Yes.* But then Tommy pulls his mouth away, rubs it along my jaw, kisses my ear, and he says, "From now on, what you do on the side, you need to keep on the side. I don't want to hear about this shit."

I think, *What?* I think, *What are you saying?* I think, *This is not what I wanted, this is not what I wanted, this is not what I want.* But Tommy's already got me by the hands, and he's pulling me toward the bedroom, and I think, *Maybe it's close enough,* even though, really, I know that it isn't. Tommy just kicks the door closed with his foot, and he's leading me toward the bed. He pulls my shirt up over my arms, and he drops down and presses his mouth against my stomach. He slides his fingers to the button of my jeans. I say, "Tommy," but he just pushes me back onto the bed and leans over me, and he's kissing me across my face, and he whispers, "Stacey. Honey. Baby. I really need you to shut up."

I don't sleep for a long time. I just lie there in the dark, clenching my teeth. I can hear Tommy breathing, and he has his arm thrown over me, his hand cupping my breast. I must fall asleep at some point, and when I wake in the morning, it's still dark out, and Tommy is already gone. I think, *Of course.* I think, *I knew it,* and I slide out of bed to pull on my clothes. There's a note on top of my bag that says, *Didn't want to wake you. Call later.* Which is bullshit because it doesn't exactly say which direction the phone is supposed to ring. I just sit on the edge of the bed with my head in my hands for a long time. I don't even have it in me to stand up and walk away.

It is a long day. The longest. When the boys are finally in bed, I pick up the phone, and of course I have no messages. I knew that I wouldn't. I think about calling Tommy, but I would never do that. I call Phillip instead.

"Hey," I say when he picks up. "Sorry for calling so late."

"It's fine," he says, but he sounds a little off. "How was your festival thing?"

"Oh, I think it was good," I say, and I shrug even though he can't see me. "All that promotion stuff isn't really my thing." I wait a second. I try to pause my way off of the subject. I say, "I was hoping you'd want to come over."

He says, "I can't, Stacey, I have an early morning."

I suck my lips in and chew on them. He's never turned me down before. I say, "Maybe this weekend then."

He says, "Yeah. I'll call you." I think he's just going to hang up then, but he says, "Sweet dreams, okay?" and I nod like he's right there in front of me. I wish he was right there in front of me. I say, "Yeah, you too."

Tommy doesn't call for two days. When he does, it's late in the morning. I can't bring myself to answer, and I don't want to call him back. He texts, *Hello? What the fuck?* in the afternoon, but I just reply, *Super busy. Call soon.* My phone rings again while I'm making the boys dinner. I'm making grilled cheese because they begged for it, and I don't feel like I can eat anyway.

"Hey," I say, but I don't think I sound happy. I'm not sure what to do with my voice.

"What is going on with you?"

"Nothing. I'm fine," I say, but it sounds like I'm actually pretty shitty, and I shake my head like I can make myself stop. I can't though.

I'm way out in the deep end, and I know it. I know it only gets worse from here.

He sighs. He says, "Is this because of the other morning? Because it was really early, Stace."

"No." I flip the first sandwich over, and it looks like I've already burned it. It looks like I'm going to be starting over.

"Okay. If you're gonna be this moody, I'll just call you later."

I take a deep breath, and I say, "I'd rather you didn't."

"Jesus Christ, Stacey." He sighs again. "I mean, you do hear how crazy you sound?"

"I'm not crazy, Tommy. I'm just tired of this."

"You're tired of what?" The tone in his voice makes me tighten my fingers around the spatula, press my teeth together. "All the shit I do for you?"

"You mean all the shit you force on me?"

"Oh, I'm so fucking sorry, Stacey." He laughs, but it isn't a nice laugh. "For all the airfare, and the dinners, and the wine, and fucking making you successful. I'm such an asshole for giving you all of that. Do you even hear yourself?"

I shake my head, chew on my lip. "I never asked you for anything."

"You've never had to. Because I give you everything." He's yelling now, and my eyes are stinging, but I can't tell if it's from him or the smoke coming off the griddle. "Everything you want, I just fucking give it to you."

"What makes you think you know what I want?" I say, but I wish I hadn't because he says, "Then tell me what you want, Stacey, because I'm getting tired of guessing."

"Jesus, Tommy, look, I just . . . I'm trying to figure out my life here."

"Bullshit. You're the same fucking mess you've always been."

"Don't," I say.

"Tell me how you're figuring shit out, Stacey. What is it you think you're getting a handle on? I would love to fucking know."

"How am I supposed to get a handle on anything with you sticking your hands in it all the time? That's the whole point, Tommy. You need to stay the fuck out of my life."

He doesn't answer, and honestly, I don't like it. I feel like taking it all back, but I know it's too late for that, so I try at least to get the edge out of my voice, and I laugh a little like I think at the end of this, we're still going to be friends. "Tommy, come on, I know you. I know how you are."

"Yeah? How is that?" he says, and the way he says it, it sounds like a trap, but I can't help myself. I walk right fucking into it.

"Are you kidding? Because every time I turn around, you're fucking someone else. And you know what, that's fine. I don't care, but I'm not twenty-two anymore. I can't stay mixed up in this shit. I'm not interested in being another way for you to pass the time."

For a minute, he doesn't say anything. It feels like forever. And then he says, "I think you're a little confused, Stacey. That sounds a lot more like how you treat your little doctor friend."

And I just say, "Fuck you," but I say it like, *I hate you.* I say it like, *I hope you fucking die.*

"You know what, honey? I think I'll pass. 'Cause you're a sweet little ride, but you ain't worth the fuckin' crazy."

And he hangs up and I think, *This is just what I expected, this is exactly how I knew it would be.*

I set my phone down on the counter, and I switch the knob on the stove to off. I leave the sandwiches on the griddle and set the spatula down on an empty plate, and then I sit down in the middle of the floor and put my head between my knees, and I cry.

"I bought you a Tofurky," Jenny announces when I pick up the phone. "But you might want to cook it at your house. There probably won't be any room in our oven." We always do Thanksgiving at Jenny's because Todd is serious about his bird, and I won't let him bring that shit into my kitchen.

"Yeah, okay," I say. I haven't really been thinking about the holidays. I've been trying not to think much at all. I spent most of the morning on the treadmill, and I'm fucking wiped out.

"Are you bringing Phillip?" she says.

"I don't know." He did come over on the weekend, after the kids were in bed, but he was kind of uptight. We just watched a movie, and then he left. "I'll call him," I say.

"I think it would be good."

I think, *What the hell would you know, Jenny?* but she wouldn't know anything. It's not really her fault.

Phillip doesn't pick up, but that doesn't mean anything. I figure he's probably with a patient, so I leave a message. I say, "What are you doing for Thanksgiving?" Honestly, he takes forever to call me back. I'm almost putting the boys to bed.

"Where have you been all day?" I say when he answers.

"I had a dinner," he says, and I say, "With who?"

He actually kind of laughs. He says, "I didn't think we had to tell each other those things, Stacey."

Shit, I think, but I just say, "Hey, you're not being fair."

"I think I could say the same to you."

"Phillip," I say, "is this about the night of the festival?" I say it like it's a genuine question, like I might be confused.

"Well, I was surprised to see you there," he says. I can almost hear him pressing his lips together in some thin, judgmental line.

"But that was work." I try to keep my voice like this is all coming as a total surprise.

"Stacey," he says, "if I was going to be spending time with a woman who had a reputation like his, I would have enough respect to tell you."

"I think it's really unfair that you're holding me accountable for his reputation. I think that, frankly, it's bullshit that I have to pay for his mistakes." Because it is bullshit, and I'm really tired of paying for Tommy's mistakes.

"Well, you certainly looked cozy, in any case."

"I've known him for two years, Phillip. And if you didn't notice, our friend Daniel was there. Are you going to accuse me of having sex with him too?"

"I didn't accuse you of having sex with anyone, Stacey." Now he's the one that sounds surprised. I'm thinking I maybe shouldn't have planted that seed, but now I'm going to have to play it out.

"Well you might as well. Clearly you think I'd be easily seduced." Which, obviously, I am. I could kick myself for being so easy.

"Now you're putting words in my mouth. I just felt like it was disrespectful."

"And I think you're being disrespectful now. You know, I don't think Thanksgiving would be such a good idea."

"Fine, I'm sure you're right," he says, and I think, *Yeah, I usually am,* but then he says, "Maybe we shouldn't see each other at all for a while."

————

Sadie calls me in a panic late Wednesday night. She says she's vegan now, but Tommy's threatening to make her eat turkey, and even the sweet potatoes are going to have marshmallows and what the hell is she going to do?

"Honey, when did you turn vegan?" I say, and really, it is pretty obvious.

"God, Stacey, I thought you of all people would understand."

"No, I totally get it," I say. "I think it's great. But I think you can see how maybe this would make your dad a little worried."

"Because I care about the planet? Because I don't believe in torturing animals?"

"Because you just got out of an eating-disorder clinic and if you're not careful, he's going to send you back." I say this pretty quickly, and then I feel a little bad because, really, it does sound harsh. "Look, I know this isn't about that, and really, I think this is a positive move that you're thinking differently about food and how you handle your body, but you know, your dad's got to be a little nervous."

She doesn't say anything. She's too busy sniffling and crying.

"Look," I say. "You can't be so focused on saying no. No turkey, no marshmallows, no bread. Tommy's not ever going to take that well. You've got to put a different spin on it. Just sit him down and give him a list, say, 'Dad, here are all of the things I would like to have instead,' and I promise, honey, he'll give them to you."

"You really think so?"

"Yes, Sadie, I do. But here's the thing, honey, you're actually going to have to eat it then. You can't push it around on your plate and act like you're full, or he will pack you up and ship you back."

"Can you talk to him?" she says, and I say, "No." I know she's going to want to ask why. I know she's going to feed me some shit like, *He always listens to you,* but I just can't even take it. I can't even have this discussion with her, so I say, "Really, if you want him to start respecting you, you're going to have to do this yourself. He loves you, but he's not going to trust you if you try to run this through me."

She says, "Fine," but then she cries a little more, and I sit on the phone with her for a long time, and I think, *How the fuck did I get here?*

The boys and I make two pies, one pumpkin and one chocolate cream, because *No one really likes pumpkin,* Stevie said, and Ben said, *Yeah, but it's a tradition.*

Todd likes pumpkin. I wonder if Phillip does too. Not that he'll be there. Though I keep feeling surprised that he hasn't called. We fought on Monday, and now it's Thursday morning, so he's not going to call.

"Are we making whipped cream, or do we have whipped cream in a can?" Stevie says.

"We're making it," I say, and he says, "Oh."

He likes the kind in the can because it's sweeter and thick.

"We can put a little sugar in it," I say.

He jumps off the stool and opens the pantry.

"You want to set the mixer up, Ben?"

He shrugs.

"Benny, what's the matter?" I say.

"Nothing." He hooks the whisk into the mixer, snaps on the bowl. "Is your boyfriend coming?" he says.

"You mean Dr. Keller? Phillip?" I say. "No."

"Good," he says, but then he tilts his head to the side. "I mean, there might not be enough pie."

"You don't like him?" I say.

"I don't care," Ben says. "He's fine, I guess."

Stevie sets the sugar on the counter. "I think he's nice," he says.

The timer beeps behind me and I open the oven, stick a knife in the center of the pumpkin pie. It doesn't come out clean.

"Just a few more minutes," I say, turning around.

"Can we put vanilla in too?" Ben nods toward the mixer.

"In the whipped cream?" I say. "Sure."

"So what's Phillip doing that he couldn't come?" Jenny asks as she pours me a glass of wine. I'd texted her not to expect him, but we haven't really had time to talk. Or I haven't. Or I've been careful about staying busy.

"I don't know," I say, taking the glass, and then, because I'm too tired to bother, I say, "We're kind of fighting."

"What? What about?"

I try to wave my hand dismissively, but it doesn't come out right. Even I don't believe it. "He ran into me and Tommy after the festival and he just, I don't know, he didn't like it." I take a sip of the wine. I think, *I hope she has another bottle of this. I hope she has like six.*

"He didn't know Tommy was going to be here, did he?" She gives me a look like, *You little shit.*

"Not so much, no." I sigh.

"Stacey," she says, and she's giving me her stern voice, her angry mom stare. "You have been dating him for almost a year. That is serious.

That is a relationship. And if you can't start to act like it, then you should let him move on."

"Yeah, that's what I hear."

"From Tommy?"

"What?"

"Do you hear that from Tommy?" she says again. "Because it seems like he's the only one you listen to, or talk to, or have room for in your life. And frankly, I'm not sure you have room for Phillip while Tommy's taking up so much space."

I just shake my head. "Can we maybe not talk about all this tonight?"

She presses her tongue into her cheek in this expression our mom always made when she was really, really pissed. "I guess you'd rather talk to Tommy about it instead."

I say, "Yeah, that would be perfect. That would be really great."

Thank god Todd yells from the kitchen, "I am ready to carve this bird," because by now, my eyes are stinging, and when Jenny turns to go in the kitchen, I tip my head back and blink as fast as I can.

I pull it together and when I walk into the dining room, Ben's sitting in the spot next to mine. He smiles at me like things are good, like this is the best holiday he's had in a while.

"I'm not having turkey," he says. "I'll eat the Tofurky with you."

"I'm having a drumstick," Stevie says.

"Mmm, carnivore," Todd says, setting a leg on Stevie's plate.

"That's disgusting and too much food for you," I say, but Stevie just grins.

He doesn't even like turkey that much. He just likes the drumsticks. They remind him of Disneyland.

———————

Daniel calls me Saturday after Thanksgiving, and when I pick up he just says, "Hey, sweetie," but his voice says, *I'm sorry you're a mess.*

I shut my eyes really tightly. "What's up?" I say, making my voice sound totally fine.

"Honey, don't bother. I already know what went down."

"It's nothing. It's no big deal," I say, and I use my nails to pinch the inside of my right wrist.

"Really? Because it's a nightmare here. Stacey, he is so pissed."

I take a deep breath and blow it out. I know Daniel can probably hear it.

"Look, honey, about next week . . ."

The premiere. "Maybe I should just miss it."

"There's no way he'll let you out of it." He sighs. "Look, he wants me to put you up in a hotel, but you know, you could just call him."

"I'm not calling him."

"And he's not calling you, and it could go on like this forever. You sure you want that?"

"You're the one who said this thing with Tommy was a bad idea."

"I said it was a bad idea a year ago, two years ago. But you went ahead and did it. And now you're in it, Stacey. You're in it, and you need to fix it. Just call him, honey. Just call him and apologize."

And then what? I think, but I already know the answer, which is basically nothing, so I say, "I can't."

DECEMBER

WHEN I GET TO LAX, I'm hoping to see Daniel. I'm hoping to see some kind of friendly face, but there's just someone at baggage claim with my name on a sign. He takes me to the hotel, and when I check in, the clerk gives me an itinerary. There's a reception event tonight, and tomorrow is the movie. Daniel has at least scribbled a note on the bottom that reads, *Sarah's already here. Call her.*

I've brought this tight sleeveless navy dress. It isn't short exactly, but it isn't long either. Not that it's cold out, but it is December, so I wear knee-high boots, and when I zip them over my calves, I am more held together. I know Tommy will not be alone, so I feel like I need that. I also feel like I need a little more bronzer, but I'm afraid of making a mess of myself, so I lay off.

I ride with Sarah and John to the restaurant. The whole place has been rented out, and it's packed with people I've never met, but there are some of the other actors, Jason, Joe, even Alan, whom I've barely seen in the past two years. Joe actually kisses me on the cheek. He says, "The buzz on this thing is good. I've been getting some nibbles. Think maybe you'd want to work with me again?"

I just laugh. "I haven't even had a drink yet, Joe. Maybe let's wait on that talk."

Sarah loops her arm through mine. "We are going to the bar," she says in this loud announcement type voice. I'm glad she's here, and I let her pull me away.

People are lined up along the bar. They're like two deep because of course it's free, but when they see that Sarah is Sarah, they let us through. I rest my foot on the brass rail, twist the heel of my shoe against it, study the scratches in the polished wood. Sarah says we're starting with tequila, and when the shots come, and I raise my head to drink it, I catch Tommy's reflection in the mirror. He's across the room. He has his arm around some girl.

"Lime?" Sarah says, but I don't even need it. I toss my head back and feel the warmth slide down my throat. Sarah whoops and says, "Let's have another," but I shake my head. I feel jittery. Light-headed.

Still, Sarah orders another round. We don't drink it though. We just carry it with us. As we move away from the bar, I see that John is talking to Tommy. John spots us, and he raises his arm up. He waves us over. I'm thinking, *I don't want to do this, I don't want to fucking do this,* but there's nothing I can say. We get close enough, and I know who the girl is. She is *the neighbor's wife.* She doesn't even have a name, but Tommy's got his arm draped across her shoulders, and she's just glowing. She wants to be seen.

"Ah, my god, my love," Sarah purrs. She holds her arms out to Tommy, and he lets go of the girl, steps forward to Sarah and tips her backwards in this dramatic kiss. And then she cries, "Not in front of my husband!" and we're all supposed to laugh. I'm sick of laughing at this shit.

Then Tommy lets her go, and he turns toward me and all the muscles in my back tense along my spine.

"Stacey." He smiles. "God, it's so good to see you, honey." He takes my hand. He kisses me on both cheeks.

I think, *You are such a fucking asshole,* but I smile. I say, "Yeah, this is great."

He nods toward my glass and says, "And I see you've already got your dinner."

I give him my very best smile, and I raise my glass to him. "Starving," I say, and he laughs like I've just said something delightful.

He says, "Yeah? You usually are."

Tommy is standing at the bar, waiting for his bourbon, resting his elbows against the wood, and I feel like this is ridiculous. This is just fucking stupid. I think, *It's just Tommy.* I think, *We can still be friends.*

I move to stand next to him, and I mimic his posture. I get the bartender's attention, and I order a shot. While I'm waiting, I turn toward Tommy and say, "Hey," and he turns his head just barely.

He says, "What?"

I twist my thumb under my fingers, press the nail against the soft pad of my ring finger. I smile. I smile really sweetly like this is all a joke. I say, "Tommy, sometimes people argue, and then if they're not complete assholes . . ."

The bartender sets down a fresh bourbon, and Tommy nods a thank-you. He takes a drink. Then he smiles at me. He looks me in the eye, and he smiles, and I feel my shoulders start to unknot.

"Stacey," he says, his voice soft, "this is not an argument. This is me not giving a fuck what you do."

He just stands there, holding his drink. He doesn't even have the decency to walk away. I just grab the back of my lip with my teeth, and I bite down until I taste a little blood. I look down at my hands, and I think, *I don't know what I'm doing here,* but I don't know where else to go. Then little miss fucking nameless walks up behind Tommy, and she slides her arms around his waist, and she says, "Hey," and she sounds all breathy and drunk. She says, "What's taking you so long? I'm getting lonely."

Tommy says, "Well, we wouldn't want that now, would we?" and he turns and kisses her real slow. He's got his hands around her face. Then the two of them walk away, and I just stand there. I think, *Of course.* I think, *Of course. Of course. Of course.*

So I get drunk, I get very drunk, much drunker than I should be. I blame Sarah, because she keeps me going, though it's not her fault really. She just thinks we're having fun. She introduces me to someone. I don't catch his name because it's loud, and I'm not really listening. What matters, anyway, is that he is tall and very, very good-looking. He has blue eyes, which I like better than green eyes, and I say this out loud. He's also young. Ridiculously so. He's nowhere near thirty. He has these long fingers, and he trails them along my wrist, and I totally let him. When I send him to the bar for another drink, I say, mostly to Sarah, "I think I will have that," and she says, "God, I wish my husband were dead." Then she slaps her hand over her mouth and says, "Oh shit, I'm so sorry," but we're both laughing. I think it's just the tequila.

When the boy comes back, because really, he's a baby, I say, "I keep forgetting your name," and he says, "What do you want to call me?"

and he says it really close in my ear. I say, "I don't want to call you anything. I just want you to take me home."

Sarah calls me first thing in the morning, and my head is pounding. I can feel my heart beating in my temple. "If you're alone," she says, "you should meet me for breakfast."

She's sitting poolside, which looks beautiful and inviting, even if it is too cold to swim. She has a full pot of coffee, and she's ordered me toast. "So?" she says, and I shrug.

A strand of her hair falls across her eyes, and she grabs it, tucks it behind her ear. I think we're the same age, but she's just so beautiful. It seems to come so easily too. I mean, she's eating a croissant.

"How was your night?" she says, and her mouth is almost twitching.

"I don't really remember," I say, though this isn't entirely true. I remember it was a little disappointing. He was rough, but not in a fun way, just in the sense that he didn't seem to understand how much pressure to put behind his hands. But whatever, he's young. I'm sure he's still learning.

Sarah frowns. "Seriously? You're giving me nothing?"

I take a bite of the toast. "What do you want to know?"

"Did you sleep with him?" and she kind of whispers. She sort of looks around to see if we're alone. It's adorable. I feel like I'm in college, and even though my head hurts, I feel better.

"What about that doctor?" she says.

"Phillip?" I say, and I shrug. "I think we broke up."

"You think?" she says. "How do you not know? You're either seeing someone or you're not." She makes a face like I'm an idiot, like it's always so simple.

In any case, he hasn't called me since the night we argued, so I guess I'm not.

John and I go in through the back to avoid the mob in front. From inside, we can see Sarah doing her red-carpet shtick. She looks beautiful, and she's wearing this simple red and black dress, but it is short, and she's showing off her legs. And she gets attention, quite a lot, stopping every few feet to answer questions, stand with her hand on one hip, now turn to the side. I almost say, *I don't know how she does it,* but actually I do. She drank a lot of champagne in the car on the way over, and I think she popped a Xanax before that. Still, it's nothing compared to when Tommy shows up. We can hear the screams for a good ten minutes before we see him. He acts like he loves it, and he walks the edge of the carpet, talking to fans, grabbing their hands. I think he poses for more fan photos than professional shots, and he kisses a lot of cheeks. When he catches up to Sarah, he puts his arm around her, and they perform this whole *Look at us, we're old friends* bit. Which of course they are, but they're miming it now, like, *Hey, it's so great to see you, it's amazing isn't it, how beautiful we are and how much we love each other.* I'm so sick of the act.

Tommy and Sarah are still making the rounds as the lights are dimmed, but John grabs my elbow to steer me toward our seats. I move a few spaces in, and he leaves a seat between us for Sarah, but when Sarah comes, she drops right into the aisle seat. I stand up to move closer to John, but then Tommy's standing at the end of our row. They both stand up to let him in, and then we're face-to-face for a second, though I can feel him not looking at me. I move a step backwards, and he sits in the next seat. I think, *Fuck,* and I look at Sarah, but she doesn't know anything, so she just smiles.

Tommy says, I guess to me because I'm the one sitting there, "I hope you like it." But I don't say anything. I don't even smile.

I do like it though. It's amazing and horrible and dark, and Sarah fills up the screen with this terrible ache. And Tommy is terrifying. He's so very, very cruel, and I don't even think it's familiar. I just think it's true.

When the credits start to roll, Tommy turns to look at me, and he says, "Well?" but then people start clapping, and everyone starts to stand. I have tears in my eyes. Sarah grabs my hand and squeezes it, and she kisses Tommy. She says, "Look at us, we did it. We pulled it off." She's holding on to both of us. We're inches apart.

In the lobby, there is champagne, and someone hands me a glass. There are too many people, and the press of them makes me unsteady. I feel myself moving a few steps from Sarah, from Tommy. I know the space will open up the farther I move from them, but there isn't anywhere I can go. Sarah keeps pulling me back, keeps asking for my attention. I don't know why she needs it when she has all these other eyes and hands, but she does. It's like she needs me to help her open a pocket of air. Between flirtations and fawning, she feeds me commentary on every person who comes close enough, every person who leaves. Then the person in front of us is Tommy's girl from last night, and I know she's just working her way past us to get to him. Her dark eyes are outlined in black, shadowed in a pale gray. Her lips are just barely reddened. They almost look naked, and her skin is flawless, unlined.

She moves away, and Sarah catches my eye, mouths, *Poor thing,* and she nods in Tommy's direction. It's terrible to watch. How he extricates himself, moves to take her hand from his arm where she's resting it. He kisses it like it could be anyone's. She starts to talk, and he leans in like he's listening, but he looks over her shoulder, he nods hellos, he fucking waves. The poor girl, she's holding her expression like it's been painted on. He shifts his weight away from her, lets her know she can step away now, and as she does, he turns back toward me, and I give him this look like, *You piece of shit.*

We're maybe ten feet apart, and he takes a step toward me. He says, "You have a problem, Stacey?"

I'm done. I'm just so done. I say, "You know what? I'm just a little sick of the show." Sarah's talking to someone important on the other side of me, but I see her stop. I see her turn her head. "This whole 'Tommy fucks a child actress,' I think we've all seen enough of that."

Tommy's still coming toward me and his jaw is tight, and he's almost whispering. "Oh, I'm so sorry. Is it hard for you to watch? Where's your little plaything from last night? He is not a doctor, by the way. He's too fucking young."

I put my hands up, and I say, "Fuck you," and I say it loud, and now there is space opening up around us, and people are turning to look.

He cocks his lower jaw out at an angle, narrows his eyes. "Thanks for the offer, honey, but I can think of better ways to pass the time."

I think, *Why are you doing this?* I think, *Why are you so fucking mean?* But I don't say anything. I wouldn't know what to say. I don't even know who I'm talking to.

"What's the matter, Stacey? You at a loss for words? You want me to write you a fucking script?"

"You're the actor, asshole. Here's Tommy DeMarco being charming. Here's Tommy DeMarco blowing off another girl. And isn't he gorgeous? Isn't he just fucking great? Your whole goddamn life is a fucking performance piece."

"Not all of it, honey," he says. "I think you're the one juggling all the roles, aren't you?" He's close now. He's got his finger in my face. "Why don't you go home and act like a good mother? Why don't you go act like some sweet little doctor's wife? Role of a lifetime, huh? You probably want to lock him down before he finds out what's in that pretty little fucked-up head of yours." He stands there, glaring at me, and everyone is staring, and for once I don't even care.

"I hate you." I say it quietly. I say it like I mean it.

He says, "Get the fuck out then," and he turns like he's looking for someone, and he yells, "Get her out. Get her fucking out."

"I don't want to be here anyway, Tommy. I never did."

But there's nowhere to go. Everyone's pressed in to watch, and we're stuck in this tight little circle. We're locked in.

I feel a hand wrap around my elbow, and I turn to see Sarah. "C'mon," she says, "let's go." She's all business now, pulling me out toward the back. A few people try to talk to her, but she just shakes her head. When the crowd thins enough, she pulls me even with her, locks my arm tight against her, and under her breath she says, "When were you going to tell me you've been fucking Tommy?" She doesn't wait for me to answer. She says, "This is a mess."

I duck my head. I feel sick.

We go out the back, and John is already there waiting with the limo. He holds the door open, and we slide in. The seats run in an L the length of the car, and I end up in the corner. Sarah's in front of me, and across from her is the bar. John sits next to me. He pats me awkwardly on the leg.

"Pour us a drink," Sarah says to him as the car pulls out. She's got her arms crossed tightly. She's pursed her lips. She turns her head like she doesn't want to look at me.

"Here." John hands her a flute of champagne, and she narrows her eyes at him. "What is this?" she says. "Are we celebrating?"

I drop my head into my hands. I don't even know what to say.

"Sarah," John starts, and he sounds reasonable, calm. "I'm not see-ing how this is all about you, so maybe you could bring it down a notch."

She sighs. "I know." She reaches out to grab my hand. "I just don't know what you were thinking."

"Oh, come on," John says. "It's Tommy. He's a very seductive man." He pats me on the back. "I know my night with Tommy really threw me for a loop too," he says, but he says it so straight that I barely hear him. It takes me a second to look up, and by then Sarah's laughing, and she says, "Oh, go to hell. Pour Stacey a glass too." Then she smiles at me and raises her glass and says, "Well, here's to fucking Tommy DeMarco."

There's a special entrance to the hotel. We get right into an elevator from the car. There's a man in it, like an actual operator, except that he's huge and more of a bouncer.

"Good evening, Ms. Nixon, Mr. Grim," he says, and he slides a pass card across a scanner and takes us all the way up. The doors slide open onto this enormous living room with ceilings that are at least two stories high. My room is just a few floors below, but it looks nothing like this. The room is full of flowers, all these ridiculous bouquets. Sarah clearly has a lot of admirers.

We step off, and Sarah immediately kicks off her shoes. She just leaves them by the door like someone will obviously pick them up, and I think, *Jesus, Sarah, you're just like my kids.*

"What are we drinking?" John says, walking to the bar.

I say, "What have you got?"

Sarah drops into one of the couches, curls her legs up beside her, and leans back against the armrest, her arm balanced just so. She looks like something out of a painting, and I don't think she means to, she just moves like this, so sure of her place in the world.

"So how did all of this happen?" she says.

"Really, Sarah, is it any of your business?" John says.

"Well, I'm sure Stacey wants to talk about it."

"If she's smart, she won't talk to you."

Sarah narrows her eyes at him and then turns to me. She pats the seat beside her on the couch.

I sit, but I don't lean back. I cross my left leg over and behind my right. I rest both elbows in my lap.

"Well?" she says.

"There's nothing to tell," I say, and I shake my head. John hands us each a glass of white wine. I take a sip. It's very dry, very crisp. "Thanks," I say.

Sarah is still just looking at me. She raises an eyebrow. I smile. "Fucking Tommy," she says.

John sits down across from us. "The question is," he says, and Sarah turns back to face him, "where do we go from here? How does it affect the movie?" Of course. He has a lot of money in this.

Sarah waves her hand. "Who cares? Tommy's always fucking somebody on a movie, and they always sell."

John gives me this look like, *Sorry. She's an asshole.* "The point is that it doesn't usually blow up like this. I mean, I've seen Tommy lose his cool, but not in public. This is different."

"I'm so sorry, John," I say. "I shouldn't have started that fight."

John makes a dismissive face. "Don't worry about it. Tommy deserves it. The guy's an asshole. I love him like a brother, but he's an asshole. We just, we need to think about how we can put more space between the two of you."

I say, "Yeah. You're probably right."

"You know what?" Sarah sits forward, her eyes wide. "I'm just going to call him. Have him come here, and we'll talk this out."

"No," John and I both say.

She's not letting go of it. She gets up and starts looking for her phone. She's got a little bounce in her step. "It'll be fine," she says. "What's a little sex between friends? You just need to clear the air."

But I feel like there's no air left inside the room. I feel like I'm in a vacuum, like there's no gravity, and I grip my knee tightly with both hands. When I open my mouth, I feel like there's nothing in my lungs to push the words out, but I say, "Sarah, if you call him, I will leave. I swear to god, I will leave."

She just stares at me for a minute, and she looks from me to John, but John is looking at the floor, and she looks back at me, and her mouth goes very round, and she just says, "Oh."

When I land in Omaha, I just get a cab, which is hard to do, because the whole fucking city only has like two. But I don't exactly have

Phillip to pick me up, and Jenny's got the kids, and I honestly don't want to see anyone anyway.

It snowed while I was gone, but they've cleared the streets. It's piled up along the curbs, and it's mixed with sand. Jenny had texted, *Snow day!* but there's nothing festive about this shit. It just looks cold and unclean. The cab drops me at the house, and I go straight to my car to go pick up the boys. I know Jenny is going to want to hear all about the premiere, and I've been prepping. I've picked out plenty of stories I can tell.

"The movie was so good," I say as she hands me a cup of tea. "I mean, they did an amazing job."

"This is so exciting. Tell me everything," she says.

"There was an awful lot of champagne," I say, "and some very nice dry white. And you should have seen the room that Sarah was in." I tell her about the elevator and how Sarah worked the red carpet. I tell her about the crowd at the restaurant party. I even tell her about the tequila and having breakfast by the pool, how beautiful the weather was, how the sun was so bright. I manage to talk for more than an hour, and I don't actually tell her much of anything. By the end of it, she really thinks I had a wonderful time.

The boys want to put up the tree, but to be honest, I don't know if I can. We skipped it the last two years and just went home to my parents'.

"Please, please, please," Ben says. "We'll do all the work."

They obviously can't drag the boxes up from the basement, so I have to do that part, and then I have to assemble the tree, but I'm sure they're going to do all the rest after that.

I'm watching them try to untangle a strand of lights when the doorbell rings.

Stevie yells, "Package!" and runs after Bear for the door, but then he calls back, "Mommy, it's Dr. Keller."

"Hi," he says when I open the door, and he's holding flowers, lilies, and they're quite lovely, so I let him in.

"I'm so sorry," he says. "I was stupid and jealous." When he puts his arms around me, I actually start to cry. "Stacey," he says.

He kisses me right in front of the boys, and I let him. I feel guilty and grateful too. I don't know which I feel more. I don't know that it matters.

"I went online and bought our tickets for this weekend," Jenny says when I pick up the phone. "We even got a sitter."

"I can take your kids. You don't need a sitter."

"You're coming with us. You and Phillip. We'll all see it together."

"Oh, I don't know," I say. I don't think I can watch it again.

"We've already got the tickets, so I guess you have to," she says.

"Great," I say.

"What is wrong with you? This is the most exciting thing that's ever happened to you and you're acting like it's some kind of chore to celebrate it."

"No. I just, after that fight with Phillip, I worry it'll be weird for him."

"Well, you're worried for nothing. I called him, and he's thrilled. He's happy for you. He's genuinely happy for you. You know, I don't even think that fight was about Tommy. I think that fight was about you not really letting him into your life." She sighs. "I know you don't like me to say it, but Michael would want you to be happy. He would want you to find someone."

It's honestly almost more than I can take. I close my eyes for a lot of it, but then I feel like Tommy's voice is too big. I feel like he's right in my ear, and that just makes it worse. Phillip keeps trying to hold my hand, which is just pissing me off. I think, *Can you not see that I am overloaded here? Can you not see that I don't have anything left?*

The movie is all building toward this one scene with Sarah where Tommy—not Tommy, Frederick—pins her down and cuts out her heart. It won't kill her though. That's the thing about this character. She's already dead. I think I'm not going to be able to watch it. I think maybe I could make an excuse to step out. But then I don't time it right, and Jenny grabs my arm, and she whispers, "Oh my god, Stacey. Oh my god." She has tears streaming down her face, and I try to look at her instead of the screen, but then she gasps, and I can't help it. I look up, and I see Tommy, and I think this is probably how I will always see him from now on, and I start to cry. I break down right in the theater. It's okay though, lots of people are crying. This movie is really sad.

The babysitter lives two blocks away, but it's dark out and cold, and Phillip offers to drive her home.

"Should I swing back after?" he says, and I say, "Of course."

The boys are already in bed, so I just peek in on them, check to see if they're sleeping. And then I walk down to the kitchen, open a bottle of red. I'm feeling sober, very sober. I'm feeling like I need a drink.

There's a tap on the glass of the sidelight, and Bear springs up from the rug with a low growl.

"Easy," I tell him. I make him sit, and I just wave Phillip in from the hallway. "Wine?" I say as he's closing the door.

"Sure," he says. He takes his coat off and folds it over the banister, and then he follows me into the kitchen. "So, I have a confession to make."

From his tone, it doesn't sound serious though, so I smile as I hand him his glass. "You didn't like the movie."

"I liked the movie," he says. He frowns. "You know I have your book."

He does. I signed it. He bought it the night that we met.

"You didn't like my book?" I laugh.

"I should read it again," he says. "You know, I didn't really get the Frankenstein connection."

"You didn't get . . ." I shake my head, but I'm smiling. "That's sort of the whole book."

"Yeah, I can see that now." He shrugs. He gives me this sheepish grin. "I'll read it again."

"I'm starting to think you're not so smart for a doctor," I say, but I set my glass down on the counter and move toward him.

"You do know you can still be a doctor even if you graduate at the bottom of your class."

"You didn't?"

He's still got his glass in one hand, but he wraps his other arm around me.

"Let's call it high middle," he says, and then he kisses me.

"Are you staying the night?"

He does sometimes, though I always kick him out before the kids wake up, and tonight I really don't want to sleep alone.

I am in charge of Christmas pajamas, and all of the cousins have to match. It's one of our traditions, or one of Jenny's traditions anyway. I put it off too long and now when I find cute ones, they don't have all the sizes I need. I grab what I can and hope I can order the rest online. I don't have time to keep messing with pajamas. I still have the boys' Christmas lists to run through, and now I feel like I have to get something for Phillip. I'm leaning toward cuff links.

My phone rings while I'm looking at Legos. I wish I'd brought the lists. I'm bound to pick the wrong sets. Or maybe I'll get two of the right sets, but they'll both be for the same person. I look down and see that it's Sarah.

"When are we going to talk about Tommy?" she says.

"Never." There are three sets I'm leaning toward. I decide it will be easiest to buy all three and then just bring the wrongest one back.

"Stacey, this shit is starting to spill over onto me. You know he's not taking my calls?"

"Maybe he's out of town."

"Maybe he's furious. Come on, Stacey. What the hell did you do?"

"Jesus, Sarah. I didn't do anything. It's just, I mean, I knew from the beginning it was a fucking mistake."

The person behind me gives me this angry "Excuse me!" and of course I haven't been paying attention. The aisle is full of kids. I try my apology face, but I don't think it's working.

"What do you mean 'beginning'? This wasn't just a one-night thing?" She makes this exasperated sigh. "How long was this going on?"

"I don't know," I say, but then it doesn't feel worth it to keep lying, so I just say, "Always."

"Oh my god," she says. "Do not tell me you blew him off for that doctor."

"I didn't blow him off, Sarah. It was just, it was time to make a decision." I grab a couple packs of these stupid role-playing cards that the boys are into and wander away from the toys into the pillows-and-sheets aisles because even one-sided there's only one conversation that sounds like this. "Tommy's not exactly a good decision."

"No shit, Stacey. That's pretty fucking obvious. You have to string him along for so long just to figure that out?"

"Fuck you. I wasn't stringing him along."

"Well, you were stringing someone along, weren't you? Or were you just hoping Tommy would get his shit together?"

"Sarah."

"Because, really, trying to have a relationship with Tommy is like playing fetch with a blind fucking dog. It's not going to work, but you're just an asshole if you get mad at the dog."

"No one's mad at him."

"Sure, that was really obvious when you were screaming at him in public. That was very, very clear."

"Look, Sarah, I didn't mean to make things hard on you, but you guys are old friends. For you, it'll blow over."

"And what about for you?" she says.

"I don't know, Sarah. I really don't know."

———————

Sadie texts me a photo, a self-portrait with candy cane, and it reads, *Help! Too many candy canes on the tree! I'm getting addicted! LOL.* She looks totally skinny, and of course I know what she's doing, hitting the sugar like it's a bump of cocaine. I bet she's eating less than eight hundred calories a day.

I walk in quick circles around the room, and then I dial Tommy's number. When I see that it's connecting though, I hit *end*, which is stupid because he's just going to see the missed call. I sit on the edge of the couch, pinch my lips between my thumbs, and I try again.

"Can't make up your mind?" he says when he picks up. I can hear voices behind him, laughing. He's never alone.

"Please don't start."

"I didn't call you, honey." His voice sounds toxic, strained.

"Sadie sent me a text. I don't think she looks very good."

"She's fine. She's doing better. She's been sucking on candy canes all day."

Uh-huh, and Red Vines got me through college, I think. "Did she eat any lunch?"

"You know what, Stacey? I don't fucking know. It's really none of your business anyway, is it?"

"She texted me," I say. I'm twisting my fingers together into knots. It's the only way I can keep myself from hanging up. "And really, for no reason. It feels like a cry for help."

He doesn't say anything for a minute. "Fine. I'll talk to her."

"I'd rather you just watch her. And Tommy," I say, "don't tell her I called."

"I wish you hadn't," he says. He sounds more tired than angry, but he still hangs up.

The gingerbread kit comes with an uneven number of jelly beans, but Ben says Stevie can have the extra. They divide the jelly beans, the miniature holly wreaths. There's only one pack of frosting, but they take turns glopping it on the roof, and then the counter, and then the floor. Bear parks himself at the base of their stools, licking it up. Stevie must have leaned his elbow into a patch of frosting. The sleeve of his sweater is crusted with white. I try not to look.

My phone rings, and Ben jerks up to see the picture that comes up. "Noni," he says, and sits back down.

"Hey, Mom," I say.

"We're just coming out of the theater," she says. "I am . . . well, I'm just overcome."

"Thanks," I say. "It's good, isn't it?"

"Tommy is an absolute genius. I mean, he's really an artist. I think I didn't give him enough credit before."

"He's a great actor," I say. Ben glances up, his expression a question I don't know how to answer.

I step away from the counter and move toward the back door, snapping my fingers for Bear to follow so I have something to do, something to think about other than *Tommy, Tommy, Tommy.* I'm so sick of everyone thinking about Tommy.

"And such an advocate for your work. I mean, the ending? If he hadn't fought for you on that ending . . ."

"Can I call you back?" I say as Bear pushes past me through the open door. "We're just in the middle of this gingerbread house. Let me call you after dinner."

I won't though. I'll wait till the morning. She always works in the morning, locks herself in her study, turns the ringer off on her phone. Sometimes I pretend I can't keep the time difference straight. *I just realized the time,* I'll say on the message, like it's an honest mistake.

We usually do Christmas morning together, hence the matching pajamas, and this is my year to host, or technically last year was, but obviously I postponed. Jenny and Todd will bring the kids over as soon as they wake up, and I've told Phillip he can come in the afternoon. I get up at five to make cinnamon rolls, and when the pan is ready I set them by the fireplace to rise. Bear is curious, so I bring a cup of coffee in and sit in the chair next to the hearth to keep him away. I curl my legs up under me and look at the tree. The ornaments are concentrated at the bottom because the boys really did do most of the decorating, and the lights they chose were the twinkling whites. These were Michael's favorites. I hate the twinkling. It makes me feel dizzy. Underneath the tree are all these packages. I bought every single thing on their lists, and it took me hours to wrap it all. I really focused on getting the folds right, making everything crisp. I know any minute now they'll wake up, they'll come running, they'll tear all of it up.

Phillip shows up at one o'clock. Jenny's crew is back home changing out of their pajamas or maybe grabbing a nap. The boys are up in their beds too, but I doubt that they're sleeping.

"Merry Christmas," Phillip says, and he kisses me.

He kisses me like he knows the boys are in their room. He pulls me tight against him, kneads his fingers into my waist. I am happy to see him.

"I have something for you," he says, and I say, "Yeah, I can tell," but he says, "Stacey," and I think he might be embarrassed.

"Come here," he says, and he pulls me to sit on the couch. He hands me a small silver box with a maroon ribbon, and I recognize the wrapping. Inside is this little gray velvet box, and I think, *Oh shit,* but when I open it, it's just a pair of earrings, these very classic pearl earrings circled with gold.

"I think I'm falling in love with you," Phillip says, and I say, "Oh."

He takes my hand in his, and I look down, study his fingers. He has these nice hands, but his skin is always dry. He has to wash his hands so much at work.

"Stacey," he says. "We've been seeing each other a long time, but I don't want to *just* keep seeing each other."

"Oh," I say again.

"I know that sounds like an ultimatum, but I don't mean . . . I just . . . I want us to be going somewhere with this."

I think I should be flattered. I should really be flattered, but I sort of feel like I want to walk out of the room. But he is so sweet. He really is so sweet. And I do think this is the right decision. I think Phillip is the smartest, best decision I could make.

I reach into the box and unclasp an earring and try it on. "So these come with a catch?"

"I wouldn't put it like that," he says.

I think, *I would,* but I just smile, and I lean forward and kiss him. I set my hand on the side of his face. "I like the earrings," I say. "Catch and all."

JANUARY

PHILLIP HAS A NEW YEAR'S PARTY. It's not a work thing exactly, but close enough. I wear the navy dress I took to L.A. It doesn't exactly have the best vibes, but it was expensive as hell, and it fits like a glove. When Phillip picks me up, he just says, "Wow."

The party is at this private house in Midtown, and there's a valet, thank god, because parking's a nightmare, and it is seriously cold. Phillip comes around to my door to help me out of the car, and he keeps hold of my arm as we walk up the steps.

"Be careful," he says. "It still looks icy."

Inside, someone takes our coats, and I notice Phillip is wearing a suit. He looks respectable, sexy. I slip my arm loosely around his waist and curl toward him, put my mouth right by his ear. I say, "I have an idea of something we could use that tie of yours for later."

"Stacey! Jeez, what if someone heard you?" he says, but his fingers do tighten a little on my waist, so I just smile.

Phillip leads me toward the bar set up in the dining room, which is enormous and full of this dark cherry furniture. Everything looks turn-of-the-century and the plaster on the ceilings is clearly original, restored obviously, but done by hand by some long-dead craftsman. Phillip gets me a glass of white wine, and as we move toward the living room, we run into a couple of the people he'd introduced me to in the spring. I don't actually remember any of their names, but I remember which ones are M.D.s, and even if I didn't, I think I could probably tell.

"I don't know if you remember Stacey," Phillip says, making the introductions.

"Oh, right, yes," says Cara the cardiologist. "I remember you were telling us about your movie. We saw it, by the way." She sort of furrows her brow line. "It was kind of disturbing."

"But good," her husband interrupts. "Disturbing in an artsy kind of way."

"Mmm, thanks," I say. I don't care what they think of the movie. It's getting great reviews because it is so fucking perfect and smart, and I don't want to think about the movie anyway. I take a drink of the wine. "This is a beautiful house, isn't it?"

Phillip nods. "The woodwork is really just amazing."

"So what's it like getting to know all of those Hollywood types? I would think they'd be intimidating," Cara's husband says.

"Some of them." I shrug. "It helps if you drink a lot."

Phillip laughs and says, "She's just kidding."

Not really, I think, but I smile, and then, because I'm feeling generous, I say, "Sarah Nixon is lovely. She's very funny and sweet."

"What about that Tommy DeMarco?" asks the woman who used to be pregnant and is still not drinking, probably because she has to go home later and nurse a baby. "He is gorgeous," she says, and she sort of fans herself. "I mean, I don't think I could be in a room with him without blushing."

I can relate to this obviously, but Phillip looks uncomfortable. "It wears off," I say.

"You're pretty close friends, right?" Phillip says, and I can see now that tonight could go either way.

"Well, we had to work pretty closely during the production, but there's not much need to keep in touch now." I smile. "We don't exactly have a ton of things in common."

We're still at the party when it strikes midnight. They have waitstaff that come around with these trays of champagne and hand out little paper horns. The whole room counts down together, and it ends in a cheer and all this honking, squawking noise. I turn toward Phillip, and he catches my lips with his. I think he wants to be discreet, but I grab the lapels of his suit to keep him from pulling away. I open my mouth against his, suck in his lip. I hold him there until I feel him kiss me back, and then I let go.

"Happy New Year," I say.

"I'm looking forward to spending all of it with you," he says.

I don't know what I want from the coming year, but I like that he says this. I like it a lot.

When the phone rings, I answer it without looking because it's early. The boys are just getting dressed for school. The only person who calls this early is Jenny, and only if someone's sick. I figure she needs me to pick up the healthy kids for school.

"Are you watching?" It's Sarah. She sounds excited.

"Watching what?"

"The nominations, you idiot. The fucking Academy Awards."

"No. Shit. I had no idea. Is that today?"

"We got a ton of them. Me, Jason, Tommy. Best picture too."

"Congratulations, that's fantastic." I open the fridge and pull out the milk for the boys' cereal.

"It's huge. John is through the roof. We'll make a pile of money on this thing."

I hear Stevie jump the last two steps to land in the hallway. When he comes into the kitchen he says, "I don't have any socks."

"Look, I've got to get the boys off to school. Let me call you later."

"Are you kidding? They can be late. This is huge. We have to plan. And talk dresses. You can borrow my stylist, of course."

"Oh no. Uh-uh. I'm not going to be there."

"Don't be stupid. You have to go. The whole thing is based on your book. We'll look like assholes if we don't take you."

"Wow, that's super generous, but look, the kids are behind sched-ule already, and if I don't get them off to school, then that means they're home with me." There is no way, absolutely no way, I'm letting that happen. I still have to take the tree down, catch up from the holiday break. "I promise, I'll call you later."

Stevie really doesn't have any clean socks in his drawer, but we do find one hidden in the bottom of his pajama drawer, and we borrow another from Ben. They don't match exactly, but he keeps his shoes on at school. It should work.

I'm meeting Jenny for lunch because it's almost her birthday. She wants to hit this new Indian place, which is stupid because we live right by an Indian place we already know we like, but it's her birthday.

I see her car when I pull up. It's possible I'm running a little late. She's sitting in a booth by the buffet, and she's already ordered me a water and a glass of white wine.

"Just one glass," she says. "We've got plenty of time before we pick up the kids."

"I think we have enough time that we could have two."

"So it's buffet, which I know you don't like, and there's no mulligatawny, but they have this tomato soup. The guy says it's vegetarian."

I wave my hand like, *Whatever.* "I'm sure it's fine."

I find some lentils that seem palatable and some kind of curry.

"So," she says when we sit back down, "the goddamn Oscars, huh?"

"Yeah." I make a swirl of lentils through the curry. "It's very exciting."

"Have you talked to them yet?"

"Sarah called first thing."

Jenny frowns. "And Tommy?"

"Not yet." I break off pieces of the naan and shove it into my design. I think it looks like a starburst.

"You and Tommy fighting?" she says.

I look up, and she's just staring. She's got that mom face again. Not the one that says she's angry, but that she's figuring something out.

I just shake my head. "I don't really want to talk about this, Jen."

"You don't want to talk about what?"

I don't answer. I keep crumbling the bread.

"Jesus Christ, Stacey. Did you sleep with him?"

"Jenny, can we not do this? It's done. It's over."

"What do you mean 'over'? How long was it going on?"

I've run out of bread to tear. My fingertips feel greasy. "I don't know. A long time."

"Why didn't you tell me? God." She sighs, shakes her head. "You have this wonderful, sweet, totally attentive guy—who is a doctor, by the way—and you want to throw all of that out for some stupid affair with some stupid actor who fucks literally everyone? Literally everyone, Stacey."

"Literally? Did you sleep with him too?"

"Don't be cute, Stacey. Don't be fucking cute." She slams her hand on the table.

"Okay, that's why I didn't fucking tell you." I drop my head into my hands. I can feel her watching me. "It's not like that."

"What is it like?" she says.

But the truth is I don't know.

"Are you in love with him?" she says finally, and she says it really quietly, like the answer matters. It doesn't. It doesn't matter at all.

"Jenny, please."

"What about Phillip?" she says.

"I care about Phillip. I do. There's no reason for him to know." I know Jenny would never say anything, but I look up at her like I'm asking anyway.

She shakes her head. "I knew that son of a bitch was trouble."

I think about defending Tommy, saying it wasn't his fault, but I don't actually believe that. He is trouble.

Jenny sits with her arms crossed for a long time, looking at the table. She hates being angry with me, so I know that it's bad.

"I know you've had a hard couple of years, but Phillip has done everything to try and make it better. And I get that Tommy is handsome and exciting, but he's not . . . real," she says finally. She holds her hands over her face and sighs into them. "I at least hope you regret it."

I do. I totally do. "It doesn't matter. Tommy's not even speaking to me."

"What do you mean he's not speaking to you? I thought you weren't speaking to him?"

"Does it make a difference?"

"Yeah, it proves how much of a dick he is."

I can tell she wants to feel bad for me now. She reaches over and pats my hand.

"He's really mean now. You remember that one really bad scene in the movie?" I say. "He's kind of like that."

The wood floors are covered in these little white mineral stains. It's all the snow and salt the kids and dog keep tracking in. It's almost not worth cleaning, but I can't stand to keep looking at it. I pull a broom out of the closet to sweep up the dog hair and cereal crumbs before mopping, and I flip the radio on. I hear Tommy's voice, and I realize it's that interview show I love, but I think about changing the channel.

"Now, your new movie is based on the book *Monsters in the Afterlife* by the poet Stacey Lane."

"That's right."

I drag the broom along the toe kick under the counters, find all the grit that's hidden there.

"I have to say, I read the book, and I thought, 'There's no way they can make a movie of this.' What made you believe it would work? And I should say, you didn't direct the movie, but you both starred in and produced it."

"Yes. And it was a project that I really pushed for. I just fell in love with it."

"But what made you think, 'This would be a great movie'?"

"I don't know. I guess I thought it would be a great anything, and movies just happen to be what I do. I read the book, and then I read it again, and then I left it on my coffee table for a week, and every time I walked into the room, I picked it back up, and I just realized that I wasn't able to let it go."

"Are you surprised at the critical reception?"

"You know, I think initially people had their doubts about the whole idea of adapting a book of poetry, and particularly this book, which isn't necessarily an easy read. And maybe that was what drew me to it, at least in part. The challenge. But you know, these are archetypal characters. There's a universality that I thought, with a different medium, we'd be able to tap into." He laughs. "And really, I wouldn't have put so much money down if I didn't think we'd be able to pull it off."

"It's interesting that while it's called a novel-in-verse, the book itself is not particularly narrative, and while the poems move from scene to scene, they really read more like meditations."

"I think that's a great way to describe it. This was one of our biggest concerns when we sat down with our screenwriter, Joe Rosen, who is just a master storyteller, and we knew he could fill in that gap."

"I understand you brought the poet, Stacey Lane, in on the project as well."

"We did. I can't imagine that we could have done it without her. I really wanted us to be guided by her vision, which is just so distilled, so sharp, and particularly, with the content of the book, I mean, it's dangerous territory. It could have gone either way."

"Definitely. There's the potential for the violence to be gratuitous or titillating even, which is what I was afraid of when I sat down to watch it."

"Right, yes, that pornographic quality that you can get in some really awful slasher flicks, and I just knew that we needed Stacey's influence to hold us back from that."

"It certainly worked because as much violence as we're subjected to, the movie doesn't seem to be about violence so much as it's about what leads to violence and what then comes out of it."

"Mm-hmm, and it's not just the effect on the victim, but what the violence does to the perpetrator, and, more subtly, what it does to those of us who witness it."

"It's interesting, isn't it, to watch this character attempting to reconstruct herself, quite literally, in the midst of this chaos?"

"I love that you use the word 'reconstruct.' You know, Stacey and I argued early on over whether our speaker is an unreliable narrator, and of course, Stacey thinks more like a poet than a novelist, so she kept dismissing the point, saying, 'She's a persona, not a narrator,' and I said, 'You can call her whatever you want, but she's still a liar.'"

"What do you mean 'liar'?"

"Well, like you say, this character is constructing herself, reconstructing herself, building this persona to use Stacey's words, and she's doing it deliberately. She's leaving a lot of the truth out."

"That's such an interesting reading. I have to tell you, I just didn't read it that way."

"I don't know that you have to, but I think you miss a certain understanding of the character if you take her at her word."

"My guest tonight is Tommy DeMarco. His new film, *Monsters in the Afterlife*, which he produced and starred in, has been nominated for seven Oscars. We'll talk more after a break."

Phillip wants to take me to dinner on Friday, and when I open the door, I feel like I'm underdressed. I'm just in jeans, but he's got on these black slacks, a tailored shirt. At least he's not wearing a jacket, but I feel like I should change. I feel like we should match.

"Should I put on something different?" I say.

"No, of course not, you look beautiful." He presses his lips against my cheek.

We drive down to Dundee and hit this very elegant, very French café, and Phillip orders this expensive-as-hell Bordeaux. It's like two hundred bucks a bottle, which is something I've never done outside of L.A. He smells the cork, he takes the obligatory sip, and then he nods to the waiter.

"Stacey," Phillip says as the waiter moves away, "I think you know how I feel about you."

The table we're sitting at is tiny, so we're already knee-to-knee, but I press my calf into his. I rest my hand on his wrist.

He reaches into his pocket and pulls out another of those little silver boxes and sets it on the table, but when he opens it, it's totally empty. "I want to fill this box with anything you want," he says.

I think this is supposed to be a romantic gesture, but I don't like jumping to conclusions, don't like the possibility of being wrong, so I don't actually say anything. I just raise my eyes from the empty box to him.

He says, "Marry me, Stacey," and I take a deep breath. It's the right thing for me to do. I know that.

"Okay," I say. "Yes."

What he puts on my finger finally is this huge round-cut diamond that's so clear it's almost blue, and it's circled with these tiny diamonds around the edge and down the band. It's set in white gold. It looks like winter against my skin.

"Oh my god," Jenny says, holding my hand in both of hers.

We'd asked them to meet us out for drinks.

"Congratulations," Todd says, and he claps Phillip on the shoulder. He looks at me. "That's a hell of a rock."

"It's pretty heavy," I say.

The bar is crowded. The place has these happy-hour deals, and there aren't many places to sit, but Phillip spots a couple stools in the corner, and he ushers Jenny onto one, holds the other for me. I sit sideways and rest my arm over the back, and when Phillip stands behind me, I lean against his chest and feel him step forward just a bit to brace me. He slides his arm down to my waist.

"What do the boys think?" Jenny says.

"We haven't said anything yet. We've got plans to take them to the arcade tomorrow. We'll tell them between rounds of laser tag."

"Ease the blow?" Todd says.

"I just want to warm them up to the news." I turn my head back to look at Phillip. "They like you, they do, but this will be weird for them."

"Okay, well, we need something to toast with," Jenny says. "I don't think the waitress is coming."

"I'll go up to the bar," Phillip says.

"White wine." Jenny waves her hand between the two of us, though I'd hoped for something stronger. "You should go with him," she says, fixing her gaze on Todd.

"Subtle," he says. He winks at me.

She watches them move through the crowd, then leans toward me. "So I'm guessing he hasn't found out?"

"Found out about what?"

"Don't play dumb, Stacey. You haven't told him about your . . ." But there isn't really a word for it, is there? "You haven't told him about Tommy yet."

"I'm not going to tell him. He doesn't need to know."

"No," she says. "He doesn't. Not if it's over and done."

I shrug. "Okay then."

"So is it over and done?"

"Jenny, please," I say like I'm brushing her off.

"Because if you fuck this up," she says. She jabs one finger down at the table. "This guy is real, and he's good, and he wants to make a life with you. And if you fuck this up because you're still in love with some daydream . . ."

"I'm not . . . I didn't say . . ." I shake my head. "Jenny, please," I say again, this time just whispering.

Todd's just a few steps away, two glasses in his hands. He sets them on the table. I don't really trust myself to talk, so I just smile a thank-you. I smile, and I mean *Thank you, thank you, thank you.*

Phillip drops a lot of money on the arcade. Stevie must blow through fifteen dollars trying to get a stuffed dog out of a claw machine. It keeps slipping out of his grasp. I put my arm around Phillip, rest my chin on his shoulder. "You'd be better off just buying him one."

Ben finishes the racing game he's been playing and stands up. He's about twenty feet away, but when he turns to face us, I can see he doesn't like the way I'm standing. He comes toward us, but he's kind of dragging his feet.

"You out of money?" I say when he gets close enough.

"No. I just don't know what else to play."

Phillip raises an eyebrow, and I say, "I'll talk to him."

As I walk toward Ben, I hear Phillip say, "You want some help with that?" and Stevie says, "Yeah. I really want the green one."

"What's going on?" I put my arm around Ben and we walk a few steps away.

"Nothing," he says. He crosses his arms over his chest. "I want to call Tommy," he says.

"What?"

"I want to talk to Tommy."

I crouch down in front of him, take his hand. "Honey, I don't really talk to Tommy these days."

"Because of him," he says.

"Because of Tommy," I say. "Because Tommy is just, he's just very far away."

He kicks his foot against the floor, the tile squeaking beneath his sneaker, and he pulls his hand out of mine. He turns just as Stevie and Phillip walk up. Phillip has his hand on Stevie's shoulder.

"Look, Mom!" Stevie says. He has a new stuffed dog in his hand. "I like this one better anyway. Orange is my third favorite color. But if they had a blue dog, I would really want that."

"You guys want an ice cream cone?" Phillip asks.

Ben just shrugs, but Stevie says, "Yeah!"

The place only has soft serve, so I tell Phillip to get them the chocolate and vanilla swirls.

"You want one?" he says.

I shake my head. "I can share yours."

I think Ben makes a face, but I ignore it and send the boys to wash their hands. While they're gone, I pick out a table at the edge of the food court. No one else is in it, so it doesn't really matter where we sit. I drop one knee onto the bench and sit on my foot. I brace my arms against the edge of the table. The boys come back first, and they sit on the bench across from me. Stevie has his new dog tucked under his arm.

When Phillip gets there with the ice cream, Stevie says, "Ice cream!" and Ben says, "Don't be such a stupid nerd."

"Ben," I say, "don't talk to your brother like that."

He doesn't say anything. He just looks at the floor.

"So," Phillip says, and he looks at me.

I don't know if I can do this. The timing is shit. The ice cream is clearly not smoothing things over, but Phillip is looking at me expectantly.

"Well, boys," I say, "you know Phillip and I have been spending a lot of time together."

"So now you're going to get married or something?" Ben says, and because he's such an idiot, Phillip says, "Yes."

It's like he's never met a pissed-off kid, and mine is eleven now. He's good at it. Ben just glares at him, and Stevie looks confused.

"Eat your ice cream, honey," I say, touching Stevie's arm, and then I turn toward Ben. "Well, we've been talking about it, sweetheart."

"Do we have to come live with you?" Stevie says to Phillip.

"I think Phillip will probably come live with us."

"Or we might buy a new house," Phillip says, and I look at him like, *Really?* because now Stevie looks like he's about to cry.

"I don't want to leave my house," he says.

"Yeah," Ben says. "We like things the way they are."

"We're not doing anything like that now," I say, and I put my hand on Phillip's arm to let him know he should keep his mouth shut. "We're not selling our house. This would just mean that Phillip would be around more, and we could spend more days together like this." I sort of hold my hands up toward all the games like, *Isn't this great?* but clearly they don't agree. They don't think it's great at all.

FEBRUARY

WHEN I SEE the phone number, I think about not answering. There is no reason in the world I would want to talk to Tommy, except curiosity. Curiosity makes me pick it up.

"What?" I say.

"Have you heard from Sadie?" He almost sounds out of breath.

"No. Why?"

"She was supposed to be on a seven a.m. flight out of New York, nonstop, but she missed it or something. She switched her ticket and then she had a connection in Chicago." His words are a jumble, everything is off tempo. "She didn't get back on. I don't know where she is."

"Have you called her?"

"Yes, I've called her. She's not fucking answering."

"Don't yell at me, Tommy." I don't need this shit at all, but I say, "What about tracking her phone?"

He's taking these deep breaths through his nose. "She must have turned it off."

"You call the Chicago airport? Try to page her? You have people looking?"

"Yeah." He sounds like he's talking through his hand. He sounds like he's going to cry.

"Look, I don't know what I can do, but I'll send her a text, and maybe if she turns her phone back on, she'll call me."

"Yeah, okay." He doesn't sound like he's going to hang up. For a minute, I just listen to him breathing, and then I say, "Look, I'd better go, but I'm sure she's going to be okay."

When I hang up, I send her a text that says, *Please call me, honey. You're killing your dad.*

Sadie does call me, but she hasn't gotten the message. She's afraid to turn her phone on, so she's calling from a security desk at the airport. They let her use it when she tells them that she's lost. It's a local call anyway. She's in Omaha.

"Can you come get me?" she says.

"Jesus, honey, what are you doing here? You're scaring your dad to death." But then I'm afraid she's going to hang up. "Never mind, just stay put. I'm coming to get you."

Phillip is supposed to be coming for dinner, but I call him. I say, "I have to cancel. It's an emergency. It's a kid thing."

"Are the boys okay?"

"Yeah, no, it's my friend's kid. She's stranded. I have to pick her up." I don't know why, but I take the ring off. I tuck it into the cabinet above the kitchen sink.

"Should I come over later?"

"No. I don't know how long all of this is going to take. I'd better go." I say this like I'm not going to be taking the phone with me, but Phillip worries about me talking and driving anyway.

I yell for the boys to put their shoes on and get in the car.

"Where are we going?" Ben says.

"We have to get Sadie."

"Tommy's Sadie?" he says.

"Tommy's here?" Stevie says, peeking over the railing.

"No. Just Sadie. C'mon, hurry up."

I grab my keys, turn the alarm on, lock the door. I almost hate to call Tommy until I have her in my sights, but the airport's thirty minutes from here. That seems cruel.

He picks up on the first ring. "Have you heard from her?"

"She's in Omaha. She called me from the airport."

"Jesus. Shit. Are you going to get her?"

"Yes, of course. I'll have her in half an hour." I pull onto Dodge. There's not much traffic. I should be on the interstate in maybe five minutes.

"Okay, yeah." I can almost see him pacing, pushing his fingers back into his hair. "Did she sound okay?"

"I don't know, Tommy. She sounds like a kid who's running away." Which is true, but I know he needs more reassurance. "She didn't sound hurt. I'm sure she's fine."

"Stace, I don't know what I would do." His voice cracks.

"Look, she's fine, and she's here, and I'm going to get her. Just start thinking about how you're going to get her home."

"Yeah, no, of course. I'll come and get her. I'll get a plane tonight."

"You know what, just let her stay here till tomorrow. She'll be fine with me. You wouldn't even get in here until late. Just come tomorrow."

"She's my kid, Stacey. I can't just sit back and have dinner. I've been out of my mind all day."

Great. Tommy's coming to Omaha. That's just what I need.

I have to park in the quick park so I can go in and get her, which is annoying. And I have to take the boys with me, which makes it even worse. Seriously, I could wring her little neck for this, but when I see her sitting by the phones in the baggage area, I pick up my pace crossing over to her, and I wrap her into my arms. Her eyes are red. I can feel her shoulder blades through her coat.

"What happened, honey?"

Her eyes fill up and spill over, down her cheek, off her lip. "I don't want to go home."

I sit down next to her. The boys are standing a few feet away. Stevie is staring. "Hey, why don't you guys go count how many red suitcases you can find on the big conveyer belt." Ben just looks at me, but I say, "C'mon, I need you to take care of your brother."

"Fine," he says under his breath.

I hold Sadie's hand. "Honey, I want you to tell me all about it, but first you're gonna have to call your dad." I hold my phone out to her. Tommy's number is already set.

"You probably already called him," she says.

"Sadie, you knew that I would." I squeeze her shoulders. "Don't you want him to come get you?"

She cries a little harder because of course she does. She wants him to swoop in and pick her up and make everything better, but he can't anymore, and that's why she's so pissed. That's why she says, "No."

I hit *dial* and hold the phone up to her. I can hear his voice when he answers. She doesn't say anything at first, but then she says, "Daddy?" and she wraps her fingers around the phone, takes it out of my hand.

By the time Tommy texts me that he's landed, Sadie's sleeping in my bed. I'm leaving the guest room open for him. I fed her black bean soup for dinner, which I let her watch me make, but when she went to the bathroom, I blended a few avocados in it, and she didn't seem to notice. She ate almost a whole cup. I sit in the front room to watch for Tommy, and when the lights of the taxi pull into the driveway, I go to the door. I don't know how I feel about opening it. Bear comes running, but I don't let him bark. I don't want him waking up all the kids.

"She's upstairs, first door on the right."

Bear tries to follow, but I grab his collar before he can slip past. I walk down the hall to wait in the kitchen. It's a few minutes before I hear Tommy's footsteps on the stairs, and Bear jumps back up to go and greet him. I hear a thud in the hallway that tells me Bear has flopped down at his feet. Tommy must have stopped to scratch him.

I pull down a bottle of bourbon and set it on the counter with a glass, and when Tommy finally walks in the room, I nod toward it. "You want that?"

Tommy doesn't go for the bottle. He crosses the room and pulls me tight against his chest, his arms wrapped around me, his chin by my ear. "Thank you," he says, and we just stand there for a few minutes. My nose is pressed against his shirt. I breathe in the smell of him, and I hold my breath.

"I don't really know how to make this apology," he says.

"It doesn't matter." I try to pull back, but he doesn't loosen his grip.

"God, Stacey, how'd we even end up like this?"

"We drink too much, and we're both a little slutty."

He laughs, and now he does let me go, and he reaches for the bourbon. He pours a little in the glass. "You having any?"

"I have an open bottle of red, but I thought you might need something stronger."

I open the cupboard for a glass, and there is Phillip's ring. I don't take it out. I leave it where it is. I take a glass down and pull the cork back out of the bottle. I pour it nice and full. I pour it like I mean it.

"So what did Sadie tell you? What made her pull this stunt?"

I turn to look at him. He's sitting on one of the stools along the island. This is where the boys sit to eat their cereal. I hope it's not sticky. I lean back against the counter, my arms crossed, the glass in my left hand. "Well, for one thing, you need to stop giving her so much money. What kind of sixteen-year-old can pay cash for a same-day ticket?" and I give him this look like, *You're stupid, Tommy.* "She didn't say much though, just that she's sick of being shuttled back and forth. And she says she hates New York."

Tommy shakes his head. "I can't really fight her mom on that."

"It doesn't sound like she'd care. Sadie says she's never even home."

"Doesn't matter. If I ask, she'll just say no. She's fucking vindictive."

"Because you're probably an asshole to her."

He rubs his thumb across his bottom lip. "Maybe. I mean, there have been times when I have been."

"If Sadie wants to live with you, you need to make it happen. She needs some attention, Tommy. She wants to be taken care of. Why do you think she set you up for this big rescue?"

He drops his elbows on the counter, holds his head in his hands. He looks worn down.

"Did you get any dinner?" I say, and he shakes his head. "I'll heat you some soup. It's really fattening though. Don't tell Sadie."

When I set the bowl in front of him, he wraps his fingers around my wrist. "I know I've been an asshole to you," he says.

I think about pulling my hand away, but I don't. "We've both been assholes. Let's just drop it."

"I don't want to drop it, Stacey. I never really did." He looks at me with those stupid green eyes of his, and he moves his fingers a little farther up my arm, and I just think, *Fuck me,* I mean, not like *Fuck me* but like, *This isn't good.* I pull my hand away and move back across the room to retrieve my wine.

He smiles, so I know he's going to say something shitty. "It's mostly my fault. I should have expected you to flip out at some point."

"I didn't flip out." I shake my head.

"No, you did," he says. He rubs his face with his hands. "But I know I handled it like a dick, and then"—he makes a dive-bomb gesture with one hand—"we went off the cliff."

"I don't really think we need to rehash all of this, Tommy. I think you just need to eat your soup."

He narrows his eyes a little dismissively, but he does take a bite. "That's really good. How does she not know this is fattening?" he says. "Anyway, I think your strategy of just not ever saying a thing out loud so that you won't have to deal with it isn't always the most effective. I get that it's how you live your life, but, you know, it's fucking annoying, Stacey."

I take a sip of my wine. "Seriously, Tommy, just eat the damn soup."

He takes a few bites—seven actually. I know because I'm counting, and I'm counting because it helps me not think about how the spoon fits against his tongue, how it slides from between his lips. I feel like the wine is going to my head. Then Tommy stands up, and he walks toward me and reaches his arms around me, rests his hands on the counter behind me. He ducks his head toward my mouth, but I turn my face to the side.

"Phillip asked me to marry him."

Tommy freezes. He's totally still, and his mouth is so close to my face. "Are you joking?"

I don't say anything. I look at the floor. I can see a few black dog hairs along the corners of the white cabinets. I think about getting a paper towel.

"This guy doesn't even know you. He can't make you happy."

"He makes me happy."

"Then we have different definitions of what that means," he says, and he steps back finally.

"We make sense," I say. "He fits in my life."

"Don't you want someone who's going to make your life bigger?"

"No," I say. Because it doesn't matter what I want. Because he doesn't mean it as an offer anyway. So I say "No" again. I say, "I don't."

Tommy just stares at me, and then he says, "Fuck. Christ. It's your fucking life."

By midnight, I've finished the red and opened another bottle, and Tommy has switched over from the bourbon because *flying with a whiskey headache is a fucking nightmare,* he says. And we've moved into the living room, where I'm tucked into a corner of the couch, my feet pulled up. I've pulled my end of the coffee table closer so I don't have to unwind myself to reach for my glass. Tommy still seems on edge, sitting forward with his elbows on his knees. He's not acting like himself. I try asking him about work, about new projects, but it doesn't take.

"I've read a lot of scripts," he says, "but nothing I want." He kind of shrugs. "I've got a small part coming up, but it's mostly a favor."

"Maybe that's good," I say. "Take some time off. Spend it with Sadie."

"You know I'm not good at that," he says. "I don't think I know how to help her."

"It's not about helping her. It's about being around."

"Doing what? She's not five. I can't take her to the zoo." He takes a drink of the wine. He swallows it like it's water.

"Don't ask me. I do take mine to the zoo, and I still suck at it. Maybe we should both give our kids to Jenny."

He kind of laughs, but then he lets his head drop down below his shoulders. "Whatever I do, I know I'm gonna fuck her up."

"Story of my life," I say.

He groans. "Shit, Stacey. I don't want to be like you."

"I know. It sucks, right? I'm a disaster."

"You really are." But when he looks up at me, he's smiling. "So how are the boys doing these days?"

"Not great. I guess it could be worse." I grip the stem of my glass and twist it through my fingers. "They're not crazy about Phillip."

Tommy laughs, and whatever he's about to say, I don't want to hear it.

"Don't," I say, and he holds his hands up like he's going to hold himself back. "You know, he's just . . . he's not their dad."

"Come off it, Stace. That isn't the reason. I mean, they fucking love me."

"Yeah, well, you put on a better show. Your 'not genuine' looks really fucking genuine and his looks like an uncomfortable mess."

"I'm totally genuine with them," he says. "Jesus, you're an asshole."

"You're not genuine with anyone, Tommy. You're just a really talented actor."

"You've just got to stand right on the edge of that cliff, don't you? See how far you can stick your toes over. It's like you can't help yourself." He doesn't sound mad though, so I just shrug.

"It was a compliment," I say, though it obviously wasn't. And suddenly I feel like maybe I did stick my toes over too far, like maybe I am losing control. "Look, it's late. I've got to go to bed."

I get up early. Sadie's still sleeping, tucked into Michael's side of the bed. It'll be hours before the sun is up, but the moon on the snow casts the backyard in this weird bluish light. I let Bear out and watch him from the window, this black monster trudging through the snow. He sniffs around the playset, checks the perimeter of the yard. I think about yoga, but today I don't have the balance. I'll wait till the house is empty, and then I'll run. I let Bear in, and I make a pot of coffee, clean up the glasses from last night. It'll be an hour still before the boys are up for school, and I don't know what to do with myself. I sit on the couch, cross my ankles under my thighs. Michael has been gone for so long now, long enough that I should be able to sleep.

When I hear the boys' alarm, I go into the kitchen. I make them oatmeal, organic rolled oats, and I stir in a little almond butter, a splash of vanilla. Stevie comes down first and plants himself in the same spot Tommy was in last night. I put the bowl of oatmeal in front of him, and he wrinkles his nose.

"I don't like almond butter," he says.

"It's good for you. Lots of protein."

"I like blueberries instead."

"Blueberries don't have protein."

"Can I have both?"

I toss the bag of frozen blueberries on the counter, and he tries to maneuver a spoonful into his bowl. His fingertips come out of the bag blue. I take it from him and shake a handful of berries onto the top of his oats. Then I make a bowl for Ben and do the same.

When Ben sits down, he just looks at the bowl and frowns. "I don't like blueberries."

I say, "You love blueberries."

"Not in oatmeal."

"Then pick them out."

"I can't now. They're all mixed in and mushy."

"I like them," Stevie says.

Even the muscles at the base of my tongue feel tight. I press my fingers hard into my palms. "You know what, just throw it out."

"Never mind. I'll eat it."

"No, if you're going to complain about it, you don't need to eat it." I can hear the tone of my voice change, but I can't actually stop it.

"I said I'll eat it," he says, but he pushes the spoon through the oats like he's not happy about it, and it takes everything in me not to reach over and pull it away.

"Hey," Tommy says, walking into the room, "what's for breakfast?" and when the boys spin in their chairs, he says, "Oh my god, you guys are so big!"

Stevie reaches him first, throwing his arms around Tommy's waist. Ben is a little slower, hanging back, but Tommy reaches out and grabs him by the back of the neck, pulling him in tight.

"God, what is she feeding you? You're huge. Are you getting into that giant dog's food?" He moves Stevie back an inch. "You," he says, "were, like, to here last time I saw you." He holds his hand right at his waist. "And now you're way up here," he says, sliding his hand up. He still has his other arm wrapped around Ben's shoulders and he gives him a little shake. "I bet it's the blueberries." Ben laughs a little, and Tommy pulls them both in for another hug and then nudges them away. "Go eat your breakfast, man."

The boys climb back into their seats, and Tommy walks around the island behind me. He rests his hand on my back and looks over my shoulder into the pot of oatmeal. "Can I have blueberries in my oatmeal?" he says, and Stevie giggles. Even Ben smiles, and I just think, *What are you trying to prove?* I feel like I need to move away from the stove. It's too warm. I need to find some space.

"Take whatever you want," I say. "You always do," but then I think, *Fuck, I shouldn't have said that,* and I turn in the opposite direction and circle back behind him toward the coffeepot. "I'll get you some coffee."

Tommy must have made some calls while I was getting the boys to school because by the time I get back, he has everything arranged. He probably just called Daniel. Either way, he and Sadie are set to fly out around noon.

"Is she awake yet?" I ask. Tommy's sitting on one of the stools in front of the counter. There are little drops of oatmeal everywhere from the boys.

"She's in the shower."

"Any breakfast?"

"Not yet."

He reaches his left arm back and rubs his neck, and the way this pulls at the fabric of his T-shirt makes me look away. I toss my keys by the coffeepot and grab a dishrag, hold it under the faucet, add soap.

"God, the boys are messy," I say, using the rag to sweep the bits of oatmeal and blueberries into my hand.

"They're good kids, Stacey," Tommy says, and he stands up, moving out of my way.

"You just like them because they like you."

"Everyone likes me. I don't like everyone back."

"I've really missed your ego," I say, but he just smiles. He says, "I know."

He walks behind me to refill his coffee, and as he passes, he squeezes my shoulder, but I don't stop wiping the counters. Oatmeal dries so quickly, I need to get every drip. He turns and leans back against the far counter, holding his coffee at his mouth and breathing in the steam.

"I feel like we need to clear the air, Stacey."

I glance up at him, then back at the counter. "I feel like everything is fine."

"You're still a bad liar," he says.

I look toward the stairs. I can't hear the shower anymore. "Maybe we should talk about this some other time."

Tommy sets his coffee on the counter, leans backwards on his hands. "Your 'some other time' is kind of bullshit, isn't it? I don't know how your whole not-talking thing works with everyone else, but that's not us. That's not how we work."

I'm just standing there, holding this rag. I still have crumbs in my hand, and I think, *We don't work, obviously.*

"Jesus." He lifts his hands and slams them back into the counter, pushes himself forward. "I am so sick of fighting with you, Stacey."

"We're not fighting."

"You're not. But I'm fucking trying here. Get invested, okay? Because I would like us to actually get past this." He's not yelling, but he's loud enough that I want him to be quieter. He's loud enough that I feel like taking a step back. "I am really fucking sorry. Okay? I don't know what you want from me."

"I don't want anything from you."

"Fuck that. When are you gonna admit that you're the asshole here? I mean, I think I've been pretty upfront with how I feel about you, but all I hear from you is how you don't give a shit about me. I mean, you'll go to bed with me over and over again, but you're never going to take me seriously."

"Take you seriously? Take what seriously? 'I don't want to know who else you're fucking'? Because, really? Fuck you for that."

"Stace, no," he says, stepping toward me, but then I hear just this whisper of a noise against the wood floor behind me, and Tommy's face totally falls, and I think, *Of course, she's so tiny, she moves like a ghost,* and I close my eyes like that's going to stop anything.

"Oh my god. You slept with my dad?"

I turn on the ball of my foot. She's standing there, her hair still wet from the shower. "Honey," I say, "no. No, it's not like that."

She obviously doesn't believe me. I am a terrible liar. She looks past me to Tommy, and he says, "Sadie, honey, you wouldn't understand."

She can't seem to close her mouth. She just stands there, staring at him. "You ruin everything," she says, and I think she's talking to Tommy, but I can't be sure.

"Honey," I say, and I start to take a step toward her, but she shakes her head and runs out of the room and back up the stairs.

It's true. I do feel ruined. I stand there, looking at the place she'd been standing, and then I turn back toward Tommy. I throw the dishrag at him, and he flinches. "You happy now?" I'm so exhausted and my hands are covered in crumbs and soap. Tommy's just standing there with his head down, staring at the rag where it's bounced off of him and landed on the floor. I walk to the sink next to him and rinse off my hands. He's standing right in front of the towel, so I shove him with my elbow. "Move," I say, and he does.

"I don't know what you want me to say," he says.

I finish wiping my hands, and I sit down at the counter and prop my head up with my elbows.

"You want me to leave?"

I think, *Yes*. I think, *Maybe*. I think, *No*. But he does. He walks upstairs, and I can hear him talking to Sadie. I can hear her crying, but I can't hear what she says. I turn my head toward the window, look at the snow. It's weeks old. It's thawed and frozen, thawed and frozen so many times that the top layer is clear as glass.

When I start the treadmill, I have my earbuds in, but I can't find a song that fits my mood. Everything is too happy or too fucking slow. I pull them out and drop my iPod down onto the carpet beside me. I turn the speed up another click. I think about pushing it higher, but I want to be able to run and run and run. I don't want to have to stop. At five miles my legs are on auto, and my head is finally clear. It's nothing but air. Three more and my right knee starts to twitch. I don't know how long I can ignore it. Probably longer than I should. I hit *stop* and step down onto the carpet, but I can't straighten my leg, can't put my weight on it without feeling this awful pinch deep in the joint. I sit on the floor, pull the leg into me, try to stretch it back out. I know it's not really an injury, it's just worn out. When Michael was alive, we used to run together on weekends. He'd plot out the routes, keep me from doing too many hills. He was faster than me by a lot, but he kept this really slow pace, so I never got ahead of myself, never got out of breath. These days, my lungs are always on fire.

Phillip calls three times between appointments, but I don't answer till it's close to five o'clock.

"Hi," I say when I finally pick up.

"Where have you been all day?" he says, but he doesn't sound suspicious.

"I was running when you called. I think I tweaked my knee." I try sort of maneuvering it around, and it still feels sore.

"You want me to look at it?"

"Maybe. I don't think it's swollen or anything."

"How's your friend's kid?"

"Oh, she's fine, you know, trying to run away, but then not really."

"Huh?"

"It's nothing," I say. "She's just being sixteen. So are you coming over tonight?"

"I don't know. It might be pretty late. I have a meeting with my realtor."

"I hope you're just talking about selling your place."

"For now, but I think we should talk about that." I can hear him tapping a pen against his desk. He's obviously nervous. "Stacey, I don't want to live in your late husband's house."

"It's not his house. It's the boys'."

"I think they can adapt."

"They are little boys, Phillip. I don't think they should have to." I twist the ring around my finger. I must be puffy from running. It feels a little tight.

He sighs. "Look, maybe we should wait to talk about this face-to-face."

"Can we please not do it tonight? I'm really . . . I'm exhausted. I just . . . I can't." I can't take another fight.

"Okay, not tonight, but we are going to talk about it, and soon." He sounds, I don't know, firm. I really don't like it on him. "Look, I'll call you when I finish up and maybe I can make it over."

There's the dull hum of the garage door opening and closing, the chime of the door as Phillip comes into the house. Michael's bay has just been sitting empty, so it made sense to give the second opener to Phillip, and now when he comes over late, I don't have to wait up. Besides, I like listening to him let himself in, the sound of his shoes on the carpeted stairs.

"You look tired," he says when he comes in the room, and he crosses to my side of the bed and sits beside me. "Let me look at your knee."

He pushes the sheet out of the way and pulls up the thin flannel of my pajama pants. He presses his fingertips gently around my knee, bends and straightens it, asks where it hurts. "It's a little swollen," he says, pulling my pant leg back down. "Did you take anything?"

"No," I say.

"I'll get you some ibuprofen. Where do you keep it?"

"Top drawer to the left," I say, pointing toward the bathroom.

He comes back with two tablets and sits back down in front of me. I take them with a swallow of the water sitting on my night table.

"No running for a while. I think you could use the break." He smiles at me, rests his hand on my cheek.

"You should get ready for bed," I say.

I turn on the TV to watch the news while he's undressing, brushing his teeth, and when he slips into bed beside me, I curl into him, let him cradle my head against his chest. He slides his hand just inside my waistband, starts to rub his fingers lower and lower on my back.

"I'm so tired, Phillip."

"Sure," he says, moving his hand back to my waist. "Okay."

Sadie calls me the next night while I'm making dinner.

"I'm not mad at you," she says. "I'm just mad at my dad."

"You shouldn't be mad at anyone," I say, but I can't really say more than that because Phillip is here, and he might act like he's reading the magazine he's holding, but I know that he's listening.

"No," she says. "He's an asshole. He treats women like they're disposable."

"Maybe you're confusing this with how you felt Matt treated you?" I try to say this in a really gentle tone so she won't get defensive.

It must work because she just sighs and says, "Maybe."

"I'm sorry he made you feel that way, honey. I really am. That's a shitty thing to do to a person."

Now I know that Phillip is listening because he gives me this look like, *Who are you talking to?* and I shake my head.

"Dad never made you feel disposable?" She says this like her relationship with Tommy hinges on my answer.

"No," I say. "Never." And when I say it, it feels like the truth. I probably would have said it anyway, but it does, it feels true.

Stevie's picking through his stir-fry and only eating the tofu.

"Baby, eat the broccoli too."

"Broccoli's really good for you. Lots of vitamin C," Phillip says, and honestly, his tone is a little *School House Rock*. I mean, the four of us could be in a fucking commercial right now.

Ben rolls his eyes, and I point my finger at him and say, "Hey," and he just looks back at his plate.

"You know who hates broccoli?" he says a minute later. He looks up, looks me in the eye, and I'm thinking, *You had better not,* but he does. He says, "Tommy."

"Well, it's good he's not here then," I say, and I take another bite like nothing's happening. *There's really nothing to see here at all.*

"But he likes blueberries," Stevie says, probably because he just doesn't like to be left out, and he kind of wiggles in his seat. "Blueberries in his oatmeal, like me."

"Just eat your dinner," I say.

Phillip hasn't said anything. He's just staring at me with this dumb look on his face.

"Yeah," Ben says, and he turns to Phillip. "That's what we all had for breakfast yesterday."

"That's enough, Benjamin." Though, really, it's way past enough.

Phillip sets his fork down. "Stacey," he says, "what's going on here?"

Ben has this little smile on his face, and Stevie's still wiggling, though he is actually eating his broccoli now.

"It's nothing," I say, and I stand up to take my plate back to the kitchen. "Finish up, boys. It's almost bedtime."

Phillip follows me, stands next to me with his arms crossed while I'm rinsing the plate. I glance over at him and smile. "Ben's just trying to upset you."

"Breakfast?" he says.

I sigh, dry my hands. "Tommy's daughter ran away, and she ended up here, and he had to come get her. I told you all of this already."

"No, Stacey, you didn't." He shakes his head. "You didn't say it was him. Or that you had breakfast."

"I didn't think it was worth mentioning."

"This didn't just slip your mind, Stacey. You decided not to tell me."

"Maybe I didn't want to upset you? Maybe I expected this?" I hold my hand out in a gesture like he's the problem. *You're the problem, Phillip,* my hand says. "Honestly, you have already been on edge about me going out for the Oscars, so maybe I didn't want to deal with the suspicion and the jealousy. I mean, you can see how your complete lack of trust feels a little disrespectful?"

"So you're lying to me to build trust? That's a stretch."

"I'm not 'lying,' Phillip, and if you really want to know everything, I'll tell you." I take a step backwards and shrug. "He came to get his daughter. He slept in the guest room."

"He slept here?"

"In the guest room. And then in the morning, he ate oatmeal, and there were blueberries, but no broccoli because he doesn't like broccoli, and apparently, neither do the boys. So that's everything. Now you know everything."

"Somehow I doubt that."

"Really?" I say. I cross my arms and turn my head to the side. I hope this looks like I'm just too angry to look at him. I hope he can't tell I'm shaking. I hope he can't tell that I'm coming apart.

"So you fly in Saturday morning," Daniel says. "We'll get you in about ten."

"Sure," I say. "That sounds fine." I'm in the grocery store, trying to find a decent mango. They're Stevie's favorite fruit, and there's a sale.

"Tommy wants you to know you can stay at the house if you want"—his voice sounds really tentative, really gentle—"or we can put you up at the same hotel as Sarah."

"Yeah, I think the hotel." I feel like I've squeezed every damn mango in the pile, but nothing is ripe.

"Stacey," Daniel says, "you have to work this shit out. This thing with you and Tommy is getting ridiculous."

"Tommy's ridiculous. Come on, Daniel, you know how he is." The woman across from me selecting apples looks up and catches my eye. She must hear something in the tone of my voice because she gives me this sad smile, and I turn away.

"I know he's different with you," he says.

"I don't really want to hear it," I say, and I know my words sound sharp, clipped. I leave the mangoes, push my cart toward the bananas, the oranges, the kinds of things that are always safe.

"Yeah, I forgot, you don't want to hear anything, do you? I warned you. I fucking warned you. But you didn't want to listen then either. And now you're all pissed off because he is who he is."

"I'm not pissed off, Daniel. I just don't need this shit."

"What shit? Honey, he fucking dotes on you. You think all this is normal for him? You think this is just what he's like?"

"Daniel," I say, but he's on a roll now, he's not shutting up, and I'm standing here, in the middle of the grocery store with my eyes closed, willing him to stop.

"I get that he's an asshole. I really do. But you know what, sweetie, you're a fucking asshole too. And at least he's trying. At least he didn't bail on you."

"Jesus, Daniel. Whose side are you on?"

"You and Tommy? There are no sides. You both want the same thing, and he's not even fighting you on it. You just need to figure out what the fuck you're going to do. Because this is it. After this weekend, he's got no reason to bring you out."

I don't know what to say, so I say, "I'm getting married," though it's actually kind of hard to get the words out.

Daniel sighs. "Yeah, I've heard all about that. You using him to get back at Tommy, or just to get away from him?"

I lean back against the display of bananas and brace my arms on the cart. I feel like I can barely hold myself up. I try to brush the tears off my cheeks, and the woman from the apples hands me a tissue. She doesn't ask, *Are you okay?* and I feel so grateful about that I almost hug her.

When he speaks again, he doesn't sound angry anymore, just sad. "Sweetie, please. He seems like a nice guy, you know. Don't drag him into this shit."

"Would you stop? Please. Would you please just stop?"

"Okay," he says finally. "The hotel. I'll set it up."

I flip the lights off in the boys' room and stand in the hallway for a long time, but tonight they aren't really talking. It's probably for the best. Lately, they have nothing good to say. Maybe none of us do. I just listen to them breathing, rolling over in their beds, and then I walk downstairs to the kitchen, pour myself a glass of wine. Phillip's in the living room watching the news, and when I walk in, he picks up the remote and turns it off.

"You want a glass?" I say, raising mine, even though I know he won't.

"I have an early morning," he says.

I turn back toward the kitchen to cork the bottle, but Phillip says, "Stacey?" and I stop. "We need to have that talk."

I turn back around to look at him, but I don't say anything. I can't place what he's talking about.

"The house," he says. "We need to talk about your house."

I just sigh. I say, "Not tonight."

"You say that every night."

"Then maybe you should stop bringing it up."

"Do you need to tell me something?" he says. "Because it seems like between Ben and the house, we've got some problems here. I mean, I don't expect all of it to be easy, but at some point we're going to have to deal with it. Right?"

"But not tonight," I say. I shake my head.

"I'm not here to just fill a vacancy," he says.

And I say, "No one asked you to."

"I don't want to live in this house, Stacey."

"Then don't," I say. "Don't live here. Leave. I don't care. But the boys and I aren't moving."

"You don't care?" He stares at me, tilts his head like he's trying to figure me out.

"I don't want to have this conversation, Phillip. How are you not getting that?" I turn and walk out of the room into the kitchen. I set my glass on the counter and lean over, holding my head in my hands, and I think, *I can't do this, I can't fucking do this.*

Tommy is hosting a party Saturday night at his house, and it's supposed to be small, just the people at the top of the food chain, producers, director, leads. Maybe the dozen or so most important people on the movie. And their dates. And me. I don't really know why they've invited me. I ride with Sarah. John won't be getting in until tomorrow, so it's just the two of us in the back of this Town Car.

"No fighting with Tommy tonight," she says, and she pats my hand.

"We're not fighting anymore," I say. "We're totally fine." Or totally done. Whatever. Either way, we won't fight.

"You sure about that?" she says. "Because this shit between you is exhausting."

"Sarah, I said it's over. Can we fucking drop it?" I look away from her, out the window.

"Oh yeah," she says. "You sound fine. This'll be great."

"Maybe you should worry about tomorrow," I say, and honestly, this is a little unfair of me. I know she's seriously worked up about tomorrow. She had me write her a speech just in case, and she's been practicing it all day. I love Sarah, but this is obnoxious.

When we pull up to the house, there's another car in front of us, and when I step out, I see that it's Jason.

He turns and spots us. "Stacey, come meet my wife." The woman beside him is blond and thin, with disproportionate breasts.

"This is Trina," he says, and I shake her hand.

While I do, Jason must look me over carefully, because he says, "Holy shit, Stacey, you getting married?" and he grabs my left hand and holds it up.

"Mm-hmm," Sarah says. "To a doctor."

"Shit, that sounds boring," Jason says, and I laugh.

There's a part of me that wishes I'd just left the ring in the hotel room, but it seems kind of stupid to take it off now.

The door is wide open because the people ahead of us haven't made it all the way in. Tommy has staff tonight, letting people in, taking bags and coats. I don't have anything to hand over. It's not Nebraska. It's not that cold.

Tommy's at the end of the hall, by the fireplace in the great room, and I don't know who he's talking to, but when he looks up, I smile, and then I turn left into the living room and go straight to the bar. I lost Sarah by the front door. She's still talking to Jason, and I didn't want to wait.

"What can I get you?" the bartender asks, and I say, "Red."

"Pinot? Malbec? Grenache . . ."

"Malbec, thanks."

Then I hear Tommy's voice over my left shoulder. "Stacey."

When I turn, he hugs me and says, "Hey, how are you?" and I don't say, *I'm so fucking miserable.* I just say, "Fine."

When he lets go, he sort of squeezes my hand, but it's my left hand, and he looks down and says, "Congratulations, honey. It's very pretty."

"Thanks," I say, and I turn to get my wine. When I turn back, Tommy's slipped off to the next group. He spends most of the night circulating. I spend most of the night pretending not to notice where he's standing, and who he's talking to, and whether she's pretty.

We have to get dressed so early on Sunday. I go up to Sarah's room, and she has a whole goddamn staff. There are two people doing her hair, which is ridiculous because in the end it just looks natural and kind of windswept. She's wearing this pale rose-colored column that plunges in the front, and her waist looks so tiny I think I could get my hands around it. I mean, she looks like a goddess. My dress is pretty simple, so purple it's almost black, and really, really fitted. It has kind of a high slit up the side, and it's basically backless. I did not show it to Phillip because I think he would have died.

"Shit, Stacey, you look gorgeous," Sarah says at first, but then she looks at me a little more critically and says, "Actually, we should work on your face and maybe do something with your hair."

She passes me off to her people and the next thing I know they're putting fake eyelashes on me and fixing the curl of my hair, but they're quick about it. They know we're on a schedule.

Sarah wants me to wear these teardrop diamond earrings and a bracelet of hers, but I say, "I don't know, they don't really go with my ring."

She sighs heavily like she can't believe what a pain in the ass I am. "So leave the ring here," she says, and I say, "Fine," and drop it in with the box of stuff she's sending down to the hotel safe.

"You ready?" Sarah says, and she turns to me and smiles. She pops open her little clutch and pulls out a pill box and says, "Xanax?"

I laugh and shake my head.

———————

Tommy texts John as he's pulling in, and we go down the back elevator to the limo. When he steps out of the back of the car in this very classic tux, I feel like I'm probably in a lot of trouble. He kisses Sarah and pats John on the arm as they both slip past him into the car. Then he holds my left arm by the wrist, and he kisses me on the cheek. He lets his hand slide down across my fingers as he lets go, and I can tell he notices that I'm not wearing the ring.

"You look beautiful," he says.

"You look pretty good yourself."

"I clean up all right," he says, and I say, "You do dirty pretty well too," and then I say, "Shit, I didn't mean to say that," because really, I shouldn't be flirting with him.

He laughs, but he isn't smiling. "Right," he says, "you have such a loose tongue. Always letting things slip." He rests his hand on my back and presses me toward the open door. "'Oops, I made a mistake,' she says. That's adorable, that is really fucking cute." He says it like he's mumbling, but he wants me to hear it.

I turn my head toward him, and I say, "Tommy," but he says, "Just get in the car."

Sarah looks up as we're climbing in. "Are we going straight or picking anyone else up? You bringing a date?"

For a second, I feel a little nauseated because I hadn't considered that, but he says, "No, we're good to go."

"We need more champagne then because I am ready to lose it," Sarah says.

"It's already open." Tommy leans forward and pours a glass for

Sarah, and then one for me, and John, and him, and when he leans back against the seat, our arms are almost touching. I can't decide which direction I should shift in, so I just fold my hands around my glass and try to be still.

Outside the window, there's the carpet, and it's all roped off and there are people maybe twenty, maybe thirty feet deep on the other side. There are cameras flashing, and these stage lights overhead, and it's all just insane. There's a line of cars ahead of us, letting people out slowly, and when the car finally stops, Tommy says, "You ready for this?" and Sarah and I both say, "No."

The difference is that as she's stepping out of the car, she turns on this smile and you'd never know. She's radiant, totally glowing. She smiles. She waves. Tommy puts his hand on my back to move me away from the car, and I look at him like *Uh-uh,* like *Please,* like *No.*

"Stacey, you've got to get that look off your face. You look panicked."

Which is fitting because I am panicked, and right now, I'd like to be as far from Tommy as possible because it's on him that everyone's so focused. There are people literally screaming his name.

John steps between us, and he reaches for my arm. "Tommy, you go ahead with Sarah. We'll hang back a few steps," he says, and I think this sounds perfect.

"I've got her," Tommy says, and before John can answer, he pushes me forward and then steps ahead of me and grabs my hand. We make it all of, I don't know, three feet before people are stopping us, and they're asking for pictures. Tommy says, "Sure," and he pulls me in close and under his breath says, "You need to smile."

As we start walking again he says, "Right now, our job is to be pretty."

"That's never my job," I say. "My job is to be smart."

"Not today. Today they're only paying for pretty." But then he smiles at me for the first time all day, and he changes his voice and says, "You got this, honey. You can do pretty in your sleep."

I know he's just trying to distract me, but it's not working. There's too much noise here, too many people. "No, I can't. I can do smart in my sleep."

"You can do both. You're a fucking triple threat."

"That's two things, not three," I say.

He leans in close to my ear. "And you're amazing in bed." I laugh, but I know he doesn't mean it. He's just looking for the right reaction because he says, "There you go. That's the smile they want. Keep that."

It gets worse the farther we go because there are all these little interview stops, and Tommy's expected to talk to everyone, and the questions are all basically the same, and then they all want to know, "Who's your date, Tommy?" and he keeps introducing me as "the poet, Stacey Lane." One woman asks, "Are you an item, then?" and Tommy just laughs and says, "No." As he says this, his hand is firmly on my back, and because my dress is backless, his hand is on my skin, and I think, *It's really fucking hot out here for February,* but it's probably just all of the lights.

"Tommy?" this voice says behind us.

Tommy turns and says, "Hey there, honey, how are you?" and the tone he uses makes me feel a little sick, but I just keep my head turned away. I don't want to look. It would be nice if I didn't have to listen, if I couldn't hear them, because she says, "When are you going to call me again?" and he says, "I don't know, honey, when do you want me to?"

I start to step a little away, not far, just to be polite, but Tommy says, "Stacey, let me introduce you." I honestly can't tell whether he's trying to be an asshole or nice. I just know that now, I'm having to shake this woman's hand. She's looking me over really closely, and I'm trying to ignore her breasts, but it's hard because they're really out there.

"Stacey's our poet," Tommy says, and she seems to like this. Obviously, poets are not all that much of a threat.

"Nice to meet you, Stacey," she says, and I smile, and then she turns back to Tommy. "Where are you heading tonight?"

"I don't know yet," Tommy says, "but I can give you my assistant's number. He'll know where to find me."

"I think I already have it," she says, and Tommy says, "Do you? You should definitely use it." And I'm like, *Jesus, this is disgusting.*

Once she's gone, Tommy puts his hand on my elbow, and he starts me moving again. "You okay?" he says.

"Of course," I say, and I say it pretty quickly. "Why wouldn't I be?"

"All the crowds," he says. "You didn't think I was talking about Rebecca, did you? I already know that kind of thing never bothers you. Does it, Stacey? I mean, it's not like I'm going to marry her, right?" And he says this so close to my ear that his lips brush against it.

I stop walking. I can't take another step. I feel like I can't breathe. I don't know if it's the crowds or Tommy. Probably Tommy. I say, "Jesus, Tommy, what are you doing to me?"

He turns to face me, and he steps close. He puts his hand on my cheek, and he leans in like he's going to kiss me, but he doesn't. He says, "Honestly, Stacey, I have no idea. You never fucking say." Then he takes a step back. "You can't just stand here, honey. God knows you don't want to make a scene."

When we get inside, they have us sitting in the third row, and Tommy's on the aisle. Sarah's next to me, and Jason's behind us—well, Jason's not yet. I don't know where he is, but his wife's sitting there.

The show starts, and it is really fucking inane. There are a couple of song-and-dance routines, and the host does the whole roasting of the most famous people in the audience. There's a particularly funny joke about how promiscuous Tommy is, which I obviously really enjoy, but Tommy just laughs like, *Of course, you're right, I'm such a whore.* Then they start giving out the awards. There are so many awards, and our movie picks up two of the smaller ones right away, but then it misses out on another, and the next one we're up for is supporting actor, and that means Tommy.

The actress presenting the award is Allison Grant. She is so talented and graceful and a total knockout. While she's reading the names of the nominees, I wonder if Tommy's ever slept with her. I know that they've been in a movie together, so I think, *Probably.*

They show clips of all the actors and then there's this long pause while she's trying to get the envelope open. They seem to cement these things shut for dramatic effect. She pulls out the card and takes this little happy breath, and then she says, "Tommy DeMarco."

Sarah screams next to me. Tommy just smiles and does this self-deprecating shake of his head. I swear I think he's been practicing.

Then we're all standing and clapping, and John reaches across Sarah and me to shake his hand, and Sarah throws her hands over both of theirs and says, "Oh, Tommy, I love you! You deserve this."

Tommy looks at me, and I take his face in my hands, and I say, "I'm so proud of you." I lean in and press my lips against his.

It's nothing. Really. Nothing more than Sarah's done a million times, but I don't get it right. Maybe I hold it too long, maybe I move my bottom lip against his, maybe it's the way I press my thumbs against his chin. Tommy pulls away from me and whispers, "You have any idea what you're doing here?" and of course I don't. Everyone is watching, and I feel like I'm going to crack in half. But Tommy takes my neck in his hands, and he pulls me toward him, and for just a second, I think about Phillip, and I don't know whether it's good that he's watching alone. Then Tommy's mouth is on mine, pressing it to open, pulling at my lip, and the people around us start to applaud. When he backs away, he smiles at me, and then he turns and jogs up to the stage.

Sarah leans over and says, "What the hell was that?" but I don't answer. I feel like I'm going to be sick, and if she keeps talking, I'm not going to be able to hold this smile. I think, *Please let the boys be in bed.* I don't know what else to hope for now.

Allison hands him the award and kisses him on the cheek, and then he leans into the microphone and says, "You'll have to give me a minute to catch my breath," and everyone laughs. I hold my fingers over my mouth and press them hard against my lips. He looks at the award for a long second, just admires it. His timing is perfect. He's hitting all his marks. "Stace," he says. "Remember when you tried to talk me out of this part?" I nod, but he's not looking at me anymore. "You are a brilliant, a brilliant poet, but you're never going to make it as an agent." More laughter. "So, I wouldn't be up here if it wasn't for my friend, my partner in crime, my brother, Jason Collier." Everyone applauds. "You are the finest director I know. The most brilliant mind. You see the world and then you bring it into focus for the rest of us. And Sarah, you are the lightning rod we all coalesced around. So generous with your talent and your art. I'm so grateful. And Stacey, Jesus, Stacey. What the hell am I supposed to say? This is for you, baby, and all those beautiful monsters in your head."

He gives a little thank-you nod and steps backwards and walks off the stage. The band starts playing, and Sarah puts her hand on my arm like she wants my attention, but I just shake my head.

It seems like he's backstage forever. There's a song and then they give out another award. I see him finally, trying to make his way back to his seat. He doesn't have far to go, but it's slow going, people are stopping him, shaking his hand, offering congratulations. I try not to watch him. I don't know what to do with my face.

When he finally sits down, Sarah reaches over me to grab his hand and squeeze it, and I push myself into the back of my seat to get out of their way. "We have so much to celebrate," she whispers before she pulls her hand away.

I keep my gaze firmly on the stage and the presenter who's talking. I'm not sure what the award is for, but I watch like it's important, like I really, really care. Tommy slides his hand under my arm and winds his fingers through mine, and he leans his shoulder against me, holds his head close and in a low voice says, "So what are your thoughts on going public with this? Because I think we just went very, very public."

When I turn to look at him, he's smiling and he just looks like himself. He looks like Tommy, my Tommy. I laugh, but my breath catches in my throat and I have to hold my mouth closed with my teeth to keep from sobbing because I feel like he meant it. I feel like he meant every word.

"Stace," he says, putting his hand on my cheek. "We're fine. I got you. You don't need to cry."

"I'm not crying," I say.

Tommy rubs his thumb under my eye. "I can see that," he says. "You'll make a mess of yourself and then you'll look like hell in all the pictures they get of you."

I laugh a real laugh this time. Tommy takes my face in his hands and leans his head against mine. I can feel his breath.

"And then I'll get all these calls, people saying, 'Tommy, who is this girl? She's a mess.' And I'll say, 'Yes, she's a fucking disaster, but god I love her.'"

"Do you?" I say.

"How can you be so stupid when you're so fucking smart? Do I love you?" He kisses me, brushes his thumb across my lips. "Baby, I love you."

I press my mouth against his over and over. I say, "I love you." I say, "I love you. I love you. I love you."

"Fuck. You better. 'Cause I don't think Rebecca's going to call me now."

"You're an ass," I say, shoving him in the chest.

"I know, but you love it," he whispers in my ear.

He turns his attention back to the stage, but he leans his body against mine, slides his hand through the slit in my skirt, rests it just above my knee, massaging his thumb along my thigh. I slip my arm under his, lean my head against his shoulder. I don't even care that people are watching, probably Rebecca is watching. *There's no space here, I want to say. There's no space for you, or anyone like you, to slip between us.*

Sarah wins too, and her little speech is a hit. She's such a natural. It seems totally off the cuff. While she's backstage, John slips into her seat and leans toward us. "Thank god," he says. "This should keep her happy for at least a week."

We both laugh, and Tommy says, "Yeah, she's a handful. Don't know how you do it, man."

John shrugs. I can tell he's looking at our hands, but he doesn't say anything. John's always cool. He gives me a smile, and he moves back to his regular seat.

Jason does not get best director, but he's already got two, so nobody feels too bad for him, though Tommy does turn and grab his arm and say, "Best fucking director I know." They miss out on best picture too, but honestly it's a big night. No one's complaining.

When the show finally ends, Sarah drags me off to the bathroom, which is a nightmare because everyone wants to stop and talk to her.

As we're walking, Sarah pulls both our phones out of her little clutch, and she hands me mine.

"Yours is flashing like a motherfucker," she says. "I wonder why."

It is. I have a lot of messages. Jenny has sent seven. First she says, *Oh my god, what are you doing?* Then, *What about Phillip?* Then, *You are a selfish, selfish brat.* Then, *That seemed like a hell of a kiss.* Then, *You're still an asshole.* Then, *I hope you're happy.* Then, *I didn't mean that sarcastically.*

Sadie just texted, *OMG! OMG! LOVE!* which as far as I'm concerned just seems like an awful lot of pressure.

Phillip did not text. He has called three times though, and he left a voice message. I don't feel like I need to listen to it. I know what it says.

"Shit," I say. "I feel like such an asshole."

"Yeah, you really are. What the hell is going on with you and Tommy anyway? I mean, one minute you're not even speaking, and then I turn around and the two of you are making out."

"We're not making out."

"Whatever, Stacey." She pushes the door to the restroom open, and there's a line of women, which is great. I love that we're stuck here. "You may not have noticed," she says, "but Tommy's not the kind of guy you can push around like that."

I've noticed, and the women around us are noticing too. They know who we're talking about, obviously. "Sarah, can we not do this here?" I say quietly.

"Oh fuck," she says, raising an eyebrow. "You think we're the only ones talking about it? It's big news, Stacey. For two people who can't make their minds up, that was a hell of a stunt."

The first stop after dinner is this nightclub, and the guests are strictly A-list, like there are not very many faces that I don't recognize. Tommy keeps his hand on me at all times, which is a relief because the crowd around us is constantly moving. It'd be really easy to get swallowed up. It's also a relief that everyone he introduces me to is famous. It makes it easier to remember their names, which is good because all the conversations are basically the same. *Where the hell did I come from? What the fuck is in Omaha?* and *How'd I manage to lock*

Tommy down? I don't know, I say to all of it, and Tommy just laughs a lot. At least he's happy. We're happy. Because suddenly we're a couple and we're happy about it. Tommy tosses around the word *girlfriend* like it's his favorite thing to say. *My girlfriend, Stacey. My girlfriend's a poet. Have you met my girlfriend?* And every time he does this, there are invitations—to lunches, and brunches, and shopping, and dinners, and to show me around L.A. I nod like I'm agreeing, though I don't really know to what.

"So how long are you in town?" Elaine Parsons asks me. Elaine Parsons. *Christ.*

"I leave tomorrow," I say, taking a sip of champagne. I wish it was vodka. Champagne is lovely and all, but it never seems to do any real work.

"Tomorrow?" she says.

She widens her eyes and glances at Tommy, who's half turned away. Someone tapped him on the shoulder and now he's standing with his back to me, really deep in conversation. It's so loud in here, I can't really tell what he's saying, but he has his fingers twisted tightly through mine, and this makes me feel—not exactly grounded—but at least held in place.

"Well, when you come back, we'll have to have lunch." She smiles broadly. "Tommy and my husband and I go way back. I'll fill you in."

"That would be great," I say, though it sounds pretty awful. I already don't like her, the way she's studying me, how she keeps glancing past me to see who else is walking by.

"Why don't you give me your number?" she says just as Tommy turns back, slipping his arm around my waist.

"Daniel has her calendar. He can set it up."

She stares at him for a minute, her smile tight. "Great," she says finally. She looks away from him, looks me straight in the eye. "Don't let Tommy keep you all to himself now."

I laugh, shake my head.

"We'll set something up," she says, patting my arm and eyeing Tommy a last time before she turns away.

"You could have told her to fuck off. You can tell any of these people to fuck off," Tommy whispers in my ear.

I turn toward him, let him brush his fingers along my neck. "I thought these were your friends."

"Tough to say," he says. "How loose a definition are we working with?"

It takes Tommy three tries to punch in the door code because we've been drinking, and now he's kissing me, and my hair is in the way. I slip under his arm and move behind him, and he hits the right buttons and pushes the door open and pulls me inside. My shoes are already in my hand, and he takes them from me, drops them on the floor.

"God, I've missed you," he says. His mouth is on mine, his fingers spread across my shoulder blades.

"How much?" I say. "Tell me how much."

He laughs, and he takes my face in his hands and kisses me over and over. He takes my hand in his and pulls me down the hall and through the great room. But when he flips on the light in the master, he says, "Fuck," and steps backwards, blocking my way.

"Let's go upstairs," he says. He flips the light off and turns to face me. "You go. I'll be right up."

I frown.

"Stacey, go upstairs," he says, but I don't. I push past him and turn the light on, and of course, there she is. That little actress, *the neighbor's wife,* naked, passed out across his bed.

"I'll get her out," he says. "Someone'll come get her. Don't let this ruin our night."

I can't seem to turn away. She's got these perky little tits, dark brown nipples.

"Stacey," he says. He puts one hand on my shoulder to nudge me out of the room, but I shake him off.

"How'd she get in here?"

"Stace, come on."

"She has a key?"

"No." He shakes his head. "I don't know. She knows the door code or something."

"You gave her the code?" I turn to look at him, but he looks at his phone.

He gestures toward the door. "C'mon. I'll take care of it."

"You've been seeing her this whole time?"

"Stacey, stop." He takes my face in his hands and leans his head against mine. "She's no one. She's nothing. I love you."

"Then what the fuck is she doing here?" I shove him back hard and walk past him into the great room, and then farther still. He's already making a call, and I don't want to listen. I go into the living room and sit in Sadie's chair. I hold my hand over my mouth and pinch my lips. I think how it will always be like this, Tommy making a mess, someone coming to clean it up.

I hear the front door open and close. It's quiet, then still quiet, and then there's a commotion in the hallway. She's half awake now, mumbling, crying. I can't hear what Tommy says to her, but his voice sounds like a threat. I wonder if they've dressed her or just thrown a blanket over her shoulders on the way out. I wonder if I'll find her clothes in the morning, tucked around the house like little clues. I close my eyes and take a deep breath.

"Hey." Tommy's voice is soft. He squats down in front of me, holds my hands in my lap. He holds my fingers up to his lips. "Stace, I know you're upset."

"Upset," I say. "You think I'm upset?" I pull my hands away and press them over my face.

Tommy keeps his hands in my lap, rubs his thumb across my thigh. "Honey, come on. The girl is unstable."

"She's not unstable," I say.

"I don't give a fuck what she is." He stands up and takes a few steps away. "Stacey, please. Let's not start this shit. Not tonight."

My fingertips are black with mascara. I try wiping my eyes with the backs of my knuckles. Tommy watches me, his arms crossed, his lip curled just slightly like he doesn't like what he sees.

"You bailed on us. That was you." He jabs one finger in my direction and then steps backwards, walks to the bar. I close my eyes, cover my face with my hands. I hear him pull a bottle down.

"Am I pouring one for you?"

I laugh through my hands, drop them into my lap. "Sure, Tommy. Pour us another drink. That'll fix everything."

"Goddamn it!" he yells, and then a shatter of glass, a million tiny bells clattering against the floor. I turn to look at him, and he's leaning hard against the bar, his head down like he's studying the broken bottle.

"There's nothing to fix," he says finally. "This just is what it is. You either want it or you don't."

"Maybe I don't," I say. I turn my head away, rub my thumb along the arm of the chair. There are tiny markings in the soft finish, and I can almost see Sadie pressing her thumbnail into the wood, feeling the give as she tunes Tommy out. I wonder if that would work for me.

"I don't know what to do," he says, but I don't have anything to offer. I don't know what to say. I just know the sound of his voice is too quiet, it's too far away. I think, *Come get me, Tommy,* but he doesn't. He slumps down against the wall, his feet sliding into the puddle of whiskey and glass.

"You'll ruin your shoes," I say quietly.

He looks up at me, shakes his head. "I can't carry this whole thing. If you're not going to be in this, really in this, I don't want it. I'm not Michael."

Sometimes I wish he was. I wish he would hold everything together and make it easy for me. Michael would never just sit there the way Tommy is, his arms balanced across his knees, waiting.

"You know this girl . . . That was not . . . You were gone," he says finally.

I nod, but then I shake my head. It feels impossible. It's all impossible. "I wish we knew how to do this," I say. I brush my fingers under my eyes and try to smile at him.

He watches me for a minute. Then he sighs, lowers his head. "It's late. You should go upstairs," he says.

I think about waking up without him, opening my eyes in the room upstairs that Sadie calls *Stacey's room,* though I've slept there exactly once. I think it would feel lonelier now. I think everything would feel lonely without Tommy.

I stand up and cross the room.

"You'll cut your feet," he says, trying to shove a clear path with his shoe.

I step through the wet of the whiskey, over his knees, and slip down into his lap, burying my face in his neck. He puts his hands on my shoulders, shifting me backwards, pushing my hair back from my face, and I lower my eyes.

"Look at me," he says.

I look at his eyes, at the skin around his eyes. He looks so tired. I put my hand on his cheek, run my fingers over the stubble along his jaw. I rub my thumb across his mouth. "Your lips are dry," I say.

"I spilled my drink," he says, and I almost smile.

"Stace," he says. "I don't know what I'm supposed to say here. I don't know what you want."

I lean into him, lean my head against him, and I feel his lips press against my forehead. I close my eyes and press my palm flat against his chest, count the dull knock of his heartbeat.

Twenty, twenty-one, twenty-two.

"All of it," I say. "I want all of it, Tommy. I want you."

NOVEMBER

WHEN I WAKE in the morning, I haven't seen Tommy in almost three weeks, but he's flying in tonight. The house feels empty without him, and of course I barely slept. When I walk out, I hear Bear's collar rattle as he stretches, steps down off the couch. He's too big to be on the furniture, and his nails are already leaving marks, but Tommy breaks all the rules for everyone. He keeps letting him up.

I have an hour still before the boys will be awake, so I make coffee, sit at the counter, fire up my laptop. Erin sent me final edits on the third manuscript two days ago, and I need to look through her changes. She's not asking a lot, shifting the order of a few of the poems, changing a line break or two. She doesn't like a few of the titles, but I'm not going to change them. It's going to press no matter what I do. I could drop a grocery list into the middle of it, and she'd still take it.

In any case, next week is Thanksgiving, so I need to be done. Jenny and her crew are all meeting us in Turks and Caicos for the holiday. Neither she nor Tommy is completely looking forward to it, though I think things are warming up. Over the summer, they spent a week with us, and she spoke to him without scowling on three separate occasions. And only once during the whole trip did she call him a fucking dick. It's possible she was holding back though. The kids were around a lot.

When my phone rings, I almost don't catch it. I've plugged it in to charge on the other side of the kitchen, and it's on silent, but I hear it vibrating against the counter.

"Hey," I say, cradling the phone with my shoulder. I move to refill my cup. "Shouldn't you be on a plane?"

"Just boarding," he says. "How much did you miss me?"

"Very little," I say.

"How's the writing?"

"It's good." I take a sip of the coffee and wander back to the glass door. It's early, but the sun's already up, throwing the shadow of the house across the patio, the pool. "I wrote a villanelle."

"That's a good form for you, all uptight and obsessive."

"I'm hanging up now," I say, and he laughs. He sounds happy. He's always happy when he comes home, and happy again when he leaves. It's the in-between we're still figuring out, how to make it through a Tuesday.

In Omaha, on an afternoon as beautiful as this, I would have walked the mile to the boys' school and they would have run ahead of me on the way home, Stevie begging to take the short cut across the golf course. *Absolutely not,* I always said.

Instead, I'm pulling up to the guard station at the front gate of their school. There's a sticker on the front window of the car, so the guy just waves me through. What their school does not have is a uniform, which strikes me as a terrible injustice every time I see Ben trudging out of the school in his black jeans and T-shirt. Who keeps buying him these black jeans? Probably Sadie.

"For thirty-five grand, they should get a uniform," I'd said after Tommy brought me to look at the campus last spring. They'd given me all these glossy brochures on clubs and activities, and I had them spread across the coffee table in the great room.

"It's not that kind of school," Tommy said, handing me a glass of wine. "And what matters is the education they'll be getting."

"I'm just saying," I said as he sat down next to me, "I wouldn't mind that sort of safe, parochial image."

"They have great security there."

"You know what I mean," I said.

"You want me to send them to religious school?"

"No." I shook my head, took a sip of the wine. "Maybe. I don't know."

Tommy put one hand on my leg and rubbed his thumb across my thigh. "Ben'll be twelve soon. You can't keep them home with you forever."

"I know that," I said, though I didn't appreciate him saying it. I hadn't wanted them to start a new school when we moved in March, so we'd just hired a tutor, and I kind of liked watching them doing their schoolwork in their bathing suits out on the patio.

"He needs to get out, get away from you, make some friends, maybe find a girlfriend."

"I hate you," I said. "I hope Sadie elopes with that fat boyfriend of hers and you end up a grandfather."

"Jesus, Stace." He laughed though. "That's a little below the belt." Tommy actually likes the fat boyfriend, probably because he is fat and completely adores her.

"Mom!" Ben pounds on the glass of the passenger window, and I startle. I hadn't even seen him come out. "Unlock the door." He rolls his eyes dramatically. "Jesus, Mom," he says as he opens it and climbs in.

"Watch your language," I say. "Where's your brother?"

"No idea." He slouches down in the seat, his thumbs folded around the phone in his lap.

"Who are you texting?"

"Sadie. She wants to know if Dad's coming home tonight. Her dad, I mean . . . Tommy." He fidgets a little, clicks the screen to black.

"He is." I reach over, smooth a curl of his hair, and he ducks his head away. It's pretty much what I expected. I pull my hand back, look past him out the window for Stevie.

"How was school?" I say.

He shrugs. I've never been good at this part. I've never had to be. Michael was the one with all the canned speeches about family. He'd put his hands on Ben's shoulder and say, *We have each other, and that's what matters.* He used to say that one a lot, and I always thought, *That's such bullshit. It's not that easy.*

"You know he loves you, Benny."

"Who?" he says, and he turns toward me like he really needs the answer. Like he needs me to tell him what I haven't been able to say.

"Both of them," I say. "Tommy. And your dad. They both do." I run my fingers through his hair again, and this time he lets me, tilting his head into it.

Stevie pops the handle on the back door, and Ben twists away from me, rubbing one fist across his eyes.

"Hey, Mom," Stevie says. "You know how to make salt dough? Because I have to make a map. It's due tomorrow."

Fuck. I glance to the left behind me and pull onto the circular drive.

"Salt dough?" I say.

I look at the clock. Tommy should have landed by now.

"You know who you should ask?" I click the call button on my phone, and it starts ringing through the speakers.

"Tommy!" Stevie squeals as soon as he picks up. "Mom says you can help me with my homework."

"Homework? Must be math. Is it like a worksheet?"

"No, I have to make a salt map."

"A salt map?" he says. "Great. Yeah. Okay. And your mom says? Can you put her on the phone?"

"You're on speaker," I say.

"Right," he says. "Why don't you pick up the handset, baby?"

"I can't," I say. "Because I'm driving. It's the law." I pull through the gates and into the line of cars turning right.

"Pick up the handset," he says again.

"Oh god, you know, the traffic here. I better go." I can't even keep the laughter out of my voice, and Ben snickers in the seat beside me.

"You are such . . ."

"I love you too," I say, and then I touch my finger to the red circle on the screen.

"Good one, Mom," Ben says.

He turns to face the window, but I catch the slow lift of his lips, the start of a smile. Behind me, Stevie's humming to himself. He kicks his feet against the back of my seat, and I don't even tell him to stop.

acknowledgments

A tremendous thank-you to my agent, Susan Golomb, who said in our first conversation, *You have a lot of work to do.* A million thanks for taking me on and making me do it. Thanks also to Krista Ingebretson, Scott Cohen, and everyone at the Susan Golomb Literary Agency and now Writers House.

Thanks, of course, to my editor, Tara Singh Carlson, and to Helen Richard. You are such smart, generous readers. Thank you for helping me shape this book.

To my earliest readers, Anne Mancini, Anne Freimuth, Ken Brosky, Stephanie Austin, and David Mainelli, thanks so much for your insight and encouragement. Endless gratitude to Katie Benns, Sarah McKinstry-Brown, and Jen Lambert. You've each read more drafts of this than any person should have to suffer through. Thanks for never telling me to fuck right off.

Thanks to the friends and family who encouraged and supported me and put up with my anxieties—those of you listed above, and also Ken Freimuth, Michele O'Donnell, Susie and Dennis Stieren ("life insurance, trust account, annuity"!), Marni Valerio, Rebecca Rotert, Steve Langan, Karen Shoemaker, and Natalia Treviño.

Thanks to my sons, Devon, Ashton, and Brandon, for putting up with a mother who is too frequently caught up in her own head. I owe you a trip to Disneyland.

And to David, who puts up with the most and hasn't left me yet, you make everything possible.